To Ide

FORCED TURNOVERS

A Novel for Racial Unity

Our friend
for life.

TONY CEBALLOS

Tony

⌐AUTHOR elite
ACADEMY

Published by Author Academy Elite
PO Box 43
Powell, OH 43035
www.AuthorAcademyElite.com

LCCN: 2019907481
ISBN: 978-1-64085-738-4 (paperback)
ISBN: 978-1-64085-739-1 (hardback)
ISBN: 978-1-64085-740-7 (ebook)

Available in paperback, hardback, e-book, and audiobook.

—Dedicated to Clayton Ricker—

Clayton, my friend on earth and in heaven.
You saw my potential when no one else did.
Your legacy far outreaches your days among us.
I move forward,
witnessing your enormous footsteps all the time,
taking joy in the fact I will see you again.

A NOTE TO THE READER

Forced Turnovers is a fictitious story set in the southern United States in the late 1960s, and I chose to employ a detailed, realistic setting for that period in my storyline. Much terminology has changed in the average-American lexicon since then, and certain words, phrases, and beliefs have been jettisoned, for good reasons. Therefore, the use of any such words and phrases, or the portrayal of such views by any characters in this book is done merely to highlight and not condone that time in American history.

—Tony Ceballos

1

Friday, February 16, 1968

The caller dials the number, hanging up after one ring. He pauses. The clock shows 12:33 a.m. Thirty seconds later, the caller dials the same number—this time, hanging up after two rings.

• • •

A man in the corner of a dark bedroom sits and listens as the phone rings once then ceases. He waits. A spiral of cigarette smoke ascends from his lips. Thirty seconds later, the phone rings twice then ceases.

The man stands to his feet and walks into the hall, opening a door leading to the basement. A single bulb illuminates the flight before him. His rugged boots announce every step on his way down. Shadows clutch the walls as the man retrieves a suitcase with care from beneath the stairs. He places the case on a nearby workbench and views the contents inside, satisfied with what he sees.

Outside, the man cautiously loads the suitcase in the passenger seat of his car. He then circles the vehicle and climbs behind the wheel before driving into the darkness.

• • •

The following afternoon is a prelude to spring. On the vast school lawn, the sight is captivating: a billion blades of uncorrupted green grass shower in sunlight, all slightly leaning thanks to a consistent breeze. The unseasonably warm, Georgia air beckons as multiple, easily distracted students heed from inside the school windows, their attention disengaged from the teacher's sluggish, mundane curriculum.

• • •

The hidden timer inches closer to its mark.

• • •

An ambiance of serenity blankets the Macon South campus, an all-black high school not because of segregation but because of the demographics on the south side of town. Gentle currents of air navigate the prolonged hallways. The school exits remain open. A backdrop of glorious light rests at the end of each corridor, a promise of the waiting afternoon. Outside, all along the property line, a chain-link fence armed atop with jagged barbed wire appears unnecessary amid such calmness.

• • •

The hidden timer inches closer to its mark.

• • •

Innumerable live oak trees accent nearby Jefferson Street, their leaves caressed by a playful gust. Lofty, corpulent clouds hover innocently at tremendous levels, rubbing shoulders with streams of sunlight that saturate the landscape below.

• • •

The hidden timer inches closer to its mark.

• • •

Full as usual are the classrooms within the belly of Macon South High School—every desk in every room occupied.

Teachers and students alike go through the motions.

A teenage boy mischievously flicks the earlobe of the dozing schoolmate in front of him.

Multiple post-lunch yawns bounce from one row to the next in a chain reaction.

A magnanimous breeze passes through an open window, the fresh air introducing itself to a young, female student. A sweet smile comes to her face.

• • •

The hidden timer inches closer to its mark.

• • •

In his office, Charles Bullock seals another familiar envelope, taking a moment to whisper a prayer over the letter before dropping it in the outbound mail. *God*, his mind toils, *I hope You know what You're doing.*

Vaulting to his feet, the principal of Macon South High School for the past two decades moves briskly to his office door. *So much to do*, he ponders. *It's a busy day and there's not enough time to....*

A disabling, crippling sensation engulfs the man, overtaking him. His skin wanes cold as if his body just exhaled all energy and life. *Something's wrong,* he senses. *Something's very, very....*

• • •

The hidden timer hits the trigger.

• • •

The explosion is merciless, heinous, bloodthirsty, first gutting wide-open the wall that concealed the evil device only an instant earlier. Huge chunks of jagged plaster displace. Debris poses as shrapnel.

Directly across the hall from the vicious blast, classroom walls buckle, the brutal force ripping through, rearing its baneful head, violently catapulting rows of desks and students for several feet—end over end. Deadly shards of glass from shattered windows take flight, lodging under both hair and skin.

Above the point of the explosion, the ceiling begins collapsing, creating a domino effect and branching through half the building. In another adjacent room, suspended-lighting easily gives way, plummeting to the ground where the free-falling mass pins an unsuspecting teacher beneath the rubble.

On the second story, students are pulled through an expanding vacuum in the crumbling floor, dropping helplessly with flailing limbs to ground level as the bodies of other students break their fall.

The detonation is deafening, letting loose what sounds to be a thousand wailing demons down the rumbling school corridors.

Numerous residents across Jefferson Street lurch from their homes, jostled by the explosion. The sound likened itself to the blast from a lightning strike, followed by piercing ripples of violent thunder, and it came from—of all places—the school. Promptly, the community's worst fears imaginable are confirmed. Tens...then scores...then hundreds of South students flee the building in a ghastly, running, shrilling panic. Onlookers in the exclusively black part of town stand fraught with fear, watching with incredulous eyes and quivering mouths as smoke and debris mushroom above the imploding schoolhouse. A sobering, horrific reality forms. Residents scamper chaotically, several rapidly descending on the scene. As they do, the closer they draw, the more hideous and bloodcurdling the cries of terror become.

Macon South High School gropes for breath and life.

• • •

"Are we still meeting, sir?" FBI Agent Dennison queries through a sliver of the doorway in Dawson's office, the two scheduled for a sit-down to cover a few mundane items.

The answer from Dawson is curt as the man glares at the phone on his desk, awaiting a ring. "Conference room in ten," Dawson snaps without looking up.

That says it all, Dennison calculates. *Something huge just went down.* The subordinate pulls the office door closed on his way out, taking the hint; his boss is clearly antagonized.

Ten minutes later, the Atlanta FBI third-floor conference room is full. Several agents are left standing along the wall.

Dennison annoyingly taps the shoulder of his colleague and friend, interrupting Maxwell's conversation with another agent. "What do you think?" Dennison queries.

"I'm not sure what's going on," Maxwell responds, leaning in, "but Dawson's asked to see me after this meeting is over."

"No kidding. The boss cancels me and books you," jabs Dennison. "You must make more money than I do."

"Yeah, right," Maxwell responds. "I don't know what he wants."

As the two agents converse while waiting for the meeting to begin, Dennison cannot contain his sinister smile. "Dawson probably wants to discuss how hideous your teeth look," Dennison snickers at Maxwell's expense. "He might be transferring you—too hard to look at."

"Get out of here." Agent Maxwell scoffs, running his tongue inside his mouth along the area where two of his teeth are missing, knocked out on his previous assignment. His car met a ditch during a pursuit, and his face met the steering wheel.

All conversation ceases as FBI Special Agent in Charge Harold Dawson enters the room. The veteran field-man wastes no time.

"Here we go. There was an explosion in Macon about an hour ago. At a high school." The man pauses. Complete silence abounds. "Early reports indicate it may have been some device, and the reason we are leaning in that direction is a party has already phoned the local newspaper down there to claim responsibility."

A handful of agents shift in their chairs at the unsettling news, and the room hangs on the man's every word.

Agent Dawson, a man who comes across all business all the time, plops a thin stack of papers on a rugged conference room table. His broad knuckles white as they press against the surface. His rough, dark eyes pan the group.

"And this is not just any ordinary high school we're talking about, men. It's Macon South High School with an enrollment of nearly 1,000, including faculty and staff, and every person there is black—not a single white in attendance or on payroll. As far as who claimed responsibility...."

Agent Dennison guesses correctly to himself before the words ever leave Dawson's lips: the *Klan.*

"Dead or wounded we don't know yet," Dawson continues, "but Macon PD and FD are on the scene and sifting through the wreckage."

The words of the lead agent are blunt, and despite a room full of stone-faced objectivity, a tangible sense of shock lingers. Today had been calm up until now.

Dennison looks around the room; he sits as confounded as anyone. At the same time, Dennison knows if such a catastrophic event would happen anywhere, Macon, Georgia fits the profile perfectly; the city a percolating caldron of racial unrest over the past twenty years. Agent Cy Dennison is quick to surmise what all this means for himself and the rest of the Atlanta Chapter of the FBI.

"I just got off the phone with 'H' in D.C.," Dawson proceeds. "We've got a green light. The National Guard is already en route for potential riot control. We're on our way to find out what happened."

• • •

The best efforts of the man cannot mitigate his rapid breathing. His chest continues to expand and contract with frantic repetition. A push of involuntary air rushes through his open mouth, the sound filling his ears. Phillip Barlow clutches his gyrating heart. Bent at the waist, he watches through a sliver between two slats of wood, hiding in his dilapidated shed in the back yard, fearful of the voices that bid him.

"Phillip! Open up! It's us!" a voice calls from the front of the home, men pacing back and forth on the porch.

"Come on, Phillip! Open the door!" a second voice chimes with irritation.

Loosely ensconced by walls and a roof of termite-riddled shiplap, the man watches and waits in silence.

Tired of waiting, the intruders force their way through the front door and begin to toss the residence. Soon, the bedroom light illuminates the night. The back door is violently pulled open from the inside as one of the men steps onto the back porch. He surveys the rural surroundings; there is nothing to see or hear save the ambient sounds of Georgia wildlife at night. The man on the back porch eyes the shed in the distance, gesturing a step in that direction. "Phillip," he bids for good measure.

From inside the shed, a pair of dilated pupils anxiously watch the man's every move.

The second wooden stair nearly snaps under the weight of the man's boot, bringing his progress to a halt. With disgust, the man gives up, cussing under his breath then muttering, "He's not here."

"He out here?" queries the second man after stepping through the back door.

"No" is the gruff response as both men walk back through the home and eventually through the front door.

Relief comes to the man in hiding at the sound of the truck's ignition turning over. Phillip steps to his right to see through another sliver of the rickety edifice. As his boot plants on a wobbly floorboard, the movement inadvertently rouses a distinct rattling sound from a darkened corner of the shed.

The man freezes.

The rattling swells, and soon the faint silhouette of an imposing, bulky, coiled snake takes shape in the darkness.

Phillip is paralyzed by the moment as the hissing crescendos. The man eventually looks to a nearby metal rake, hanging from a nail in a beam. Slowly, the man reaches. He cautiously secures the weathered, wooden handle as rattling fills the inside of the shed; the snake gave its warning and has now slithered into position.

With a firm grip, the man begins an aggressive assault, striking mercilessly at the snake before it can strike him. The rattler lunges but misses. Other tools and objects go airborne from the confined battle. Three, four, five fatal hits with the rake and the rattling begins to wane, but so does the sound of the once idling truck out front—the ignition is now off.

Phillip ceases all breathing as he looks and listens: there is nothing..., nothing. Following a period of stillness, the truck starts again and soon thereafter pulls off the property.

A huge exhale escapes the man's chest. On the floor to his right is the dying rattlesnake; its body flops under the iron teeth of the rake. One final time, Phillip strikes and claims victory.

The shed door opens. After looking in every direction, Phillip walks the distance to his home and enters through the back door. To his left, he finds his mattress on the floor. His closet door hangs from its hinges--they knew he would be hiding from them. The rest of the home has been tossed as well as he quickly peruses, stopping to peer through the front curtains.

The paranoid man gingerly pries the front door ajar, looking into the night, not sure if they will return. Cautiously, Phillip crosses the threshold and the wood planks bow and creak with his every step. All seems well until catching his peripheral vision is the sudden silhouette of another man, causing the homeowner to gasp and nearly fall backward.

Seated eerily yet calmly in a chair a few feet away, the uninvited man stares back, the jagged scar on the right side of his face coming fully into view in the moonlight. "Phillip," the man speaks. "Why are you hiding from us?"

Simultaneously, the calloused hand of a second man reaches over Phillip Barlow's shoulder from behind, applying firm pressure.

2

Saturday, March 2
Georgia Boys Basketball State Title Game
Augusta Christian Academy vs. Savannah Memorial
Alexander Memorial Coliseum, Atlanta, Georgia

Mindfully observing the game clock, Kevin Stevens ushers the ball across half court—less than two minutes remain. Poised and collected, the 17-year-old point guard knows full well his ability. An aura of confidence envelops the athletic teenager. An uncanny coolness is about him. A wreath of certainty laps over his shoulders and hangs from his neck. Assuredness graces the parquet floor in his every advancing step. A formidable expression of nonchalance paints his façade as he strolls calmly toward the jagged teeth of the waiting defense—no worries, no pressure.

His mastery over the ball is evident. Dribbling is profoundly routine to the young man, second nature, as customary as his next breath—right…left…right…between the legs…right…left. The leather sphere is simply an extension of his hand; one does not end, nor the other begin. Inseparable is the union between the two. Already an excellent ball-handler, Kevin reinvested his life in the art of dribbling once he saw Pete Maravich in person in a North Carolina gym. Kevin and his father made the trip once news spread the phenom would be there. The down-and-back to Raleigh was worth every ounce of effort in Kevin's opinion; the trip more of a life-changing pilgrimage than anything else.

As for tonight, this is Kevin's game, his night. The capacity crowd of 10,000 is at his mercy, as are the five players donning enemy jerseys.

A salvo of flashbulbs illuminates press row—over 50 photographers are present. The barrage of light is momentarily blinding, surfacing for an instant before disappearing just as quickly, immediately increasing the courtside temperature by five degrees. Even so, Kevin pays no mind.

Fanatical cries and resonant clamor cascade down from the bleachers, descending on the athletes in heavy, rolling sheets; even so, Kevin pays no mind.

Despite what for most would be an overwhelming crush of distraction, only a single, predetermined idea harbors the young man's focus at this crucial juncture: somehow, someway scoring on this trip downcourt, no matter what.

All eyes are fixed on the consummate high school point guard. The young man is playing in his second consecutive State title game, and the butterflies that once inhabited his stomach have been supplanted by nerves of steel. Kevin is the ultimate floor general, serving as another coach on the court. Recently, the young man was named All-City for the third straight season, All-State for the second, and earlier this evening in a special pre-game ceremony, Kevin Stevens was honored as Mr. Basketball in the State of Georgia for the '67-'68 season. All these accolades and Kevin is still only in his junior season.

An incessant number of college scouts pepper the arena on the campus of Georgia Tech tonight and understandably so—their bulbous eyes thick throughout. They have converged on the capital city in full force this weekend, igniting a low drone about the place upon arrival. Their agenda is simple: they are here to see the man coach and his son play, the two together representing the ultimate package deal.

• • •

Surveying with pinpoint scrutiny, Roger Stevens scours every minute detail from the sideline, casting a wide net of basketball knowledge. Calculating, calculating, calculating, the veteran coach ponders a streamline of possible scenarios that could unfold and confront his team: a made basket, a missed basket, a rebound, a blocked-shot, a loose ball, a turnover, an out-of-bounds play, a time out, an untied shoelace. Nothing evades his keen sense of the game; no stone is left unturned. A geometry teacher by day, the man relishes the opportunity to see every angle of the game; he prides himself in always being two steps ahead. The situation before him is not foreign. Tonight is not the first time one of his teams has played for the coveted Georgia State Championship. He knows what is at stake, what is on the line, and, more importantly, what it takes to win.

Roger Stevens has mastered the helm for the Augusta Christian Academy Patriots for ten seasons. During that span, the man has assembled an astounding and unimpeachable run: six state titles, nine city championships, and an overall record of 190-29 (a .860 winning percentage). In short, Roger Stevens has compiled an untouchable resume that would cause any high school coach to salivate.

Upon Roger's arrival at Augusta Christian, the institution began to witness a transformation, a radical reversal, the revival of a basketball program which had been lifeless for several years. The Academy did an about-face. Seemingly overnight, the school became synonymous with winning, renowned on a state level and beyond, a basketball powerhouse, a factory for producing great teams and individual talent alike, a roundball haven, a dynasty to be feared and respected by all. As a result,

Roger Stevens became known as the best and most sought-after high school coach in the Southeastern United States. Head coaches, athletic directors and even university presidents from Memphis to Miami caught wind of him. They heard of his magic touch, opening tall the floodgates to a massive recruiting frenzy—a frenzy to one day secure the son as a college player and the father as a college assistant coach.

Even so, Roger has always been one to keep first things first. He has held the recruiting frenzy in check, keeping things in proper perspective regardless of how enticing, seductive and intoxicating the whole process became. He made perfectly clear to all comers his plan, that Roger would remain at Augusta Christian until the day of his son's graduation. Then, once that day comes and goes, the two will assess their future options as a tandem—as father and son.

Regardless of where Stevens and his son will take their high-flying basketball show two seasons from now, some unfinished business remains open tonight. More specifically, standing in the way is a pesky, relentless team from Savannah Memorial High School, the lone obstacle preventing another championship banner from finding the Academy rafters back in Augusta.

From the opening tip, the title game has simulated a heavy-weight fight, both teams trading staggering blows—the score nip and tuck all the way. Currently, Coach Stevens and his Patriots narrowly cling to a three-point lead with 1:40 left, and the venerable coach watches intently as the ball resides in the hands of his best player.

Adhering to his father's beleaguered, raspy voice which has steadily depreciated over the course of the night, Kevin floats to the left side of the floor. Once on the wing, he signals for a clear-out, isolating himself at 6'4" versus his much smaller counterpart.

The Savannah player is weary, exhausted, his legs rubbery from a long night of physical punishment. He continues to surrender seven inches in height to the towering, Patriot point guard. Complicating the issue further are the four fouls etched by the Savannah player's name in the scorebook, forcing him to play it safe, close to the vest, allowing the aggressor to have his way.

Kevin shows patience and discipline—time is on his side. Dribble by dribble he prods the smaller opponent toward the goal while keeping an eye out for the double team.

Savannah is at a loss; the Gator defense is still perplexed. How do they guard this stellar marksman? Whenever they run to double or even triple-team Stevens, he always finds the open man and usually for an easy basket. Whenever they play Stevens straight up, leaving their player on an island with him, he burns them as well, evident by his 27 points so far. Either way the result has been the same: every time Kevin Stevens touches the ball, something good happens for the Patriots—the team goes as he goes.

After penetrating the heart of the defense, a mere ten feet from the basket on the left side of the floor, the Academy's best player makes his move. With no double team in sight, Kevin takes a hard dribble toward the middle, his slender body drifting just outside the paint.

"Help!" bellows the Savannah Coach from the nearby sideline, signaling his defense, reminding them of what they discussed during the last time out.

At that instant, two additional defenders rush the advancing ballhandler in a ravenous pack, leaving their defensive assignments to run across the lane.

Instinctively, Kevin responds to the converging traffic by spinning away in the opposite direction toward the baseline, in a whirlwind toward his *go-to* move: a turnaround, midrange, baseline jumper while moving left. As he faces up, the subtle bump he gave the defender grants the necessary separation. Kevin rises confidently in the air, well above the outstretched arm of his counterpart and the triple-team that never got set, rendering his defenders ineffective. The jump shot ascends, then descends in effortless fashion, the ball fluffing the net as it passes through—two points.

The roar of the crowd reaches deafening heights in light of Kevin's gracefulness. Meanwhile the Patriots, now leading 53-48, retreat to the defensive end of the floor.

Roger clenches both fists energetically. The father and son have perfected that very move over an infinite number of hours in the Augusta gymnasium. "So smooth," the coach comments to himself, safely under his breath; privately, so only he and the One who gave Kevin his talents can hear.

Urgency abounds as the diminutive Savannah point guard pushes the ball. The voice of his coach barks the next order, the command finding the player's ear.

Resembling a cat on its hind legs, Kevin assumes his defensive stance, crouching low, ready to pounce. As the smaller opponent crosses the timeline, the coach's son is there to meet him—the way it has been from the start.

After pestering the Savannah counterpart for the entire game, hounding him at every turn, there are three facts Kevin knows for certain about the player he is covering. One, his last name is Wilson. Two, he is a solid point guard in his own right with explosive quickness, compensating for his lack of height. Three, just as the rest of his teammates, his coach and the countless faithful representing Savannah Memorial High School tonight, Wilson is black; a configuration in stark contrast with the Augusta Christian roster—its coach, players, and fans reflect the other end of the spectrum.

On this night, the concept of having different colored uniforms to distinguish between the two teams has proven pointless. Much the same, the encompassing arena crowd remains divided in spirit as well as race, making it easy to determine who is cheering for whom.

Keeping a close eye on all off-the-court activity is a legion of Atlanta's finest, men in dark blue who pepper the facility. There was a rumor before the game Reverend King might be in attendance to see a distant relative play for Savannah, and the local PD have prepared themselves inside and outside the building for all crowd-related contingencies.

Wilson eludes Kevin with a quick move to his left then passes to the wing. Making the catch, the Savannah small forward immediately looks inside; his intentions obvious. The Gators want the ball in one place: down low on the block in the hands of the muscular, 6'6", 240-pound center who is the focal point of their offensive attack.

Drawing the undesirable assignment of guarding this stalwart opponent, Reynolds Green, the August center, offers valiant resistance. Despite possessing good size at 6'6" as well, Reynolds is still significantly overmatched, outweighed, and ultimately unable to maneuver around his counterpart's immense torso. The Savannah player is simply too strong, his legs fashioned after tree trunks; huge, grounded, cemented, immovable. His upper body is much the same: massive, packed, solid through and through.

"Watch the clear-out, ref!" Roger blasts from the Academy bench at the sight of the struggle in the paint, channeling his anxiety toward the nearest official. "He's holding him off!"

By his fire-breathing tone, it is clear the coach means business. No one is more serious about winning than Roger Stevens. Every time he assumes the sideline, white-hot competitiveness wells up and blazes from his sternum. Even now his face takes on a stunning shade of bright red; his voice searing, his protest vehement. Regardless, the man's resounding petition falls on deaf ears—the officials allowing the physical play to persist.

The Savannah wingman spots a crease in the defense and delivers a crisp pass inside. From there, his wide-bodied teammate takes over, the Savannah center wasting no time in bending a quick, assertive move to the goal despite all opposition.

Reynolds feels helpless, exposed. The All-State player from Savannah is too much to handle one on one. All the Augusta center can do now is foul and foul hard. Putting his thoughts into action, Reynolds saddles the opponent, practically jumping on his back, wrapping both arms around the opponent's robust frame, denying the shot a chance to get airborne.

A shrilling whistle intervenes. The baseline official had no choice; Reynolds made it easy for him.

"Good foul, Reynolds! Roger is heard applauding from the team bench. "That's okay!" he declares, content with sending the opposing center to the line rather than giving him a layup.

With a chance to cut into the Augusta lead, Savannah Memorial's top scorer steps to the free throw line. Sweat pours mercilessly over the ridge of his brow. Desperately, the player searches for a dry section of his uniform to wipe his hands—there is none.

The crowd noise is vociferous, like thunder as the first free throw goes up…and in, the ball catching the inside of the rim before spinning rapidly through. The basket cuts the lead to four.

In between foul shots, Kevin rallies his teammates, keenly forewarning them of the inevitable full-court press that is sure to come.

The Savannah center eyes the target again. His concentration is intense, almost spiritual as he tries to remain impervious to the throbbing, swelling uproar around him; most of the distraction coming from the Augusta fans behind the basket, the throng frantically waving their arms back and forth, beseeching a miss. Standing tall at the line, the physical stature of the young black man is impressive, enhanced, making the senior in his final game of high school appear much older than 18 years of age. However, regardless of his mature, external features, the hulking adolescent is unable to hide the frightened look in his glazing eyes.

After much meditation, the second attempt lifts and hangs.

The crowd noise ceases as all eyes cling to the leather sphere floating toward the goal with just a touch of backspin. This time, the ball finds the heel of the rim and kicks off, ricocheting high into the air where it suspends in taunting fashion above the conglomerate of uniforms waiting below; the bodies jostle for position. Sweat flies. Grunts grunt. No calls are made. Elbows are liberal—the fight is on.

The ball descends into the fray and is tipped, tipped, and tipped again.

Breathless is the capacity crowd, all throats gripped firmly by a glove of tension.

For what feels like an eternity, the basketball volleys from one hand to the next. Finally, the ball squirts from the pack, finding a home. Unfortunately for the Patriots, home is in the hands of the bulky Savannah center who had ironically stayed put, not budging from the free throw line during the entire fracas.

Coach Stevens is beside himself. A sharp pain shoots up his spine. His teeth grit. His fists clench again; this time, not from joy. Veins protrude from his neck as the man suffers mental and physical anguish over a loose ball falling into enemy hands, the man knowing how critical every single bounce can be.

Following the mad scramble, Kevin realizes an opponent has been left wide-open beneath the basket, the player waving his arms vigorously, looking for an easy score. The Augusta point guard scurries to cover the open man—the Savannah small forward.

With Kevin now blanketing a new man, Trevor Hopkins, the Augusta small forward, must step out and switch, covering the much shorter, much quicker point guard, Wilson.

"Stay with him, Trevor! I've got yours!" Kevin calls out in support; albeit, surveying a situation of which he does not approve.

Trevor immediately finds himself on his heels, no match for the catlike quickness of the 135-pound opponent.

Wilson wastes no time in exploiting the matchup. The Savannah guard jukes right, then left, then right in a flurry of movements, displaying great ball control at the top of the key. After briefly toying with the taller and less coordinated defender, the electrifying guard blows past Trevor with a hard, driving, first step, throttling unimpeded to the hole, beating all help and rotation and laying the ball over the front of the rim for two.

It is now the Savannah faithful who catapult to their feet. The basket breathes new life into their school. The score is 53-51; Augusta barely in front.

Following the made basket, the Gators surprise no one by resuming their trademark, hyper-aggressive, full-court press.

Roger watches helplessly as his Patriots struggle to inbound the basketball.

Kevin is shrouded by two defenders—one in front and one in back—who are with him wherever he goes. After a tiresome effort, the point guard successfully eludes the dogged double team, possessing the ball deep in the corner, dubiously circumscribed by both the baseline and sideline. The coach's son pivots and views the disheartening, 80-some-odd-foot separation between him and the Augusta basket. Also, the vicious, swarming double team is prompt to return, complete with flailing arms, waving hands and quick feet.

The baseline official continues his count: five..., six....

Roger stands powerless on the sideline with zero timeouts at his disposal, his team in trouble.

The Savannah defense is a blanket spread over the entire dimension of the arena floor; every Patriot is covered.

Running dangerously low on time, Kevin must decide. Zealously, he scans the hardwood, focusing on the first friendly jersey he spots at half-court, looking to Trevor who is the only outlet in sight.

Contrary to Kevin's knowledge, out of view, lurking inconspicuously behind Trevor is the enemy. The defender has been locked into Kevin's eyes from the beginning, shifting in every direction the Augusta point guard has glanced, ready to force the turnover.

To the dismay of this eager defender and the shock of every eye in the arena, Kevin recants his actions and craftily refuses to launch a cross-court pass. Instead, the veteran point guard pulls the ball back down into his chest, watching as the two surrounding defenders explode vertically into the air. It was only a fake, an excellent pump fake at that, and the Savannah defense bought it hook, line and sinker.

With his would-be captors now airborne, the wide-open sideline appears to Kevin as the break of day. Taking the clear path, he seizes the opportunity unscathed, scooting past the timeline and beating the referee's count by less than a second.

"Oh, come on, Ref!" the Savannah coach wails in a fit of disgust, flinging his clipboard down the team bench, nearly decapitating two of his reserves. "That was ten!"

The unruly symptoms of panic shown by the man are understandable. The balance of the Gator season has been reduced to a mere 45-second window of opportunity. The only remaining option is to foul; foul and pray for a barrage of Patriot free throws to miss the mark.

"Foul! Foul!" the Savannah Coach commands.

"Spread! Spread!" the Augusta Coach counters.

In spontaneous response to their general's clamoring instructions, the Academy players deploy accordingly. Positioned near the right hash mark of the frontcourt, Kevin now secures the basketball with confidence, simply waiting for a defender to give chase.

The two Savannah players from the backcourt return humiliated. With outstretched arms, they run full speed at the Academy ball-handler. Despite their best intentions, they are unable to reach him before the mindful point guard whips a pass to Trevor Hopkins.

Two different defenders react abruptly. They too pursue the Augusta forward out of desperation, likewise, failing to reach him in time.

Trevor is quick to rid himself of the basketball, finding Reynolds at the top of the key.

With swift success, the Patriot offense swings the ball from spot to spot, point to point, player to player.

Roger watches intently from the sideline, ecstatic with the crisp ball-movement on display, his eyes continuously shifting back and forth between the action and the game clock. "That's it! Swing it! Swing it!"

The basketball comes full circle, working its way back to Kevin at the right hash.

The seconds erode—22...21...20....

The Academy point guard watches as the seconds dissolve, the clock refusing to show mercy on Savannah Memorial.

Discomfited, the opposition scrambles furiously, feverishly, as if pursuing the sole antidote to a recently digested poison.

Kevin's mind shifts into attack mode as he surveys the hectic scene before him—*it's time*. Looking diagonally across the court, he identifies Trevor wide-open amid the chaos; a Savannah player not within 20-feet of him.

Quick to read the eyes of his teammate and friend, Trevor breaks toward the goal without hesitation, signaling for the ball as he does without an obstacle in his path.

Roger watches from the sideline as the golden opportunity plays out. "Now!" his lungs discharge.

On cue, Kevin fires a scorching, cross-court laser, hitting the recipient in perfect stride.

Upon delivery of the pass, Trevor turns his attention skyward. Pushing from the hardwood with his left foot, he elevates, extending toward the goal with his right hand in textbook fashion, gently laying the basketball off the backboard and looking back as the leather sphere drops innocently through the hoop, causing the Patriot lead to drift out of reach.

An uproar consumes the capacity crowd; an eruption of joy from some, an eruption of agony from others. From floor to ceiling, the Atlanta arena embodies hysteria, the decibel-reading ascending to the stratosphere. The bleachers quake from the ear-splitting bedlam, most of the ruckus caused by crazed Augusta fans who can smell and all but taste victory.

On the sideline, however, in a peculiar display, even with victory now in hand, Roger Stevens suddenly is the calmest person in the building. Oddly subdued, he reminds himself of something, the same introspection of which he has reminded himself on six prior occasions. *Remember this moment, Roger. Remember it. You may never get here again.*

Down by four with under ten seconds left, Savannah Memorial continues to display the persistence and tenacity that have brought them this far.

With basketball in hand, Wilson jets upcourt, weaving through a maze of taller bodies who futilely attempt to decelerate the whisking guard. Even so, the valiant effort is too-little-too-late, as Wilson's pull-up, 15-foot jumper finds only rim, the final rebound landing appropriately in Kevin's arms.

Showing great presence of mind, the Augusta point guard wisely heaves the ball high into the air and well out of reach, thus allowing time to expire and another State championship to become a reality.

At last, the arena horn gives off a powerful, booming, long-sustained blast. The game is over: Augusta Christian Academy 55, Savannah Memorial 51.

What ensues next is nothing less than a mob scene. Augusta players, cheerleaders, and fans spill uncontrollably onto the hardwood floor in a mass of bodies; the assemblage bouncing up and down in unpolished, unrehearsed rhythm. Pushed into the roaring cluster of celebration as well, Roger Stevens suddenly finds himself among the faithful.

Amid the multitude, a father and son lock eyes; the head coach and the best player on the team. Immediately, the two begin making their way past all obstacles, striving toward each other, struggling past grasping hands before finally melding in a hearty embrace.

With all the crazed hoopla surrounding Roger and his son, the thoughts running through the man's mind do so at a dizzying pace.

"Two in a row, Dad!" Kevin exclaims over the excessive clamor while intentionally messing up his father's hair, jubilation coursing through the veins of the teenager. "We did it!"

Roger fights hard to keep his eyes from filling, warding off any signs of perceived weakness. "Yes, we did, Kev," he replies in wonder. "Praise God: yes, we did."

Perfect. A perfect moment in time. Roger and his son cleave to one another at center-court, relishing not so much in another state championship but in their love for one another and the rare opportunity they have been given.

The moment holds, and then, as all moments do, it passes as something else catches Roger's eye. In the distance, through the partying Augusta teammates and fans, the man beholds the players from Savannah Memorial. He notices many of them either sitting or lying on the court, their heads hanging in despair as their coach, parents, and supporters try to offer solace. A sizeable section of the hardwood floor now resembles a depleted war zone; a battlefield, littered with bodies wounded in spirit.

With empathy now in the driver's seat, Roger parts from his son and motions for him to follow. The two wade through the jovial drove around them. As they do, one Savannah player comes into view, the young black man lying face down on the court, his body plagued from head to toe by both exhaustion and sorrow. Upon drawing closer, Roger recognizes the player: Wilson.

Eventually, the August coach kneels beside the diminutive point guard from Savannah.

Reduced to tears, Wilson gave all the strength and energy he could muster this night.

Roger reaches down, placing a strong yet tender hand on the young man's jersey number. "You played a great game, son. Gave us all we could handle," the Augusta Coach conveys, searching for the right words knowing full well such words are few and far between at a time such as this.

Contrary to what most people know about Roger Stevens, regardless of his bulletproof reputation and despite his teams reveling in success over the past decade, winning has not always come easily for the man. Life, in general, has not always come easily for the man. Roger knows all too well what losing is about. He has been there. He can empathize with what this young man from Savannah is experiencing. It is the worst, the lowest, to try as hard as you can and still fall short, face-first; to feel inadequate, not good enough. Roger has felt the venomous sting of defeat too many times to count, mostly as a small-college player and an upstart high school coach. More than anything, the man is aware how supposed words of encouragement are anything but at a time like this. He knows there is no such thing as the right thing to say, and he realizes the only effective remedy is a heavy dose of time in which to recover.

Unsure if his words are making a difference, unsure if the depleted Savannah player is even listening, Roger continues. "But if you can honestly say you left everything you had to give right here on this floor...if there is nothing left in the tank, then you have done all that was asked of you. You can sleep well tonight."

Indeed, Wilson heard every word. Furthermore, despite the plague of a devastating loss, an ointment of encouragement begins to salve the player's bereavement, even if for a few moments, causing the appreciative young man to lift his head from the floor to hear the man conclude.

"I wish you had been on my team this year, son. I could have used you." Sincere are the words from Roger's heart. Even so, the man fails to grasp the significance of the moment. Roger fails to realize his words of encouragement serve as more than a simple extension of cordial sportsmanship. Much more than that, his words are the kindest this young black man has ever received from a white man. These words, as simple as they may be, Jacob Wilson will never forget.

"Thank you, sir," the youth replies in humility, the tears on his cheeks beginning to dry. "You've gotta' good team there."

As Roger kneels, a pair of glossy, well-polished dress shoes come to a halt beside him. Looking up, the coach from Augusta Christian recognizes his counterpart, the coach from Savannah Memorial.

"Congratulations, Coach," offers the black gentleman with white blended in his hair and beard, his hand extended.

Roger springs to his feet and accepts his hand and token of goodwill while declaring, "Coach, you stay right here. My boys have something to say to you and your team."

Whether the Academy players are finished celebrating or not is of no concern to Roger. Instead, the adamant coach walks intrepidly into the assemblage, manually removing those in Patriot uniform one by one. His instructions are specific and non-negotiable.

Pleasantly surprised, the head coach from Savannah Memorial watches as a single-file line of Augusta players soon emerges, humbly approaching him and his team, wishing to congratulate them on a hard-fought and well-played game. It had not been automatic this season that a squad of all white players felt the need to grace the Gators in unpretentious fashion, and the man welcomes the gesture with open arms.

Roger Stevens leads the way, and his son follows.

3

Agent Nathan Maxwell peers around the corner of the building. The night hides him well. He eyes the officer in his patrol car. The policeman is at a distance but still close enough to see everything if Maxwell plays his cards right.

Across the street in downtown Decatur is a group of black pedestrians, young people hanging out and enjoying the cool evening air.

Maxwell determines now will be as good a time as any. He steps behind the building again and removes the bottle of whiskey. The man takes a deep breath then a big swig, washing the liquor around in his mouth for a few seconds before spitting it out as far as he can. He next douses his shirt with alcohol over both shoulders and tosses the bottle in a nearby trash can.

As the FBI Agent crosses the street, he can tell he has no one's attention. Maxwell begins to sway as he walks to create a scene.

The officer spots the odd behavior from behind the wheel, tracking the man as he draws near the group of blacks standing under a streetlight.

Maxwell pries his way into the innocent cluster.

"Hey, man," blurts one in the group, angry at Maxwell for his rudeness.

"Sorry, man," Maxwell responds. "I just…."

The officer watches from his patrol car as the seemingly drunk white man swings and hits one of the young black men across the face.

"Hey! Hey!" Shouts from onlookers interrupt what was a pleasant night. "Grab him!"

Maxwell falls to the ground to cover up, making it difficult for anyone to grasp his arm. "I'm sorry. I'm sorry," Maxwell pleads with the group.

"Sorry doesn't cut it!" is the response from the young man who was punched.

"All right! Break it up!"

Those in the group turn to see the approaching white officer, causing them to hesitate. "We were just standing here!"

"Get back!" The officer wades through the crowd.

"He punched me, man!"

"I saw what he did. Step back!" is the officer's monotone response.

Maxwell remains curled up next to the curb like an innocent victim.

"He's a crazy drunk, sir. You need to lock him up!"

"I'll take care of it!" the officer announces, reaching down for Maxwell's arm.

"Well, what are you gonna' do with him?" asks another, the group clearly dissatisfied by the officer's lack of urgency.

"I said get back!" the officer declares, raising his tone and placing a hand on the end of his night stick for good measure.

Those in the group look to each other before a voice of reason prevails. "Come on, Jimmy. Let's go, man."

One by one, the young black men step away and give space.

The officer stands tall.

Maxwell continues to lie in the street.

"That's not right, man," a voice is heard as the group heads in the opposite direction.

With any threat from the group put down, the officer turns his attention back to the drunk in the street. "All right. Get up."

Maxwell stumbles to his feet and intentionally falls into the officer, breathing across his face.

"Oh!" The officer turns his head at the overwhelming gust of liquor. "That's terrible."

"I apologize, Officer," Maxwell offers with a mixture of belching and babbling. "Just...up in the sky...Maryland."

Witnesses look on as the Decatur policeman leads the public drunk down the sidewalk.

"Come on." The policemen strong arms the undercover agent. "Get in the car."

Maxwell plops into the back seat on his side. "Thank you, sir. I'll sleep here tonight."

With a look of disgust, the officer closes the back door and slides behind the wheel. As he pulls onto the street, the policeman radios a call to headquarters.

Maxwell's eyes and ears focus as he listens intently.

"This is Unit-5 to base. I'm bringing a drunk to the station. Get a cell ready."

● ● ●

Roger rubs his eyes. They are itchy, sore, tired from a tedious night of traveling. Roger glances to his right. There slouches Kevin fast asleep in the passenger seat, failing the duty of navigator. *Looks comfortable*, the weary captain ponders. *That'll be me soon enough.*

As the man staves off yawn after yawn, the fact that he was able to round up a replacement for tomorrow—make that later this morning—is huge. Roger Stevens, a long-time, dedicated Sunday school teacher who only moonlights as a basketball coach, contemplated arriving for church and his class on a mere two hours of rest. However, Karen, his better and smarter half, reminded him of how futile he is on anything less than six.

He missed her. It had not been the same without her in Atlanta. Prior to this weekend, she had not missed a single game in his entire coaching career or Kevin's playing career, and of all the games to miss—the State championship. Roger, regardless, stood firm, having it no other way. Karen needed to be with her mother—end of discussion. There would always be more games and, God willing, more State Championships.

When it came to marrying Karen, Roger knew he had struck gold. Never in recorded history has there been a woman so full of tolerance, kindness, love, gentleness, compassion and the list is perpetual. She is world-class to the man, top-notch, first-rate, a Godsend and so are her parents, which makes the situation involving Karen's mother even more difficult to bear. The man loves his in-laws dearly, and from day one they have been an enormous blessing.

Karen grew up the oldest of three sisters, and all three married within the tight span of 16 months as young women. Before the ladies knew it, not only were they newlyweds, but all three had little ones on the way. Roger and Karen were first with Kevin. The other two sisters had married brothers and settled in Columbia, South Carolina, and their babies were just months behind. Ultimately, Karen's parents decided to move to South Carolina to be near Karen's sisters. Roger and Karen were not offended in the least by this decision since Karen's sisters had seven children between them, and Roger and Karen only had Kevin. It was a simple numbers game and made sense to everyone.

However, upon their departure from the Augusta area, Karen's parents displayed a great act of generosity. After many conversations and much convincing, Karen's parents overwhelmed Roger and Karen with their kindness. Roger eventually swallowed his pride and accepted the keys to the home where Karen and her sisters were raised: a gorgeous, palatial, three-story, pre-Civil War home; an eight-bedroom beauty on 10 acres of rustic Augusta countryside.

The gesture was difficult for a man like Roger to receive; he had never been big on handouts. Not only was Roger from the school of hard knocks, but he graduated at the top of his class. Part of him knew it was important to receive a blessing; otherwise, the blessing could never be given. Another part of him viewed charity as something for someone else. In the end, with great hesitation and much thankfulness, he agreed.

The car turns onto a familiar road. Roger looks to the right and sees the never-changing Savannah River. The water is stellar scenery as a half-moon hovers just above the sparkling, glass-top surface. The homes are few and far between along this country road which matches the riverbank curve for curve. Ahead, however, there are signs of life.

As the Plymouth Fury draws near the residence, a distinctively long, gravel drive grades downhill to meet the rural highway. From the edge of the drive, Roger looks toward the house and becomes ecstatic. "She's home!" he blurts aloud, seeing Karen's car parked through the darkness. He was not expecting her until tomorrow.

With eagerness, the husband shoots the car rapidly up the drive, causing a bumpy ride; one that rudely jostles Kevin's body, waking him for good.

"Huh…, what?" the boy mutters.

"I said you mom's home," the man repeats; although, the enthusiasm he feels is clearly one-sided. "Maybe she's still up."

At the sound of Roger's Plymouth rumbling up the drive, gravel peeling and scattering wildly under its tires, the vestibule light kicks on and then the porch light. Soon, the front door opens…and there she is.

Karen descends from the porch with her customary shoulder-length blonde hair, her energetic bounce, and, most of all, her smile—the smile Roger has been rushing home to see for two decades.

From a safe distance, she observes her husband jolt the car to a sudden stop, the man vaulting through the driver-side door while neglecting to throw the Plymouth fully into park.

Bursting out in laughter, Karen watches as the man frantically attempts to slide his large frame back in the car as it begins to recede down the drive; Roger has one leg in and one leg out, their son still in the passenger seat.

The emergency brake is desperately applied, giving way to a nasty screech. Just that quickly, the man reappears. "When did you get here," he queries.

"Earlier tonight…or last night…or whenever it was," she replies. "Surprised?"

"Absolutely!"

After jogging around the automobile—the now parked automobile—the husband takes his wife in an almost rough embrace as if just returning from war. He next delivers an equally passionate kiss, causing her head and body to tilt backward.

"Missed you," he says in a muffled voice, his lips still pressed against hers.

"Missed you, too," she responds.

Despite Roger's thrill to see the love of his life, there is a burning question he must ask, and it cannot wait.

"How's Mom?"

Karen deflects. "What about the game?"

"No, later on that," Roger demands. "How's Mom?"

The smile on Karen's face wanes. After glancing down, she looks up again, trying to walk the line between optimism and honesty. "Could be better." Her sigh accompanies the diagnosis. "It's still her kidneys. They are failing."

Quietly with her husband, Karen shares a handful of poignant details, and she was correct: the news is not good. Rather, the truth is blunt and the outlook harsh.

Roger takes a deep breath as the world grinds to a halt. He thought he had braced himself for bad news but not this bad. Automatically, his mind begins to play the game of worst-possible-scenario.

"We'll just have to keep praying," Karen counters, attempting to thwart the discouraging particulars with a slightly energetic tone. Looking up at her husband, she reads his countenance well. "Hey." She tugs at the ends of his shirt collar. "God's in control. He'll take care of it," she reminds her mate for life with confidence. "Remember Kevin?"

Coming out of his trance, Roger offers a partial nod. His wife's inference, *remember Kevin*, saddled his attention; a tool both have used through the years when the other is running low on faith.

At birth, Kevin's left foot was twisted inwardly. The hope the boy would simply grow out of it, or the problem would correct itself, was incorrect. The prognosis given by one doctor had the toddler all but fitted with a corrective brace for most of his youth. However, before any further action was taken, Roger and Karen did something else: they prayed. Even more, the Stevens Family put their faith in action, bringing Kevin forward in church where they and their pastor beseeched God for a miracle.

As a result, the same doctor who had been confident in his original prediction quickly changed course. Kevin Stevens never wore a brace on his foot, which is a primary reason why Roger and Karen and their pastor always went to great lengths to see Kevin play basketball. They wanted to see Kevin play but not only because of his talent. They also wanted to see the boy play as a visible reminder that God still heals.

Therefore, whenever Roger or Karen needs a lift, a shot of faith in the arm amid tough circumstances, they remind one another with the words, *remember Kevin.*

Right on cue, the sluggish teenager emerges from the Plymouth half-conscious, wearing an impression of the car's vinyl interior on the side of his face.

"Hey, you!" his mother calls, always glad to see her *baby*, a pet name the 17-year-old detests.

"Hi, Mom."

Karen, after looking around for help but getting none, addresses the elephant in the driveway. "Is someone going to tell me about the game or what?"

Kevin offers a mischievous grin, "55-51."

"Ugh! Win or lose?"

"We won."

"Yes!" Karen shouts, throwing her arms in the air and then around the neck of her much taller son, and, being that she is only 5'3", she stands on the tips of her toes to do so.

One look at the Stevens Family and it is clear from which parent Kevin gets what. The boy clearly favors his father's 6'5" stature. At the same time, Roger failed to pass his brown hair and darker features down the line. Instead, this is where Karen stakes her claim. Kevin bears his mother's sapphire blue eyes and golden blonde hair, which Kevin keeps conveniently chopped into a crew cut just like all the boys at the Academy.

"Let's celebrate!" exclaims the jubilant wife and mother. "Who's hungry?"

Neither Roger nor Kevin are quite sure what time it is, neither do they know for which meal to be hungry. Drawing from past experiences, all they know is never decline a delicious, home-cooked meal when Karen Stevens is offering.

• • •

One hour later, Kevin is upstairs and in bed—out cold.

Roger is in the living room, mindlessly sorting through his briefcase—not because there is any work to do in these pre-dawn hours but mostly out of habit. The delectable meal his wife made settles peacefully in his stomach, weighing him down like a warm boulder. Roger offered to help clean up following the glorious, impromptu feast. However, his wife declined his assistance.

Running on fumes, melting into the sofa, Roger decrees, "Forget this junk," plopping his briefcase onto the adjacent coffee table. Upon impact, three envelopes jettison from the mess and fall to the floor. Roger reaches down, recognizing who the envelopes are from—the return address stamped firmly in the upper-left corner. Even more, Roger recognizes what these envelopes have come to represent.

The man is unable to prevent a groan from escaping. His face is quick to contort; not due to any pain or stiffness. Rather, his discomfort manifests once he discerns the all-too-familiar penmanship inked across the front of the envelopes. These letters have become a thorn lodged firmly in his side ever since the first envelope arrived several weeks ago.

Except for the news about his ailing mother-in-law, Roger had considered today a great day until now. At least the letters had slipped his mind for a while. He had hardly given them any thought this weekend. Maybe it was God's way of giving him a break, cutting him some slack. Otherwise, this situation has been constantly on the coach's mind for weeks, entangling him, ensnaring him. The envelopes even hurt to see. The sight of them scrapes at his heart, scours his soul. Roger cannot remember when such a supposed non-issue has emotionally and mentally assailed him in this way. The whole scenario sickens him to his stomach, especially after the horrid, woeful, poisonous episode reported in the news from two weeks ago.

Karen switches off the kitchen light and graces the living room.

Roger senses her approach and immediately tosses the envelopes face-down on the table. The last thing he wants to do is burden her even more on a night like this. She has been through so much with her mother—they all have.

From behind, Karen closes the distance with haste and wraps her arms around her much larger man, enjoying the warmth. "So…, did you miss me these past few days?"

Quickly, the husband shifts from solemn to sarcastic. "Yeah, I guess."

"You guess?" Mrs. Stevens responds. "How's that couch looking right about now, Mister?"

Roger wheels around, smiling mischievously. "Not as good as you."

4

Should be anytime now, Agent Dennison entertains wishfully at one end of the office.

It better be anytime now, Special Agent in Charge Dawson stews behind his desk, the venerable man from the Bureau staring at the telephone, as if he can will the phone to ring via his dogged mind power.

Phase one of the D.C. plan is complete. Agent Maxwell infiltrated the Klan, but he told Dawson it was a hard sell. The suspicion of the Klan leaders has been on the rise since the FBI arrived in Macon, and Maxwell said it took his arrest in Decatur to pry his way inside. The fact that Maxwell had a public arrest record for assaulting a black man was key. D.C. and Dawson knew the Klan might research Maxwell's background, and the Klan certainly did; everyone in the group seems to have a cousin or a friend in every city in the South. Thanks to the flawless driver's license produced by the document specialists at the Atlanta FBI, the Macon chapter of the Klan welcomed Agent Maxwell under his false identity: Frederick "Freddy" Collins.

Tired of sitting, Agent Dennison stands and begins to pace. Through the blinds, he sees agents from Atlanta, Charlotte, and Memphis, all laboring side by side and scurrying about the makeshift office.

The piercing squall of the telephone rips the boredom in two. "This is Dawson," the man gruffly answers. "Yeah, what do you got?"

There's Maxwell, Dennison affirms to himself, ambling back across the office to resume his seat, listening intently. Concerned for his co-worker and friend in the Bureau, on the one hand, Dennison also knows if anyone can blend with the average citizens of Macon, it is Maxwell. Dennison just wants Maxwell to come back in one piece.

Behind his desk, Agent Dawson furiously scribbles while Maxwell spills his best stuff. "Go on…" The scribbling continues. "Then what I need is your best hunch. What's your gut telling you?" The subsequent pause is a long one. "That's what I needed. Get back to me with anything new and be careful."

Dennison awaits the news, any news. "Maxwell?"

"Yeah," Dawson responds while still etching notes from the phone conversation. The venerable agent takes a deep breath, leaning back in his chair; the details are gnawing at him. "Maxwell said Macon P.D. discovered a body this morning: Phillip Barlow, a known Klan member around these parts, dead in the cab of his truck on the outskirts of town from an apparent self-inflicted wound—a revolver in the seat next to him. Macon P.D. proceeded to Barlow's home, and it gets even better: large quantities of fertilizer, fuel, wires, bomb-making paraphernalia—everything a growing boy needs to craft a device, along with a typed note."

"How did the note read?"

"*I'm sorry*, basically. *I'm sorry for bombing the school.*"

Dennison, a quick study, states the obvious. "Sounds pretty tidy."

Dawson thumps his fingers on the desk in contemplation. "It could be just that simple, you know? Sometimes it is."

"That would be very tidy," Dennison responds. "Too tidy. It screams set up."

A pound at the office door interrupts. Agent Blaine Wheeler, the lone black agent on site in Macon, does not wait to be waved in—his information is too urgent.

"Sir."

"Yes, Wheeler," Dawson acknowledges.

"Sir, I have Macon P.D. on the line, they say they might have a break for us."

Dennison reads the mind of his superior, both men exchanging a half-smile and both men knowing Maxwell's intel is always faster than that of the local P.D. "I'll take it," Dennison volunteers, standing to his feet to follow Wheeler out the door.

With a furrowed brow, Dawson reaches for the receiver and begins dialing. It is clear to him Dennison is not buying the details regarding this Phillip Barlow, and Dawson's superior probably will not either. The call quickly filters through a switchboard operator in D.C., and Dawson soon shares a five-digit code with an additional operator. After a few seconds of silence, a voice emerges on the other end to which Dawson responds.

"Sir, this is Dawson," the Special Agent in Charge reports with ostensible reverence in his tone. "I have an update for you."

● ● ●

The next day, Jerry makes his normal morning rounds on the restaurant floor, armed twofold with a pot of coffee and a huge grin.

"Hello, Jerry.... Hi, Jerry." The familiar voices of his patrons salute the man in typical fashion.

Not to be outdone in kindness, Jerry, Owner of Jerry's Restaurant, returns each gesture by filling every cup to the brim; this is the part of the job he loves, mingling with the people, his customers, talking about weather, politics, and, of course, The Bulldogs. However, regardless of how pleasant this morning has been for the man, his day swiftly undergoes a turn.

The front door to the restaurant swings open. Two black men enter the restaurant. Carefree, they walk past the spot where Jerry's sign used to be and find themselves a booth.

The sight is infuriating to Jerry. The owner's blood percolates much like the pot of coffee in his hand. Even so, Jerry keeps smiling. He proceeds past the two new patrons without a glance; a cup of coffee for them is out of the question. Truth be known, the owner would much rather pour the searing liquid on their heads than serve them. Instead, Jerry will get his waitress to take their orders.

Exiting the dining area, Jerry walks the length of the kitchen and moves toward the back of the restaurant. He stops at the door leading into the banquet hall. Before entering, he hesitates and exhales, gathering himself before crossing the threshold.

A man oddly sits in the center of a large room, occupying one table in the middle of a dozen or so empty tables—he has the entire banquet hall to himself. His face is behind the morning edition of The Macon Telegraph; his breakfast plate now empty.

Jerry approaches the man with deference and does his best to calm his jittering right hand, allowing him to pour the man a refill.

"How was everything?" the owner inquires.

"Wonderful, Jerry. Always wonderful." The customer's tone and demeanor are polite, uncharacteristic for someone who evokes such fear.

Jerry, with the two of them in private, speaks freely as he gestures toward the newspaper in the patron's hand.

"So, what do you think of the front page?"

The reply from behind the paper is blunt. "What's there to think about? They told it like it is."

"It's too bad about Phillip," Jerry offers in a remorseful tone.

"Yes. Too bad." With those words, Raymond Huddler lowers the morning paper for another sip of coffee. As he does, coming into full view is the jagged scar on the right side of his face.

Jerry tries not to look at it, but there is nowhere else to look.

No one, including Jerry, dares to ask Raymond Huddler about the scar on his face, and even Huddler fully acknowledges the scar is not pleasant to the eye. However, the mark also serves as a battle scar of which Raymond is very proud; the result of a knife fight he had with a black man many years ago—a black man who is no longer alive.

"Phillip will be missed," Huddler continues in an exhortative tone. "But remember, Jerry, all things work together for good to those who love God...to those called according to His purpose."

In Jerry's opinion, the only thing more sinister than getting on Raymond Huddler's bad side is to hear Raymond Huddler quote scripture. Jerry believes if the Bible is the *Good Book*, it sounds anything but good when passing through the lips of this man.

"All is well," Huddler adds. "We just need to go underground for a little while, that's all. This happens every so often. We have to let our friends in the FBI feel like they are winning for a change."

Jerry decides to change the subject. "By the way, two black guys just walked in my restaurant like they own the place." The restaurant owner sulks, shrinking childishly in his chair. "I really miss my sign."

Raymond Huddler stops everything to look the owner of Jerry's Restaurant in the eye. "I'm sorry to hear that, Jerry. Make sure you bring me their food before you serve it to them, okay?"

5

Roger Stevens takes a different route home from work this day; he told his wife he would be a little late. Kevin rode off with some friends following the celebratory championship rally at the Academy, and Roger finds himself alone with extra time at his disposal. The coach eases his car into the familiar parking lot of Hillside Christian Church, thinking to himself, *it's as if time stands still at this place.*

"Knock, knock," he announces once entering the church doors.

"I'm here," a voice calls from around the corner.

Roger steps into the office of Reverend Jordan, and there he is: Roger's pastor for life. Reverend Jordan officiated Roger and Karen's wedding and was there to welcome Kevin into the world—just to name a couple of highlights through the years.

Roger has learned, while carrying a position of high local visibility, one loyal confidant is worth more than a thousand flattering tongues. Furthermore, if anyone has proven to be and even surpassed that of a loyal confidant in Roger's life, it has been Reverend Jordan.

"Roger," the near-elderly man proclaims, standing joyfully to his feet.

"Hope I'm not interrupting," Roger offers as the men embrace briefly.

"Never." Even if Roger were interrupting, the reverend would never allude to the fact. "Are you caught up on your rest?" the minister asks gleefully. "Recovered from the playoff push?"

"It takes a while," Roger the part-time insomniac responds. "I'll get there eventually."

"Probably already thinking about next season, aren't you?"

Next season, the coach ponders. *What an ironic question.* "I'm...trying not to think about next season actually." *What am I even doing here?* Roger badgers himself in silence. *What is this kind man supposed to tell me? Short of suggesting prayer, what revelation can he possibly have? It's not his problem; not his responsibility.* Roger speaks up to break from his trance, realizing he has lapsed into an elongated pause. "Not quite there is what I mean."

The seasoned minister takes the hint. "I understand. Let's talk about something else then."

Something else, Roger scoffs internally. *There is nothing else right now. What else is there? My entire life has become only about this.* "Agreed." Roger has trouble concealing a sigh. "Let's talk about something else, Pastor."

Reverend Jordan discerns a hitch, a speedbump in Roger's tone and demeanor—odd behavior for a man who just celebrated another glorious state title. Even so, the pastor opts to let Roger initiate from here. The reverend simply sits across his desk with a supportive smile.

Normally a man of poise, to try and uphold his composure for the sake of reputation would take more energy than Roger Stevens can muster today. Instead, the man uncharacteristically struggles with his breathing before running both hands firmly through his hair. Roger next slumps forward in his chair, choosing to stare at the floor rather than the pair of eyes across the desk. "I... I'm not," Roger searches for the right way to start his sentence but falls short. "Not sure where to begin."

Pastor Jordan does not bail the man out. He simply continues to sit and smile.

"I can't believe I'm going to say what I'm going to say," Roger offers amid a sarcastic chuckle, reluctant to broach the subject; the last thing he wants to do is give his burden validity. Roger knows once he brings it up, it is no longer just in his mind; he is acknowledging the burden exists.

With great apprehension, his tone fragile and quivering, Roger surmises there is no better place to start than the beginning. "I apologize if I become long-winded...."

The Reverend acquiesces with a courteous wave, settling in his chair, knowing it is unlike Roger to intentionally monopolize anyone's time.

"So," Roger gives a final, beleaguered pause, "A few months ago, we were in Columbia, visiting Karen's parents, and I bumped into a gentleman at a gas station in town. We started an innocent conversation and, come to find out, he is a high school principal from Macon...."

• • •

The unfamiliar vehicle first catches Karen's eye as she passes through the living room. *Whoever it is,* Karen observes, *they're pulling up the drive.* Karen tries to identify the driver, but she cannot. *Might just be a turnaround,* she considers, even though their driveway is not the most logical place for such a purpose. *It could be someone who simply likes the house*—they get those from time to time. Karen knows, however, when most people observe the home, they do so from a polite distance, from the road and not from the Stevens' property.

It is a large car—a Cadillac, solid white with out of State plates. It draws near the house and finally stops.

Karen, the only one home, proceeds with caution to the front door where she can inconspicuously peer through the curtains. She observes the older gentleman as he steps from the car, the man wearing a full Stetson, his hat almost blocking the sun. The older man does not seem like a physical threat, but Karen is prudent regardless.

The man sizes up the home from the driveway. He begins to curiously pace back and forth as if he wants to walk around the impressive structure but stops short of doing so.

Karen walks from the living room to the dining room and back again. She mirrors the steps of the man from safely inside her home. Ultimately, Karen decides to act.

The front door swings open, and Karen steps onto the front porch while maintaining a safe distance. "Can I help you?" she asks and warns at the same time.

Despite having a sweet voice, Karen startles the stranger. The older man quickly removes his hat and clutches it to his chest at the sight of the woman of the house.

"Oh, hello there, ma'am," he stammers as if suddenly embarrassed by his forward actions. "I apologize. I hope I didn't disturb you."

Karen smiles politely but with the look of someone who feels owed an explanation.

• • •

For the most part, the Augusta Christian parking lot emptied quickly following the Championship rally. Only a few cars remain, giving Bart Newhouse, Sr. and his son plenty of parking options.

The driver, the father, the coach—Bart Newhouse, Sr.—steps from the car, closes his door, gazes at the school building and ceremoniously states, "The mighty Augusta Christian Academy...in the flesh."

His son steps from the passenger's side and stares in anticipation as well; both had only heard of the place but never seen it in person.

Despite the respect felt by Newhouse, Sr., his reverence is not enough to overshadow his brimming self-confidence. "Won't they be surprised to see us?"

6

He did it. Roger told Reverend Jordan everything. Roger told him about the chance, out-of-town encounters on two separate occasions with Principal Charles Bullock from Macon South High School. One encounter was in Columbia and the other in Alpharetta, Georgia while Roger was visiting a coaching colleague. In retrospect, Roger knew the odds of both men, one from Augusta and one from Macon, independently arriving at the same places at the same times on two separate occasions—well, needless to state, Roger, a Geometry teacher and not a statistician, would still be impressed with the math. That is, unless someone like Roger wants to label the entire scenario a hoax.

Besides recalling the two encounters with the principal from Macon, Roger informed the reverend of the subsequent letters. More specifically, Roger recounted the most difficult aspect of it all: his constant, repetitive, persistent thoughts of Principal Bullock and his school—day after day after day.

Reverend Jordan, a minister seldom caught off guard, is admittedly taken back by Roger's recounting of the past few months. Pastor Jordan had no idea. *Amazing* is the reverend's private assessment: the same man Roger encountered on two occasions on the road is the same principal whose school was ripped apart by the evil explosion in Macon—the slightest reminder of the story causes the reverend's heart to lurch. Everyone in Georgia and the nation knew of the bombing of the all-black school by now—another dark stain on the reputation of the South and particularly Georgia. *Those poor children*, the reverend cannot help but think to himself. On the other hand, the reverend considers the fact no one was killed in the bombing as nothing less than a miracle. *Thank you, God.*

As the two men sit across from each other, Reverend Jordan does his best to listen and not prod. It is clear to the veteran pastor, given the fact he has known Roger Stevens for most of Roger's life, something profound is at work within Roger's heart.

Eventually, Coach Stevens grows weary of speaking.

Reverend Jordan breaks a long bout of silence with a question: "He actually asked you to come to Macon South to coach basketball?"

Roger nods, mildly chuckling at the thought—chuckling because the idea seems ludicrous, yet with each passing day Roger thinks about the premise more and more.

"What happened to the previous coach?"

"He is the coach. Well, that is, he took over two years ago when the other coach resigned and Principal Bullock couldn't find anyone else to take the job, so he did it himself, which I admire, actually."

"That's quite a commitment," lauds the pastor. "Principal and basketball coach."

"I have to tell you, my hat's off to the man," Roger proclaims as he sits back in his chair, placing his hands atop his head, still fidgety. "I don't know how he's done it, not to mention all the pressure and turmoil and tragedy he and the school have endured and must endure every day. He seems to be a unique man. I'll give him that."

"Does he believe in God?"

Despite Roger's best efforts, he cannot prevent the conversation from going where he wants to avoid. "Yes, I mean, he claims to believe in God. He does, well, I think he believes in God," Roger stammers through it all. "Yes. He believes in God." As much as Roger wants to paint the high school principal from Macon as delusional, Roger, with sincerity, cannot. "He seems to be a very good man. A very faithful man. Well, he would have to be, right, given all he has been through?" Roger keeps blathering on, trying to head off an unwanted destiny at the pass. "Yes. Principal Bullock believes I should come to Macon…. He believes that is what God has next for his school…and my life."

"He said that?" queries the pastor. "He said those exact words?"

"Not exactly. He didn't say *my life* as in what's best for me." Roger lurches forward again, now looking to the floor as he spews a laborious amalgam of both facts and conjecture, his body language clearly jittery. "He feels it's time to resurrect the school's morale, especially after the tragedy…, and he believes a resurgent basketball program could do that for them, as a rallying point. He said I would be the perfect man for the job."

Reverend Jordan pauses, not wanting to come across too strongly or overwhelm a man who is already overwhelmed.

Roger pauses as well, not wanting to share any unnecessary information. Roger views each word as a trap—not set by his pastor, but set by himself. More than anything, Roger wants to avoid all traps potentially set by God. Roger considers God a saving God, a healing God, a loving God, but also a God who is masterful at bridling the strong will of those He loves.

"Does this gentleman…?"

"Principal Bullock." Roger blurts sharply while shifting nervously in his chair again, interrupting the reverend. "Sorry," Roger apologizes, trying to mask his anxiety.

"Yes, thank you. Does Principal Bullock know you going to Macon might be way off your radar at this stage of your career? Unless, it's not off your radar."

Roger smiles the best he can, looking to the ceiling again, his left knee bouncing nervously, the man speaking as if chewing imaginary gum. "I have no desire to coach at another high school. No. I have no plans to coach anywhere else—high school or even college—until after next season which will be Kevin's senior season. That's been my plan all along."

The reverend listens as the man's tone steadily elevates from annoyed to angry.

Finally, Roger looks Pastor Jordan in the eyes and begins to vent, his hands gesticulating as if conducting an invisible orchestra. "There are so many parts to this whole thing that are way off base. I can't be asked to make less than a lateral move to another high school and start from scratch. I can't leave the Academy on a whim without warning. I can't ask Kevin to transfer to another school the summer before his senior year. His friends and teammates have built something very special here. I can't take my wife farther away from her ailing mother. I can't ask my son or my wife to go with me to an unsafe place where I might not be able to protect them. Besides, I'm sure Principal Bullock can't even come close to paying me what...."

The verbal barrage ceases. Roger lowers his hands. He made his point. Roger had not realized it until now, but his tone has ascended to that of clamorous, unbecoming the civil conversation between a man and his amiable pastor. If Roger did not know better, Roger would think he is trying to compile a list of excuses to defend his case. *It's not Pastor Jordan's fault*, Roger considers. *He doesn't deserve such treatment. It's not Karen's or Kevin's fault—or even Principal Bullock's fault. This is my problem.*

Roger discharges a hard exhale, causing his cheeks and lips to vibrate as he pushes through the air—a roaring engine rumbling to a halt.

Reverend Jordan sits calmly. The veteran minister has always believed every pressure cooker must let off steam at some point. Based on the details of Roger's account, the pastor discerns the following. This Principal Bullock does not seem to be a delusional man, and, in fact, he deserves the benefit of the doubt considering all the man has endured and seen. Even so, Principal Bullock is probably out of his depth in asking a much-accomplished, much-respected, very expensive coach like Roger Stevens to leave everything and move to such an unstable location. Maybe the principal has been through so much he feels he has nothing to lose by asking. The *chance* or assumed *chance meetings* are intriguing; the odds of the two men crossing paths out of town more than once would be remarkable. In the end, the entire situation has clearly besieged Roger, a man normally quite adept at navigating life, which makes the coach's unnerved behavior even more peculiar today. Either Roger is suffering from guilt and remorse at the thought of the people of Macon South or there is the possibility God is speaking through all this.

The veteran minister is well-versed in looking for red flags when people come to him for guidance. On many occasions, people have assured him God told them this or that. Reverend Jordan's response has always been consistent in such instances: *let God confirm His voice. If it is indeed the voice of God, God will confirm it in another way. Most notably, God will never speak contrary to His written Word because God is not the author of confusion. What benefit is there in God trying to confuse those who seek Him for wisdom?*

Regarding Roger and his unique situation, there has been something else Pastor Jordan has garnered during their conversation: Roger keeps speaking emphatically of *his plan*, which again is out of character for Roger. Reverend Jordan knows Roger is only human, but the pastor also knows Roger is a rarity. Very few people who are so accomplished speak of themselves less than Roger does. It is not in his nature. Roger is not one to draw attention to himself. It has always been God who has placed attention and recognition on the life of Roger Stevens, probably because God knows the man will always channel all honor and tribute back to God. So, for Reverend Jordan to hear Roger force his plan with such determination is an anomaly.

All these observations made by the seasoned minister come as a result of a long, personal relationship with the man before him, a relationship developed over decades. It is relationships such as these, relationships that endure the battle of time, that Reverend Jordan believes are worth more than gold; to develop trust; a bond of honesty; to love each other in good times and bad; to see a person at their best and worst and still love them. Few and far between are such valuable relationships in the mind of Pastor Jordan, and the relationship between him and Roger Stevens is a much-labored tapestry.

Roger rubs his eyes, severing the silence. "I can't even see straight, Pastor Jordan. I'm exhausted." After everything Roger has spouted, the man musters the courage to sit back in his chair and ask his lifelong pastor a fateful question. "What do you think about all this?"

The reverend smiles, choosing his words carefully. "More than anything, Roger, I can tell you are quite burdened."

Yeah, you think, Roger harbors within, proud of himself for not blurting those words like he has everything else.

"I think we have to draw a line of distinction here," continues the veteran minister. "Is this something…, this situation with Principal Bullock and his school, is this compassion you are feeling toward him…or is this compulsion?"

Roger displays a befuddled expression across the desk. "What do you mean, Pastor?"

"I ask because it's important for us to know the difference. There are times in our lives when we see an obvious need, and we act out of compassion. In other words, we see the opportunity to do something good, and we have the ability to act, so we act because it makes sense. Then, there are times when new roads or opportunities present themselves in key seasons, and we sense urgency, we sense pulling or pushing to go down these roads. These are open doors and decisions meant to shape our lives as a whole, and we are meant to walk through certain doors at the right times. For example, who to marry, the city we should live in, the career we should choose. Thus, we feel compelled to do it, not just because it is the compassionate thing to do, but because these choices are necessary to keep the big picture of our lives on track, keeping us in alignment with the plan of God for our lives. That's what I mean by distinguishing between compassion and compulsion."

Good question, Roger acknowledges. *Good point*. "Both. I think…both. I feel terribly for the man, for him to work and live in that environment, day after day." Roger snickers. "Makes my problems look small. Yes, I want to help him. I want to help anyone in a bad situation, within reason, that is. As far as compulsion: I don't know. I just don't know….I have never felt compelled by Charles," Roger corrects himself, "by Principal Bullock to go to Macon. He can't compel me. No one can compel me."

Reverend Jordan leans forward and clasps his hands on his desk, speaking tenderly. "Roger, please look at me."

With just enough cooperation, Roger obliges as Reverend Jordan asks his final question: "Roger, do you feel compelled by God to go to Macon?"

The question stops everything, hitting Roger with a mental sledgehammer. With eyes on his pastor, Roger shifts his body weight forward, leaning into the conversation for the first time and not resisting it. Void of excuses, void of energy, void of coherent explanations and politically-correct speech, Roger states the overriding point he desperately desires to convey.

"Pastor Jordan, I'm just one man. I am just…one…white… man. What do I know about working with black people?"

Reverend Jordan gives his answer some time. Ultimately, the pastor responds with truth laced in kindness, sending a smile back the coach's way. "Roger, I think the keyword is *people*."

7

Conversations with Reverend Jordan, according to Roger, are always productive; a little too productive at times, meaning the minister always has a knack for helping Roger get to the heart of a matter, the root of an issue, whether Roger wants to get there or not. During his drive back to the school to retrieve a few items, the Championship rally seems like forever ago. Little did everyone else know, Coach Stevens had a difficult time enjoying the season-ending celebration. *If all these people only knew,* Roger thought during the festivities. *If all these people only knew what was on my mind, my heart and how heavy I feel. It's a good thing they don't. It would be the blandest, deadest, shortest celebration on record.*

Two men talk at the entrance of the Augusta Christian Academy. As Roger parks and approaches the building, he easily recognizes one of the men as Principal Mize, a good man who has become a good friend over the years. The other gentleman, a black gentleman, Roger does not recognize.

"Here's Coach Stevens now" the principal announces. "We were just talking about you."

"I hope it was good," the coach responds.

"How could it not be?" the other gentleman affirms while extending a hand.

"Coach Roger Stevens," Principal Mize oversees the introductions, "this is a friend of mine from college, Ernest Compton."

"Nice to meet you." Roger gladly receives the man.

"The pleasure is mine," Mr. Compton insists. "We were just concluding the tour of the Academy, and we finished with the gym and talking about your basketball season. Congratulations."

"Thank you very much," Roger humbly accepts.

"Coach," Principal Mize interjects, slightly hesitating while placing his index finger above his upper lip, trying to find the right way to say the following. "I want to inform the staff of this soon, but I might as well bounce it off you first because I value your opinion. My former college-mate here, Mr. Compton, is soon to join our faculty at the Academy."

Roger's eyes come alive, refreshingly surprised by the announcement. "Great. That's great. Welcome aboard." Roger swiftly extends a second handshake. Elated, Roger wants to show full support of this monumental moment in the history of the Academy. The fact is Mr. Compton would be the first-ever black faculty member at Augusta Christian Academy, which has been a threshold Roger and Karen desired to see the school cross for years.

"Well," Principal Mize proceeds, speaking freely among friends. "I've been thinking quite a bit lately about the need to expand our horizons here at the school and embrace change."

• • •

By the time Roger arrives home, he is not in a good place emotionally. He passes through the front door unannounced, tossing his things on the dining room table, dropping himself on the couch.

Karen hears the disturbance and enters the living room to find her husband's face in his hands.

"Roger?"

Roger Stevens lifts his head; a perturbed countenance gives way to a phony smile. "Yes, yes…, it's me."

"Is everything okay?"

Tired of pretending, lacking strength or interest in hiding how he feels any longer, the man looks at his wife and answers her candidly. "No, Karen. Everything's not okay."

Karen finds a spot beside her husband.

"No," Roger protests what he perceives as sympathy, standing and exiting the room.

"Roger," she calls from behind, perplexed. "What is it? What's going on?"

Roger next finds a chair at the kitchen table, not thrilled when his wife takes the seat across from him.

"Is it Kevin? Where is he?"

"Kevin's fine. He's with Reynolds."

"Then what's going on?"

"I don't want to talk about it."

"Well, you don't just storm out of a room and say everything's not okay and not expect to talk about it."

Roger begins to put his face in his hands again then quickly withdraws them—it has become his *go-to* posture in life. He knows he must quit portraying a man in crisis or else it will just draw more attention, and attention is the last thing the man desires. "Look, honey, I'm sorry. I didn't mean to alarm you. It's not been a good day."

Karen gets it, believing everyone is entitled to a bad day. Thus, she gives her husband room to speak his mind.

"I," Roger blurts. "I didn't mean to barge in and mess up your day, too, which seems to be the only thing I'm good at doing lately."

"You're not messing me up. Just fill me in."

Silence settles except for monotonous ticking from the kitchen clock. The secondhand moves slowly, as if hindered by a ball and chain.

Well, the cat's out of the bag, Roger acquiesces. Not only is he going through this wilderness, but now he is dragging everyone he loves through it, too. He sighs, thinking of the best place to start.

Karen reaches across the table and takes his hand, smiling gently.

He exhales, finding a temporary oasis in Karen's eyes. "I love you."

"You know I love you," she gently confirms. "So, talk to me."

After another pause, Roger begins. "I don't.... I'm so bogged down right now, Karen: I don't know where to start. I honestly feel like God has it in for me."

His opening statement is shocking. Karen perceives her husband as one of the most blessed men on earth, the fingerprints of God tangibly on his life. "Why would you say that? You know that's not true."

Roger looks to the ceiling, revealing the underbelly of his bloodshot eyeballs, continuing to hold his wife's hands across the table. "I think...." *Dare I say it*, Roger warns himself. "I think God might be trying to get me out of Augusta."

The words of her husband are piercing, poignant. Karen maintains a visage of objectivity for his sake; however, Karen's pulse quickens. Even so, the woman refuses to tip her hand. "What do you mean, out of Augusta? The school or the city?"

"Both," he responds adamantly." Get me out of the school, get me out of town, get me out of this house. It's ridiculous for me even to mention it, but...." Roger pulls himself to his feet and lumbers to the kitchen window, gazing across the serene beauty of their back property.

"What is it, Roger?"

After a substantial exhale, the man faces his wife again. "I wonder if God wants me to leave here and coach basketball in Macon."

"Macon?"

"Yes, Macon. At Macon South High School?"

Macon South? She tries to wrap her mind around Roger's scattered explanation. *Another high school?* Karen, a naturally-born multi-tasker, keeps the conversation going as her mind takes her somewhere else. What Roger said about the house: it registers with her. Such news should be shocking to the woman, but, oddly, it is not. Of course, Roger had previously told her of the chance meetings in other cities with the principal from Macon South, Bullock she believes is his name, the surprising job offer and the subsequent letters; she even read them herself. Of course, like everyone else, her heart broke for the school and families and children as she followed the story of Macon South from afar. Even so, Karen never considered herself to be intimately attached to the situation.

"What are you saying, Roger? Coach...at Macon South? Are you sure?"

"I don't want to be sure," he snaps at the innocent woman. "That's the problem. I want God to tell me I'm crazy, that I've made all this up in my mind, that I'm connecting dots in my head that aren't there..., but my heart...." The man's voice dissipates.

Karen stands from her seat and draws near her husband across the room, softly taking his arm. "Your heart, Roger?"

● ● ●

Time passes in the Stevens' kitchen, and Karen grants her husband ample opportunity to get to the bottom of everything.

Roger discerns his wife's generous allotment of grace. *What a kind, gentle woman,* he affirms to himself. Furthermore, Roger determines they have come too far for him to be anything less than completely honest, and anything less than sharing his whole heart with Karen would be unacceptable. *She deserves to know everything.*

Despite the pressing weight atop his shoulders and the heart-crushing sensation within his chest, after uttering a thousand words connected to a thousand contradicting emotions,

Roger manifests a delirious chuckle. *How did it get this far*, he wonders? *How did life come to this point*? "Honestly," he resumes. "I don't want to think anymore...because when I do...I think more about going than staying."

Karen is numb from the details of their conversation. "Let me ask you something, Roger. Obviously, your heart goes out to this man. All of our hearts do. I know you've been praying for him and so have I. But, honey, there's a difference between praying for people and uprooting and leaving your home to live side by side with them."

The longtime-Geometry teacher has surveyed every angle of the situation before him ad nauseam, and he still cannot figure it out, and he certainly cannot see what God—if God is up to something—is trying to do. It does not make any earthly sense to the man.

"In my opinion," Karen continues, the woman becoming irritated herself, "I'm not sure how Principal Bullock could even ask you to do that. I mean, he knows you have a family, right?"

"He has a family, too, Karen."

"Yes, I understand." She humbles her words. "That's not what I mean. I just mean your family is here."

"I don't want to go, Karen," the man emphatically states while pounding the table with his fist. "Do you want to hear me say it? I don't want to go. I don't think it's wise to go. I don't think it's safe to go. For a million reasons, I don't want to go."

"But you're thinking about going?" she retorts. "You're thinking about going before your son's final year of high school when he's about to graduate with his friends?"

"Believe me, Karen, I know. I know." Roger had calmed down briefly, but, once again, the man feels his temperature escalate—the emotional-rollercoaster continues. Roger next marches from the kitchen to the dining room as his wife follows.

"All right," Roger resumes. "I'm going to tell you something, and if I'm imagining all of this or if I'm crazy, then tell me—and I hope I am." He gathers his thoughts as the two sit on the couch again. "I went and spoke with Pastor Jordan today and laid everything out for him. I told him that I had two *chance*...or what I believed to be *chance* encounters with Principal Bullock while traveling. I told Pastor how the man both called and wrote, asking to see me. I told Pastor what I didn't tell you yet—that while you were with your mother one week I drove halfway to meet with Principal Bullock, and it was there he first asked me to move to Macon and coach at his school, and I'm very sorry I didn't tell you. I just wanted to discard the whole thing and move on."

Karen is upset but remains under control. She is trying her best to cut her husband some slack, knowing full well such behavior is far outside the norm for him. Instead of taking the heated conversation in another combustible direction, the wife of 20 years decides to stay on course. "So, how did you answer him? What did you say?"

"I was respectful but truthful. I told the man I was flattered with his proposal, but I have no plans of leaving the Academy until after Kevin finishes. Yes, I admit the man and his school have stayed on my mind since then, but that's in large part due to the shock I felt that he even asked me the question in the first place. And that's what makes it so hard to distinguish between my sympathy for the man and what God might be instructing me to do. And I've asked God, Karen, I've asked God to take this man off my mind. I've asked time and time and time again for all of this to leave my mind, and it won't. It just won't. So, either I'm obsessed with this man and his school...or God...."

Karen listens as her husband's heart pours forth. "Has he contacted you since the bombing?"

Roger grimaces. "No."

"Have you contacted him?"

A look of shame surfaces as Roger answers. "Once I heard he was still alive and well, I sent him a letter; an encouragement card." Embarrassed, Roger knows his response was not in correct proportion to the tragedy that befell the man and his students. "But that's the thing, Karen: I can't get involved in this, and I don't want to give the man hope if there's none to give. That's just cruel, and he needs to go on with his life and find his next coach and just…just stay alive."

Roger and Karen share the same thought simultaneously. *If this doesn't involve us…, then why are we having this conversation?*

Karen simmers in frustration as she learns important details for the first time. However, more than anything, Karen's heart goes out to her obviously anxiety-riddled husband; the man is simply attempting to make sense of it all.

"Here's what doesn't help," Roger proceeds. "And you know me, Karen. I've never heard the audible voice of God, yet I believe in Him more than ever. Whenever God has spoken to me through the years, spoken to my heart, He has always backed up what He's tried to tell me in some other way. Not so much with a sign but a seal; a seal of His presence in the details of my life. So, if I'm making all this up in my mind, that would be the end of it, correct? God wouldn't show up in the details of this situation."

Karen concurs. "I see your point."

"After my meeting with Pastor today, I drove back to the school to get a few things, and there's Principal Mize with another man, a black man; the two of them went to college together."

"Oh, that's nice. Is he in town visiting?"

Roger looks his wife in the eyes, "He's coming on staff. Principal Mize is hiring him as the new History Teacher at Augusta Christian. Principal Mize said it is time to expand the horizons of the Academy and embrace change."

"Wow!" Karen cannot help but display her surprise, the woman knowing full well such a hire would mark the first-ever black man or woman at Augusta Christian. "That's wonderful. We've always wanted that, and it's about time."

"I agree. I agree whole-heartedly. It's just…"

"What?"

"It's just when Principal Mize said the words *expand horizons and embrace change*, it's as if his words were suspended in air above our conversation, and then the words rang over and over and over in my ears. I almost didn't hear anything else he said after that."

"But just because the Academy is hiring a black man doesn't mean God is sending you somewhere else to coach at a black school, honey."

"I know, Karen. By itself, it doesn't mean anything other than an answer to our prayers for the Academy, and Mr. Compton seems like a great man with great accomplishments, and he'll fit in perfectly at the school, but Mr. Compton wasn't the only visitor at the school today."

"What do you mean? Who?"

Roger smiles incredulously. "Remember Bart Newhouse from Atlanta Chapel?"

It takes a moment, but Karen soon recalls. "Newhouse? The basketball coach?" Her memory sharpens. "The arrogant guy?"

"Well," Roger chuckles, "I apologize. If I said *arrogant*. I should have said *confident*. And, yes: that's the guy."

"What was he doing at the school?"

This story just keeps getting better, Roger ruminates. "He was there with his son. They were visiting the school. His family is relocating to Augusta, and his son is transferring to the Academy in the fall. His boy will be on the team next season."

"Well, that's okay, isn't it? Is his son a good player?"

"His boy is very good," Roger affirms, "And Bart is a quality coach. It just doesn't make sense for him to move his son and family here before his son's senior year." Roger pauses and thinks, *That was an ironic comment if there ever was one.*

"What else did Newhouse tell you?"

"He didn't tell me anything. I wasn't there while he was there. Principal Mize asked me to hang around and spoke with me after Mr. Compton left."

"What did Principal Mize say?"

"He said that Bart said he's doing it for exposure for his son. Bart said the team he coached at Atlanta Chapel lost a bunch of seniors and his son would be the only quality player on the team. They finished third in the State behind us and Savannah Memorial this season. He said he's been thinking about leaving for some time now, and he thinks *we'll* make it back to the State tournament again next season. Get it? *We.* I asked Principal Mize if he actually said *we*, and Principal Mize confirmed Newhouse said we."

"Well, that's a little forward of him," Karen agrees. "But all that sounds okay. You can't have too many good players."

On the surface, Roger considers, *yes, she is correct.* The problem is little in Roger's life has seemed okay for some time now. It just does not make sense to the man. The timing is too loaded. Of all the seasons, of all the times, for Bart Newhouse to arrive unannounced at the Academy now—just one more area of life that does not jibe with Roger.

"Are you afraid he's going to ask to help coach?"

The man pauses before dropping yet another bombshell on his wife. "Actually, Karen, I wonder if God's brought Newhouse here to move me out."

"What? No," Karen reacts boldly. "Principal Mize is not going to replace you."

"No, sweetheart, Principal Mize would never fire me, but Bart Newhouse would be a very worthy replacement if God calls me to leave. That's always been a desire of my heart, and God knows it. I have always wanted to leave the Academy in good hands. It's just...I don't want to leave."

• • •

"Let's move! This car!" Agent Dawson motions to Agent Dennison in the parking lot of the FBI Macon branch.

Several other agents jump in company cars as well, and abruptly the FBI caravan stretches down Route 49.

Dennison got Maxwell's call fifteen minutes ago when Maxwell could not reach Dawson. Dennison then phoned Dawson; hence, the processional of FBI vehicles races into the night.

"So, a potential Klan meeting outside of town, huh?" queries Dawson.

"That's the word from Maxwell," replies Dennison.

"Then it must be solid intel," Dawson concludes. "Maxwell doesn't miss much."

The lead car heads due west for twenty minutes with the remaining vehicles in tow. Eventually, the caravan abandons the highway for a spate of dirt roads, finally entering what appears to be an open field before finding cover behind an adjacent tree line. Dawson kills the headlights and engine and steps from the car; the remaining agents follow suit. There, they wait.

• • •

Kevin called earlier and asked to stay over at Reynold's. Roger and Karen said *yes; great timing*, they thought. The two now have all night to talk if need be. They talk straight through dinner; neither of them was hungry. The couple moves from room to room during their conversation. Mostly, it is Roger exuding restlessness and Karen following him. Roger has stood and sat repeatedly. Karen has tried to remain calm and supportive, but then Roger would say something else to make that impossible. Neither of them knows where all this is going, but, after the words they have spoken tonight, it seems life will never be the same.

Karen's strategy has been to allow Roger to unload everything on his heart. This would be best in her opinion since she has been withholding a bombshell of her own.

Roger's once frenetic verbal pace slows to a crawl; his energy spent.

Now, Karen discerns. "Okay, Roger, it's my turn to tell you something you don't know."

Karen has the attention of her husband. He knows that tone of voice.

"You weren't the only one who had an unexpected visitor today."

"What do you mean? Who?"

"I saw a car pull up our drive this afternoon and watched an older gentleman get out to look around."

"Who was he?"

"He introduced himself as Wayne Ridgely from Oklahoma, and he looked every bit the part."

"What did he want?"

Karen hesitates and smooths the back of her hair while looking to the ground. This time it is Karen who is guilty of avoiding eye contact. Nevertheless, she speaks. "To buy our home."

Roger is numb as the words wash over him. He waits to respond, giving Karen a chance to reveal her poor attempt at humor, but she does not.

"Buy our home? Are you kidding? What are you talk....?"

"He asked if our home was for sale."

Of all the drama Roger brought to the table tonight, Karen just wadded it up and threw it out the back door. Roger trips over his thoughts and words. "How..., I mean what..., how does a person even start that conversation, Karen? *I want to buy your home?* What did he say exactly?"

Karen strives to keep her tone calm. Her husband is a very godly and mild-mannered man, never violent. However, lately, it seems a single spark can light his fuse. "Like I said, I saw him pacing in front of the house, so I opened the door...."

"Which door?"

"The front door, and I...."

"Did he knock?"

"No, he didn't knock, and I...."

"What did he say?"

"He introduced himself and told me how beautiful our home is and...."

"What did you say?"

"Roger, please! Let me finish." Her words back the man down. "He said..., well, he actually went on and on about our home and how beautiful he thought it was, that he was from

Tulsa or near there and that he is relocating to the area. He didn't brag, but he mentioned the oil business."

"Was he pushy?"

"Not in the least. He was a very nice, older, grandfatherly man. He has grown children and grandchildren in Augusta, and he wants to move closer to them. He said his wife recently died, the poor man. He said he wants to make up for lost time from all the years he worked, and he would like a big home and yard where his grandkids can run free."

Roger holds his tongue the best he can. The portrait his wife paints makes the mystery man likable and his story somewhat within reason. "I'm sorry about his wife," Roger interjects as delicately as he can, "but it's rude, Karen, to show up on someone's doorstep out of the blue and ask if their home is for sale."

"I don't think he meant to be rude. I just think he liked our home from a distance and kept driving closer." On cue, Karen removes a folded piece of paper from the apron she donned for the dinner she never cooked. She next places the paper in her husband's hand as the two share the living room couch.

"What's this?" Roger looks at the folded paper with great suspicion. "His phone number?"

Karen pauses. "Not his phone number…but it's a number."

Roger's face waxes hot. "He made…, he had the nerve to make an offer on the house…, on our house?" Roger refuses to look inside; annoyance wells, then anger, then fury. "I don't need to look at this," Roger decrees, dropping the paper to the floor, declaring, "I can't take this seriously."

"You might want to take a look at *this*," his wife strongly urges, picking up the paper and following him into the kitchen. There are many rooms in the sizeable Stevens' home, and Karen is willing to follow Roger into every one of them if need be.

Roger wheels around. "Do you want to move, Karen? Is that it? Do you want us to leave Augusta, our home, our lives?"

Karen scoffs; Roger's question is preposterous to her. "That's ridiculous, Roger. Let's stay on point. I didn't ask this man to come to our home. I'm not making this up."

The husband turns his back to his wife for the last time—
she's had enough. Karen circles Roger's much-larger frame in
her own surge of frustration.

"Quit turning your back on me. We need to talk about this,
Roger. This is serious—all of it. You are struggling with leaving
the school, leaving our home to take us to Macon of all places
where there have been bombs and the Klan and who knows
what else, and a man just drove up out of nowhere and offered
to buy our home when it's not for sale. All that doesn't happen
every day," Karen unloads. "Especially when that man offers you
four times what your home is worth!" Karen forcefully stamps
the piece of paper back in her husband's hand. This time, it is
Karen who barges out of the room, returning the favor.

The man looks down at the still-folded piece of paper in his
hand, pondering, *Did she just say four times?* Roger unfolds the
paper. *Wow*, the man calculates. *That's a big number.* In many
cases, such news might be a wonderful, marvelous, magnificent,
earth-shattering, and bountiful surprise. In this case, accepting
such news would only seal Roger's fate. "God," Roger whispers
within an otherwise empty room, "I think you want me out."

• • •

Dawson stares at the open field.

The worst part of the job, Dennison privately affirms as he
waits near Dawson, as everyone waits. *Two hours...and nothing.*

Agent Blaine Wheeler leans against a company vehicle on
the other side of Dennison. In Dennison's opinion, Wheeler—a
seemingly good man—has done a quality job of keeping any
personal feelings out of the investigation into Klan activity.
However, Dennison can only guess Wheeler—the lone black
agent serving in Macon—has as much vested interest as anyone
to bring those involved in the Macon South bombing to justice,
and like Dennison and all the remaining agents, Wheeler is
not buying the death of Phillip Barlow as the end of the story.

Standing on the other side of Wheeler, Agent Travis Hopper leans his back against his company car, disinterested, smoking a cigarette, his seventh of the night. Hopper mumbles a cuss word here and there to let everyone know what a waste of time he finds the entire stakeout to be, and the bugs do not help.

Finally, in the distance, there is movement. Agents motion to each other in the direction of two o'clock—headlights from an approaching vehicle.

Watching Dawson, the agents mimic his lead, each of them stepping fully out of sight and drawing their weapons.

The pickup truck turns from the connecting dirt road and enters the far edge of the open field; headlights and the rumble of a poor exhaust system fill the night.

The clandestine agents tuck further behind their company cars as the truck gains speed and bolts across the field directly toward the men.

"Be ready," Dawson prepares the men with an authoritative whisper, beams of oncoming light shining across his face.

Could be a lookout, Dennison ponders.

The passenger door opens before the truck fully stops, and a man of indeterminate age lurches from the vehicle, approaching the tree line with purpose.

They know we're here, Dennison and several of the agents conclude.

The man steps into better moonlight, a younger man, stopping in front of a bush; the unzipping of his pants can be heard for miles in the stillness.

The squawk of a Bureau-issued radio startles the young man as the guilty agent reaches for his hip. The young man freezes, gripping either side of his pants as the agents remain still, and the young man squints for a better look. He squints harder, and eventually, the moonlight reveals the silhouettes of multiple men crouching in the dark in the near distance.

Muttering incoherently, the young man immediately turns and runs in the opposite direction.

"Go! Go!" Dawson commands, unleashing a fury of action.

"Jed," the shell-shocked young man calls out to the driver of the truck. "Drive!"

The driver looks over his shoulder through the rear window of his truck. Behind him is his friend in a dead sprint with a barrage of flashing red lights illuminating the tree line.

"Oh! Woah!" The truck lunges forward. "Get in! Get in!"

"Drive! Drive!"

At least four FBI cars close quickly, allowing no time for an escape.

"Look out!" the passenger shouts as another vehicle swerves in front of them. An agent leaps from his vehicle and displays a revolver, firing the weapon in the air.

The truck careens wildly to the left before coming to an abrupt halt.

The same agent approaches through the duet of darkness and moonlight, his gun no longer pointed toward the sky but directly at the cab of the truck.

"Hands! Show me your hands!"

The driver and passenger instantly comply, their hands shaking high above their heads.

The remaining agents surround the pickup. Flashlights blind both the driver and passenger as a dozen FBI men converge step by step on the truck with weapons drawn.

"Out, slowly!" Dawson commands.

Both doors open. "Okay, don't shoot. Please don't shoot us," the driver pleads. Once the young men exit the vehicle, they are taken to the ground by adrenalized agents.

"Sorry...we're sorry!"

"Face down!" Agent Dawson is not interested in blubbering apologies, clearly irritated with their blown cover. "Search the truck! Let me see their ID's."

Agents immediately sift through the vehicle.

"You boys headed to a rally?" Dennison inquires.

The young men hesitate long enough to look at each other before answering. "No...no, sir."

"Then what are you doing out here?"

"Just pulled over to…just needed to pull over, sir."

"Anything?" Dawson calls out.

"Just some liquor, sir," one of the agents answers while displaying a bottle found in the floorboard.

Another agent hands Dawson the wallets of those from the truck; nothing looks out of the ordinary to the man as he makes a mental note of both names.

"Hold on," calls out another agent as he checks the bed of the truck. "Got a gun here—a rifle.

"You purchase that gun legally?" Dennison asks.

Lying face down, the driver pauses, then responds with what sounds to Dennison like a rehearsed answer. "It's my hunting gun, sir."

"That's not what I asked you," Dennison insists while kneeling close to the driver's ear.

The young man on the ground clearly stalls for time. "I lost my paperwork, sir. I'm sorry."

Dennison scoffs. "That's convenient."

The agent who removed the rifle from the truck brings it to Dawson.

After giving it a once-over, Dawson hands the rifle to Dennison.

Cy Dennison, the renown firearms expert of the group, earned high proficiency marks on the range at the Bureau Academy. Undoubtedly, Dennison's background as a marksman derived from his early days as an amateur in the winter biathlon, nearly qualifying for the U.S. Olympic Team in '52 for the Oslo games. Before that, Dennison cut his teeth hunting with his father in the Adirondacks in upstate New York. "How much money you make?" Dennison sarcastically inquires of the driver as the agent analyzes the high-quality rifle. "I ask because the price of this sleek firearm doesn't jibe with the value of your beat-up truck."

The young man on the ground twists his neck at the question. "What do you mean?"

Dennison snaps back. "I mean this gun is above your pay-grade. Where did you get it?

The two young men on the ground look at each other again before a final answer is given by the driver—the same response as before. "I lost my paperwork, sir?"

"Young punk," Dawson mutters.

Dennison hands the rifle back to his superior, stating, "I don't know what those etches are beneath the barrel."

"I'll throw all the liquor out," the truck passenger attempts to negotiate.

Irritated, Dawson kneels to be heard clearly. "Hey, punk, I don't care if you stirred that stuff in your grandmother's bathtub. What I care about is you wasting my time. Do you understand me?"

"Yes, sir. I'm sorry, sir."

An exasperated Dawson stands to his feet. "Take them in until they can prove legal ownership of this rifle," he commands as he begins to walk away from the commotion, signaling for Dennison to join him.

"Yes, sir," Agent Wheeler responds. "Get up," he orders both young men with the assistance of another agent. As Wheeler corrals one of the suspects to his feet, he sees Agent Hopper, seemingly disinterested, standing a good distance from the action. "Here, Hopper. Have one."

Hopper takes the arm of the driver. "Sure…. Glad to help."

Meanwhile, Dawson mutters a few profane words as he leads Dennison several feet away from the scene.

"I thought the intel was good?" Dennison offers tentatively, drawing alongside his superior.

"I'm sure the intel was good," assesses Dawson. "Maxwell's intel is always good. These dumb young punks must have missed the update that the meeting must have been moved."

Dennison can only guess what his boss must be thinking. *The group is not here because they knew we were coming. Someone tipped them off.*

8

The next morning, Roger waves from the front porch as his wife and son leave for an impromptu visit to South Carolina. Karen desires to see her ailing mother more and more of late, and the trip gives Kevin the opportunity to do the same. Besides, Roger could use some time alone, and, truthfully, everyone could use some time away from him in his opinion.

Once Kevin, Karen and Karen's car leave his sight in the distance, Roger turns and re-enters the suddenly vacant home. His plan for the day: spend time in prayer on what to do next. However, *what's the rush?* he determines. He will pray eventually. In the meantime, he plans to catch up on other pressing items around the house that eluded him during basketball season.

Tending to the first item on his list, Roger eyes the pesky transition piece between the dining and living rooms. He bends, kneels and then the robust man pauses, staring at the floor before him, quickly lost in a trance. His eyes suddenly moisten. He rubs them in haste, attempting to avert any distractions from his work. He clears his throat as he battles an oncoming lump. The man wags his head, trying to regain clear thought, but he is losing the fight. It is obvious to Roger Stevens—he will not get anything else done today. Instead, he yields to the lone, overwhelming compulsion to pray.

"Oh," the man clutches his chest from heaviness. He considers vaulting from his knees to his feet. Instead, Roger's body slowly stretches forward, his forearms keeping his face from dragging across the floor. Soon he lays flat, his face in his hands. It is not long before a muffled wail resonates from the lungs of the beleaguered combatant, resigning himself to the following concession: *There's no one else here, so why try to hide it?*

An outburst of moaning and sobbing fills the room; an undulating, swelling groan absorbed by the walls. Roger contorts his body, laying the left side of his head on the floor as his hands grasp both shoulders, curling his knees, almost in a fetal position. *Look at me*, he considers. *A grown man, look how weak and pitiful.*

Roger is normally an emotional stalwart, going through life with the specialized gift of motivating and strengthening others. This display, however, is humiliating to the man, but since he is alone in this enormous house, Roger decides to let it rip in a vociferous tone.

"I'm so angry at you, God! Are you satisfied? Are you happy? I'm broken. Nothing I desire carries any weight with you at this moment, and You've made it this way."

The only interruption in the man's onslaught of prayer is to catch his breath amid spewing a mixture of words, gasps, and groans. "I'm humiliated. Is this what you wanted? To reduce me to nothing? I can't do anything until we make this right, and I don't want to make it right with you because I know what you're trying to do. I just want you to leave me alone. Why can't you just leave me alone?"

"Everyone thinks it's so wonderful serving You, but sometimes it's the worst feeling on earth, and I'm there now. Why would You possibly ask me to do this, to lead my family to such a place, such a violent place? If it's just me, and You want to kill me, if you want me dead and out of the way, then so be it, but don't do this to Karen and Kevin. They have nothing to do with this. Please, God, leave them out of it. Don't harm them at my expense. Don't harm anyone else but me."

• • •

A few miles away at Hillside Christian Church, a reverend, making his Saturday preparations in time for Sunday, stops to pray. "Father, please soften Roger's heart toward you. Be merciful, God. Be merciful."

• • •

As the morning progresses, Roger lifts himself from the floor. He awakes from an unplanned nap on the couch, and it takes him a few seconds to get his bearings. The tears have subsided. The buildup in his chest and throat have broken free. He blinks in a flurry. His thought pattern seems clearer. There, at eye-level, across the room on a shelf, he recognizes the birthday gift Pastor Jordan gave him many years ago. Though having read the inscription several times before, Roger tilts his head to reread it, the glass frame displaying a picture of an artist's rendition of Jesus kneeling in the Garden of Gethsemane to pray.

"He went a little farther and fell on His face, and prayed, saying, 'O My Father, if it is possible, let this cup pass from Me....'"

Roger does not need to read the rest of the verse since he already knows the scripture by heart. Standing to his feet, stretching his body, he concedes and speaks the remaining portion of the text aloud from memory. "I know. I know. 'Nevertheless, not as I will, but as You will.'"

• • •

"Last night was too close for comfort," a voice shares later that night from a poorly-lit alley behind a tavern in Macon. "Word has it there were a dozen agents out there waiting for us. What if we had been there?" Agitated, Raymond Huddler addresses a crop of plain-clothes Klansmen just before midnight. "Now, how did they know to be there?" Huddler poses his question, focusing on one young recruit.

The young man takes a moment to look at those on either side of him for help. "I don't know how that happened, sir."

Unimpressed and unconvinced, the leader continues to walk the alley, staring down his subordinates one at a time, cigarette smoke billowing high into the night air above the gathering. Huddler stops, projecting a suspicious glare in the eyes of another young man, causing the recruit to tremble lightly.

"The problem is," Huddler continues, "I changed the meeting place almost at the last second, which leaves me rather perplexed. It makes me go back in my mind to consider who I spoke with yesterday."

The men on trial along the wall nervously look to one another, each one interested in outing the snitch to keep the wrath of Raymond Huddler from befalling them all.

Raymond ambles to the end of the line. He comes face to face with Frederick Collins, known to the Macon Klan as Freddy but unknown by his real name: Agent Nathan Maxwell of the Atlanta FBI. "Freddy...?"

Maxwell keeps direct eye contact to quell all suspicion. "Yes, sir."

"What should I do if I uncover an ideological adulterer in our midst?"

Without hesitation, Maxwell responds resolutely. "Kill him, sir."

Huddler is intrigued by what he hears; his eyes flare at the words. "Yes. I concur. And what if that adulterer is our midst right now?" The man motions to the rest of the group.

Maxwell looks at Huddler and then glances down the line at the other men; all of them look precariously back at him. Maxwell does not hold his tongue for long; he cannot afford it. Instead, he answers Huddler's question with equal certainty as before. "Splatter his blood all over this alley wall."

The eyes of Raymond Huddler grow large, the man displaying a wry grin. "I concur again."

With those words, Raymond Huddler takes a step back and reaches beneath his jacket, swiftly removing a handgun and immediately pointing the firearm at Maxwell's face, between his eyes.

Maxwell cannot keep from disguising the knot in his throat as he swallows hard.

The moonlight illuminates the steel barrel of the gun. Huddler closes the distance, his eyes coruscating with madness in the reflection of the alley light overhead. The gunman stops a foot in front of Maxwell and presses the gun against his forehead. Next, Raymond points the muzzle at one eye, then the other, down to Maxwell's lips, and back to his forehead in the form of a cross.

"In the name of the Father," Huddler whispers coldly as his finger draws tension against the trigger. "Let this be lesson to everyone," he exhorts.

"That would be a mistake, sir," Maxwell stammers. "I'm not your man."

"Are you saying I'm wrong, Freddy?" He presses the handgun more firmly against Maxwell's forehead, gritting his teeth in anger at being questioned, forcing the back of Maxwell's head against the brick wall. "Are you calling me a liar, a bearer of false witness?"

Maxwell closes his eyes momentarily…then reopens them. "Not a liar, sir. Just saying you have the wrong man. I'm here to serve you and the cause faithfully, sir."

As Maxwell looks into Huddler's eyes, it is as if the Klan leader is somewhere else, and wherever it is, it is glorious to the man. Even so, Huddler eventually returns.

"I apologize, Freddy," Huddler offers as he drops the gun then conceals the pistol under his jacket again. "This adulterer, whoever he is, has caused me apprehension even among my best men." Raymond Huddler places his right hand on Maxwell's shoulder, the delusional gaze from a few moments ago replaced with a sober and appreciative smile. "But when I find him...."

Maxwell chooses not to smile but to remain solemn. "I understand, sir."

Raymond Huddler pauses for a few moments before emphatically instructing, "Let's go!" On that note, the group takes little time in dispersing to find their vehicles, driving off into the night.

9

Seated on the family porch swing, a now docile Roger Stevens—following more than a day of prayer—considers the picturesque, tranquil Sunday evening before him—the best the Augusta countryside has to offer. Unfortunately, he knows only a small number of such moments remain. As he ruminates, he has every opportunity to reconsider his decision. The man gazes skyward on occasion as if looking for a sign from God; some indication that he passed the test and God is soon to release him from his choice. No such sign is given.

While sitting in peace for three hours or so, Roger has observed only a small number of vehicles on their county road. Eventually, here comes the one he desires to see.

Karen and Kevin ascend the inclined drive to the Stevens' home. Kevin is first to step from the car.

"Hey, buddy." Roger salutes his son.

"Hey, Dad."

The two briefly lock in a side hug. "Thanks for going with your mother."

"No problem. There was good food."

Roger smiles. He next greets Karen as she emerges. "Hello, ma'am."

"Hello, sir," she responds.

"How'd it go? How's Mom?"

"Oh, you know: nothing new." Karen gathers herself before responding with a question of her own. "And you? How's was your time alone?"

Roger presents the best smile he can. "Productive."

Karen discerns a favorable countenance on her husband; not necessarily one of joy but at least one of peace. "Good. I missed you."

"I missed you, too." Roger holds Karen and offers a kiss and an apology. "I am very sorry for the way I acted and how I've acted in general for I don't know how long. I ask your forgiveness."

"It's okay, sweetheart. You're human. We're all human. It happens to the best of us." Karen pulls back and fixes her eyes, very much wanting Roger to understand her heart: "I just want you to know, I'm with you no matter what."

The words of his wife nearly bring the man to tears again. *How can she possibly go along with me on this one? How can anybody possibly go along with me?* Roger pulls Karen close again, causing her face to bury in his chest as he immerses his face in her hair. "I love you, Karen. And I'm sorry. I'm so very sorry."

Karen can feel his heart beating—beating with strength. During the long drive, the wife and mother had time for God to deal with her as well. "How can I possibly blame you for doing what God would have you to do?"

A sense of relief tides the couple on the front porch—they are a far cry from where they were two nights ago. The husband and wife lock eyes one final time before Roger suggests to Karen, "Should we go talk to Kevin? Let him know what's going on?"

"Yes," she acknowledges. "It's time."

Roger and Karen Stevens enter the front door of their home, the only home Karen has ever known, the only home Kevin has ever known, and the only home Roger wants to know.

• • •

Raymond Huddler enters Jerry's restaurant, expeditiously proceeding through the diner and toward the banquet hall.

Jerry observes from the kitchen, watching as Huddler produces a key then as he unlocks multiple deadbolts to a rarely used door at the far end of the banquet hall, the man ultimately pulling the door closed behind him.

Now out of sight, Raymond takes a flashlight in hand and carefully descends a short flight of rickety steps. As he illuminates the dark passage before him, a musty smell pervades. A wayward rat skirts past his shoes, but the man is unphased. Eventually, Raymond Huddler ascends another set of shoddy steps and unlocks another door, leading to a sub-room. There, in an odd portrait of submission, the man kneels near a closed air vent, and he waits.

Two minutes later, footsteps approach—not from behind but from the front. A substantial two-foot by two-foot grille is removed from the other side, allowing a rush of light to invade through a litany of miniature squares, shining onto the face of Raymond Huddler, the man humbling crouching as if in a confessional booth.

A pair of black dress shoes stand before him through the air vent, which is all Huddler can see of the other party. After a few moments of silence from both men, Raymond Huddler speaks. "We're at a stalemate. Things will be quiet for a while, but the war is not over."

The man's words are met with further silence before the other voice finally replies. "Anything else?"

"The FBI will remain for a time, but then they will leave."

Again, stillness fills the air.

"Anything else?"

"That's it."

With those words, the air vent is quickly covered and clicks into place. Not a man to be patronized, Raymond Huddler cannot help but think to himself, *Very fortunate. He is very fortunate to speak to me in such a way; very fortunate I must kneel to communicate with him.*

Opening the door to the sub-room, closing the same door and descending the decades-old wooden steps, Raymond Huddler walks several feet in the direction from which he came, strolling through the passage by flashlight that connects Jerry's Restaurant to the office of the Mayor of Macon, Georgia.

• • •

Agent Dennison sticks his head through the office door. "I'm heading out for the night unless you need anything else, boss."

Special Agent in Charge Harold Dawson does not bother to look up. He knows who it is. "I'm good. See you tomorrow."

Dennison can only guess Dawson's level of restlessness. It has been a frustrating ordeal for everyone. None of the locals are talking and even Maxwell's intel has dried up.

"See ya, Wheeler," Dennison offers in passing on his way out the door, saluting his fellow agent who is covering the night shift.

"All right, Cy."

As Dennison prepares to enter the stairwell and exit the makeshift FBI headquarters in Macon, footsteps whisper in the distance. Dennison halts to peer down a dark hallway to see a nearly-inconspicuous Agent Hopper.

Dennison thought everyone else was gone.

Hopper thought the same.

The two agents look at each other from opposite ends of the hallway. No words are spoken.

Dennison nods.

Hopper musters the friendliest grin possible, which is not much, and nods as well.

The two agents go about their business.

10

Thursday, August 15

The summer of '68 in Georgia has been down the middle; not warmer than usual, not cooler than usual but just plain hot.

Roger, Karen and Kevin Stevens rumble down the highway in their Plymouth Fury, the faithful automobile gobbling every painted, white line in its path. The City of Augusta is well in the rearview mirror. A posted sign whips past the family at 55 mph: *Entering Bibb County*; each passing road sign shouts to the Stevens family, reminding the trio they are farther from home than ever before or so it seems.

Roger has attempted to keep the mood light, but his conversation-starters have fallen short. It quickly became clear the man should not press the issue. The husband and father is torn apart at the thought of his wife and son suffering at the hands of his choices.

As the drive unveils new scenery to the Stevens family, churning are Roger's thoughts. He never knew what it would be like to leave the Academy, but he had a rough idea, and his idea was certainly more ceremonious than the hurried, impromptu sendoff he and his family received last week. Roger blames no one. The decision to move was made with short notice, and he was the one who decided to leave. School was already out for the summer. Several of the families from Augusta Christian were vacationing, along with several staff members. The tea, coffee and punch reception held by the school certainly was a kind gesture. However, Roger felt badly because the event was clearly thrown together. No one thought the man's tenure and his family's impactful stay at The Academy would end on a hot, mundane Augusta night with thirty or so well-wishers in attendance. Even those present looked puzzled at best by Roger's decision to leave, not to mention the destination of his choosing, and it was challenging for even his closest friends to buy in and whole-heartedly show their support. All the years, all the accomplishments, all the memories, all the friends and all of it ended for Roger like a vague, distant whimper in the night.

Karen was saddened by the sendoff as well. She was disappointed not for herself but for her husband and son. Karen did not blame anyone either, but to say the event was *anticlimactic* was a vast understatement in her opinion.

Possibly the most difficult part of the move for Karen was packing their home. During the process, the wife and mother had to step to the back porch several times to shed nostalgic tears in private. The thought of someone else living in their home seemed inconceivable. In addition, there was a mix up with the delivery date of the furniture belonging to Mr. Ridgley, the kind new owner. The moving truck arrived a week earlier than Mr. Ridgley planned, and the Stevens family had yet to move out. Karen was the only one home when she cordially accepted the delivery. Rather than send the innocent movers away in a huff, Karen graciously allowed the men to set the furniture to the side in her living room. There the items sat for days—someone else's furniture in the Stevens' home, and Karen could not bring herself to look at any of it.

In the back seat of the Plymouth Fury, Kevin Stevens is not only fighting sadness but anger, regret, and animosity all at once.

Considering all the hurdles the Stevens Family jumped to get to this point, the toughest for both Roger and Karen was breaking the news to Kevin. Roger and Karen laid out everything before their son, assuring Kevin they had no idea what lies beyond his graduation, which is only nine months away. However, Kevin's parents could not mitigate the fact that a young man's senior year is typically a most glorious year, and despite the righteous cause of leaving for Macon South, it still did not change the truth: Kevin had one shot—one shot in a lifetime—to be a senior in high school with his friends. Kevin had one shot to see the culmination of three prior years—the meticulous laying of an illustrious foundation—come to fruition at Augusta Christian. Kevin had one shot at a senior year to finish what the team started. The Patriots were set to win back to back State Titles. Kevin was set to be All-city for the fourth time, achieving a feat never witnessed before in the City of Augusta. Kevin was most likely to be named All-State for the third straight season, and Kevin even had the opportunity to be named player of the year in the State of Georgia for a second straight season, joining a very elite group—the Mount Rushmore of Georgia High School basketball. Now, those opportunities are gone.

As unreasonable as the prospect of moving has been, Kevin, amid a surge of emotion, had to admit his parents tried to be as reasonable as possible. Roger and Karen ultimately laid the decision for their son to move at Kevin's feet. Roger and Karen agreed to leave Kevin with Reynolds and his family for the school year, and as much as Roger disliked the idea of Kevin playing basketball for someone as smug as Bart Newhouse, Roger would have done it for Kevin's sake.

In the end, it was Kevin who agreed to go, and just as his parents felt about their decision to leave Augusta, none of the Stevens Family made the choice because it was what they wanted to do—not by a longshot.

Entering Macon, Georgia reads the latest sign.

"Macon, Georgia," Roger announces in a half-optimistic tone, trying to generate some sort of enthusiasm upon their arrival.

In the passenger seat, Karen conjures her best smile.

In the backseat, Kevin conjures nothing.

Fifteen minutes later and the Plymouth Fury pulls into the parking lot of the Roosevelt Center, a building constructed over two decades ago as a depot for U.S. provisions in World War II. Principal Bullock gave Roger the rundown over the phone. Several runways, beginning in the early '40s, were built in Georgia to train Air Force units to defend against potential enemy submarine attacks in the Gulf of Mexico. War provisions were housed in one half of the enormous building and military personnel in the other on the south side of Macon. Now, thanks in part to a hesitant Mayor with strong urging from Washington D.C., the historical edifice will serve as the make-shift home for staff and students of Macon South until a new school can be built. Privately, despite his public endorsement, the Mayor of Macon was much more in favor of leaving the landmark as is and canceling both upcoming semesters at South. Whether he would admit it or not, the Mayor of Macon never has been a frequent visitor to this side of town.

As the Stevens family drives across a large, empty parking lot, a man stands in the distance near the front doors of the Roosevelt Center. It does not take long for Roger to identify the individual. Roger finds it impossible to overlook such a grand smile exuding from such a well-dressed man in one-hundred-degree heat. Roger shakes his head and ponders, *how can a man smile like that after all he has experienced? It must mean the man knows something many people don't.*

"That's him," Roger announces in subdued fashion to Karen and Kevin. "That's Principal Bullock."

Karen prepares her best smile, meanwhile partially holding the principal responsible for everything.

Kevin would much rather despise the man than meet him.

The father, mother, and son step from the automobile and quickly stretch; their vehicle is filled to the brim with their belongings.

Charles Bullock rapidly circles the car to the driver's side, his hand extended. "Coach Stevens. Welcome back to Macon." The principal references the previous trip Roger made to town during his decision-making process.

Roger receives the man with a smile. In his heart, Roger sincerely likes Charles Bullock, which made the decision to come here slightly easier. "Good to see you, Principal Bullock." Roger looks past the principal to the large building behind him. "How is the new building working out?"

"Well, not exactly new but extremely accommodating as far as square-footage." Principal Bullock places a hand on his heart and pauses, wanting to convey gratitude for the building God has provided. "The entire school and I are most grateful for a place to call home—for now."

The principal next turns his attention to the other important passengers. "Mrs. Stevens, it's so good to see you again. And, Kevin, what a pleasure to finally meet you. I've heard so much about you."

Karen responds in kind.

Kevin does his best just to keep it together.

Roger steers the subject in a new direction. "How are the buses coming along?"

The principal responds again with a smile and enthusiastic tone, his hand still resting on his heart. "Let me show you." The man leads the Stevens family around a nearby corner of the building where a handful of secondhand yet well-maintained school buses come into view. "We almost have the new routes ready to go for the school year. As I said, God has been so gracious to provide, and how He worked through your former school was such an unexpected blessing."

Upon Roger's decision to leave the Academy in Augusta, the man had a heart-to-heart talk with Principal Mize. News of the family's departure was as surreal to Roger's former boss as it was to Roger. However, when all was said and done, not only did Principal Mize give Roger his blessing, but Principal Mize pledged to do whatever he could to help. The interracial kingdom of God had become important to Principal Mize of late; hence, the hiring of a new black history teacher at the Academy. Moreover, Principal Mize quickly gained a heart for Roger's new endeavor as well, and the principal expressed his support in the form of a most magnanimous recommendation to the Academy School Board. Principal Mize suggested sending the Academy's well-maintained, small fleet of used buses to Macon South with Roger Stevens, all shipped from Augusta to Macon with the help of generous volunteers. The Academy could then sacrifice and buy other buses to replace the donation.

The news was Christmas morning to Charles Bullock. Of course, Macon South never needed buses in the past. The school had always been in the heart of the South community. However, with the former building decimated, even though the Roosevelt Center is located on the southern edge of town, the walking-distance would still be impractical for every student. Therefore, the donated buses have been a most welcome surprise to the South Principal—a blessing from heaven, as he called it.

"Doesn't that look impressive?" Principal Bullock states with pride, motioning toward the buses aligned uniformly in a row.

"Yes, great," Roger replies, trying to keep pace with the man's enthusiasm.

Principal Bullock is beaming. "Now, let me show you my favorite bus." Once again leading the Stevens family with vigor, Charles Bullock navigates between the buses. Toward the back of the fleet sits the newly-adorned Macon South basketball team bus, fully and audaciously painted in blue and brown. Painted down one side of the bus are the words *Macon South*. Painted down the other side of the bus are the words *Go Muskrats*.

"Who are the Muskrats," whispers Kevin in the background.

"We are," Roger quickly answers to deter Kevin's incredulous tone. "We are the Muskrats."

"Yes, we are!" chimes Principal Bullock with a swing of his fist—all the man is missing are pom-poms.

The Stevens family basks in the light of a team bus that undoubtedly screams over-the-top team spirit. At first glance, the team bus is a little much on the eyes, especially for Karen who has a taste for quality décor and color schemes.

So much for keeping a low profile, Roger thinks to himself. *They'll see us coming from a mile away.* Despite his opinion of the salient and semi-outrageous team bus, Roger is warmed by the grin on the principal's face. Charles Bullock and the school have been through so much, Roger considers. They deserve every emotional victory they can get.

"Looks like it's ready to roll," Roger gives his best assessment, glancing back at Karen and Kevin for help.

"Sure does," Karen concurs.

Kevin cannot take much more.

The principal discerns the hardship on Kevin's face. Charles Bullock steps forward to stand before all three members of the Stevens Family. "I know I've said this before, but I just can't say it enough. Thank you. Thank you, Stevens Family, Roger, Karen, and Kevin, for everything: not merely the donation of the buses but thank you for donating your lives. I know this must be very, very challenging for all of you. But from the bottom of my heart, I thank you for trusting God."

If you only knew, Roger thinks to himself as the men firmly shake hands again. Quickly, Roger retracts his original, self-serving thought. If anyone knows how to trust God, it is the man standing before him now, and as great as the Stevens Family believes their sacrifice to be, their sacrifice—in Roger's mind—does not surmount the living sacrifice that is Principal Charles Bullock.

"Well," the principal clasps his hands in joy, "I would next like to show you the inside of our nearly-new school building?"

• • •

Thirty minutes later and Roger, Karen and Kevin are back in their car. The tour was impressive; better than Roger anticipated. The building had certainly received great attention from the Macon South community; the volunteers did wonders in Roger's opinion. Of course, there is no gymnasium in the Roosevelt Center; a huge problem for an aspiring basketball program. However, thanks to the surprising generosity of Roger's long-time friend Tom Chaney, a former college teammate and Head Coach at Ridgewood High School across town, Roger and his team have a standing offer to use the Ridgewood gymnasium for practices and home games. *Again*, Roger marvels, *all that has been needed has been provided.*

"Everything seems to be on track," Roger suggests from behind the wheel.

Karen must agree. "It seems they are trying their best."

Roger glances in the rearview mirror; Kevin does not want any part of the conversation. Roger lets it go. The fact that Kevin has come to Macon without understanding all the reasons why displays great maturity on behalf of the young man, and Roger could not ask for more from his son.

After another fifteen-or-so-minute drive, the Stevens family arrive at the place they will call home for the school year. In nostalgic and pleasant fashion, Roger and Karen immediately discern similarities between the home coming into view and the home they left in August—not in terms of size or even beauty but in subtle ways. This new home is in the Macon countryside. There is a decent amount of land. There is even a long, gravel drive descending from the house to the road; *very familiar.*

Kevin has yet to see their temporary home until this moment; his father and mother saw no need to add insult to injury by dragging him down to Macon prematurely for a tour. Even so, Roger and Karen fully realize access to this temporary home, much like many details along the precarious journey to Macon, developed marvelously.

The property is owned by the Andersons, a husband and wife in their late-sixties—one of the more affluent black couples in Macon. Mr. and Mrs. Anderson could never get a loan from a bank despite their profitable earnings as soybean growers. Nevertheless, the couple built equity on their own through faith in God and diligence, and, in the end, the couple never had to pay back any interest on any loan from any bank. Thus, the Andersons have been thankful for the doors God opened and for the doors God sealed shut. When the Andersons— friends with Principal Bullock for years—heard the Stevens were moving to Macon and heard of the glorious reason why they were moving to Macon, the Andersons expressed the desire to get involved. The couple offered their home as living quarters, knowing they themselves would have ample room in the adjacent cottage for a handful of months.

Roger and Karen were most grateful for the extremely kind gesture, but they suggested it should be them, the Stevens family, who should stay in the cottage instead of uprooting the homeowners. The Andersons would have it no other way.

Still, despite the favorable circumstances falling into place, Roger and Karen know none of it may be enough to surmount the heaviness of Kevin's heart, save possibly one amenity. Roger and Karen are hoping one feature on the property will appeal to their son. The couple is depending on a long shot, one potentially redeeming quality, and the object can be seen from the road as the Stevens turn toward the Anderson home.

At the top of the driveway, secured firmly above the garage, weathered but durable, off-white more than white, rusted more than orange, is a regulation backboard with a hoop and a net.

"Can you see it, Kev?" Roger asks his son with subtle optimism. "Mr. Anderson put up that hoop for his son many years ago."

Kevin sees the emblem of reverence from a distance. Despite the doldrums of his soul, Kevin must admit the sight of a basketball goal sparks hope and a reminder of home.

It never mattered where the Stevens family have been in their travels, no matter what city in what state: the sight of a serviceable backboard and hoop has always brought comfort to

Kevin. Whether in the countryside or on the downtown pavement, whether inside a beautiful arena like Alexander Coliseum or attached to a barn above a lonely plot of dirt, something about a basketball goal does Kevin's heart good. The sight of it makes him want to find a basketball, any basketball…and just play. Whether five-on-five, three-on-three, one-on-one or just a game of H-O-R-S-E; it does not matter to Kevin. It is an escape, an oasis, even a sanctuary. It does not matter what type of day Kevin had today or what tomorrow holds, a basketball court always offered him freedom from all worry and concern: *putting the ball in the basket; that's all that matters.*

"What do you think, Kevin?" his mother dares to ask.

After a substantial pause, Kevin Stevens finally speaks: "I think I'll be spending most of my time out there," quips the teenager.

His mother looks at his father. They both rationalize quickly in their minds: his reaction could have been worse, much worse, and they can live with his response.

● ● ●

The Stevens' first night in their interim home is uneventful, which is good in the opinion of both Roger and Karen; there is *no need for any further drama.* The past few months have supplied plenty of emotion and, certainly, the next few months will also. Kevin chooses the living room couch on this first night. There, the teenager lies on his back, tossing the basketball straight up in the air, working on his release, follow-through, and backspin.

"You sure you want to sleep on the sofa?" his mother queries for the umpteenth time.

"I'm fine, Mom."

"He's fine," Roger whispers from the kitchen table.

Karen takes the hint and plops in the chair opposite her husband. "Welcome home," she utters in semi-sarcastic fashion.

Roger leans forward and smiles at his lifelong companion. "Home is wherever we are…as long as God is watching." With those words, the man slips his wife a note, reminiscent of their actions in high school.

"What's this?" Karen turns over the paper and reads the penmanship of Reverend Jordan; on the note is no commentary, just one scripture in ink:

> The name of the Lord is a strong tower;
> The righteous run to it and are safe
> Proverbs 18:10.

"I found this note in my stuff. I think he slipped it in my briefcase when I wasn't looking, for just the right time."

Karen offers a genuine smile. "This is the right time, isn't it?"

The scripture and familiar handwriting of her lifelong pastor brings an encouraging smile to her face. Looking up, she finds her husband presenting his hand to her across the table. As a sign of agreement, Karen takes his hand.

11

Tuesday, September 3

"It's going to go well today," Karen decrees as she sends the two men in her life out the door for the first time to Macon South High School.

"Of course, it is," Roger affirms.

Of course, it is, Kevin privately entertains sarcasm. Still, the teen has decided to give it his best. He is just unsure how effective his best will be.

"I have been up praying for both of you since early this morning," Karen peppers her husband and son with optimism, "And I will keep praying throughout the day."

Roger smiles, looking at his son and patting him on the shoulder, "It's going to go well." The man kisses his wife, and he and his son are off.

• • •

The Plymouth finds a parking spot and rumbles to a halt as Roger and Kevin arrive 45 minutes before school. Just that quickly, Roger's far-fetched wish to remain inconspicuous goes up in smoke. The man planned an early arrival to avoid a crowd. Conversely, Roger did not account for early arrivals all the way around, many parents and students descending on the Roosevelt Center extra-early to familiarize themselves with the foreign building. Instead of slipping through the doors with minimal attention, innumerable eyes find the Stevens men immediately. As Roger and Kevin step from the car, the white man and his white son become the talk of Macon South, circumscribed by curious eyeballs, prodding elbows and whispering voices.

Well, Roger considers, their cover blown, *so much for a sneak attack.* The coach and teacher turns to his son; Kevin looks uneasy, to say the least. Roger smiles to calm the moment. "Here we go. You ready?" *That was a dumb question,* Roger criticizes himself.

Kevin would prefer to sit in the car all day, but he knows he cannot. Instead, he motions toward the school doors, trying to get them both inside as soon as possible.

Roger takes the hint, and Kevin follows. The Stevens men have never felt taller, their towering frames impossible to hide. They both sense it: every eye is on them. Roger chooses not to stare in return, taking a business-as-usual approach, radiating a smile in the direction of every face he sees, meanwhile gripping his briefcase tightly. Kevin, on the other hand, stares at the ground, suddenly reconsidering the idea of moving to Macon—only one minute into the experiment.

Pleasantries are few and far between this morning; not out of intentional rudeness but out of shock. Many of the South students heard there would be a new basketball coach, and his son would be with him, and they would be white. This is different, however. Seeing them is different. That was a rumor, but this is a fact. This is them in the flesh.

Roger Stevens attempts to sever the awkward silence the best he can. "Good morning. Good morning," he salutes several students. *There's no going back now,* the man concludes to himself, leading his son through the ever-growing crowd, down the longest hallway of their lives and toward the office of Principal Bullock.

Black teenager after black teenager stare as the man and son walk past. Whisper after whisper swirls. Roger's skin has never felt and looked so white to him as it does right now.

The first face in the Office of the Principal is a friendly one: the Principal's Secretary. "Coach Stevens, good morning," the matronly woman greets the Stevens men while coming to her feet, almost doing a curtsy in their honor. "Please take a seat and I will get...."

Before the kind woman can summon her superior, Principal Bullock nearly bolts through his office door, radiating with optimism as usual. "Coach Stevens: first day of school," the principal announces with his hand extended.

"Good morning, sir," Roger responds, and he is proud of his son for doing the same thing.

"The day has finally come," Charles Bullock declares, fully believing the impact of this day will have far-reaching ramifications, propelling Macon South into a future much greater than its past. In Roger's opinion, the principal has enough enthusiasm for everyone in the room and school and community, for that matter, and enough enthusiasm to contradict anyone who thinks hiring a white basketball coach at an all-black school will not work.

"We are here and ready, sir," Roger speaks with respect and in faith.

The Principal places a firm hand on the coach's shoulder, non-verbally reminding him of everything it has taken to get them to this point. "Let me lead you to the assembly."

• • •

The largest room in the building is in the center of the converted depot, and over 1,000 students and parents have begun gathering. Principal Bullock leads Coach Stevens and his son to the front row. *Might as well lead us to the highest point in*

Macon for all to see, Kevin concludes in his heart and mind. Near the front, the principal begins introducing Roger and his son to several faculty members at South, a majority of which are exceptionally gracious and kind; the lone exceptions being those whose apprehension can be seen and felt, as if they want to ask, *is this whole idea going to make things better or worse?*

The previously oversized space quickly fills, and after showing Roger and Kevin to their seats, the principal walks intrepidly to the microphone and stands tall before the bustling crowd. The commotion wanes quieter and quieter until silence falls. Thus, Principal Bullock speaks his first words of the 1968 school year to Macon South High.

"Here we are," his voice ricochets from wall to wall. "Here we are, Macon South High School." Principal Bullock opens his arms wide as if to embrace the building itself and everyone in it. "Here we are, and no bomb, no explosion, no attack, no evil plan has kept us from getting here. I think God deserves praise for that very fact this morning."

A man who is not ashamed or embarrassed in the least about his faith in God, Principal Bullock initiates the round of applause himself. Soon, the entire room joins him in a chorus of clapping, and just when the applause begins to slow, Principal Bullock personally keeps it going, which causes the crowd to keep it going as well.

Despite Roger's personal, high-level of awkwardness this morning, it is understandable to him: the optimism and rejuvenation felt and expressed by Charles Bullock. On the other hand, Roger assesses, it is equally understandable: the overall trepidation surely felt by a large percentage of faculty, students and parents in this expansive room. The last time school convened at Macon South, an explosive device detonated, and a heinous blast ripped through a building filled with hundreds of young black people with one clear intention: to kill them all. With the vivid memory of those sights and sounds still fresh, it would not surprise Roger if hundreds of uneasy South faithful are subconsciously looking over their shoulders this morning, despite their fearless leader's tone of bravery.

"Regardless of what happened," Principal Bullock barrels forward, "We made it this far. Even though we had to cancel the final weeks of school last year for the underclassmen and even though last year's senior class had to finish their studies at Second Baptist Church, we made it through. And before we go any further and step into a new school year, I want to pray."

Pray: what a refreshing word, Roger and Kevin both consider silently. No matter where the two are, no matter if they find themselves at the ends of the earth, the father and son know they can always pray.

"I have invited my pastor—a man who is even a pastor to many of you—to join us. Reverend Jenkins, please come forward and lead us in prayer."

With those words, a black minister complete with a black shirt, black pants, black coat, and a white collar arrives at the microphone. The room assumes a reverent hush as the man clears his throat...and in a gravelly voice begins to pray.

"Lord God, You are great...and greatly to be praised. We thank you for bringing us this far. We thank you for causing us to survive the toils of yesterday by the strength of your right arm. And because you are an everlasting God, You are the same today as you were yesterday, and You will be the same forever, and You will yet again protect and preserves us, Your people, by the strength of your right arm...."

"Amen," Principal Bullock proudly seconds.

Amen, Roger silently agrees in his heart.

"And last but not least, Lord God, we know, in fact, we are certain, that what has been meant for harm, You, God, will turn for good. We offer this prayer to you in the name of Your Son Jesus. And all God's people in the room, said, 'Amen.'"

"Amen!" The agreement is more pronounced throughout the assembly, accompanied by a round of applause.

"Thank you, Reverend," Principal Bullock salutes and resumes the duties at the microphone. "Of course, I don't have to tell you we are undergoing a few changes this school year: a different address, a different building, different-looking classrooms, and a different and new and highly-esteemed basketball coach."

Roger chokes on air, a lump dropping into his throat from nowhere as Principal Bullock lightly motions in his direction.

Next to Roger, Kevin almost passes out. Capacity crowds normally do not bother the young man. This crowd, however, does. The teen fraught with fear leans toward his father and pleads through a whisper, "He's not going to call you up there, is he? Or me?"

Trying to display composure, Roger whispers in a calm attempt to quell his son's anxiety. "No, I don't think he will call...."

"I want to welcome our new Head Basketball Coach Roger Stevens and his son Kevin, and I want them to join me up front right now."

Coach Stevens, and especially his son, become lifeless, Roger catatonically thinking, *what is he doing? I am trying to draw as little attention to us as possible, and he is going to parade us in front of the entire school?* Completely put on the spot, Roger offers a humble smile, as if to say, *thanks but no thanks, Principal. You have it under control.*

To no avail, the ebullient principal waves them on, Charles Bullock igniting another round of applause on his own, the man clapping wildly; his visage one of childlike enthusiasm.

Roger offers a final, non-verbal decline, desperately hoping Mr. Bullock will reconsider. The principal does not. Reluctantly putting his best foot forward, Roger stands and signals for his fright-stricken teenager to follow, both father and son walking toward the principal who, blatantly enough, takes a huge step back and motions for the new coach to assume the microphone.

Kevin shuffles forward on a death-march with his hands in his front pockets, trying to go somewhere else mentally.

Coach Stevens steps before the mic and gives his son a quick glance to make sure the teenager has not hit the floor.

"Ummm" is the initial, ineloquent stammer escaping Roger's chest—the microphone stand is a little short to suit his height.

Springing into action, Charles Bullock darts in front of Roger to adjust the height of the metal pole. "Let me get that for you," offers the effervescent principal. A nearby amplifier pops and squeals. "There you go. Say hello," he encourages the new coach with a slap on the back before lunging out of the way.

Roger emits a smile out of the side of his mouth while simultaneously holding the thought: *I could punch you right now, Charles.*

Kevin cannot believe this is happening.

All eyes are on the white man and his son.

With the mic in his face, Roger concludes: what else can he do but speak? "Thank you, Principal Bullock. It's...good..., I mean it's great to be here at Macon South. My name is Coach Stevens, and not only do I coach basketball, but I also teach Geometry. So, if you ever want to talk obtuse angles in your spare time, I'm your guy." Roger's lame attempt at humor is only good for a muffled cough in the distance and the squeaking of a shifting chair. "This is my son, Kevin, by the way."

You're acting obtuse, Dad, is the thought in Kevin's mind; the teen feels about ready to die.

"Ummm." Normally an effective public speaker, Roger verbally fumbles about as an infinite number of black faces fill his vision. He cannot believe he is here and neither can they, and nothing could have adequately prepared the man for this moment. All Roger can do is embrace and experience it. *Help me, God,* is his only thought.

With that, Roger pivots to get momentum going. "Just a quick announcement...if Principal Bullock doesn't mind."

The jolly Principal gives his new coach a vote of confidence with an overt thumbs up.

"I am aware there will not be a football program this fall at South in light of the big move from the school to this building. But I have some good news. Today, after school at three, anyone interested in playing basketball this season can meet us for our first offseason workout and scrimmage. We have been blessed by Ridgewood High School and their basketball coach, an old friend of mine, to use their gymnasium for practices and home games this season."

Roger's announcement does not generate much excitement—he thought it would be perceived as good news. Instead, the man just aroused more anxiety than calm; the Ridgewood area commonly known as an unwelcomed place to people from the South side of town. Roger dubiously observes as several in attendance turn and whisper to one another.

"Now, this is not an official practice because," the man tries to get back on track, "the first practice of the season is not until the first week of November. This is simply an opportunity to throw the ball in the air and play some basketball. My son...."

Kevin gives his father a foreboding stare as if to say *don't you dare.*

"Will be there, and I will be there as well. So, any boys from grades nine through twelve who want to play, please meet us at the new team bus out back, and we'll go play." The man has run out of words. "And...I guess that's it."

Coach Stevens turns the microphone back to Mr. Bullock as the principal ensues with more wild clapping. To Roger it is evident: Principal Bullock is the only one in the room who believes in him as the new hire. Everyone else will need proof.

As Roger and Kevin take their seats, Roger reflects, *I think that was the hardest thing I've ever done.*

Principal Bullock soon concludes the assembly, and teachers are dismissed a few minutes early to arrive at their classrooms in advance of their students.

Exercising keen foresight, Roger scheduled Kevin's first-period class to be with his father in the Geometry room. Therefore, Kevin stands and exits the assembly tucked behind his father.

Upon arriving in his father's classroom, Kevin has his choice of seating. He opts not for the front, nor the back. He also chooses against the center of the room. Instead, Kevin settles for the side of the room farthest from the door and toward the middle—his best attempt to remain low-key.

As the young black faces begin to filter through the door, Roger makes a point to greet everyone with a smile, leaning casually against his desk to seem as non-threatening as possible. In return, he gets some smiles, some blank stares, and a few suspicious glances.

The bell rings. Roger takes a deep breath and begins his teaching career at Macon South High School by introducing himself to the class and choosing a predictable exercise. "Everyone, please share your name as we go around the room."

The students comply, and soon the fateful moment arrives. All eyes look to Kevin as the young man sits up straightly and clears his throat.

"My name is Kevin..., Kevin Stevens..., and I am the teacher's..., Mr. Stevens there..., I am his father."

The class bursts in laughter.

Kevin catches his mistake. "I mean he's my teacher....my father."

The class laughs again.

"Okay," Roger intervenes. "I think we know what he means. That's my son, Kevin. All right. Who's next?" The man swings the conversation to the next student.

Oh, that was bad, Kevin laments privately, sweat beading just below his hairline.

The first hour of the first day comes and goes. Roger noticed his students spent more time staring blankly at him than comprehending the Geometry he was teaching, staring at Kevin as well, but that was the worst of it. As the bell sounds at the end of the first period, Kevin lingers and is soon the last student in his father's class. The two engage in a private conversation that ends with the father patting his son on the shoulder, neither of them wanting to embrace to draw extra attention to the white teenager who already feels under the microscope.

"Check in with me later. Let's have lunch," the father suggests.

"We'll see how it goes." Kevin exits the room and enters the hallway.

Roger can only watch, his heart exiting with his son as well.

• • •

As the second-period bell rings, Kevin carries the stares from the assembly and first period with him to the next class, and the same would happen for third period and beyond. By fourth period, just when Kevin thought the awkwardness of day-one could not escalate, the lone white kid at Macon South enters history class and draws the attention of a group of boys. Kevin instantly feels the weight of the group's collective stare on his way to an open desk at the back of the room.

The once talkative pack of boys draws silent, stunned at the sight of the coach's kid—the white kid—in their midst.

As Kevin takes a seat, a muffled comment is made followed by snickering from the group, their heads and eyes turned in curiosity to observe the white kid's every move. Kevin's response is right down the middle: he does not stare back, but he does not look away, refusing to cower in fear. He simply gives the group an occasional glance to make them aware he is aware.

The History teacher calls fourth period to order. All eyes and bodies shift to the front of the class in concert, and even the boys in the group adhere to the instructions, except for one. A young black man, obviously tough and well-muscled, wearing a solid white t-shirt and blue jeans, does not move an inch. Instead, he continues to stare straight through Kevin Stevens. Every student in the room now faces the front except for the coach's son and this brazen teenager.

Kevin gives another glance and then another, trying to help the brash teen realize how rude he is acting, but the young black man is not concerned with feelings or decorum or courtesy or anything of the like. Instead, the larger black teen is in a trance, and the white boy is the target.

"Mr. Taylor," the female teacher claps her hands to get the attention of the young man; she, too, can tell he is up to no good. "Something more interesting to you than American History?"

Without breaking his stare, the rough and tumble teen disrespectfully answers with his back to the teacher, "There's a lot of things more interesting than American History."

The other teens around the shameless youth respond in laughter—it is clear they live in a world that revolves around the muscular young man.

"Maybe Principal Bullock's office would be more interesting to you?" the teacher counters.

The class cackles and hisses at the undertone of tension; everyone caught in the middle between the authority figure and the rugged youth.

Eventually, the young black man surrenders his stare-down, slowly turning his body to face the front of the class.

Kevin wonders, "*What's this guy's problem?*" As time goes on and more glances from the black teen persist, Kevin is left to conclude, "*I guess I am.*"

The never-ending period finally ends, and the staring session spills into the hallway. Kevin keeps his head up yet minds his own business. He can sense the group from History class behind him thanks to their not-so-quiet whispering and laughter. Kevin strides confidently—not too fast, not too slow. All eyes are on the tall, slender, white teenager as he wades through the otherwise all-black student body. Teenagers part the hall before Kevin and remain parted at the sight of the group behind him; many can sense something is brewing.

A friendly kid, Kevin would normally smile at the passing faces, but right now he is singularly focused on passing through the doors straight ahead—the cafeteria. Kevin was originally heading for his father's classroom for lunch, but he has changed course. The last signal he wants to send is he is running to daddy with this pack of boys behind him and emitting the scent of fear.

Kevin arrives at the cafeteria, breaking his stoic countenance to nod respectfully at the teacher standing at the double doors; the man reciprocates respect to the teen.

Mr. Dawkins, the P.E. teacher at Macon South, next turns his focus to the pack in pursuit of the new coach's son, the man taking an exaggerated step to end their momentum. "Gentlemen, are you in this lunch period?"

The group collectively comes to a halt. One of the boys looks around and then stammers on behalf of everyone. "Uh, no, sir, Mr. Dawkins. We're just walking by. We have second lunch."

With their progressed impeded, the biggest teen, the obvious leader of the group looks past Mr. Dawkins, over the man's shoulder, as if the man's not standing there, watching as the bodies in the cafeteria begin to ensconce the white kid by sheer number.

"Well, then," Mr. Dawkins deduces, "I guess I'll be seeing you gentlemen at second lunch." Mr. Dawkins has the attention of everyone in the group except for one. Contact with the final young man is established when Mr. Dawkins steps directly in front of the teenager and calls him by name to break his trance—Mr. Dawkins, an athletically built man at 6'2" is just shy of reaching eye-level with the 6'4" student. "You hear me, Billy?"

Billy Taylor concedes and turns his attention away from the white kid and toward Mr. Dawkins. Agitated by the interruption, Billy is slow to acknowledge the man, refusing to answer his question on purpose.

Mr. Dawkins detects insubordination and quickly rises to the occasion, not afraid of the bigger teen one iota. "So, get lost," is Mr. Dawkins instruction.

Billy is under the skin of the man, and, for now, that is good enough for Billy. The muscular teen looks past the teacher one final time. The white kid is out of view. Therefore, Billy Taylor flashes a confident smile and responds with one word before he and his group resume their amble down the hall. "Cool."

12

Day one is complete. Roger checks it off his mental list—at least the school-portion is complete.

Kevin appears in his father's classroom a few seconds after 3 p.m., standing by the wall as the other students exit seventh-period Geometry.

"How'd it go?" the father inquires.

"It went," his son responds minus any bells or whistles. "School is school."

"Well, we made it through the first day," his father affirms, closing his briefcase emphatically. "Now, let's go play some ball."

Kevin mildly shrugs his shoulders. He cannot argue with his father; basketball always seems to help.

Fifteen minutes later and not knowing what to expect, Coach Stevens enjoys a pleasant surprise as he and Kevin find approximately ten boys hanging around the Muskrat team bus, ready for the first off-season workout. "Wonderful, men" is the cheerful, unrehearsed greeting blurted by the man; Roger did not know if any would show up. "Great turnout."

The group of teens collectively stands straighter at the sight and voice of the head coach. "I'm Coach Stevens." *They already knew that* he tells himself. *No need for the new white basketball coach to introduce himself.* "Climb on and let's go shoot some hoops."

The teens step aboard, and the suddenly optimistic coach checks his watch one final time before joining them.

"Hello again, Rufus," Roger salutes the gentleman behind the wheel, a heavy set, loquacious, black man to whom Principal Bullock introduced him earlier in the day.

"Good to see you, Coach."

"Ridgewood High School, please."

"You got it, sir."

The bus doors squeak as they close, and the vehicle quickly falls in gear. Coach Stevens turns to address the riders from the front of the bus, rubbing his hands together while brandishing a smile. "Okay, gentlemen. I welcome you aboard our new team bus."

All young black faces plus one white face show deference as the man speaks.

"The first thing I want to do is learn everyone's name, so I...."

The bus brakes unexpectedly, causing Roger nearly to lose his balance. Rufus apologetically interrupts the man's first-ever team address. "Sorry, Coach. Looks like you've got a few more."

Roger pivots to see four more young men at the bus doors.

"You want them on or off?" Rufus asks. "They're late."

Never a man to condone lateness by his players, still, Roger knows if ever there is a day to extend a pardon, today is the day—a little mercy to get things on the right foot. "That's okay, Rufus. Let them on."

Kevin watches from a distant, imperfect view as his father addresses the belated arrivals. "Hi, men." His father extends a warm invitation down the short set of bus stairs. "Climb aboard. Take a seat."

At that moment, as far as Kevin is concerned, the optimistic mood of the afternoon just escaped through the open bus windows.

The large literal and figurative head of Billy Taylor is first to appear as the athletic, 6'4" teenager stomps demonstratively up the steps in no hurry. Once at the top, the ultra-confident teen pauses to survey the passengers from the front of the bus, taking the time to make eye contact with all those on board. His scan of the riders, however, stops with the coach's son, and Billy immediately lapses into his same trance as before, his staring session only to be interrupted by the voice of the driver.

"You're late," Rufus announces, unimpressed with Billy's dramatic entrance.

Billy does not care for the driver's admonition and rewards him no response.

Roger's not sure what the deal is with this kid, so the man gives him another chance to listen and obey. "Let's find a seat, men."

"Today!" Rufus adds curtly, displaying less patience than Coach Stevens. Rufus draws a less-than-thrilled look from Billy Taylor, and Billy's first inclination is to comment on the overall flabbiness of the driver. Instead, the muscular youth in a solid white t-shirt turns and strolls down the center aisle of the bus. As Billy draws even with Kevin's seat, the black teen takes a moment to stop and stare again.

Again, Kevin remains strong, returning a stare of his own.

The other teens on the bus observe in silence, discerning some bad blood already.

Roger does not understand the young man's problem, and just before the coach can admonish him a second time, Billy eventually moves past the white kid and settles for a different seat.

Another young man makes the mistake of leaving his feet in Billy's way.

"You best move 'em" is Billy's only warning—a successful warning.

The remaining young men traveling in a pack with Billy take their seats, as well.

Roger observes the brazen young man still staring at his son from across the aisle. "Name?" the coach calls out to interrupt the moment. No answer is given. "Name!" Roger calls out more pronounced, not about to be ignored by a potential player.

The newcomer breaks his trance and answers. "Billy."

Billy. The coach makes a mental notation before jotting the name on his clipboard.

• • •

"Roger Stevens," the voice of a longtime friend beckons as soon as Roger steps into sight, the team bus now on the property of Ridgewood High School.

"Tom! Great to see you."

The men meld in a semi-embrace. "Here you are in Macon, Georgia," decrees the Ridgewood Coach.

"Here I am," Coach Stevens responds tentatively under his breath. "And I can't tell you how much I appreciate all you're doing by letting us use your gym."

Tom Chaney places a supportive hand on his colleague's back, steering him toward the gym while using a tone of discretion. "Don't mention it. You're the one making all the sacrifices. How was your first day?"

Roger discharges a sigh. "Not bad, not terrible. There must be a first day before there can be a second day, right? You know how it is: first day, first practice, first game—first everything."

"I hear you, partner," Coach Chaney empathizes. "We all have to start somewhere...or start over somewhere." The man fun-lovingly grips and wrestles the back of the neck of his longtime friend. "You're a rookie again."

Roger snorts. "Feels like it."

"Come on. Let me show you the gym, and then I'm going to get out of here because I don't think you want me scouting your team or anything."

Coach Stevens chuckles. "I wouldn't put it past you."

Meanwhile, the players from South have exited the bus and follow the two men, Billy Taylor eyeing Kevin Stevens the whole way.

• • •

Basketballs pound the hardwood—sweet music to Roger Stevens; *feels like home*, the man ruminates. The shrill of his whistle is also soothing to his ears. "Everybody over here!" Players surrounded the veteran coach on all sides. "First, I want to thank all of you for being here. Just a reminder: this is not an official practice. This is simply an opportunity to roll the ball on the court and get some exercise."

As the man gives instructions, he again notices the athletic black teenager, Billy, staring at his son from across the huddle. *What's the deal with this guy?* Roger considers while concluding his brief speech.

"I'm just here to watch. Alright, let's shoot free throws for teams—first five versus second five. Whoever's not in has next game."

Kevin hangs back, allowing the other players to step to the line first; part of him wants to see how the teams sort out.

After several attempts at some offseason, rusty-free-throw shooting, the squads take shape. Kevin lands with the first five. Billy lands with the second five.

"First five go shirts. Next five go skins," instructs Coach Stevens.

Billy is the first player to strip his shirt, and he does so with supreme confidence, unabashedly, the young man displaying a muscular, 6'4" frame with little body fat and a V-shaped upper back. He tosses his shirt to the side, but the shirt does not make it all the way off the court. Instead, one of his lackeys grabs it for him and pitches it out of bounds.

God's gift to the world, Roger assesses. The veteran coach has seen his type before.

On the shirted-squad, Kevin discerns the faces around him: none of them knowing quite what to do. "Kevin…. I'm Kevin," the veteran point guard takes the initiative and bounces from player to player on his squad with a handshake to break the ice. After making the rounds, Kevin continues to lead by stepping to mid-court for the jump ball.

When Billy sees the coach's son move to the center, he excitedly brushes past the surrounding players on his team, entering the center circle as well, very eager to match up head to head with the white kid.

Roger observes everything—Billy eyeing Kevin and Kevin eyeing Billy. The coach next places his whistle in his mouth and gives one final instruction before the ball goes airborne. "Let's keep it clean, gentlemen."

The ball goes up and both the coach and his All-State son watch in awe as Billy explodes vertically, high in the air to easily control the tip at the height of the toss, out-leaping Kevin by the length of a forearm, redirecting the ball cleanly to a teammate behind him.

Kevin barely had time to get off the floor.

Roger barely had time to adjust his eyes at the spectacle.

Coming back down, Billy unexpectedly sprints ahead of the pack and toward the goal. "Ball!" he commands.

Kevin's squad is slow to react, including Kevin.

Billy's friend and teammate responds by lofting a football pass over the heads of everyone. Suddenly, out in front thanks to a combustible burst of speed, Billy catches the ball cleanly about 12-feet from the basket, takes a hard dribble and shows no remorse in forcefully dunking the basketball with two hands.

"Oooo," the boys on the sideline ring out at the display of athleticism.

"Okay," Rufus commentates from a chair near the gym exit door.

Kevin barely reached the free line in pursuit of his opponent, and as Billy runs past Kevin, the muscular teen speaks in the ear of the coach's son: "Where you at?"

Kevin feels his breath but does nothing. As Kevin turns, he glances at his father.

Roger stands wide-eyed, his whistle dangling from his lips—the whole sequence happened fast. Roger overlooks the swagger of the athletic teen and instead entertains the thought, *We've got a player on our hands.*

Kevin shakes off the shock. Taking the ball out of bounds, he passes to a brave soul willing to play point guard. Kevin is the consummate high school point guard; however, there are no stakes in this game, and, with nothing to prove on this first day, Kevin wants to get everyone some touches.

Leaning against the stage in the Ridgewood gym, Coach Stevens maintains an eye on the matchup between his son and this new kid, Billy, for multiple reasons.

As the bodies flow from one end of the floor to the other, Billy waits for Kevin at half court, granting Kevin a not-so-friendly bump as he crosses from the backcourt to the frontcourt.

"Keep it clean," the coach repeats from a distance, not wanting to bail out his son because of how it might look. Roger knows Kevin can handle himself.

Meanwhile, Billy lifts his hands in the air to give the impression he is not doing anything wrong, suddenly playing the innocent part but playing it poorly.

Kevin keeps his cool, even smiling to calm the mood.

The ballhandler at the point is picked up by his defender.

Kevin watches from the block to see which direction the ballhandler will choose. With no one else eager to move to the basketball, Kevin dips in the lane to set up his man…then uses the player in front of him as an unknowing screen, shearing off the player's back and popping out to the wing.

The kid playing the point sees Kevin open on the wing and picks up his dribble to pass on the move but not quickly enough.

Billy jumps the screen and floods the passing lane, knocking the ball ahead. The basketball careens toward the sideline, but Billy makes another athletic move to tip the ball and keep it in play while impressively tight-roping the sideline with excellent balance.

The point guard who threw the errant pass wears his mistake and sprints at an angle to cut off Billy's head of steam. To no avail, when the player lunges in front of Billy, Billy effortlessly dribbles around his back, leaving the defender grasping at air, spinning the defender completely around. Meanwhile, Billy coasts in for another uncontested, two-handed dunk.

Coach Stevens continues to watch in pleasant dismay; part of him is bothered by the cockiness, the other part of him is thrilled with such promising signs of talent on the court and on the first day.

Kevin feels like he is moving in slow motion, as if his feet are embedded in cinder blocks. As Billy approaches him on his way downcourt, Kevin drops his head and turns to jog in the same direction.

Again, Billy jogs alongside the white kid to give him the business. "That's two for me."

Roger did not hear what Billy said to his son, but one more display like that and the coach is prepared to intervene.

Kevin defers the point again.

The same player brings the ball across half court, wanting to redeem himself for the intercepted pass and show he is not soft. The ballhandler tries to do it alone by putting a move on his man before getting to the wing to launch a quick jump shot.

Coach Stevens shakes his head; the man has never been thrilled with zero passes and a contested 17-foot jumper to start the offense.

The shot banks left, finding the rim.

Out of nowhere, falling out of the sky, Billy snares the rebound high above the traffic below. "Give me that," he shouts, slapping his hand on the ball for all to hear.

Kevin and the rest of the defense are in full retreat.

Billy holds up this time, choosing not to force the fast break. Instead, he gathers himself before crossing half court, taking his time, allowing both teams to get down the floor and set up.

Billy wants to slow down and enjoy the moment, thinking to himself, *no need to run the white kid off the court so fast.*

Billy controls the ball nonchalantly down the middle of the court, eyeing Kevin all the way. Next, Billy stops several feet in front of his defender and begins to dribble back and forth, switching hands again and again—a non-verbal way of calling out the coach's son.

Playing it cool, Kevin awaits Billy at the top of the key in his defensive stance.

Billy smiles at the sight of his defender settling into his crouch and decides to take him on. Dribbling closer, Billy blades his body to protect the ball, allowing him to talk to the white kid at the same time.

"This is going to be three for me," Billy forewarns. "You ready for it?"

Kevin hears but does not acknowledge. Instead, the coach's son studies the rhythm of Billy's ball-handling, looking for a telltale sign, and Kevin sees one.

Under the impression he is about to juke and blow past his defender, Billy steps back, lurches and fakes his body to the left before cutting to his right but leaving his dribble too high.

Kevin recognizes the poor technique and instinctively drops his body closer to the floor, reaching in with a darting hand and tapping the ball in the opposite direction of Billy's momentum.

Billy looks down at his right hand: the ball is gone. He glances over his shoulder: the coach's son picked him cleanly.

"Nice pick," Roger whispers from the stage, trying to hide his smile.

Kevin swiftly pushes the dribble ahead, showing a burst of his own.

The anger within Billy wells instantly, blood rushing to his face. Enraged, the teen mutters something, pivots and turns on the jets, exploding in Kevin's direction with one thought in mind: running him down.

Kevin knows he must be fast; the closing speed of his opponent no doubt lethal.

Billy knows he can run the white kid down because Billy knows he can run down anyone.

Roger shifts his body weight forward with a look of alarm. He has two players charging full speed downcourt, one chasing the other with the look of vengeance.

Kevin picks up his dribble at the free throw line, relying on his long strides to carry him the rest of the way, pitching his body more forward than up. He knows his defender will elevate high, no doubt looking for a soft toss to tattoo against the backboard.

As the coach's son lengthens his steps, Billy shortens his steps, chopping up the hardwood, looking to time the release point, closing at a reckless pace.

The two players go airborne with much force.

As they do, Coach Stevens utters from the sideline: "Oh, no."

Billy ascends quicker than Kevin, poised to redeem his pride, his right arm raised high in the air.

Kevin senses the defender and contorts his body to manipulate the trajectory of the ball, making it difficult to block.

Billy is not playing the ball, however, and—with swift judgment—his heavy right arm falls like a gavel, missing the basketball completely and striking Kevin across the upper torso, tomahawking his shoulder.

The initial impact takes Kevin's feet from under him, and the offensive player is suddenly exposed and vulnerable.

Billy's chest presses against Kevin's left shoulder in midair, and the weight of the defender's body drives the coach's son with a downward thrust into the unforgiving surface of the basketball court.

Roger helplessly watches as Billy plants his body atop Kevin's body, both boys crashing to the floor. The collision of bodies is violent and felt by everyone in the gym, and the coach sprints in that direction.

Kevin, at first, does not feel anything, but soon the sense of shock gives way to a shooting pain in his shoulder and the absence of breath, the air pried from his lungs, his caving chest gasping with desperation. Kevin cannot speak. He can only groan.

Billy immediately bounces to his feet, the body of the white kid propping him up like a mattress. Billy looks fine, uninjured by the impact.

Kevin writhes on the court, rolling from his back to his stomach and to his back again.

Roger arrives with fury, enraged not only by the overaggressive play but by the fact that Billy now stands over his son in taunting fashion; Billy shows no remorse for what he did to the coach's son.

Acting more like a father than a coach, Roger wedges his way between the two bodies, giving Billy a generous bump to make room.

"Kev! You okay, Kevin?"

There is no response, just more writhing and groaning.

Instead, the only words Roger hears are those of Billy behind him. "Gotta' get up higher than that."

With as much restraint as he can tap, the fuming coach spins away from his son's body and comes nose to nose with Billy Taylor. "Out of here!" Roger yells in his face, Billy feeling the heat of the man's breath. "Now! Out of here!" The coach has his hands against Billy's chest and begins to back him up.

Billy's instincts kick in. He clutches the hands of the white man, ready to throw them off. Before he does, Billy recognizes the coach's suddenly bloodshot eyes—he really got to the man. For now, Billy will leave it at that, and Billy loosens his grip, allowing the coach to make his point.

As Roger confronts the reckless teen, after a moment of rage, the coach returns to his senses, although, part of the man wants to throw the punk to the ground in the same way he did his son. Relinquishing his hands, the man does not abandon his tone. "Move it! You won't get away with that here!"

Billy brazenly retorts, "Sure, man. Sure."

"That's Coach Stevens to you," Roger emphatically decrees from an inch in height above the rogue teenager.

The cavalier teen exudes a wry grin. "Not my coach." Billy takes a few steps back while maintaining eye contact with the incensed father, saving one final glance for the man's son who is supine on the court, Kevin trying to catch his breath. "Come on, boys," Billy summons. "Let's jet."

On cue, the three other boys who run in Billy's pack grab their shirts and follow his lead. One of the boys jogs past Kevin, glancing down at him on his way to the door. "Mmmm," he mutters as if to convey what a sad spectacle the white boy is lying on the ground.

The other boys can be heard snickering as they exit the gym. "You got him good, Billy."

Rufus and his scowl have risen from his chair near the exit atop his corpulent legs to glare at the boys. "Done lost your mind, you fool?" he grills Billy as the unsympathetic teen struts past him. "Get outside."

"You get outside!" is Billy's response, the teen done with all the petty comments of the bus driver, stopping long enough to stare Rufus down.

"Come on, Billy. Let's go." One of Billy's friends nudges him from behind.

Still seething, Roger's thoughts begin to clear as the pulse in his eardrums subsides. The man regains his composure, realizing he cannot simply kick the boys out of the gym—*we're not at Macon South right now. The boys just can't walk home from here.* "Rufus!" he calls out to the driver near the exit. "Make sure those boys get on the bus and wait for us there."

"Yes, sir."

Feeling like a horrible father, Roger finally turns his attention to his son. "Kevin. I'm so sorry, kid. Are you okay?"

With each second, breath returns to Kevin's chest.

"Does anything feel broken?"

Aware of his dad's concern yet aware of his peers, Kevin rolls away from his father and pushes from the floor.

"Careful. Take it slow."

Kevin rests on his knees for a few moments. "I'm good," he offers a gravelly utterance.

The remaining boys in the gym watch as Kevin struggles for footing, everyone shocked by what transpired.

"Come off the court for a few minutes," the coach leads his beleaguered player and son toward the gym stage.

As much as Kevin wants to ignore what happened and quit drawing attention to himself, wooziness has the better of him, and he obliges his father by lumbering off the court.

The veteran coach is relieved; his son seems to be okay. Roger turns and looks at the rest of the group. The remaining boys seem genuinely concerned with Kevin's welfare, which is a comforting gesture. It appears the troublemakers are all gone.

"Sorry, Coach," Rufus calls from the gym doors upon reentering. "They're gone."

'What?" The coach queries as he jogs toward Rufus and the door.

"They wouldn't listen. Young fools."

Rufus props the gym door for Roger as the coach steps into the sunlight. From a distance, he watches as Billy and the others strut across the Ridgewood school property.

"Hey!" Roger beckons futilely. The boys look back but nothing more.

Oh, no, Roger contemplates. *There they go.*

"Not a good part of town for this," Rufus adds behind Coach Stevens.

What a day! Roger can only ponder and observe as those for whom he is responsible bleed into the background of the Ridgewood community. "We need to go pick them up," Roger states.

"No disrespect, sir," Rufus gives his input. "They made up their minds to walk out."

"I know, but we still need to pick them up. I'll grab the rest of the players."

13

An hour later, there is no sight of Billy and his lackeys.

"Where are they?" Roger quietly speaks through gritted teeth, a very unnerving feeling tiding over him. *Of all the things that could have happened*, the man stews to himself. *Of all the things that could have happened on day one, and we're driving around town looking for a group of rogue players. Unbelievable.*

Near the back of the bus, Kevin sits alone, still recuperating but much better.

"Maybe they went on back to South," Rufus speculates aloud. "Maybe they called someone to come get them."

"I don't know what they did," Roger replies, still visibly frustrated.

"Where would you like me to drive next, coach?"

Roger does not know what to say; this is not his part of town, nor is it the part of town where Rufus and the kids from South spend their spare time. "Maybe you're right, Rufus," the coach concedes. "Let's take the rest of our boys back to South. I will come look for them in my car if I have must."

Rufus soon turns down the main Ridgewood thoroughfare, and in the distance, a sight, a disturbance, a commotion on the side of the road harnesses the driver's attention, then the coach's, and then everyone's on the South bus. For Roger, it is difficult to discern what exactly is happening up ahead, but as the bus draws closer, the sight of multiple Ridgewood squad cars and a group of young black men causes the coach's stomach to drop. "No," Roger utters.

There, sitting on the curb, surrounded by three Police Officers and the County Sherriff, are four young black men with their hands cuffed behind their backs, and Roger recognizes one of them right away: *Billy*.

"Stop the bus!" demands Coach Stevens.

"You sure, sir?" the driver asks, not so much out of insensitivity but out of insecurity.

"Stop the bus!" Roger repeats, vaulting to his feet and walking toward the front steps of the vehicle, waiting for the driver to pull to the side of the road.

Chatter ricochets from one row to the next as several riders move across the aisle for a better look.

Kevin, too, is caught up in the action, although, he is more concerned for his father than anyone. How many times over the years have the boy and his mother watched the man spring into the middle of a hostile situation, no one knowing what Roger was about to do, including Roger? Too many to count. Kevin always knew his father to be a brave man—not a careless man but a fearless man and, even more so, a man of peace. With that considered, what the man is about to do, his son has no idea. From Kevin's vantage point, given the heavy police presence, it looks like Billy and his buddies got themselves in trouble, which is probably what they deserved.

As Rufus opens the doors, the driver offers one final piece of advice: "Not a good part of town for trouble."

Roger Stevens steps from the bus.

Kevin and the rest of the boys from South fixate their eyes on their head coach, watching as the man walks alongside the length of the bus on approach to talk with Ridgewood authorities.

• • •

The audacious blue and brown bus easily garnered the attention of the Ridgewood Officers at first sight. The litany of black faces on board was spotted immediately by the policemen as well. The white face that exited the bus, however, on approach straight toward them, is a surprise.

"Who's this?" one officer asks another.

"Beats me."

• • •

As Billy watched the South bus drive past, part of the young man desired to call out for help from the curb; yet, Billy's pride would not allow it. The confident, athletic teenager sits subdued, humiliated by the PD and their cuffs. Simmering in anger, refusing to look up, Billy stares at the asphalt before him as the coach approaches.

• • •

From the bus, Kevin and the others listen intently to interpret the muffled voices. One of the teens goes so far as to hang his head completely out the window.

"Pull your head inside the window like a sane person would!" Rufus fires from the front. "That's none of your business out there."

The boy responds accordingly.

"Jeremiah Jenkins!" Rufus calls to a different teen passenger.

The young man turns his head toward the bus driver at the mention of his name.

"I know your father's a pastor, and I know you know how to pray. So, you best start."

Kevin continues to watch and tries to listen. He cannot interpret what is being said. He just knows it does not look or sound good.

• • •

Thirty minutes later and after much conversation at the side of the road, the police officers begin standing the young black men to their feet, turning them around and removing handcuffs from all four.

A sense of relief is felt on the South bus, even though many of the passengers do not like Billy Taylor.

Billy and his crew can be seen rubbing their wrists, their skin raw from the metal. Each of them is glad to be free, and it was the new coach who negotiated on their behalf.

Roger says something to the four young men and points toward the bus. This time, with no resistance, all four teens concede and follow instructions—even Billy—their heads hanging low. They are greeted with the gruff salutation of a furious bus driver as the doors swing open.

"Were you born stupid or did you become stupid over time?" blasts Rufus. "Get your butts on this bus." Rufus is not finished as the troublesome teens slink past him. "Out your minds! I'll personally drive by every one of your homes and honk 'til your families come out, and I will tell them. I don't care. I will tell them what you did. And that goes for your grandmother, too, Billy Taylor."

Billy Taylor, Kevin ruminates. His name is out in the open.

The once-tough teenager scoffs silently, refusing to have eye contact with the driver, opting to look out of the window from his seat.

A few minutes and a few handshakes later, it is Roger Stevens leaving the presence of the police officers and walking alongside the team bus. Climbing aboard, he presents himself front and center, peering at the audience of young faces. *There's no need to say anything else*, he determines; he can see the humiliation in many of their eyes. Instead, the man sighs. "Let's go home, Rufus" are his only words before turning and taking his same seat at the front.

"Yes, sir," Rufus responds, still glaring at the culprits via his rearview mirror.

• • •

A couple of the Ridgewood officers watch incredulously as the eye-sore of a blue and brown bus rumbles down the road, exiting the community of Ridgewood.

"Never thought I'd see the day," one officer says to another. "I can't wait to make a call."

14

Roger did not need to call Charles Bullock last night since the principal rang the Stevens' residence a few minutes after Roger arrived home. Principal Bullock was yet unaware of the events in Ridgewood. Instead, he was placing a courtesy call simply to see how the first day went for the Stevens men at South. Roger hated raining on the man's parade by sharing the news, revealing some of the boys—of all things—fell into the hands of Ridgewood law enforcement. Furthermore, it was Roger, the basketball coach, who kicked them out of the scrimmage, banishing them to wander an unfriendly part of town for young black men. In his defense, Roger did not intend for that to happen, but little materialized the way the man desired on his first day on the job.

During his and his son's commute to the school on this new day, Roger recalls the vote of confidence he received last night during the phone conversation with his boss. Principal Bullock was extremely supportive and understanding, free of all accusation, the man in large part realizing the character of the teens involved; he knows Billy Taylor and his group. The two men spoke for thirty minutes, and Principal Bullock informed Roger that, as Principal, he would call a meeting in his office first thing in the morning with all relevant parties, boys and guardians, to set the record straight. Roger obviously agreed to attend, and the two wished each other a good night.

"You can wait here until class starts," Roger offers Kevin as they enter his Geometry class.

"I'm fine, dad."

"You sure?"

"I'm good. I hope your meeting goes well."

Kevin's mood is calm, even understanding, and Roger is in awe of the young man's resilience and approach to this new day. Yesterday was rough for everyone, including Karen at the retelling, but especially for Kevin, the coach's son at the crux of the entire issue, culminating in the teen being violently knocked to the floor by Billy Taylor. Still, to his father's incessant amazement, as is the case with most young people, the teen's body seemed to heal overnight—Roger remembers those days.

Roger parts the school hallways again on his second day, almost every student stepping aside to see if the white coach and teacher is real or a figment of their imaginations. Even so, the fact that he is a walking spectacle does not register with Roger as much today as it did yesterday.

The makeshift South offices are busy this morning. As he enters, Coach Stevens finds many visitors aligning the walls with all eyes immediately on him; he thought he was early but maybe not. Instantly, he recognizes the boys, the culprits from yesterday—*no Billy, though.*

Roger's appearance stirs awkwardness for him and everyone who is waiting. The coach smiles; it is all he can think to do. Some faces look friendly and some do not. Thankfully for Roger, the wait is short as the door to the Principal's office opens.

"Good morning, everyone," chimes Mr. Bullock, the man still jovial but with more of a business attitude than usual. "Please come in. There are plenty of chairs."

As the principal stands to the side and allows everyone to enter, Roger sees past the man into his office, and there is Billy already present for the meeting. Roger and Billy make eye contact past the small crowd; the young black man seems less than thrilled to be here. Next to Billy is an older woman, a grandmother perhaps. Principal Bullock apparently wanted to meet with the boy and his guardian first.

Coach Stevens politely waits for everyone to enter the office before he does. Wisely, Mr. Bullock has a chair reserved for his basketball coach on the principal's side of the desk to present a unified front. Roger appreciates the fact that he will not be served up as a sacrificial lamb on his second day of official employment.

"I want to thank all of you for joining us at this special meeting," the principal wastes no time in beginning. "And I don't know how many of you were able to attend the open assembly yesterday, but this gentleman is Roger Stevens, our new Head Basketball Coach."

As a matter of fact, none of these parents were at the assembly yesterday. Nevertheless, none of them need to guess who Roger Stevens is. Word travels fast around these parts. Plus, he is the only white man in the building, so...one plus one. Again, the glances Roger receives from the guardians at the announcement of his name are a mixture; some looks are courteous and some curious. The teenagers in the room, however, do not look up at all. There is a different aura about the young men today, not arrogance but reservation, maybe even a touch of humility, which Roger finds refreshing.

"I would like to begin by formally stating the facts from yesterday, and then I will be glad to answer any questions." Principal Bullock continues to speak as he takes the seat behind his desk. "As you know, Coach Stevens took those boys who wanted to scrimmage on our new team bus to Ridgewood High School yesterday afternoon. Ridgewood High opened their doors to us in large part thanks to Coach Stevens and his relationship with the High School Basketball Coach there. The afternoon started on the right foot; however, the scrimmage quickly became overly aggressive."

The principal shifts his eyes toward Billy, obviously unafraid to single anyone out. "To quell any further problems, Coach Stevens dismissed Billy Taylor from the gym, and your boys followed. After second thought and realizing it wasn't best for our young men from South to set out on foot in a strange part of town, while also trying to tend to his injured son, Coach Stevens instructed Rufus the bus driver to instruct the boys to remain on the team bus. They did not. Instead, the boys opted to walk from there."

"And they shouldn't have been in Ridgewood in the first place!" blurts the father of one of the teenagers, his tone ripping the calm atmosphere in two.

"Excuse me, Mr. Battier," Bullock assertively regains control. "I will allow ample time for everyone to speak shortly. For now, it's best we all hear the facts."

Not satisfied in the least, Mr. Battier crosses his arms in a huff and falls back in his chair in protest, his furrowed brow speaking volumes. Next to Mr. Battier appears to be his son— one of the teens Roger recognizes from yesterday. It is unclear to Roger whether the young man is embarrassed by his actions from yesterday or by his father's demonstration today.

With the exception of Mr. Battier, the rest of the parents seem more upset with their boys than with the new basketball coach, one father going as far as to elbow his son upon learning the teen played *follow the leader* yesterday, tagging along behind Billy Taylor like a mindless, pitiful puppy—they've had this discussion before.

"Therefore," Mr. Bullock continues, "When Coach Stevens stepped from the Ridgewood gym, your boys were on their way. At that point, Coach Stevens felt compelled to get your boys back the bus. However, by the time he loaded the rest of the boys and went to look for your boys, your boys were gone, and Coach Stevens and Rufus and the remaining boys on the bus scoured the Ridgewood part of town looking for them. They did not have success until the ride home, during which

Coach Stevens witnessed your boys on the side of the road in handcuffs and surrounded by the Ridgewood police."

Mr. Battier cannot resist. "And they never would have been in cuffs if he...." The father interrupts again, this time aggressively pointing his finger toward the white man seated next to Principal Bullock.

"Mr. Battier, I'm not going to tell you again." The principal matches the man's volume.

The tension in the office is suddenly palpable, and Roger cannot help but feel responsible. However, Principal Bullock fully has his coach's back this morning.

"Before anyone tries to lay blame at the feet of Coach Stevens, I think it would behoove each of you to hear the whole story. Once Coach Stevens spotted the boys on the side of the road, it was Coach Stevens who stepped on the scene, determined to get to the bottom of the ordeal. Furthermore— and I want everyone to be aware of this fact—Coach Stevens spent the next half hour providing an alibi and defending your boys in the face of law enforcement. Why? Because said law enforcement apprehended your boys on suspicion of robbery, based on an allegation made by a local store owner not far from Ridgewood High School."

The words of the principal induce shock. Multiple parents turn to look at their sons for answers. The guilt-ridden expressions on their young faces reveal the truth; the teens did not tell the whole story to their parents.

"Not to mention the store owner—not surprisingly a white man—seemed to have a personal vendetta against those who allegedly stole from his business, and he implicated your boys for the crime." The authoritative finger of the principal scans all the teens seated before him. Mr. Bullock now has the strict attention of all the parents, and no one dares interrupt the principal again.

"And, no, your boys didn't do what they were accused of doing. However, we in this room are all wise enough to know there's a fine line between guilt and innocence in the eye of the beholder, depending on the part of town." The room remains still—a bullet was dodged yesterday. "Once questioned, your boys attempted to explain their whereabouts to the officers, but the alibis of your boys fell on deaf ears as you can imagine. In fact, the Ridgewood Police were one step away from taking your boys to a holding cell in the Macon City Jail until Coach Stevens arrived and went to bat for your boys, keeping all of us from a very long night."

Coach Stevens looks to the ground, trying to avoid any perceived gloating, the man still ashamed by the events from yesterday.

"I know yesterday afternoon did not materialize in the way any of us wanted, which is an understatement. Even so, I feel an expression of gratitude from all of us toward Coach Stevens is in order. The truth is Coach Stevens stuck up for our boys in the face of those who don't think much of our boys and who probably don't think much of Coach Stevens, if you can use your imaginations again. So, given all the circumstances regarding the situation," the eyes of the principal find Billy Taylor once more, "I think Coach Stevens acted accordingly on all counts."

The explanation from Principal Bullock is well-rounded yet to the point, leaving little room for dispute.

"Coach Stevens," the silence is unexpectedly severed by the father of one of the other teens, the man speaking for the first time. "I would like to thank you for protecting my son yesterday, and my son would like to thank you, as well." The man nudges his son who bashfully stands to his feet, an action he and his parents obviously rehearsed for such a time as this.

"Thank you, Coach Stevens," quakes the voice of the penitent teenager, "for standing up for me in front of the police." The boy glances down at his father who gives him a nod to continue. "And I want to apologize for leaving the gym in the first place and for following my friends…and not listening to you. I'm very sorry." Another nod grants the teenager permission to sit again.

Roger is moved by the show of the humility. "Thank you, son. Forgiven. It's over."

Another teenage boy stands to his feet. "Me, too, Coach. I mean, I'm sorry, and thanks for sticking up for me in front of the police."

"Forgiven, son. Thank you."

The mother of the same teen speaks. "Coach Stevens, I thank you as well. My husband, my son's daddy, died a few years ago, and my son needs all the positive male influence he can get. Even if you are..., I mean...."

Coach Stevens grins and nods, understanding exactly what she means, but he does not make her say it.

"You seem to be a good man is what I mean, and I'm glad you're here in Macon."

The man is overwhelmed with unexpected emotion, deeming the woman's words as some of the kindest he has heard in a long time. "Thank you, ma'am. God bless you."

The display of gratitude from some of the parents and their sons has broken the ice in the room. On the other end of the spectrum, Mr. Battier refuses to budge from his position of bitterness, staring straight ahead, his arms firmly crossed. Darrell, his son, sits next to his father and stares at the floor.

At the end of the row of parents and boys, the matron of the room, the older woman sitting with Billy Taylor, finally speaks. "Coach Stevens," offers the voice both coarse and sweet, aged yet tender, "I would like to speak in private with you if you have a moment after. But I want to publicly state my appreciation for what you did for not just our boys but your boys. These are your boys now, and you stood up for them."

The woman's face might be weathered from years, but her eyes remain soft. Seated next to the older woman, Billy Taylor does not carry quite the same air of confidence as yesterday, although, it is still clear he thinks this meeting is a waste of his time.

Roger obliges the polite, elderly woman. "Certainly, ma'am. I'll be glad to speak with you after."

Principal Bullock waits for a few more seconds to see if anyone has anything else to say.

"Just one more comment, Principal Bullock," Roger graciously interjects. "All of your sons are still welcome to play on the basketball team. We have another scrimmage tomorrow at 3 pm and every Tuesday and Thursday after school until November when the season officially begins."

The guardians in the room did not predict such a gesture of forgiveness, and even the teenagers who bolted yesterday are caught off guard by the coach's kindness. The facial expressions of the young men seem to ask, *That's it? No strings attached? Back on the team? After what we did?*

"Most kind of you, Coach Stevens," salutes the principal with a smile of approval before standing from his desk. "All right, then. I thank all of you for coming, and I hope everyone has a much better day."

Roger Stevens stands to his feet as multiple parents grant him a handshake as they pass through the door, the lone exception being a cantankerous Mr. Battier; the man chooses to look past everyone, his face contorted from disgust as he stomps out, practically dragging his son behind him.

"Coach Stevens," Principal Bullock states, "I need to step out briefly. Feel free to use my office."

"Thank you, sir."

On cue, the eldest guardian steps in front of Roger. "Sir, I'm Betty Hodges, and I think you know my grandson Billy."

Roger smiles, accepting her hand, acknowledging Billy as well; Billy does his best to return the acknowledgment.

"The reason why I wanted to speak to you in private is I wanted to sincerely thank you for standing up for Billy...even after what Billy did yesterday."

"Thank you, ma'am. That's very much appreciated."

Over the older woman's shoulder, Billy does his best to flash a momentary smile at the coach, but it is clear to Roger smiling is not this tough guy's forte.

"Billy lives with me," Betty continues. "His mother died giving birth to him many years ago, and his father...."

"Grandma!" The teen finally speaks through his teeth, trying to derail and discourage the older woman from saying too much.

"Let me finish." The otherwise-tender woman's reply is terse. "I'm having this conversation right now."

Billy acquiesces, looking away, his countenance suddenly unbecoming the toughest kid in school.

Betty resumes. "And his father is my son, and he left a few years ago...."

"Grandma!" Billy can't stand idly by.

"Leave for the hall if this is gonna' be a problem for you," she responds to his second interruption, the woman displaying the ability to go from kind grandmother to enforcer at the drop of a hat. "I said I'm going to have this conversation."

Billy takes the opportunity and exits the room, clearly uncomfortable by what the woman is about to say.

"I'm sorry about that. He's not...he can be a good boy. It's just hard to see it when he acts so tough. His father left a few years ago, left town, left all of us. He left Billy. Said he couldn't handle livin' in the South, livin' in poverty no mo.' When the chance came, he left to work a good-payin' job up north, left to take a job workin' for a wealthy white man. Never heard from him again. Just...gone."

The story hurts Roger to hear it, and Roger is only left to guess: *no wonder Billy has a shell. No wonder Billy doesn't care much for Kevin or me.*

"So, Billy isn't too thrilled with anyone in authority, but he's especially not thrilled with white men in authority. That might shed light on how he responds to you being here."

"Yes, ma'am. That's....his life has been hard, and it breaks my heart."

"Now, he's gonna' apologize to you, but I would prefer for him to initiate rather than me just make him do it. But one way or another, he's going to apologize."

"I understand, and I thank you, ma'am. I agree. Let's not force anything. Let's just see how it goes."

"And he's gonna' apologize to your son also for bangin' him around like he did. I'm so sorry about that, and I hope your boy's okay. Billy can be a beast of a big kid."

'I appreciate it, ma'am. My son's fine. Let's just take it all as it comes."

"You let me know if there are any further situations," the older woman gives a final decree.

As Roger and Betty exit the office for the hallway, the grandmother looks around and does not see Billy. "Must have gone to class," she says aloud. "Well, it was nice meeting you and thank you for your time," she salutes the coach with a soft handshake though her skin is haggard.

"The pleasure was mine, ma'am."

Roger exhales. The meeting went better than he ever thought it would. He whispers, "Thank you, God."

● ● ●

Raymond Huddler enters the front of Jerry's restaurant and moves expeditiously through the dining area to the banquet room.

The restaurant owner watches intently from the kitchen then follows the man with stealth, observing as Huddler disappears behind the rarely-used door at the far side of the banquet room.

With flashlight in hand, Huddler descends and—a few seconds later—ascends several short steps. Entering the familiar sub room, he pulls the door firmly behind him, once again crouching before the air vent.

Footsteps soon approach from the other side—the Mayor's side—and the grille is removed.

"Hello, Raymond," the voice speaks.

Huddler wastes no time in spilling his thoughts. "I don't know if you've heard, but there is a new resident in Macon... on the south side of town."

"I am aware," the voice replies.

"Is the FBI aware?" Raymond inquires.

On that note, more footsteps are unexpectedly heard by Huddler, the steps again approaching from the Mayor's side. Through the infinite number of small grids in the air vent, Raymond observes as an additional pair of dress shoes come into focus.

"We are aware," answers the other voice. On this occasion, not just the grille but the entire air vent is removed from the side of the office of the Mayor of Macon, causing no further separation between the three men—light shines on the familiar scar on the right side of Huddler's face. "Join us, Raymond," the third man's voice beckons with his hand extended. "Let's talk for a while."

Raymond Huddler takes the hand, and the hand brings the Klan leader through to the other side.

15

"I don't mean to badger you, but you sure you're up to scrimmaging today?" Roger asks Kevin as the two walk from the school to the team bus on Thursday afternoon.

"Dad, I'm good."

"Okay. Just checking," the man backs off, knowing it is hard to be a parent without sounding like a parent.

The father and son approach the bus, and the coach has no idea what to expect. Will fewer boys return today, keeping in mind all that happened and how he threw Billy out? What about the run-in with the Ridgewood Police, the handcuffs? On the heels of that episode, will any boys show up today? Will any South parents let their boys play for such a man? Is this entire experiment finished before it gets off the ground?

As the father and son circle to the passenger side of the bus, the coach's worst fears are confirmed: no boys stand ready to board; not one. Roger stops in his tracks at the sight of zero players. He checks his watch; he and Kevin are right on time. The veteran coach cannot help but slump his shoulders, exuding a deflated sigh. "Well," he looks at his son and musters the slightest of smiles, trying to make the best of it. "Why don't you and I get in a good individual workout, like the old days?

That's not the end of the world, the teen thinks to himself. "Sure," Kevin responds, feeling badly for his father; he knows the man is trying his best.

"Good afternoon, Coach," Rufus salutes heartily through the open doors.

At least Rufus is ready to roll, Roger considers.

"We're ready," declares the driver.

"*We're ready?*" Roger considers. *What does he mean by "we're ready?" Is Rufus personifying the bus?* Roger has known people in the South to name their trucks and tractors. Maybe Rufus has already named the team bus.

As Coach Stevens steps aboard, he quickly sees what Rufus is referencing: one, two, five, seven, eleven boys on board, all of them looking attentively at the man.

Roger felt like his heart dropped off a cliff when he did not see anyone outside, but they were already inside, and Coach Stevens is almost at a loss for words. The man maintains his composure and acts as if he expected every one of them to be present, addressing the group with a very matter-of-fact cadence. "Good to see you, men. Thanks for being on time. Let's go, Rufus."

"You got it, Coach."

Kevin—also encouraged by the showing—instinctively assumes a leadership role and moves to the middle of the bus instead of the rear, plopping in an empty seat among the players, and the players notice, a few of them thinking in concert: *the white kid is back today. He must be pretty tough.*

Roger takes his customary seat at the front. During his speedy cursory count, he made a mental calculation. *Two of the boys from Billy's crew are back today. No Billy, though, and no Darrell.* "This is going to come together," Roger whispers.

The doors close, and the shamelessly blue-and-brown-adorned team bus eases out of the South lot.

• • •

What a difference a couple of days can make! Coach Stevens reflects; a much better vibe permeates the gym this afternoon.

Roger annually held pre-season scrimmages back in Augusta simply to roll the ball out for the players to get loose and get to know one another. True: he knew the term *team-building* to be clichéd at times. Still, that is what his pre-season scrimmages have been meant to do: develop familiarity and enhance chemistry among the kids. It might sound silly to others, but Roger fully believed a key pass to a specific spot on the floor in February could be the result of two guys playing together during the previous September. The first scrimmage at South on Tuesday, unfortunately, seemed to be the antithesis of team-building. Tuesday was nearly team-destruction. Even so, most of the boys returned today.

Two young men are present for the first time. Privately, the parents of the new teenagers took a wait-and-see approach, using the first scrimmage as a social experiment before committing. News of the dramatic event involving Billy, his friends, and the police made the rounds quickly. Yet, what Roger thought would be an appalling account and cause a further rift between him and the citizenry of Macon South had the opposite effect. Conversely, in the eyes of most South residents, the new white basketball coach stood in the gap between their boys and the police and—in the process—became a hero overnight.

Roger, as a new arrival to town, is not intimate with the dynamics of the South community, but he is learning on the job. What is glaringly ostensible to the man is the friction between the people of South and the local authorities, especially outside of the South boundaries, and *friction* seems to be a euphemism for turmoil, hostility, and tumult. From hard experience, the residents of South have instructed their children at an early age how to conduct themselves if an officer of the law addresses them, down to the very words to use and the body language to employ. Therefore, the fact that Coach Stevens stood in the presence of white law enforcement and lobbied on behalf of four black kids was ground-breaking news at Macon South.

Just earlier this week, it was Roger telling Karen of his frustration with God; God seemingly unhelpful in getting the scrimmages off to a good start. A few days later and how things have turned. Roger could not have imagined garnering such support from the South community so quickly, and the respect the man thought would take months to earn has, in many respects, come to him instantly. It seems what was meant for harm has been turned for good.

Kevin, also, has seen his stock rise among his new peers. In their eyes, not only did the white kid make Billy of all people look badly on the basketball court, but he took Billy's best shot when knocked to the ground. Then, Kevin got up, shook it off and returned today. The cherry on top was the ball-handling and shooting Kevin displayed on Tuesday while everyone was shooting around before the ill-fated scrimmage, bedazzlement the South boys had never seen with a basketball, especially by a white kid. They had all heard rumors of a guy named Maravich in the South, but they never knew such skill was possible.

As for the two new players, Roger has watched today as the talent pool at South just increased. One teenager's name is Tyler, and Tyler looked great the moment he got off the bus; 6'6" and lean. One fact is clear during the second-day scrimmage: Tyler is a shot blocker, and when the young man is not blocking shots, he is altering shots because of his presence around the basket; looming, hovering in the lane, rushing shots, and Roger loves every minute of it. Kevin and Tyler have been on the same team for a few games this afternoon, and the two developed quick chemistry.

Tyler only seemed to have one form of kryptonite on the court, and it did not come in the form of another taller player. Instead, it arrived in the form of a human bowling ball, a 6'3", as-wide-as-he-is-tall young man by the name of Leonard. Leonard, who came out of the womb ready to play football, would do so if Macon South had a team. However, a football coach's loss in this instance is Roger's gain, and the man marveled from the sideline as the husky teen with two anvils for shoulders moved people at his will. A couple of players learned the hard way during today's scrimmage, and their bodies went flying from contact with Leonard's airborne torso.

Leonard and Tyler have alternated success on the offensive and defensive boards, at times getting the best of one another. Occasionally, Tyler would outleap Leonard for the rebound, but just as quickly Leonard would establish position and keep Tyler off balance, allowing Leonard and his wide base to snare the ball.

Wow! Coach Stevens thinks to himself, although no one would know he is impressed. The man continues to stand and simply watch, leaning against the stage with his arms crossed and his countenance unamused. Privately, the man's player analysis is running wild. *Unbelievable athleticism and strength,* he calculates while watching Tyler and Leonard go to work. Roger knew Kevin would be Kevin this season, but the man had no idea he would find competent replacements for Trevor and Reynolds from the team back in Augusta.

The teams break for water as Kevin hits another game-winner. The coach's son jogs to where his father is standing and keeps his back to the other players, shielding his conversation with his father from the rest of the group. The intuitive point guard takes the words right out of his father's mouth. "Tyler and Leonard are good."

The man blades his body as well to conceal his words. "Not bad, huh? It looks like we've got something to work with this year. More than I thought." The man lifts his whistle to his lips and chirps two short blasts. "Good work, gentlemen. Good sweat. Let's call it a day."

• • •

As the bus rolls back into the South parking lot, the coast is clear, save one man standing near the Stevens' Plymouth. The black man seems young but not young enough to be a student. He also looks vaguely familiar to Roger, yet Roger has met innumerable staff and parents this week, and many of the names are running together in his mind.

"Rufus, do you know who that young man is."

"That's Reggie Dawkins. Used to go to school here. Used to play here," Rufus places the young man well. "He teaches P.E. at the school now."

That's it, Roger's memory kicks in. "Thank you for the ride, Rufus," salutes the coach as the bus slows to a stop. Roger stands and pivots to address the passengers behind him. "Thank you for your time today, men. Good workout. We'll do it all again next time."

Roger and Kevin wait for all the players to exit, sending them off with smiles as the coach thinks to himself, *today was a thousand times better than the first scrimmage.* As the Stevens' men approach their vehicle, the young teacher waiting for them comes to attention.

"Coach Stevens."

"Hello," Roger offers a warm greeting. "I know we have seen each other in passing."

"Yes, sir. My name is Reggie Dawkins. I'm the Phys-Ed teacher."

"Glad to finally meet you face to face, Mr. Dawkins. This is my son Kevin."

All three take the time to shake hands.

Mr. Dawkins continues. "Sorry to be rude, standing at your car like this. I just wanted to catch you."

"No problem. We just finished a scrimmage; so, good timing."

"Well, that's what I want to talk with you about, coach. I used to play here at South, and, I don't mean to pry, I just thought I would ask...."

Roger listens patiently as the young teacher speaks. *He can't be a day out of his mid-twenties.*

"I don't know what you have in the way of help, sir, as in assistant coaches; not that you need an assistant coach," Mr.

Dawkins quickly explains, wanting desperately not to offend the veteran coach.

Roger's heart warms at the idea of some much-needed help.

"I mean, it's up to you, sir. You're the coach," Mr. Dawkins addresses with courtesy. "Just thought I would offer."

Reggie Dawkins is caught off guard by the blunt question posed to him by Coach Stevens. "Are you free for dinner tonight, Mr. Dawkins? Dinner at our home?"

Reggie Dawkins forgets his name, stammering, "Tonight? Dinner? Uh, no, I mean, yes. I mean, no problem. Yes, I'm available."

"Great," Roger replies. "It will give us some time to talk and see if this could work out. Are you free to follow us? We are going that way now."

"Absolutely. I'm…, I'm." The young teacher looks across the parking lot as if he is going to point out his automobile. In honesty, he cannot. Looking back at Coach Stevens, he confesses, "Truthfully, I don't have a car, sir. I live pretty nearby, so I walk to the school."

A man who remembers what it is like to start from meager beginnings, Roger does not flinch at the young man's explanation. "Then hop in with us. I'll take you home after dinner."

A countenance of surprise gets the best of Reggie Dawkins. "Are you sure, sir?"

"I am sure, and I am hungry. Let's go."

"Take the front," Kevin relinquishes his normal seat.

The three men head for dinner in the Macon countryside.

16

For the first time in a very long time, the Stevens family dress to attend church at a place other than Hillside Christian. The time is 9 a.m. Roger would be teaching his Sunday morning class right now back in Augusta, he calculates. Instead, there is a calm, casual pace to this Sunday morning as Roger, Karen and Kevin get ready to join Tom Chaney and his family for church in Ridgewood.

"Aren't you a little nervous about going back to Ridgewood today," Karen inquires of her husband while putting on her earrings.

"I will go to Ridgewood almost every day, honey."

"I know, but this is different. This is a big Baptist church in that part of town; t-h-e big Baptist church in that part of town."

Roger pours on the adolescent teasing while adjusting his Windsor knot in front of the mirror. "Oh, I just thought it was a big Baptist church. I didn't know it was t-h-e big Baptist church."

Karen says something under her breath while walking away.

"I'm kidding, Karen." The man follows his wife across their bedroom. "I don't think there's any reason to be nervous. Sure, there could be some popular or affluent people from

Ridgewood who attend the church. There might even be some of the policemen from the other day. But for crying out loud, isn't church the one place we can go to be free and think the best of one another?"

Karen sighs and sits on the edge of their bed. "It's just the fact that everything's different: different home, different school, different church. Just one of these changes would be a huge deal, Roger, but everything has changed. Nothing transferred from Augusta with us."

"We did," Roger concludes, sitting next to his wife, placing a supportive arm around her. "You, me, and Kevin. Also, God transferred with us. Isn't that the most important part?"

"Yes" is Karen's simple acknowledgment of the truth. "It still doesn't make it easy. Plus, who knows if they will like us or not at this church—you know, with you coaching at Macon South."

"I don't have the slightest idea," Roger admits. "I hope they do. But let's keep moving forward, regardless. Besides, God hasn't brought us this far to leave us."

Kevin appears at the door.

Karen quickly swings her focus to an even bigger issue. "Kevin, that shirt."

"What?" is the teen's confounded response.

Once Karen pushes from the bed and comes face to face with her son, she spins the teen and reverses his direction, walking with him down the hall. "We are going to a new church, and we can do better than this shirt."

"You mean a rich church?" Kevin counters.

On the edge of the bed, Roger breaks a smile as his wife and son debate down the hall.

● ● ●

Ridgewood Baptist is huge, and the pristinely white edifice rivals a picturesque church painting from the late 19th century. The parking lot is almost full, and Roger nearly settles for a spot in the back when a familiar face stops them in time.

"There's Tom right there," says Karen.

"Good morning, Tom." Roger rolls down his window.

"Roger, Karen, Kevin," Tom Chaney offers with a smile. "There is visitor parking up front. Go this way."

"Oh, we're fine here," Roger comments. "No big deal."

"No," Tom insists. "Please, park up front. Those open spots just sit there otherwise. Please."

"Okay," Roger concedes, pulling past several pedestrians as they drive cautiously through the lot.

"Look at the cars at this church," Karen comments at the row of luxury automobiles to her right.

"Told you it was a rich church," Kevin emphasizes from the back seat.

"Here we are, guys," Roger announces while steering the conversation as well as the Plymouth Fury into a visitor's parking spot.

Roger steps from the car. "Good morning," he extends to a couple walking directly past the Stevens' family car.

The couple looks up in surprised fashion, smiling awkwardly.

Tom, however, is a friendly face, and the man and his wife kindly escort Roger, Karen, and Kevin inside.

• • •

The opening hymn commences, and the Stevens family joins the congregation in rising to their feet. Roger admits silently to himself: *it's nice to hear a familiar song this morning—one we sing back home. However,* the man continues to ponder as he listens, *it sounds a little stale and overly formal. Oh, well. That might just be their style.*

Roger smiles at Karen and Kevin at the sound of the familiar chorus.

Karen smiles back.

Kevin, less than thrilled to be at a new church, acknowledges his father's smile, but that is it—not disrespectful, yet not enthusiastic.

The entire assembly faces forward. The song ends, and the Pastor of Ridgewood Baptist walks to the pulpit. "Let us pray."

In unison, the congregation collectively bows their heads as the minister leads.

Roger, an unconventional Christian at times, cannot resist but cut against the grain, and as those around him bow their heads in prayer, the new resident of Macon discreetly scans the sanctuary for any familiar faces, especially looking for the Ridgewood officers from the other day. As he looks over the crowd, he recognizes no one.

Every head is still down as Roger pans to his left and assesses privately: *nope, no one familiar.* Roger keeps panning left, and all heads remain bowed in the congregation...except for one.

Roger unintentionally stares directly at the man simply because the man is staring back at Roger.

● ● ●

Looking back across the middle aisle of the sanctuary, the man holds his head high, his body leaning slightly back to get an unobstructed view of the first-time visitor. Even so, the man knows exactly who Roger Stevens is.

● ● ●

Roger is caught off guard by the glare of the man—a stern countenance which seems out of place for a church setting. More than that, Roger is galvanized by the notable, jagged scar on the right side of the man's face; Roger could see it from a mile away.

The moment becomes awkward. It is obvious the man across the aisle has no intention of breaking his stare at Roger.

Roger attempts to bring levity to the standoff by offering a smile and a friendly nod.

The man across the aisle does not reciprocate; the scar on his face appears angry as well.

Eventually, Roger takes the high road and bows his head to pray as the intense man continues his glare.

17

The Mayor of Macon parks his Cadillac in the usual spot to start the morning. The people he passes on the sidewalk and front steps of City Hall show great deference, wishing their mayor a wonderful day. The man pulls his heavyset body toward his second-floor office, breathing heavily. Similar greetings are given by staffers and his secretary who even interrupts her conversation with a man. The Mayor mundanely reciprocates with the same salutation. "Mornin'...mornin'...."

After prying his keys from his suit pants, the Mayor opens his office door and is shocked by the sight.

Raymond Huddler and the FBI agent stand in the middle of the office, in the middle of the decorative office rug. Huddler becomes instantly agitated by the interruption and barks with an angry, red face at the Mayor of Macon. "Get out of here!"

The Mayor backpedals and sheepishly obliges, pulling the door shut.

The man's secretary looks to see what might be wrong. "Everything okay, Mr. Mayor?"

"Yes," he improvises. "Yes, I just...forgot something. I'll be right back."

"Can I help?" offers his loyal assistant.

"No, no; not necessary. I'll be back."

The secretary watches as the Mayor disappears around a nearby corner.

• • •

"This is ridiculous," Huddler gnashes, "And if you don't do something about it, I will."

The agent seeks clarity. "What does that mean?"

"You know what that means. It means I will get this done. There is no way Stevens should be allowed to go about his life as if nothing is wrong. His sins are egregious."

"Tell me how you really feel, Raymond."

Raymond Huddler narrows his glare at the agent, unamused by his levity. "He mocked the house of God. He walked right through the church doors and sat among the people of God."

The FBI agent has no response.

"That's the problem, isn't it? You don't feel the same...."

"Here is how I feel, Raymond," the agent replies without hesitation, trying to steer Huddler from conjuring a holy war. "We have a deadline upcoming, a very lucrative deadline, and we are almost there. How I feel is concerned; concerned that you can't keep it emotionally together until that deadline comes and goes."

"Are you calling me emotionally unstable?" Huddler fires back.

"I'm calling you over-aggressive, to say the least, and if you push this too far and do something to this man, more light will be back on Macon and you...."

"And you," Huddler grins and sneers at the same time.

"On all of us," the agent concurs. "Now, if you can exercise restraint, then our plan will go through, payment will be received, and then you can do whatever you want to the man. But you must know, I can't protect you if you do anything prematurely."

Raymond Huddler clearly does not enjoy being told what to do as he moves toward the large vent at the far side of the room. "I don't need your protection." The Klan leader hunches and lowers himself through the opening. Before disappearing, Raymond Huddler fires off one last command. "And make sure the fat man keeps his mouth shut! He'd better not blow this!"

"Duly noted, Raymond," the agent replies.

• • •

The Mayor of Macon stands out of sight with his back to the wall. He waits and listens, wiping the sweat from his brow. The door to an ancillary room, adjacent to his office, opens and closes. The Mayor slowly and safely peers around the corner... in time to see a glimpse of the back of the FBI Agent as the agent exits the floor via the emergency stairwell.

• • •

"This doesn't feel right, Cy," Agent Wheeler offers his unsettled opinion to his fellow agent.

Dennison sits in the passenger seat, watching intently through his side mirror, doing so behind the cup of coffee he keeps bringing to his face. "I hope it's nothing," Dennison emphasizes. "Believe me when I say that."

Approximately 150-feet behind their company vehicle, Agent Travis Hopper comes into view as he exits Macon City Hall.

"There he is," Dennison confirms.

"Is it him?"

Dennison peers with greater focus. "Yep. That's Hopper..., hanging around at City Hall...and for what?"

Wheeler observes as well, trying to find a way to keep from implicating another FBI agent so freely. "I don't know," Wheeler interjects. "Word has it he's dating the Mayor's Secretary; nothing wrong with that."

"Nothing at all, especially when it serves as a nice cover for frequenting the Mayor's Office at will." Dennison looks Wheeler in the eye. "A Mayor who we know is a Klan-sympathizer."

Agent Wheeler shakes his head. "Look, Cy, I don't have a soft spot in my heart for Hopper, and neither does anyone else. The guy's a jerk. But it's a huge jump from jerk to Klan informant without evidence."

"That's why we're gathering evidence."

"Gathering...or manufacturing?"

The agents glare at each other. "Look," Dennison goes on defense, "I'm just following a hunch, and I need to know whether it's correct or not. Like I said, I hope it's not." Dennison turns to watch Hopper take a seat behind the wheel in the distant automobile. "I just find it strange, that's all. We can't seem to get close to the Klan despite good intel. And Maxwell always gives good intel. Someone is a step ahead of us...from the inside."

"Maybe the Klan knows about Maxwell," Wheeler speculates, "Or maybe they are paranoid of someone like Maxwell and keep switching things around. There's got to be another reason. Maybe it's because this town is so small, and everyone is afraid—no one wants to sell each other out."

Dennison does not respond as he continues to observe his fellow agent in the background.

"Look," Wheeler persists. "We're all frustrated, Cy. We can't seem to catch a break or get momentum. But we can't lose our common sense in...."

"I got it. I got it," Dennison capitulates. "Thanks for obliging me."

Agent Hopper eases in his Bureau-issued car onto Main Street in front of City Hall and drives in the direction of the Macon FBI Office.

Dennison gives the okay. "All right. Let's get out of here."

• • •

The final bell rings and Roger rushes out of his classroom on the heels of his students; the man is excited to see a repeat of the talent from last Thursday. Once in the hall, he hears a voice from behind him. "Coach Stevens." The man turns, surprised by who it is.

Billy Taylor stands before the man—the man whose son Billy roughed up in the gym only a week ago. The usually ultra-confident young man does not appear quite as brash this afternoon.

"Can I speak with you...for a moment, sir?" Billy asks, glancing over his shoulder to ensure no one is looking or listening; his bulletproof reputation is on the line.

The fact that the young man used the word *sir* comes across as unfitting for Billy. Still, Roger is uncertain if the young man wants to chat with him or choke him.

"Sure, what can I do for you, Billy?"

"I just want to...." The words of Billy Taylor are awkward and strenuous, offered in a deep, low tone. "I want to thank you. Thank you for coming to my defense in front of the police last week...you know, while we were in Ridgewood."

The show of humbleness is a shock, though Roger lets it play out.

"Those white policemen were getting pretty rough with me and the boys before you showed up, tellin' us all they were going to do to us; gonna' send us to jail and everything, tellin' us there's men in the jail who might beat us up if we didn't come clean."

Roger senses escalation in Billy's tone: the eyes of the young man flare as he recalls the white policemen. The verbal pace of the teenager quickens as he recounts that afternoon in Ridgewood.

Billy senses it too. He pauses and hangs his head for a few moments before lifting it again. "And I'm sorry about coming down hard on your son. I was just going up...."

Don't do that, Roger thinks to himself. *You're doing so well. Just be humble and apologize.*

Wisely, Billy stops and recants. "What I'm saying is...I apologize for knocking down your boy. I shouldn't have done that..., and I hope he's okay."

Roger finds it paradoxical: a rough and tumble kid acting in such a submissive manner—at least playing the part the best he can. As far as this veteran coach and teacher is concerned, the scene is refreshing, the man knowing from experience God gives grace to the humble; as a recipient of much grace, Roger chooses to give it.

Coach Stevens speaks succinctly. "Forgiven. Thank you for your words. Feel free to speak to my son personally. He will respect that."

Billy pauses.

Roger observes to see how Billy will handle a little dose of instruction.

"Yes, sir. I will talk to him."

"Great...and thank you for speaking with me." The coach smiles while placing a brief, supportive hand on Billy's shoulder. "Have a good day."

"Coach Stevens," the words of the teenager cause Roger to stop and turn for a second time. "Can I still play basketball for the team? I mean...play for you? Please, sir?"

Expecting a long, drawn-out, heavy-handed lecture, Billy Taylor is shocked by the pithy, three-word answer he receives from Roger Stevens: "Sure. Let's go."

• • •

Kevin is already on the team bus and getting to know the other players. The son notices his father approaching..., and his father is not alone. Kevin is left to guess, *what's going on?*

Inside the bus, the necks of curious players twist for a better view at the astonishing sight: Coach Stevens and Billy Taylor walking side by side.

"Hey, Rufus," Roger chimes, as if nothing is out of the ordinary. With those words, the coach and tough teenager climb aboard.

"Hello, Coach," Rufus acknowledges, keeping his good eye on Billy. Neither Billy nor Rufus exchange greetings but nod at each other instead.

"Good to see you, men!" Roger declares from the front of the bus. "Thanks for being here. Billy's joining us today."

Roger takes his normal seat and suggests Billy find one as well.

Walking the aisle, the imposing teen heads for the back, but before that, he stops halfway and pivots toward the coach's son.

All the players watch eagerly as does a coach and a bus driver who has laser-focus through his rearview mirror.

Billy senses the tension and looks around him, almost wanting to scold everyone and ask, *what are you all lookin' at!*

Kevin remains cool; not sure where all this is going.

"Uh, yeah," Billy starts. "I just want to say I'm sorry for the other day... for knockin' you down...and everything else that happened."

Kevin sits with all eyes on him, every player watching to see what is next. It is obvious Billy went with the quick blanket apology instead of a prolonged statement, which is no problem to Kevin. In the end, Billy seems to be sincere, and Kevin can live with that.

For good measure, Kevin stands to his feet, his height matching the height of his former nemesis. "Uh, sure," Kevin gives an equally-succinct response. "No problem."

As the surprises today keep coming, Billy offers the cherry on top by extending his hand.

Kevin receives it and shakes.

The remaining players watch in awe as Billy and Kevin sit directly across the aisle from each other, allowing for two very different worlds to merge.

Roger looks on, touched by the gesture yet amused by the awkwardness of the encounter. "Good deal," he speaks in a soft tone. "Let's roll, Rufus. Thank you, sir."

• • •

Out of nowhere, what seemed to be the world's craziest decision, leaving a proven commodity like Augusta Christian to—of all places—coach at Macon South, does not seem so crazy after all. Roger realizes basketball season is not here yet, and school has only been in session for two weeks. Still, the man senses a turnaround, and he is certainly optimistic given the pound-for-pound talent on the court—the kids from Macon South passing the eye test with high-flying colors. Of course, a million other variables surround Roger and his family, and many of those variables he knows he cannot control. What the longtime coach feels he can control, however, is what happens on the court—and with this group, the sky is the limit.

The awe-inspired man watches from his usual spot against the Ridgewood stage, mentally developing profiles for his players as he does.

Tyler is a leaper, a presence inside, a guy who can score around the rim on offense and patrol the paint on defense. *If we can just add a consistent fifteen-foot jumper to his game,* Roger calculates, *Tyler will be lethal.*

Leonard grabs every rebound Tyler does not. The coach has lost count of how many players have bounced off Leonard's torso this afternoon. There is nothing dirty about the way Leonard plays, and the bulky teenager comes across as a nice and quiet kid. *He's just being Leonard, and Leonard owns whatever space Leonard occupies at that time* is Roger's assessment of the player.

As formidable as Tyler and Leonard are, they are no match for the two players on the opposing squad during the scrimmage. Billy and Kevin landed on the same team, and—from the moment the two began playing together—there has been no answer to stop the duo. Both Billy and Kevin are simply too athletic and too skilled, and they offset the size of Tyler and Leonard by getting out and running. Even after made baskets, Kevin keeps taking the ball and immediately looks downcourt for Billy who keeps leaking out; this connection has worked half-a-dozen times or so. In addition, Kevin has begun learning the spots on the floor where Billy likes the ball; Tyler and Leonard cannot stay with Billy in terms of lateral quickness. When all else fails, Kevin gets his shot whenever he wants; none of the opposing guards can do anything with him.

Roger continues to observe from his spot in coaching heaven: height, speed, rebounding, athleticism.... The team has everything he needs. The buffet of talent at Macon South is open for business.

As Roger ponders the unexpected allotment of basketball ability in his hands for this season, the coach has reached a conclusion: even though the man is not completely sold on what he is doing at Macon South High School, maybe there is an outside chance God knows what He is doing. Furthermore, if Billy Taylor of all people can be humble, Roger feels he can do the same thing?

Standing with his arms crossed, leaning against the stage, Roger looks to the gym ceiling..., looks to heaven and states quietly, "Thank You, Father. I still trust You."

18

"Eyes down," Roger instructs his Geometry students. "Do your own work. Don't ask for help." The class seems to be doing just that as Roger quietly opens the door and lets himself out, next scooting across the hall. It has been such a busy day the man has not even stopped for a restroom break.

As the teacher and coach enters the restroom, he is caught off guard by the presence of Darrell Battier. At first, Roger displays a cordial smile. "Hi, Darre...."

Darrell is caught off guard as well, and the young man does not have enough time to hide the multiple bruises and cuts on the right side of his face.

Roger stands flat-footed, quickly left to guess, *was it a fight?* Roger's thoughts transition. *No, it feels like something else. It feels like...Darrell's father.*

Angry and ashamed, Darrell rushes past Roger and bolts through the restroom door.

"Darrell?" Roger calls, stepping into the hallway behind the teen. "Darrell, are you okay? I'm free to talk." All Roger can see of Darrell Battier now is the young man's back as he turns the corner and disappears. Roger is left saddened in the middle of the hall. His only thought is to whisper a prayer for the troubled young man.

• • •

Not sure if I should be doing this, Roger ruminates—the sole passenger in the car. He learned the details from Principal Bullock. Darrell Battier arrived at school battered yesterday. Therefore, Roger saw the teen after he already healed for at least twenty-four hours. Even so, the bruises and cuts still looked fresh.

It has been impossible for the coach and teacher to think of anyone else other than Darrell. Roger could sense the anger in Mr. Battier at the parent meeting following the Ridgewood incident, and Roger's fear is Darrell is taking the brunt of it all.

The car eases to a stop. The address matches the one on the piece of paper in Roger's hand. The home is small and somewhat run down. It is difficult for Roger to discern what color the house is. The man steps from the car and surveils his surroundings. There is no sign of anyone. "Hello, Mr. Battier. Is anyone here?"

Roger would walk to the front door, but a gate at the edge of the yard causes all visitors to stop. A used, half-filled beer bottle sits on the fencepost. "Hello," Roger calls again. The gate does not appear to be locked, and he cautiously lifts the latch. Upon closing the gate behind him and turning around, Roger's heart drops as an oncoming dog appears out of nowhere. Roger stumbles backward, but the gate he just closed holds him up.

The eyes of the rottweiler narrow as it bounds wildly toward the intruder; the sound of the man's voice woke it from sleep. Saliva hangs from both sides of the dog's mouth as its paws dig hard into the ground.

"Oh, God, please" are Roger's only words before a chain that had been laying in the grass pulls tightly, yanking the dog backward and ending its dead sprint. The dog whimpers then resorts to an uncontrollable bark, filling the neighborhood.

Roger cuts his hand on the gate and winces, looking at his wound and keeping an eye on the attack dog at the same time.

The front door to the home bursts open. "Who's that?" Mr. Battier commands, striding from his home with a tire iron in hand. "Who's that?" he repeats.

Roger can hardly form his words. "It's me, Coach Stevens."

Mr. Battier appears slow to recognize Roger. Once he does, however, the homeowner seems to charge more vigorously than his dog did. "What are...?" The man does not bother to finish his sentence. He has Roger Stevens on his property, and Mr. Battier is within his rights to act accordingly in his mind.

As the dog continues to bark at full throat, Roger realizes the man is not stopping his march toward him. Roger fumbles with the latch but cannot get it to work this time. With Mr. Battier ten feet away, the coach clumsily hoists his body over the gate to the other side, cutting his leg, side and arm as he does. The pain, however, is a small price to pay compared to the blunt end of a weapon.

"Get out of here!" blares the iron-wielding homeowner. "You're trespassing!" Emphatically, Darrell's father swings at the bottle on the fencepost and shatters it on impact, spraying the unwelcome visitor with glass and warm beer.

"I'm sorry, Mr. Battier," Roger apologizes and retreats at the same time. "I just wanted to...."

It is obvious to Roger Mr. Battier has no interest in a civil exchange. Instead, Darrell's father wants a piece of the man.

Roger takes the hint and circles his car, and by the time the aggressor steps to the curb, the Plymouth makes haste.

Mr. Battier steps into the middle of the street and watches the white coach from Macon South drive away to the sound of a ferociously barking dog.

Roger glances down to see blood seeping through his white dress shirt. He grimaces as he looks in his rearview mirror. There stands Darrell Battier's father with an iron object hanging at his side.

• • •

The following Sunday, the idea of attending church with so many families connected to Macon South has its pluses and minuses in Roger's opinion. Several boys on the team attend Second Baptist of Macon, and Roger does not want to encumber his players on Sundays—they see his face and hear his whistle all week long. He, as much as anyone, believes the kids deserve a break from him. On the other hand, Roger knows attending church with not only some of the team but others from the South community can lend to the bonding and strengthening of important relationships. The bottom line for the Stevens family as they walk through the doors of Second Baptist on this Sunday morning is as follows: After several failed attempts since moving to town, Roger and Karen have been unable to find a church to their liking; not a perfect church because both Roger and Karen know there is no such thing. Rather, a church familiar in vision and spirit.

Quickly, the nervousness of walking into yet another unknown assembly dissipates as many familiar faces greet the Stevens family on arrival. Emphasizing this fact is the decision by Pastor Jenkins—whose son plays on the basketball team for Roger—to postpone the start of service for two minutes, giving the jubilant ruckus surrounding the Stevens family time to settle.

The music begins, the congregation stands and several more people from the community of South Macon find the Stevens for a final hug or handshake.

A shuffle beat percolates from the rhythm section of the band.

An organ begins to chirp.

A woman steps from the choir and begins to sing, "I love the Lord."

The choir echoes, "I love the Lord."

The woman sings again, "He heard my cry."

"He heard my cry."

Roger and Karen look at each other, both smiling widely from the love they feel this morning while surrounded by the body of Christ; even Kevin looks more relaxed in a church than he has in some time

As he sometimes does, Roger scans the church and ruminates. *Not a fancy building*, he observes. *Could use some paint and new pews..., but it's the best church I've seen yet.*

19

Monday, November 4

The first day of official basketball practice arrives, and, finally, the man can coach again. It was possibly the most challenging feat in the world: to sit and lean against the stage in the Ridgewood gym as a mere spectator, unable to make corrections regarding the form of a jump shot, a less than textbook box out or the incorrect angle of an entry pass into the post. There were times the coach had to take an anxious walk up and down the sideline to keep from saying something, but he did it, which means he kept his coaching and comments to himself. Roger knew there would be plenty of time for commentary later, and *later* starts today.

"You ready, coach," Roger asks the first-time assistant.

"Yes, sir," Reggie Dawkins replies, trying to suppress his nerves, the young man officially returning to the Macon South basketball program for the first time in nearly a decade. Coach Stevens had already formally introduced Coach Dawkins to the team at a pre-season scrimmage. Therefore, the only action left to take is to get the season rolling.

A total of twelve young men stand before Coaches Stevens and Dawkins now, and other than Thanksgiving Day and the Friday after, for the next month until the first game, Monday through Friday, 3:15 to 6 p.m., they belong to Roger. The team of all black players and one white player dons the matching practice apparel; white t-shirts, black shorts, white socks, and white sneakers. When it became obvious not everyone on the team had the necessary gear, Roger and Karen donated to the school to see to it. Coach Stevens' philosophy: everyone is the same. Everyone deserves equal-footing to start because everyone is held to the same level of hard work, and it is time to begin.

"Men, Coach Dawkins and I will call you men because we're going to treat you like men. There aren't many promises I can make in this world, but I promise you this: we will get better. At the end of this season, we won't play anything like we play today." Roger's early-season address is already in mid-season form. "You will get better…or you will not play. The reason why you won't play is because the player next to you will get better whether you choose to get better or not. And even if you ask yourself, 'What if none of us chooses to get better?' Then my response to you is I would rather not have a team than have a team who refuses to get better. So…," the man pauses to scan each player, "We might as well get better."

A litany of nods agrees with the man.

The veteran coach concludes his speech: "Let's go get better."

Sounds easy enough, several young men think to themselves except for one.

There's going to be nothing easy about it, Kevin acknowledges as his memory hearkens back many years while playing for his coach and father. *I wonder if these guys have any idea.*

Roger officially begins the 68'-69' season by taking the basketball in his hands and, with perfect form, drop-kicking the leather sphere 30-or-so feet, the ball landing on the Ridgewood stage and rolling out of sight, knocking something over in the distance.

The faces of the players are glazed with puzzlement as they are left to wonder, *What was that all about?*

"We won't be needing that for a while," explains the coach. "I'll let you know when we do."

Before the young men figure out what is happening, a shrilling whistle intervenes, scaring them straight.

"Everyone in that corner where the sideline meets the baseline!" thunders the voice of the new head coach at Macon South. "As fast as you can! Let's go!"

Outside of Kevin's dead sprint, several of the boys move quickly, but obviously not quickly enough. The whistle blasts again. "That's not as fast as you can run, men. Everybody on the baseline."

Oh no, the young men collectively begin to appraise the coach: *he's already upset.*

I knew they weren't ready, Kevin tells himself.

"Two groups of 6: group one and group two!" Roger continues to yell.

Kevin motions to help get everyone organized.

"Group-one, sprint to the other end, touch the baseline and sprint back! Go on the whistle!"

The man's whistle is in clear command of the practice. Kevin and group-one explode into an all-out sprint; however, they do not reach half-court before the whistle shrills again. "Group-one: go back! Group-two: you are running first! Do you know why?" The man does not give the second group time to answer. "Because you don't just stand there and watch! Put your hands together! Clap! Encourage your teammates as they run! Support your teammates! They are going to play at a higher level if you lift them!"

Group-one arrives back at the starting point.

"Group-two, here we go! Go on the whistle!" The whistle gives the order. This time, as group-two accelerates, group-one catches on and begins clapping ferociously from behind the baseline. "That's more like it," the man interjects. "I can't stand a quiet gym! This gym should never be quiet."

Ten seconds later, group-two returns from full-flight.

"Group-one: on the whistle!"

Group-two takes the hint, filling the gym with encouraging volume as group-one hustles to the other end. Group-one returns.

"Group-two: you're up!"

"Group-one: you're up!"

A once quiet gymnasium now clamors with palms slapping together and squeaking sneaker tread; a few of the players are already doubled-over from the conditioning drills.

"Group-two: again!"

"Group-one: again!"

As the final group stumbles across the baseline following their third down-and-back, Coach Stevens steps to the free throw line and exhorts. "Just a warning to the wise, men. I didn't come out here to watch anybody walk. Everything we do, we do to our maximum effort because maximum effort is the only way to reach maximum potential. And if there's something else I can't stand, it's leaving potential on the floor at the end of a game. Do you understand?"

Kevin Stevens is the only player to respond. "Yes, coach."

"Excuse me!" Roger bids the entire team.

"Yes, Coach!" they ring out in unison this time, some doing so while bent at the waist, trying to keep anything down that might come up.

"Good. So, as I said before, I want everyone in that corner!" The shriek of his whistle abounds yet again.

Every player arrives instantaneously in the right spot as Roger calls out to his assistant. "Coach Dawkins, isn't funny how running line drills gets the message across?"

"Yes, sir, Coach Stevens," concurs Reggie Dawkins.

"This drill is called slide and sprint," Roger explains. "You begin by facing me in a defensive stance; knees bent with good balance. On my whistle you will slide to the right, bringing your feet together but never crossing them. I want your head up on defense. Also, your right hand should be up and your left hand down. Once you slide to half court, I will blow the whistle again. When you hear the second whistle, turn your hips and sprint the rest of the way to the far baseline. When the first man reaches half court and hears the whistle to sprint, that same whistle signifies the next man in line to start his slide, and so on. Once you reach the far baseline, jog the length of the baseline to Coach Dawkins in the opposite corner, touch his hand and sprint back to this baseline. Then, get in line with me and do it all over again. You got it? Kevin will start first. Here we go!"

A spate of whistles sends player after player down the court, the sight similar to a line of parachutists jumping from a plane. Basketball season is officially underway.

• • •

The first fifteen minutes have the South players longing for a water break and the sight of a basketball, but neither is granted.

"This next exercise is called a shuttle drill, and many football teams use it," Roger bellows as Coach Dawkins positions orange cones throughout the court. "We'll have two groups, one at each end of the floor. One man from each group will go simultaneously. The reason for this drill is to build quickness and agility for our full court press. This drill will also help get you in shape because it doesn't do any good to run a full court press with a bunch of guys who aren't in shape. Again, Kevin will demonstrate the drill for everyone to see."

• • •

The first water break could not come quickly enough; a couple of players feel they are already down two or three pounds in sweat. *Welcome to a practice run by Roger Stevens,* Kevin Stevens would gladly tell them.

Unfortunately for the South players, the coach's shrilling whistle summons all bodies back to center court.

"Men, on defense we will learn to keep the players we are guarding in front of us. This next drill is a shadowing drill. No basketball is necessary. In fact, it's another football drill, simulating a defensive back in coverage versus a receiver. You will need to use the footwork you learned in both the slide-and-sprint drill and the shuttle drill to cover your man. And, by the way, if you're not breathing heavily during this drill, you're not doing it right. I'm going to match you up. On the baseline, let's go!"

● ● ●

After two-plus hours of physical exertion, after countless defensive drills, football drills, military-type drills and no basketball in sight, the first practice of the season wanes to a close, and the young men are ready to collapse. However, Roger knows there is one base left to cover.

"Let's go. Two fastest guys in the gym; one from each team," Coach Stevens calls out. "I need a guy from group-one and a guy from group-two. Your groups decide who's going to represent you."

Group-two holds no discussion. Billy Taylor takes one look at the others and voluntarily steps to the baseline; no one in his group thinks to oppose his decision.

Following brief deliberation, both Coach Stevens and his son are surprised when group-one pushes Kevin to the front of the pack. Kevin is caught off guard by the confidence of his teammates. Normally very assertive on the court, Kevin seems oddly tentative, as if to ask his teammates, *Me? Are you sure?*

Kevin steps to the baseline, and there stands Billy, lean and mean, ready to run, ready to race, ready to win.

Billy is as surprised as anyone that group-one has sent the coach's son to challenge him head to head. Even so, Billy cannot help but smile, thinking to himself, *it doesn't matter who they send to race me.*

This should be interesting, Coach Stevens contemplates as he steps to the free throw line and creates a lane between the athletes, much like the scene at a drag strip. "We'll go on the whistle, men. Baseline and back. Whoever touches my hand first on your way back wins. It will give you time to slow down and keep from running through the wall."

Kevin looks at the ground.

Billy looks at Kevin.

The whistle blares, and both group-one and group-two erupt as the participants explode out of the gates.

Billy crosses half-court in the blink of an eye, decelerating slightly as he confidently approaches the opposite baseline. While reaching down to touch the floor, he is shocked to find the coach's son nearly neck-and-neck with him—*fast kid!*

Kevin thinks about nothing else but running his hardest. His only desire is to make the race respectable and not be completely blown out.

Both groups get louder as the race appears even at the turn. "Yeah, Kevin," a player yells from group-one. "Beat him! Beat him!"

Billy hears the enthusiasm of a close race and takes offense. Not messing around anymore, the athletic teen puts his head down to dig deeper. Despite his best efforts, he can sense Kevin next to him..., and Billy can even see Kevin out the corner of his eye.

With half the court to go, the cheering from their teammates reaches full volume.

The eyes of Coach Stevens grow large watching the two young men coming at him full speed.

Both players extend for the coach's hand.

Billy gets there first before smoothly slowing to an impressive coast.

Kevin's teammates form a safety net to keep him from crashing into the wall.

Everyone saw what happened. Billy won...but not by much. All the buzz is around Kevin now as his teammates swarm to congratulate him as if he won the race.

Only one player comes to Billy's side, one of his lackeys, Dwayne. The exchange looks awkward as Billy brushes off the thanks. Instead, the members of group-two stand and elbow each other in awe, no one saying it but everyone thinking it: *someone almost beat Billy in a race, and it was a white kid.*

Billy picks up on the sentiment. Coach Stevens does as well. "Good job, Billy," the coach declares as he attempts to draw some attention away from his son. The words of the coach manage to garner Billy's attention. Roger adds, "I wish I had timed that."

Billy smiles and nods, appreciating the recognition.

"Everybody, get in here!" Coach Stevens puts his left hand straight out in front of him. The players are quick to follow his lead, forming a pack around the man and extending their hands toward the middle, burying Roger's hand underneath. "Good first day, men. Same time tomorrow. Show up ready to get better."

The man closes his comments by placing his right hand on top of the stack of hands. This has always been a practice of his as coach: he likes to personally have one hand on the bottom of the pile and his other hand on top, signifying he has his players covered by his support. "Here's what we do. I will say, 'South on three.' Then, after I count to three, we will all yell 'South' together."

The eyes around him get it.

"South on three! One! Two! Three…!"

A collective outburst simultaneously fills the gymnasium from floor to ceiling: "South!"

The thick, humid air has produced a cluster of sweaty bodies. As the players begin to disperse and move off the court, Kevin unexpectedly finds himself confronted, face to face with Billy—always a daunting proposition.

"Nice run, man," Billy offers.

"Thanks" is all Kevin can think to say in return.

"Who taught you to run like that?" Billy queries.

Kevin shrugs his shoulders in honesty. "I don't know. I just run as fast as I can."

Billy can get with that. He smiles and nods. "Right on, man. Right on." Billy suspends his right hand in the air and waits for Kevin's hand.

Kevin extends his hand palm-up and catches Billy's hand on the way down. The two then walk off the court together and looking on is their head coach.

• • •

As daylight wanes, Karen and Mrs. Anderson work the Anderson's garden, knowing Thanksgiving will be here in a few weeks. The sun sets behind the two ladies as they enjoy the company of one another, sharing stories of family and friends.

Mr. Anderson—in the background and not far from the two women—moves at a steady pace on the tractor.

• • •

A man stands in the distance, his presence unknown to those on the Anderson property. He focuses on Karen, watching as she works alongside the black woman. The man sees no sign of anyone else at home—no sign of any other men other than the driver of the tractor.

After ten minutes or so of observation, the man walks to his vehicle in the distance and drives away.

Neither Karen nor the Andersons saw the man, but he saw them.

20

"You see this, men?" queries Coach Stevens, holding a basketball in the palm of his right hand.

Not again, stew the players; they know what is next.

"We won't need this again today." With that, the man drop kicks the ball onto the gymnasium stage. "You will find you will spend more time without the basketball than with it. Of the ten players on the court during a game, only one can have the basketball at one time. That means ninety percent of the players on the floor will not have the ball at a given time. So, if your satisfaction is solely contingent on you having the ball in your hands, then you are in for a rude awakening. Most of the game will be played without the ball in your hands, and the same goes for the best players in high school, college, and even the pros. You must learn to be productive one-hundred-percent of the time instead of just ten percent of the time."

Makes sense, according to the faces of the Macon South players. *Never thought of it that way.*

"Let's get better today," Coach Stevens announces before blowing his by-now infamous whistle. "By the way, one of these nights, you will start hearing this whistle in your sleep," he declares while holding it high for them to see. "If you don't, then I'm doing something wrong."

• • •

Practices on days three, four, and five all begin the same way to the dread of the South roster.

"You see this, men?" Roger gleefully dangles the basketball before his team again before punting the ball onto the Ridgewood Stage.

"You see this, men?"

"You see this, men?"

• • •

As the final sequence of defensive drills comes to an end on Friday afternoon, the sound of the whistle brings everyone together. The players arrive panting, many of them again bent at the waist and using the bottom of their shorts to hold them up.

"We're getting in shape, men. We're getting ready. We're getting better. Great first week of practice." The coach next extends his hand into the thicket of sweaty players. The man's hand goes on the bottom, followed by all the hands of his team, followed by his other hand on top. "And guess what? We're going to get better next week, too. Have a great weekend, and I'll see you on Monday. Remember: show up ready to get better. South on three: one...two...three...."

"South!"

As Coach Stevens and Dawkins gather their things and prepare to exit the Ridgewood gym, Roger listens as his assistant throws an idea his way; Coach Stevens enjoys the love for the game Reggie Dawkins holds in his heart, reminding Roger of himself many moons ago. Up ahead, Coach Stevens notices some horseplay; no big deal to the man, *just boys being boys*. The head coach also sees Tyler and Leonard walking and talking together. What causes Roger to smile the most, however, is the sight of Kevin and Billy goofing around, tossing behind-the-back passes to each other as they walk toward the door, leading Roger to appraise the situation with optimism: *this team is coming together.*

● ● ●

Though it has been a long week, a tough week, Roger and Kevin have a little extra life in their bones because it is Friday.

"I'm sleeping in tomorrow; I'll tell you that," Kevin announces from the passenger seat.

Roger cannot debate the point. "I'm right there with you."

The Plymouth Fury parks outside the Anderson home.

Roger and Kevin enter the backdoor as is customary.

"Karen," Roger calls; she is usually in the kitchen at this time of day. "Karen." There is no answer.

The back door opens behind Roger and Kevin, and Karen appears, her countenance confirming something is off.

"Hi," Roger offers, puzzled by her look. "Everything okay?"

Karen pulls it together to give Kevin a quick hug. "Yes," she answers. "We are eating at the Anderson's cottage tonight."

"Oh, okay." The information and his wife's demeanor continue to confuse the man. "That's fine. Is that everything?"

Karen throws her eyes in the direction of the other room while Kevin has his back to her. Roger takes the hint and switches the subject. "Kev, it sounds like we're eating next door. What do you say we throw our stuff upstairs and head over to the Andersons? I know we're both hungry."

Roger slips out of the kitchen and finds Karen in the living room. The man lowers his tone. "What is it?"

Karen's lips are pursed. She takes an envelope she has been hiding from behind her back and hands it to her husband.

Roger observers the writing, and other than the Stevens' name and address across the front, the rest of the envelope is unmarked; no return address; only a postage stamp and a processing stamp by the Postal Service branch in Macon. "What is this," he asks.

Karen does not answer.

Roger removes the lone piece of paper from inside, unfolding it as he does. He studies what he sees and pauses in confusion. He looks up at his wife then looks back at the paper in his hand.

Etched is a drawing; no words, no information, just a drawing: an angry pair of eyes drawn in heavy pencil with formidable, dark, heavy eyebrows, and the eyes are looking back at Roger. He flips the paper over to see nothing else. He examines the envelope again to find nothing else. He next looks to his wife.

"I don't understand. What is this? Where did it come from?" Roger asks again.

"I found it in the mail today."

"The mailman brought it?"

"Yes."

"Did you ask him about it?"

"No. I didn't hear him when he arrived, so he just left it in our box."

Perplexed, Roger looks at the drawing again. An eerie sensation accompanies the picture, created by an unknown hand.

"What does it mean, Roger?" Karen asks as she moves cautiously to his side.

"I...I don't know."

Staring through the man, the sinister eyes observe whoever holds the paper, watching closely.

21

Wednesday, November 27

As the final bell rings, Principal Bullock appears in the doorway of Roger's Geometry classroom. Roger attempts to discern the look on his superior's face.

"Please, come in, sir."

Charles Bullock ominously closes the door of the now empty classroom behind him and eventually stands before his staff member. "Roger, I just want you to know because I think you would want to know...Darrell Battier ran away from home a couple of days ago."

"Oh, no." Roger's shoulders droop. "Any idea where he is?"

"No," the principal responds with pessimism. "In fact, Mr. Battier came here looking for him, spewing crazy accusations about us hiding his son."

Roger is overcome with sadness for Darrell and the entire Battier family. "That's...that's terrible. I..." Roger's personal involvement comes to mind. "I shouldn't have...I shouldn't have gone to their home. I went to the Battier home to try and talk with Darrell's father and..."

"And it didn't go well," the principal interrupts. "I know. Mr. Battier told me as much. He thought you went there to fight him."

Roger's eyes open wide. "Fight him? Oh, no. Charles, I did not go...."

"I know, Roger. I didn't believe him. Too much alcohol does bad things to people."

Firmly running his hands through his hair, Roger's mind goes back to Darrell. "What about Darrell? Any thoughts on where he might be? Any at all?"

The principal's expression offers little hope. "It's sad, Coach Stevens. It's very, very sad."

Roger agrees wholeheartedly. He hates this feeling. The feeling he must do something but cannot do anything. Instinctively, Roger extends a hand to his boss. "Let's pray, Principal Bullock. Let's pray for the Battier family. There seems to be so much pain there."

Charles Bullock receives the hand of Roger Stevens as the two men pray together.

● ● ●

Karen scurries around the kitchen with a smidgen of flour on her cheek. She knows, but little do the players on the team know they are coming to the Anderson home tonight for a special, pre-Thanksgiving holiday dinner. Roger will break the news to the squad at the end of practice in a matter of minutes. Meanwhile, Karen cannot get a pulse on why she is so nervous: possibly because it is amazingly already the Thanksgiving-season; perhaps because she is cooking for the team for the first time and wants to do her best. More than anything, what bothers Karen is cooking in another woman's kitchen.

Mrs. Anderson re-enters the back door with a batch of vegetables in tow. "What do you think, sweetheart," the matron inquires of her younger counterpart.

"I think I'm nervous," Karen answers.

"Oh, why's that?"

Karen sighs while scouring a potato. "Not sure. Maybe because I'm cooking in someone else's kitchen or because we're spending our first Thanksgiving away from home. Moving to Macon. All of it I guess."

Mrs. Anderson smiles and sympathizes while washing greens under the faucet. "All things considered, sweetheart, you're doing a wonderful job, supporting your husband like you do, being willing to up and move and do what the Lord has called you to do."

"You're too kind. I'm trying my best, and I know Roger and Kevin are trying their best as well."

"That's all God asks, isn't it, that we do our best?" Mrs. Anderson casts a calm visage in Karen's direction. "He'll do the rest."

"Right," Karen concurs. "You are exactly right. Thanks for reminding me." Mrs. Stevens returns the smile and glances down to see what Mrs. Anderson is doing. Puzzled at first, Karen inquires, "And what are those?"

"Greens, sweetheart. You're from Georgia, aren't you?

"Yes. Yes, but...."

"Never served greens before."

Karen feels somewhat embarrassed. "Not exactly. I've heard of them, of course."

"Well, these are them," Mrs. Anderson proclaims, "And I have a feeling the boys will like these tonight."

Silenced and humbled by her omission, Karen chastens herself privately for not considering a better-contoured menu while keeping the boys on the team in mind. "I'm so glad you thought of that..., and I'm embarrassed I didn't."

"That's okay, sweetheart. Just the way we do things down here."

According to Karen, Mrs. Anderson is as golden as they come; the woman hardened by life yet maintaining a sweetness about her.

"Let me tell you how greens came to our table when I was a girl," digresses Mrs. Anderson. "When I grew up in Alabama, my father would help the local butcher, a white man in town. My father noticed all the parts of the cow and pig that were thrown out and wasted at the end of the day. So, he asked the butcher if he would mind my daddy salvaging what was left and bringing it home because my daddy and momma knew how to stretch a meal. The butcher agreed, and my father would bring home all kinds of leftovers. We would eat pigs feet, chitlins and the like and mix them with greens from the field, okra, black-eyed peas and make a whole meal out of everything. It got us through some lean times. Got us through the years."

"I never knew that," Karen admits. "That's...a great idea. I should have known that."

"And God always provided, too. And God still provides for my family and me to this day. And God will provide everything you need, sweetheart if you continue to trust Him."

Karen can discern she is in the presence of a great woman of God; a woman who has been through the test to acquire a true testimony.

"I guess what I need God to provide most is peace of mind," Karen confides in her newfound friend. She pauses and turns her back to the sink. "I'm okay as long as I keep my mind off everything. It's when I start dwelling on the whole situation..., that's when I start to get overwhelmed."

"That's because that's how life is," Mrs. Anderson chimes in without hesitation. "Remember, it was when Peter took his eyes off Jesus, when he looked at the waves, that Peter started sinking. As long as he kept his eyes on Jesus, Peter walked above the situation before him."

Karen smiles with moistening eyes. She had read that account many times in the Bible, but today it has taken on new meaning.

"You know, speaking of waves," Mrs. Anderson does not skip a beat while washing more vegetables in the sink, "The more they study these hurricanes with their newfangled instruments, the more fascinating it becomes. Did you know they say the most peaceful part of the storm is the eye of the storm? When I think of that, it makes me think of God's eye looking down on His child in the storm."

Karen nods gratefully, thankful for the encouragement.

"And that's where I believe you are, Karen; you and your family. All of you are in the eye of the storm, but that's where it's the most peaceful because God has His eye on you."

• • •

As Karen and Mrs. Anderson prepare a feast at the Anderson home, knowledge and sweat are flying in the Ridgewood gym.

Roger Stevens indoctrinates the young minds around him, teaching them to respect the game and respect each other.

"Men, when we play man-to-man defense..."

"Men, when we play zone defense...."

"Men, when we face a man-to-man defense...."

"Men, when we face a zone defense...."

"Cut..., cut...."

"Swing the ball, Kevin...."

"Don't reach, Billy! Don't reach! Slide your feet...!"

"Come on, Leonard! You're better than that! Box out...!"

"Stay down, Tyler! Don't go for that pump fake...!"

"Set good screens...."

"Faster, men. We've got to play faster...!"

"I told you on day-one: I didn't come out here to watch you guys walk...!"

• • •

"Bring it in, men," Roger signals.

Surprised, to say the least, several of the players notice the large clock on the wall in the Ridgewood gym, causing them to ponder, *it's only 4:30. Coach sounds like he's done with practice..., but Coach never ends practice early.*

"Good work, men. I'm proud of you. You've been great this whole month of November. I think we're almost ready for the start of the season. Not quite…but almost."

Will he do it? His players salivate at the notion. *Is he ending practice early? It's the day before Thanksgiving, after all.*

"In fact, I'm so impressed…I have a surprise."

Previously tired eyes around the coach suddenly become wide with great expectation.

"I know something you don't know. My wife has been in contact with your families, and I am ending practice early this afternoon because all of you are coming back to our home at the Anderson's for a team Thanksgiving dinner. We're going all out, or I guess I should say my wife and Mrs. Anderson are going all out: turkey, mashed potatoes, all the sides you could want."

Excitement erupts among the sweaty pack of hungry teenage boys.

"So, let's get back to South, get showered, and then let's go eat."

Before the man can put his hand in the middle of the group, Billy Taylor beats him to it. Roger hesitates and nearly stammers, pleasantly surprised.

Billy discerns he caught his coach off guard based on the man's countenance. Thus, Billy withdraws his hand just as quickly. 'Sorry, coach," he offers penitently.

Roger quickly moves to salvage the moment. "No, no, Billy. You're fine. Go ahead. Lead us. Break us down."

Billy moves his hand back to the middle, and Roger places his hand on top of Billy's with the rest of the squad following their lead, the players looking at each other as if communicating telepathically, *Coach is letting one of us lead the team chant.*

Kevin's hands are immersed in the nest of hands as well, both black and white. He looks to his father, recognizing a surprised yet enlivened spark in the man's eye.

Roger looks to Billy, ready to follow his leadership…as do the rest of the boys. Privately, Roger realizes: *this is one of those moments. I'll remember this for a long time; the first time Billy became a leader.*

Billy Taylor emphatically calls out: "South on three! One! Two! Three…!"

"South!"

22

Roger could not believe the calendar as the week began: *December is here.*

Coach Stevens can sense heightened tension in the atmosphere, and so can his team, today's practice serving as the final practice before the first game of the season tomorrow night. The South players absorbed every word they could from the veteran coach for a solid month. If nothing else, Kevin, Billy, Tyler, Leonard, Dwayne, Jeremiah, and the entire squad know more about the game of basketball than ever before, and there is a collective desire to roll the ball out to see what they can do.

Roger shares the same sentiment: *it's time. It's time to quit beating up on each other and turn our aggression outwardly.* The man feels he has extracted as much as possible from his team during the pre-season, at least he hopes he has.

The addition of Coach Dawkins has been a blessing to Roger and the team. Not pushy or precocious by any means, Reggie Dawkins has wisely watched and learned. Roger has observed Coach Dawkins interacting with the young men. They respond to him. They respect him, especially the way Reggie Dawkins can still step on the court and make it happen when necessary—the young man's jumper is still there.

Of course, the change in Billy Taylor's attitude has been nothing short of a miracle, and day by day Roger has watched an unthinkable bond develop between Billy and his son. Roger would never admit it, but he was afraid of Billy when he first met the young man—-6'4" of muscle with the meanest scowl in the world. Roger would like to think he had something to do with the transformation. Instead, the man is quick to recognize the two-fold source: God and Billy's grandmother Betty; the older woman in her seventies not intimidated in the least by the hulking teenager in her house.

Then, there is Kevin—the coach's son. The kid's talent, desire, passion, work ethic, athleticism: Roger knows to have one or two of these qualities is plenty, *but to have the whole package?* Roger knows how good the son makes the father look as a coach.

Following another physically demanding practice (par for the course), the man blows a final whistle to signify the end of the pre-season. His players jog to him this afternoon, tired but not beleaguered. An aura of confidence permeates the gymnasium. These young men, thanks to the tutelage of Coach Stevens, feel on their way to something great.

The South players have exercised faith, heeding the instructions of their wise coach. As a result, they have watched fruit come to pass. The hard work seems to be paying off in the minds of the young men. Even beyond basketball, both Roger and the players agree: something special is happening not just on the team but in the school—even in the community of South Macon.

"You did it, men. Congratulations!" Coach Stevens addresses his players with certainty. "When you walk off the court in a few moments, the pre-season is officially over, and the real thing starts tomorrow night."

A solemn vibe flows from one player to the next as the young men envelop their coach—his words gospel to them.

"Remember, shirt and tie tomorrow at school. Pre-game snack in the cafeteria at 3:30 p.m. Bags packed, ready to roll at

4:30 p.m. Don't let your teammates down. Arrive everywhere you need to be in advance. To be on time is to be late. To be early is to be on time. Everybody get your hands in here."

The head coach places his hand on the bottom and top of the stack. Before he calls out the countdown, he takes a moment to survey the young, wide eyes before him. Suddenly, the events of the past several weeks race before him in a blur. The moment is surreal. How did he get here, he examines? How is it these teenagers believe in him? What does tomorrow hold? So many lessons already learned. Yet, there are many questions leading his team and his family into the unknown.

The perspiring players look to him, ready to follow his veteran leadership into battle. He has their back. They have his. Roger ends practice with the following: "Let' go out and do something nobody thought we could do this season. What do you say, men!"

"Yes, coach," they bark in unison."

"South on three: one, two, three...."

"South!"

23

Friday, December 6
Game One
Macon South vs. Jeffersonville
Record: 0-0

The bus ride to Jeffersonville High School is a quiet one, solemn. *This is really happening,* some of the boys ponder privately. *We are showing up to play Jeffersonville High with our white coach, his white son and the rest of us black kids.*

The coach ponders privately near the front of the bus. *We are showing up at Jeffersonville High School. A white man, his white son and a group of black players.* The closer the South bus draws to the opposing school, playing a basketball game is the least of the man's worries.

Roger might be less anxious had he not spoken with Principal Bullock earlier today. In an unprecedented act of good faith, the Principal of Macon South, a man who unadvisedly gives others the benefit of the doubt, assuming everyone is as excited about this inter-racial project as he is, directly contacted the Principal of Jeffersonville to confirm the Muskrat's itinerary and wish the Jeffersonville team well. Though no name-calling ensued, the reception of the call and the subsequent conversation was less than warm and fuzzy. "I think we're on our own," Mr. Bullock shared with Roger following the phone call. "In other words, don't expect anyone to go out of their way to be hospitable." In conclusion, the Coach and Principal agreed Roger would be the school designee to make such calls in the future.

"On our own," the coach whispers to himself as the bus ride draws near completion. "I'm sure there's more where that came from."

Rufus pulls the team bus onto the Jeffersonville lot, easing the blue and brown zeppelin look-alike to a stop about fifty feet from a set of double doors.

Roger knows he must lead with strength. His players will take all cues from him. The man confidently stands to his feet at the front of the bus. "Let's go, men."

As the bus doors swing open, time stands still. *So much for approach by stealth* is Roger's quick deduction. In real time, seemingly a thousand eyes on the Jeffersonville campus are fixed, riveted, galvanized. The arrival of the Macon South team has preceded them. The students at Jeffersonville heard about the white coach and his black players. However, now the faithful Jeffersonville fans are seeing and digesting all of it for the first time.

"Lotta' starin' eyeballs," Rufus commentates; the man always with a flare to state the obvious.

Coach Stevens feels the heat and weight of the collective glare. He holds at the bottom bus step for a few moments, surveying, looking for a rep. from the host school to greet them. Glancing at his watch, he confirms what he already knows: *We're right on time.* The words spoken by Principal Bullock were indeed prescient: the team from Macon South is on its own.

Roger notices the line behind him has backed up on the bus; everyone is waiting for him. Quietly, he conveys a message to his assistant coach. "I'll lead, Coach Dawkins. Please bring up the rear and let's keep the boys between us." Roger next raises his voice for the entire team to hear, reasserting his intentions. "Let's go." The man steps from the bus onto the property of Jeffersonville High, leading his team onward and upward.

As the group consisting of a white coach, his white son and several large young black men paces toward the fieldhouse, the bodies of spectators begin to backpedal slowly and part before them. Some in the Jeffersonville contingent consider jeering at the sight. However, the size of the young men from Macon South makes the onlookers think twice before speaking.

Just before the team reaches the fieldhouse doors, an indiscernible comment comes from the crowd, followed by snickering. It is not clear what was said, but it was not kind, and the comment did not escape the ears of Billy Taylor.

Ever-confident and having never met a confrontation he did not like, Billy stops to address the situation, a line of players bumping into each other behind him. "Problem?" Billy offers a blunt, one-word question to the apparent culprit in the crowd.

The Jeffersonville teen looks up at Billy's 6'4", broad-shouldered build, and the white kid is at a loss for words. Other young men from Jeffersonville slowly begin to close ranks around their fellow student at the sight of trouble, and trouble is brewing.

Roger discerns and diffuses the situation. "Billy! Inside! Now!"

The voice of his coach garners Billy's attention. The South player looks in the direction of his coach then looks back at the Jeffersonville teen one final time, flashing a smile that conveys, *you've been spared. This is your lucky day.*

The Jeffersonville teen swallows hard as Billy pivots and resumes his cadence with the rest of the team. Another comment springs from the crowd, but this time the group from South keeps moving forward.

Roger decides to hang back just in case. "Kevin," he gets the attention of his son. "Lead us through those doors."

Kevin honors his father and moves to the front, soon grabbing the metal handle to swing the doors open wide.

The gym is quiet, save a handful of people rustling, sweeping, wrestling with wires, getting things ready for tonight. Predictably, the sight of the South team brings all bustling to a momentary standstill. One man, in particular, leaves his post and walks in the direction of Roger and his team.

"You must be Coach Stevens," the Jeffersonville JV Coach ventures an obvious guess.

"Yes, I am," Roger responds, though the man cannot contain his disappointment. "We let ourselves in because no one greeted us at the curb?"

The younger man is taken back at the blunt statement, even slightly offended. However, over the shoulder of the Coach from Macon is a group of rather large, young men at his back. "Yes…, sorry about that. We are busy preparing final details for tonight. Let me show you and your team to your locker room."

Not a very good explanation, the veteran coach deduces, but it will have to do. Again, the words of Charles Bullock have proven true: The Muskrats should not expect much in the way of hospitality tonight.

• • •

"There's a good crowd out there tonight, Rufus tells Coach Dawkins through the locker room door.

"There's a good crowd out there tonight," Coach Dawkins turns and relays to Coach Stevens.

"Is there?" Roger responds. "I wasn't sure what to expect."

As the well-experienced coach reviews his game notes, the man is soon to embark on his eleventh high school basketball coaching campaign. His players appear anxious, which is nothing out of the ordinary; there are always jitters before the first game of the season. Yet with Coach Stevens at the helm and his son Kevin and Billy Taylor both present, there is enough experience and confidence in the room to cover a multitude of uncertainty. At the same time, the venerable coach finds the display of nerves by his kids entertaining: one of them swaying continuously, one of them repeatedly tossing a basketball in the air to himself, one of them stretching for the fiftieth time, one of them jumping up and down in place.

"Okay, men." At his words, the entire team takes a seat on the locker room bench before the coach and a well-worn chalkboard. "It's like I told you. Jeffersonville is a quality team. They were one game away from advancing out of their district last season." Coach Stevens' scouting report is courtesy of his friend Tom Chaney from Ridgewood High. His friend told him the first scouting report is on the house, but Roger's on his own after that.

"Jeffersonville is returning half their squad from last season. They have some height, and they have some outside shooting, which will be more than enough to keep us honest. We'll start in man-to-man to make them beat our athleticism. Listen to me: play them straight up. Don't bail them out by being overaggressive and picking up early fouls. I need to see what type of game these officials are going to call." The man is curious about the officials from both a stylistic perspective and a biased perspective. Add the fact tonight's crowd should be ninety-five percent against his team, and Roger knows how susceptible referees can be to home-cooking—especially here and especially tonight.

"We're starting with Kevin at the point, Dwyane at the two, Billy on the wing, Leonard at the four and Tyler at center."

The eyes of his team look back at Roger Stevens, hanging on his every word, trusting him with more than just tonight's game: trusting him to get them home from Jeffersonville in one piece.

Roger looks at his team and smiles. He is glad for them. Granted, the man knows there is much controversy swirling around the team, which is his fault and not theirs. Yes, these kids will undoubtedly deal with comments, abrasiveness, even threats during the season. However, the Muskrats are soon to step on the court, and the basketball court is the one place where a coach and his players can break free from the rest of their lives and just coach and play the game. Roger knows it is a time to forget your problems; forget if your boss is mad at you, if your wife is mad at you, or if you had a bad day at school. It is time to forget everything else and step on the boards of hardwood and play the game.

The man is done speaking; there is nothing left to say. Coach Stevens extends his hand to the middle of the group. Kevin takes the lead, standing to his feet and placing his hand on top of his father's. The rest of the South roster follows. Coach Stevens then places his other hand on top, ready to defend every hand in the stack, each representing a young man and a life full of promise. He wants them to know desperately God has created them for a purpose and not even the sky is the limit. The man and semi-retired Sunday school teacher could almost break into a message right now. Somehow, someway, despite all the apprehension and reluctance, despite the hesitation and resistance regarding the move to Macon, despite uprooting his precious family and bringing them directly into the line of fire, suddenly, those emotions are somewhere in the distance. What Roger knows is this: his heart has begun to make room for the names and faces before him now. As he scans the group, he cannot help but ponder their dark features, their skin, and hair, acknowledging, *they are exactly the way God intended them to be.*

The thoughts of the man suspend in time. *I wonder what they think when they look at me,* Roger considers. *I hope they don't see me as just another white man trying to be in charge of them. I hope they see me as a coach who cares, maybe even a father figure, especially to those who don't have one.*

"Who believes you can win?" the coach snaps into action with a tone and countenance of ferocity. Before anyone can answer, Roger answers his question. "I believe you can win." The man affirms, laying a mantle of confidence over his team. "I believe you can win."

"It's we win, Coach," Leonard speaks up. "It's we. You in this too."

"Yes, Leonard. I'm in this too. And you know what: I'm glad to be in it with you."

The smiles in the locker room encircle the man.

"I'm going to ask again; who believes we can win?"

This time a salvo of agreement and emotion and motivation almost lifts the man off the ground.

"Then let's do this. South on three: one, two, three...."

"South!"

• • •

The Macon South Muskrats jog from the visiting locker room to an anticipated chorus of boos, the jeers cascade from the rafters of the capacity gym, serving a twofold purpose. For some, the expression is simply born of playful gamesmanship. For others, the sentiment is genuine, born out of disgust for the white coach and his black players. Jeffersonville High shows great attendance tonight not only because it is the season-home opener but because no one in town is going to miss this spectacle; many in the stands want the home team to stick it to Macon South badly.

As Kevin leads Macon South in warmup drills at one end of the floor, Coach Stevens walks to half court to formally greet his counterpart as is customary. Roger finds his Jeffersonville counterpart to be a man of few words...or at least he comes across that way on this night. The half-smile the man gives Roger is less than a half-hearted attempt at cordial respect, and the salutation ends almost as quickly as it begins.

No problem, Coach Stevens thinks to himself in response to the less than friendly gesture. *Let's see how your team holds up tonight.* As much as Roger attempts to be a respectful diplomat of the game, a competitive streak runs through the man and that streak, at times, can be merciless.

Roger turns his focus to his team during warmups. He notices wandering eyes and a lack of attention to detail as most of his players keep glancing at the crush of spectators filling the bleachers.

"You're goin' down tonight, boys!" yells a Jeffersonville student while cupping his hands around his mouth. "Might as well leave town!" yells another. "And take the dumb-lookin' white kid with you."

Kevin notices Billy looking over his shoulder at the crowd, the muscular teen clenching and opening his fists by his side as he does.

"Better get home by dark" mocks another random voice.

"Don't get drawn into that, Billy," Kevin intercedes from behind his teammate. "We'll take care of everything on the court."

"You know they're talkin' about you, too?" Billy offers.

"You think?" Kevin replies with a comically confused look. "I thought you were the dumb-lookin' white kid."

Both players smile at each other and proceed through the layup line.

"Focus on what you're doing," the coach wrangles his team's attention, re-centering them.

Despite the hostile majority in attendance, the spirits of Roger and his squad lift at the sight forming behind the team bench. A better than expected contingent of South supporters is gathering and carving out a section of their own. Square in the middle of the group is the notable presence of Principal Bullock. The man is obviously amid the faithful not only to keep an eye on the game but to keep an eye on the South crowd as well—to protect and prevent.

Also in attendance, Roger takes a moment to flash a smile at the best-looking woman in the gym, and Karen—who traveled to the game with Pastor Jenkins and his wife—responds with a wave from the bleachers.

Coach Stevens walks to the baseline for some final words with his assistant, both surveying the opponent as they go through warm-ups at the far end.

Before the squad from South know it, the horn gives a 60-second warning before the tip.

"Let's head to the bench, men," Roger decrees while considering to himself. *It's time. There's no going back.*

"Ladies and gentlemen," the public address announcer squawks over the sound system. "Please join us by rising for our National Anthem?"

In unison, approximately 1,500 people stand, removing their hats accordingly. As the Jeffersonville band begins the familiar music, Coach Stevens begins to zone out as usual. Roger is a very patriotic man, yes. However, whenever the National Anthem begins, out of longstanding habit, the man slips into his final pregame thoughts, covering all the bases, racing through all-things basketball A-Z. One night at a Braves game in Atlanta last year, again out of habit, the coach fell into his pregame trance while surrounded by 20,000 people. Roger had to remind himself he was out for a night of entertainment, and later Hank Aaron homered twice.

Roger breaks from protocol for one night to observe his surroundings. The crowd, of course, is predominantly white; however, the fans from Macon South are here to represent with pride, standing equally as tall for the National Anthem. The man ruminates: *this will be the only time all these people agree on anything tonight.*

The anthem ends, the crowd applauds, and the lead official blows his whistle to get things rolling.

Roger huddles with his roster in front of the South bench. The starting five extricate themselves from their modest warm-up tops and pants purchased with an equally-modest school budget. "Everything we've worked on up to this point… make it work out on the court," Roger thunders above the clamor. "Forget the crowd. Forget the noise. Do what you know to do and make the other team play our game. I'm telling you the truth: you guys are ready for this night. Now, let's go to work. Offensive tip! Go up and get the ball, Tyler! South on three," the man barks, his hands on the bottom and top of the stack. "One, two, three…."

"South!"

Kevin leads the way onto the court as the Muskrats from Macon South don their visiting uniforms: dark blue trimmed in brown; a sight Karen only tolerates because she loves the boys so much. Kevin also leads his teammates in offering quick, pre-tip, cordial handshakes to the Jeffersonville starting five as well as the referees near the half-court circle. Billy, Dwayne, Leonard and Tyler follow the example of the coach's son. The Jeffersonville players all return the gesture, albeit sometimes awkwardly, except for one player: the big Jeffersonville center in the middle of the circle. Kevin approaches the formidable 6'6" figure.

The center from Jeffersonville looks down at Kevin's hand, leaving it suspended in air. The center then looks Kevin Stevens in the face, expressionless, as if Kevin's not worth nor deserves any reaction whatsoever.

Kevin holds the would-be handshake for a while, then withdraws.

On cue, Billy appears on the scene, standing beside his teammate. Unafraid, Billy poses one question: "Is there a problem here?"

The Jeffersonville player turns his attention from Kevin to the black kid, gladly staring down Billy next.

"Easy, boys," the referee senses conflict as well. "Step out of the circle if you're not jumping."

Kevin puts his hand across Billy's chest to walk them both backward. As the two players from Macon step out, Tyler steps in, ready to represent the Muskrats at mid-court and jump out of the gym.

The officials are ready.

The Jeffersonville fans are ready.

The Macon South fans are ready.

Principal Bullock is ready.

Karen is ready.

Kevin is ready.

Roger is ready as he begins his eleventh season as head coach; never did he think his next season would start as coach of the Macon South Muskrats, nevertheless, here he is. The only thought managing to run through his mind now: *Here we go, God.*

With all formalities out of the way, the striped-shirted official chirps his whistle, and the 1968-'69 high school basketball season begins.

The ball ascends, and Tyler has no problem going up to get it, out leaping his opponent and tapping the ball straight back to Kevin.

With perfect timing, Billy leaks out and gets ten feet behind the Jeffersonville defense in a split-second.

On point, Kevin releases an over the top pass to Billy at the top of the key.

The nearest Jeffersonville opponent puts his head down and sprints...but to no avail; Billy will not be caught.

The athletic player from Macon South takes the over shoulder pass and puts the ball on the floor once.

Roger watches from the sideline, the opening play unfolding perfectly as planned.

Deep in the paint, Billy's elevates off his right foot. Soon his head soars seemingly near the rim, his athletic frame unrestrained by gravity.

The once frenzied crowd falls silent as everything happens so quickly.

Billy proceeds to start the game by doing something many have heard of but never seen in these parts: Billy dunks the basketball forcefully with two hands, causing the backboard to reverberate.

The fans from South exhale in awe and jubilation.

The fans from Jeffersonville inhale from awe and shock.

The shrill of the whistle intervenes as the lead official races in Billy's direction. "Technical foul!" the man yells above the clamoring noise, pointing straight at Billy.

The Jeffersonville crowd responds with an explosion of endorsement.

Billy lifts both hands in the air as if to say, *What'd I do?* Billy next looks to his coach on the bench with the same expression.

"What?" Roger blurts incredulously. "What are you talking about!"

The ref jogs to the scorer's table, facing the scorekeeper, straddling the center line as Roger walks out to meet him. "Technical foul! Number thirty-three from Macon! Illegal dunking! One shot, Jeffersonville."

"Illegal dunking! What?" Roger cannot speak his words fast enough. "That's ridiculous!" He follows the referee onto the court.

Not about to put up with any antics, the lead official turns to address Coach Stevens eye to eye. "Your player dunked the basketball. Didn't you see him?" the ref chimes sarcastically.

"Of course, I saw him do it," Roger barks back. "What's wrong with that?"

"It's illegal to dunk in this gym!"

"Says who?"

"Says the rules of this gym!"

"What rules of the gym?" Roger stammers. He cannot believe what he is hearing. "No one.... You never told me that!"

"You never asked," is the ref's response.

Roger is fuming now. "Are you out of your mind! You're the ref! You're supposed to tell us the rules of the gym!"

The crowd begins to grow annoyed at the sight of the coach and ref squaring off eight seconds into the game.

Coach Dawkins has moved in behind his head coach, speaking calmly into his ear.

"Let's step back, Coach."

Roger resists, not giving an inch.

"No one ever dunks so there's no need to cover it," the ref continues to stand firm.

"Is it because no one dunks or because my team dunks?"

Roger is quickly falling out of favor with the lead official as the man warns the coach with a penetrating glare but no words.

Roger Stevens, however, is not done. "Then don't give my team a technical unless you tell us the rule first. Don't be stupid."

The ref has had enough and gives another short blast of his whistle. "Technical foul on the coach from Macon."

The crowd noise crescendos again.

"Are you out of your...." Roger cannot say what he wants to say and stay in the game.

The official stands his ground and glares, waiting for the Macon Coach to give him one more reason.

"Coach..., Coach," pleads Reggie Dawkins. "Let's step back."

This time, Roger allows his assistant to pull him gently in the opposite direction.

"Do you believe that?" the head coach asks his assistant. "Isn't that ridiculous?"

"Yes, sir. But we need you. It's just the battle—not the war."

Roger acknowledges his assistant is correct. "Get over here, guys," Roger commands his team.

Karen watches from behind the South bench, recognizing the antagonized look on her husband's face.

Roger wheels around in frustration, catching a glimpse of Karen in the stands. His wife gestures softly with her hands, encouraging the man to bring it down.

Coach Stevens grabs a quick drink from the team water cooler and turns to address his team with as much composure as he can muster. The cheer of the crowd breaks his team's attention as the opponent sinks the first of two free-throw attempts.

"Don't worry about him," Roger claps in front of their faces. "Look at me. Don't worry about him and don't worry about the refs. Stay aggressive. I'm telling you....

"Ridiculous call, man," Billy interrupts, drawing the ire of his coach.

"Look at me, Billy! This doesn't change anything. I'm telling you this: if we play harder than them, we'll win. We'll get

there. Just play our game. Let's go! South on three! One...,
two..., three: South!"

As the huddle breaks, the Jeffersonville shooter misses his
second shot.

The official tosses the ball to another official who grants
the home team the ball out of bounds.

Despite the calls in favor of their team, the Jeffersonville
fans remain in a state of surreal disbelief. Many of them have
heard of dunking and even seen the feat on television. They
had never seen it done in person, though, and Billy Taylor's
opening authoritative statement has sent shockwaves through
the gymnasium.

As he and his teammates step on the court to go on defense,
Kevin pulls a veteran move. With the opposing point guard
just beyond the half court line, Kevin turns his back to him,
lulling both the opposing inbound player and point guard to
sleep. Next, with impeccable timing, the Macon South point
guard whirls and sprints quickly enough to get a hand on the
inbound pass, knocking it past his flat-footed counterpart.

The Macon South bench, already energized, leap to their
feet as the coach's son races down the court with no one in
his path.

"What are we doing?" wails the Jeffersonville coach from
the sideline.

Roger watches with wide eyes as his son's slender frame
closes on the basket then rises in the air, dunking the basketball
with two hands, causing a new frenzy to overtake the crowd.

The same official runs toward Kevin while frantically blowing his whistle. "Technical foul! Right there! Technical foul!"

Roger looks on incredulously. "Kevin," he says under his
breath, "what are you doing?"

The rest of the Muskrat squad is confounded as well as
the coach's son jogs to the bench, everyone waiting for some
semblance of explanation from the star player.

Kevin arrives at the team bench, looking at his father in both repentance and confidence. "Sorry, Coach. I dunked that one for Billy."

Confusion becomes unity as a collective smile radiates among the squad from South. The rest of the players start to get it: Kevin is one of them now.

Billy steps next to Kevin, displaying the biggest smile of all, rubbing the point guard's blonde crewcut. "Yeah, boy," Billy affirms to Kevin.

The remaining Muskrat players follow suit, all of them stepping forward to rub Kevin's head.

It begins to dawn on Roger what his son just did. He led. Kevin led, and the response from his teammates is priceless. Therefore, instead of scolding Kevin for picking up a third technical foul for the team in the first fifteen seconds, Coach Stevens jumps on board with the vibe of unity.

"Okay, okay. Settle down. Let's start over. Hands in the middle."

All hands energetically take part.

"Just one thing," the coach stipulates to his team with a grin. "No more dunking, okay?"

"Yes, coach," they collectively respond in laughter.

"That's more technicals than me and my teams got in ten years in Augusta," offers Roger.

"You're not in Augusta anymore," Billy counters.

Roger smiles. "You're not kidding. South on three: one..., two..., three..., South!"

Although the Muskrats do not show any more dunks to the crowd, there is no need. Macon South soon overwhelms Jeffersonville on their home court, and the Jeffersonville Coach is unable to counter the onslaught of athleticism with an adequate game plan.

Tyler blocks three shots, and Leonard hauls down four rebounds in the first quarter. Billy and Kevin combine for fifteen points in the opening frame. Macon South races out to a ten-point lead which extends to 17 by halftime.

Much like the first half, Jeffersonville has no answers in the second half.

The South crowd is elated.

The Jeffersonville crowd is left reeling.

The lead swells to twenty-three during the third quarter. Nothing is working for Jeffersonville, and everything is going the way of the Muskrats. The South players are feeling it—especially Billy.

Late in the third quarter, one of the Jeffersonville guards drives to the basket and fails to see the athletic wingman from South closing from behind. The Jeffersonville player shoots, only to have Billy Taylor spring from the court and launch the shot into the second row of the bleachers.

"No, you don't" Billy screams at the Jeffersonville player following the block and release of adrenaline.

The whistle of the nearest official fills the gym, the ref pointing at Billy.

The big center from Jeffersonville takes exception, stepping between his teammate and who he views as the *arrogant black kid from Macon South.*

Billy does not flinch; his eyes, in fact, welcome the confrontation. "What?" Billy sharply asks the taller player. "I'll block your trash, too!"

The Jeffersonville center gets a hand on Billy's chest. "Shut up." Before a shoving match ensues, Kevin is there to yank Billy back quickly.

"Oh, no," argues Billy, struggling to get free from Kevin's grasp, looking past the bodies to see the Jeffersonville big man. "He's not putting his hands on me."

Leonard offers support, assisting Kevin in holding Billy back.

By this time the refs have intervened as well. "That's it!" proclaims the lead official, glaring at Billy. "You're done. Get out!"

The home crowd is already tired of Billy, and with the South player ejected, the Jeffersonville fan base lets him have it.

Roger steps father onto the court, taking Billy from Kevin and Leonard who delivers their teammate out of harm's way.

However, whatever problems Billy thought he might have pale in comparison to the one he has now.

The countenance of Coach Stevens says it all, the man doing what few people are brave enough to do. He takes Billy Taylor firmly by the arm, escorting him to the end of the team bench. "Coach Dawkins?" Roger shouts. "Take over!"

Reggie Dawkins gets his bearings and steps to the front.

Roger walks Billy to the end of the bench and forces the kid with huge biceps to sit down. "Look at me, Billy."

Billy is slow to respond, still peering at the court, his eyes searching for the center on the other team.

Coach Stevens grits his teeth and speaks with force, leaning in front of his player. "Look at me!"

Not thrilled; still, Billy gives in.

"That's not how the game is played, and you will not represent me like that. Do you understand?"

Billy does not speak.

Roger can see the young man trying to calm down. Still, the coach does not cede his point. "Do you understand me, Billy? You will respect the game of basketball if you want to play for me. You will think of your teammates before you think of yourself. Do you understand me?"

Secretly, Roger never thought he would muster the courage to rake Billy Taylor over the coals like this.

Still refusing to speak, Billy nods, and Roger settles for that, releasing his player's muscular arm and standing to walk in the other direction.

• • •

By the end of the night, South posts a substantial road-victory even their Head Coach did not anticipate: 61-39. Even more, Roger never once considered a scenario where he would have to call off the dogs in the final quarter. All twelve players on the South roster logged minutes in the first contest of the season.

At the final horn, as the two teams meet in two lines at midcourt for the customary postgame handshake, the squad from Jeffersonville approaches Roger and his team with much more humbleness than before the game. There are only two exceptions.

The Jeffersonville Coach cannot hide his disgust, believing Roger allowed his team to run up the score—a humiliating loss on opening night.

Roger does not expect much when he extends his hand to his counterpart, and he does not get much. *Want to play again?* Roger sarcastically considers to himself, part of him willing to give the Jeffersonville Coach and his team another try if the man is unconvinced the better team won. Yet, following a quick conviction of the heart, Roger tones down his thoughts and feelings, knowing from experience pride goes before a fall.

The only other member of Jeffersonville who shows no interest in good sportsmanship is the team's center. The big man sulking and walking past the line to the locker room; he could only muster seven points and four rebounds along with five fouls.

As Roger turns to gather his players and direct them to the locker room, the visiting crowd from Macon South come into full view, all of whom are on their feet in applause as their team jogs past. Several fans wave to Coach Stevens as well, including an extremely-pleased principal who gives an enthusiastic thumbs up. Roger waves back. Finally, an over-joyed yet subdued blonde female in the row behind the team bench catches his attention. Part of Karen wants to be a good sport and not a braggart. Part of her wants to act as if the win is just business as usual, but another part of her knows this is a big deal, a huge deal.

Roger enters an understandably festive team locker room. Dwayne stands on the bench in front of the chalkboard giving high fives as the rest of the team enters. The Coach slaps hands with the young man before instructing his team to settle down and come together.

"Okay, guys, okay. Take a seat and listen to me for a minute."

The players submit, curious to hear the thoughts of their leader following a great night.

"Great win. You started early. You overcame adversity. You never let up. Everyone played. And other than Billy and Kevin trying to get us kicked out of the gym by dunking the basketball...."

The room explodes in laughter with the teens playfully shoving one another.

"All things considered I am extremely pleased with how we played tonight. So, every one of you give someone else a high five."

The congratulatory atmosphere continues; smiles all around.

"Now, listen," the man lowers his tone somewhat. "If we think every game is going to be this easy, we are sadly mistaken. Enjoy this victory, but realize we still have a long, long way to go. Remember, when we play, we are not only going to have to beat the other team, but we'll have to beat the refs, too. There were some bad calls tonight, but we were out in front by enough that it didn't alter the outcome of the game. There will be tougher games than this, I'm telling you. But as for tonight, like I said: great win, great night and my wife arranged for tacos for you back in the South cafeteria tonight."

If the locker room had not erupted before, it erupts now at the news of a postgame meal.

"South on three," the Head Coach calls while placing his hand in the center.

The remaining hands find their way to the middle, gladly, triumphantly.

"One, two, three...South!"

24

Tuesday, December 10
Game Two
Macon South vs. Duncan
Record: 1-0

What was already destined to be an eager crowd at the Macon South home-opener doubled in size once word spread about the Muskrats' impressive debut versus Jeffersonville. It appears the entire South community has made the trip across town to Ridgewood for the first home game; their temporary home away from home. Of course, Ridgewood is not a place people from South frequent for multiple reasons, but the Muskrat fans have wisely traveled in packs this night, knowing there is safety in numbers.

Also traveling to Ridgewood tonight has been the opponent: Duncan High School who also won their season opener. Even so, from the outset, it is clear Duncan is unable to handle Coach Stevens' team, and the primary problem for Duncan proves to be the sheer height, strength and overall athleticism of Macon South. Just as in practice, whatever rebound Tyler does not get,

Leonard does. Whatever rebound Leonard does not grab, Billy does. Not to mention, Macon South has an athletic 6'4" guard in Kevin Stevens who rebounds extremely well from the point.

Tyler, an ordinarily passive kid despite standing 6'6", has found confidence playing behind the personalities of Billy and Kevin. Tyler also benefits greatly from the strength of Leonard on the opposite block. In this the second game of the season, the South center has been putting it all together, bursting out of the gate versus Duncan by scoring the first ten points for his team on his own, converting on designed plays and offensive put-backs; none of the opponents have been able to elevate with him.

As the fourth quarter wares on for Duncan High, Billy and Kevin's dual presence proves to be too much. The tandem provides fluid scoring, even distribution of the basketball and staunch defense. Duncan sees the writing on the wall and tries to push the tempo in the final quarter. However, they do so to no avail, and Duncan simply runs out of gas.

Once again, the Muskrat backups get quality reps toward the end of the game as South pulls away. In the end, Macon has fired on all cylinders for a second straight contest. The final score: Macon South 62, Duncan High 43.

A serious man about all phases of the game, Coach Stevens is not thrilled with the opponent reaching the 40's on offense, but how can the man complain about the results? His team is exceeding expectations. Yes, he more than anyone acknowledges it is still early in the season. At the same time, Roger has no doubt: something special can happen this season at Macon South High School.

The South crowd displays their glowing approval as the boys jog off the court at the end of the game to head for the locker room.

"Good job, Coach! Great game, Coach Stevens!" are the shouts from the home stands as the coach strolls past. Suddenly, oddly, Roger Stevens is the most popular man on the south side of Macon, causing him to ruminate at the sound of the cheers: *How quickly things can change!*

• • •

Maxwell and the other plain-clothes Klansmen work feverishly by night. The train is endless. The wooden crates are endless.

Raymond Huddler scrutinizes the laborers from a distance, keeping a strict eye on Freddy Collins more than anyone. Huddler, an already paranoid man, has been increasingly agitated of late—someone among his chapter is communicating with the outside.

A bulky, rough and tumble man steps to Huddler's side. Not sheepish in the least, the man next to Huddler holds a baseball bat in his grip. "Do you want to do this now?" asks the man with weapon in hand.

Maxwell constantly monitors Huddler with his peripheral vision, and Maxwell now monitors the man next to Huddler as well.

Huddler surveils Freddy. "He's a good worker," Huddler states. "But a little too good. Yeah, let's do this now."

The man with the ball bat nods and grins; he likes this part of the job. The two approach Freddy near the rail cars.

Maxwell sees them coming. Immediately, the undercover FBI Agent begins to analyze any weaknesses Huddler's henchman might have. *He looks a little bulky*, Maxwell considers. *He might be strong, but he might be slow as well. If I can get him leaning, I can get him to the ground. I'll shoot if I must.*

Some of the men working near Freddy see the look in Huddler's eyes and sense trouble is coming. Those nearby peddle backward and leave the three men to their business.

"Good work, Freddy," Huddler compliments the Klansman.

"Thank you, sir," Maxwell replies with his best southern dialect while wiping sweat from his brow.

"There's only one problem."

"Sir?"

"You. You're the problem," Huddlers tone grows terse.

Maxwell identifies all means of escape as he continues the conversation. "I...don't know what...."

"You're a liar, Freddy. You told me you were from Decatur. I have friends on the force in that part of the State, and they've never heard of a Frederick Collins, nor is there a record of you assaulting a black man in public."

The Klansman next to Huddler positions his hands as would an angry batter, ready to unleash as soon as Huddler says the word.

"So," Huddler continues, "I'm going to have you beaten to death in front of these men as an example."

The man with the bat advances on Maxwell as the agent interjects, "Alabama, sir." His words cause the would-be attacker to pause.

The interruption puzzles Huddler as well. "What did you say?"

"I'm from Decatur, Alabama," Maxwell swiftly states for the record. "I'm from just over the Tennessee River and down the road from Huntsville. I am not from Georgia, sir."

Huddler narrows his glare at Freddy Collins. "Alabama?"

"Yes, sir."

The bulky man with the baseball bat is caught in the middle, thinking to himself, *do I get to do this or not?* "Well?" he questions Huddler.

Raymond Huddler continues to stare. "Then...I almost made a terrible mistake. I almost lost a good man this night." Huddler's countenance goes from crazed to amicable at an alarming rate. "That's good to know."

Maxwell keeps his cool as his pulse races.

"Keep up the good work, Freddy," Huddler encourages as he and his disappointed associate turn and walk in the opposite direction.

Maxwell does not dare show his back until he feels safe. This is the second time he has encountered the euphorically evil look in the eyes of Raymond Huddler.

After several paces, Huddler pivots to address Maxwell again. "Freddy, you wouldn't lie to me, would you?"

Maxwell responds, "Sir, if I *wuz* lying, you would have known it by now."

• • •

Dawson is first to the office the next morning, and his phone is already ringing. "Dawson," he succinctly answers.

"I gotta' be fast," Maxwell delivers breathlessly. "I think they're on to me."

"Are you sure?"

"I just feel it. They know about Decatur. They checked once. They're going to check again—you can count on it." The agent speaks hurriedly from a pay phone outside an empty gas station by morning light.

"Do I need to pull you out?"

"I need you to pick up the pace," Maxwell responds. "Whatever you're going to do, do it soon...or I won't be around to see it."

Dawson is distracted by motion outside his office.

Agent Hopper walks slowly past Dawson's door. Hopper worked the night shift and will soon call it a day. The lingering agent offers a nod to greet his superior this morning. Hopper heard Dawson's phone ring and thought he would see what was happening.

Dawson does not care about politeness, nearly closing his door in Hopper's face.

Hopper stands in place for a moment longer. "All right," he utters to himself before ambling across the office.

25

Games 3–5
Record: 2-0

A game within the game has emerged for Macon South as the Muskrats continued to trounce all comers in the first five games of the season.

Roger believes the best competition thus far has been in practice. Case in point, watching Billy and Kevin go head to head has been a showstopper. It seems everyone drops everything any time the two square-off, whether it is one-on-one or the most fundamental of drills.

It is clear the two players have embraced the challenge of competing against one another. Billy does not back down from Kevin because Billy backs down from no one. This fact has been great for Kevin as well, and Roger realizes Billy is the best thing to happen to Kevin. Not to diminish his son's work ethic in the least, but Roger knew Kevin was set for cruise control for his senior year in Augusta. The red carpet would have been surely rolled out everywhere the Academy and Kevin played. Instead, this season has been about getting back to the basics for Kevin, nothing but a leather ball and a sweaty gym, working hard to get better every day, competing against athletes who are just as good if not better than he is, causing Kevin to sharpen every tool in the shed.

Whether Billy Taylor's pride—at the same time—would allow him to admit it or not, Kevin has been great for Billy as well. An immense talent, the supremely athletic young man from the far south side of Macon was prepared to sit out this basketball season altogether. The program at Macon South had been shoddy over the past several years, leaving Principal Bullock to coach the team because there was no one else. People around the community would reminisce about the '60 South team on which Reggie Dawkins played, one of the better teams in recent memory. Still, that season was meteoric, and the program returned to the doldrums quickly after that. However, when the kid heard a white coach was coming to Macon, Billy knew he had to go out for the team, even if his motives were not pure. Ever-confident in his ability, Billy considered showcasing his talents just enough to get the new coach excited and then quitting, getting the man's hopes up just to let them down, all of this before ever meeting Roger Stevens.

Instead, a change of heart began to churn in Billy, especially after the Ridgewood incident on the first day of scrimmages. Soon, the coach and his knowledge of the game impressed the rogue young man, and, moreover, the ability of the coach's son caught Billy by surprise as well; he had never met a white kid with skills like Kevin. In fact, the more Billy learns of Kevin's impressive resume in Augusta, the more Billy wants to take him down. The difference is—unlike in his early days on the team—Billy wants to take Kevin down but in a friendly way, out of respect—rivalry among teammates. The animosity Billy once harbored toward the white coach and his son has waned over the weeks. Billy—if his pride would allow it—would be the first to admit the coach's son has pushed him to be better, and, as a result, the two players have formed a tandem no other team has been able to solve—not even close.

The greatest challenge for Roger has been keeping Billy on the court from the standpoint of good sportsmanship. The athleticism and aggressiveness with which the young man plays are unprecedented as far as Roger is concerned. Roger Stevens has seen innumerable players over many years while coaching and even playing the game himself as a young man. Still, Roger has never seen a specimen like Billy Taylor. Opponents have seemed scared to stand up to him, and, if they do, he destroys them. There has been no match for the muscular, 6'4" athlete. He is faster, quicker, stronger and more explosive than anyone the team has faced.

Case in point was the fifth game of the season. Billy scored inside. Billy scored outside. Billy hauled down one-handed rebounds. Billy blocked multiple shots. Billy showed-off a fade-away jumper. Billy went around the back with the dribble in traffic a couple of times. More than once, Billy Taylor has looked like the best player on the South roster, which includes Kevin Stevens, reigning Mr. Basketball in the State of Georgia.

According to Roger's understanding of different players, Billy's problem is not his ability. Billy's problem is keeping an unpredictable surge of frustration and hostility under control. In five games, Billy has picked up three technical fouls. Roger sat him down for nearly the entire second half of the fourth game, another blowout win. The man hoped his tough stance would positively impact the kid, but Roger has realized the rage with which Billy plays did not germinate overnight; thus, it will not recede overnight—this project will take time. Roger has often wondered if Billy plays basketball as an excuse to dominate and humiliate people physically. It seems to be an outlet of fury for the young man. Still, Roger must conclude, having Billy Taylor on the team—despite his baggage—is better than playing against Billy Taylor.

Overall, Roger has watched his entire team flourish, and, truthfully, the coach must admit he had no idea his team could be this good.

"This might be the best team I've ever had," he told his wife privately. Karen might not be the foremost authority on the game of basketball, but given the fact she has seen every team her husband has coached, she knows such a statement on his part to be significant. In addition, Karen has discerned an unexpected level of joy about her husband while coaching at Macon South.

Roger often taught students in his Sunday school class the axiom, *Either God is God, or He isn't.* As the man is faced with practicing what he preaches, could it be God knew how talented this Macon South team would be? Could it be God knew the team just needed a leader to pave the way to their greatness? Thus, if Roger had said *no* and resisted the move to Macon South, would Roger have missed the opportunity to coach his best team yet? Of all the teams, of all the city and State titles, would Roger have forfeited coaching his best team of all?

The man would admit it has been a struggle. It has been a challenge, yes. It has been increasingly difficult and almost unbearable at times. Even so, Roger has sensed satisfaction. He has experienced the temporary fulfillment of peace; not only from the success on the court but from new relationships. He is getting to know the players, getting to know their parents, and getting to know the South teachers and the staff and Charles Bullock. As surreal as it may seem to him, Roger has difficulty remembering what life was like before Macon, Georgia.

Amid a time in his life of uncertainty and vacillating emotions, here is what the veteran coach knows: as of mid-December, Roger and the Macon South Muskrats are 5-0, and none of the games have been close. Only one game remains before Christmas break.

26

"Billy," Coach Stevens summons the young man as they step off the team bus following practice, "The school office said your grandmother called. She needs me to give you a ride home today."

Nine times out of ten, Kevin would ride home from practice with his father. However, Karen swung by and grabbed Kevin as soon as the team arrived back at the school. She needed the extra muscle for a few errands, which leaves just Coach Stevens and Billy on this rare occasion. Given the tumultuous start to their relationship (Billy knocking Kevin to the ground and Roger throwing Billy out of practice), neither the white coach nor the young black man could have guessed they would be sharing a car ride only months later. Roger must admit, he certainly did not.

The first portion of the ten-minute drive is mostly silent. Roger has hoped desperately for a chance to bond with Billy off the court, the man desiring to build a bride. Finally, the opportunity is here, and the man is at a loss for words.

Billy quietly looks through the passenger window.

"Are you excited for Christmas," Roger inquires, hoping Billy will jump all over that question.

"Christmas is all right," Billy answers uneventfully. "It's better when you're a kid. My grandmother still gets into it."

"Your grandmother is a good woman," Roger shares while searching for common ground.

"Yeah, she is," the teen must confess. "Still tough, though. So, don't let her fool you."

Roger snickers. "That's how you know she loves you.'

"I guess. Take a right here, coach."

Roger ruminates behind the wheel, wondering if he should delve into a deep conversation or keep things harmlessly on the surface. "That's what I've learned, Billy. If someone cares for you, they will tell you when you're doing right…, and they'll tell you when you're doing wrong."

A complicated young man in Roger's opinion, there seems to be much to unpack with Billy Taylor, but given the limited information Betty shared with Roger, the man can understand why. He can understand how years of disappointments and hardships can add layers of hardened skin, causing a calloused heart. Tough times can make a person old before their time. However, Billy is still a teenager, and it saddens Roger to see the cruelty of life come to this youth.

"Make a left here, coach."

As the car turns into Billy's neighborhood, Roger Stevens takes a flier. "How's everything going, Billy? Anything new?"

The teen continues to look through the passenger window at the passing scenery. "Not much, Coach. Just playin' ball."

"Now you're speaking my language," the man responds with a smile. "I love this time of year. While everyone else is complaining about the weather and the cold and feeling miserable, I'm in heaven. There's always a warm gym somewhere."

Not one to give compliments freely, Billy expounds the coach's comment. "I can tell. You know everything there is to know about the game of basketball."

A great orator, Roger falls speechless; the man is completely taken back by Billy's glowing opinion of him. Roger always thought Billy was unconvinced of the man's wisdom, and Roger has categorized their relationship as improving yet still aloof, but for Billy to say what Billy just said....

"Thank you for your kind words, Billy," the man struggles to drive and offer the correct reply at the same time. "I have been blessed to coach for many years, many good players, many good teams, and I am thankful for the opportunity."

"How do we stack up, Coach? To the other teams you've coached?"

Billy's sudden loquacious and curious personality gets the better of Roger, catching him flat-footed. "You men are off to a great start, and you men have great potential as a team, and you have great potential as well, Billy."

Billy can live with that assessment; the confident teen knows he can ball.

Roger brings the car to a stop in front of an extremely modest house that cannot possibly have more than two bedrooms. The size of the home and square footage of the lot are comparable to the others in the neighborhood. At the sight of the humble property, Roger cannot help but think to himself, *some people work hard their whole lives and have so little.* Regardless of the humbleness of the abode, the man's heart is warmed by the modest Christmas wreath on the front door.

"Thanks for the ride, Coach," Billy spouts, promptly grabbing the handle and prying the passenger door ajar.

"Billy," Roger interjects, deciding to go for broke.

The young man stays put.

The coach swivels to face his player. "The truth is, Billy, I don't just think you can be a great player." Roger pauses, allowing transparency to win out. "I think you can be one of the best high school players I've ever seen, and that includes my son."

It is now Billy who is caught off guard. He does not know whether to listen or run; he has received such little praise throughout his young life, and certainly not from a man like this.

"But I would like to ask you a question," Roger continues. "I've noticed it's as if you are angry when you're on the court.

Don't get me wrong. I love the intensity. I am just curious what's going on in your mind when you play."

The seemingly impenetrable young man hesitates; he is not good in situations like this. It is much easier for Billy to go through life with a chip on his shoulder. People either stay away or they challenge him, and he always beats those who challenge him.

"I don't know, Coach. I guess I do play angry." The young man seems annoyed either by the question or by the thought of his answer. Even so, Billy's reply is candid. "I think when you've seen the stuff I've seen and gone through what I have, you might be angry, too."

Well said is Roger's assessment. "And you feel you bring those feelings on the court?"

"I don't know if I try to bring it with me or it just comes out of me." Billy quickly takes on an accelerated cadence. "When your mom dies when you're young, when she's young, and your dad bails and leaves town rather than stick it out with you, leaves town because he'd rather work for a white...." The young man's commentary ceases. Instead, Billy opts to turn and look through the passenger window again. "When you're black and living in Georgia...."

Roger sees the vein in the left temple of the young man starting to protrude. Billy's show of frustration takes Roger back to the rough teen the coach knew at the beginning—short-fused, quick-tempered. Roger begins to second-guess himself. Maybe he is pushing Billy too far with his line of questioning.

"Sorry, Billy. You don't have to answer me. I just want to understand where you're coming from."

The contemplative teenager continues to stare through the glass and through time. "When your dad chooses a white man's money over you, it can...it can make you feel not worth very much. So, I can be sad, or I can be mad. And since I'm not weak, I would rather be mad." The cadence picks up again. "Just like when those policemen started pushin' us around in

Ridgewood, tryin' to rough us up. We didn't do nothin', and they knew we didn't do nothin'. They were testin' us, pushin' us around." With those words, Billy turns his eyes back in the direction of his coach and answers the original question bluntly. "So, yeah. I do play angry…especially against white boys."

Roger realizes he has pushed the conversation to the edge. Softly, he tries to diffuse the suddenly volatile atmosphere. "I'm not going to keep you any longer, Billy. I know we both need to get going. I just want to throw something your way, something for you to consider."

The young man keeps his eyes locked on his coach.

"I'm not going to sit here and tell you I know how you feel…because I don't want to insult you."

Billy appreciates the comment by his coach, thinking, *there's no way you can know.*

"First, I want to encourage you to understand that not all white people are the same. And what I have learned is this: life doesn't discriminate. Life does all of us wrong. I know some seem to suffer more than others, but my point is it rains on the just and the unjust, and the sun shines on the just and the unjust. So, son: we might not have the power to change everything that has happened to us, but we have the power to move on and not be a slave to our past any longer."

Billy's eyes widen for a moment and then recede.

Roger's heart stops: he did not mean to use the word *slave.* *Why did I use that word?* He has said too much, and Roger attempts to save his explanation.

"What I'm saying, son, is we can all be slaves or prisoners to the past, no matter our color, and we all must think about letting go. I'm not saying it's easy, but I'm saying the freedom you will feel will be worth it. So, just think about it, okay?"

As Billy continues to peer at Roger, the coach does not know if he just led the young man closer to freedom or offended him beyond repair. Roger stops a huge gulp from passing through his throat.

After a prolonged silence, Billy speaks. "Sure, Coach. I'll think about it."

A great sense of relief washes over Roger's heart, hidden behind the man's firm eyes and resolute tone.

"But you don't want me gettin' soft, do you?"

Roger is confused and amused by the quick wit of the paradoxical teenager; the kid can go from fuming to fun on a dime. The coach smiles. "Billy, if you play angry, just don't be angry at me. Okay?"

Billy returns the smile. "Right on."

"See you tomorrow, son."

"See you, Coach."

Roger watches as the athletic teenager jogs through the yard to the front door, the sun setting behind the small home on this winter evening. Before entering the house, standing on the front porch, Billy pauses, turns, smiles and waves.

Roger waves back and speaks aloud to himself in the car. "God, I think I'm beginning to love these kids."

27

"Elvin! Phone!" A police officer calls across the Ridgewood station lobby, interrupting a conversation among other officers.

Elvin Butler leaves the group and picks up a nearby courtesy phone. "This is Officer Butler."

"It's time to follow up," instructs the man on the other end.

Elvin recognizes the voice and processes the directive. "Sure. Tonight?"

"Tonight." The voice is gone swiftly; the line is dead.

• • •

At 9:40 p.m., Billy is in his room doing pushups before bed. He has his window cracked the way he likes it, letting the southern winter air cool him down—an Otis Redding song playing on the radio.

Across the hall, his grandmother sleeps.

The knock at the front door of the home is demanding.

Billy opens his bedroom door and halts, listening.

Across the hall, Betty's door is shut, but her light flicks on under the crack of her door.

The knocking resumes, even bolder.

Billy checks the time as his grandmother emerges from her room; the elderly woman fidgets with her robe and straightens her glasses.

"Who could that…?" she incredulously inquires before her grandson quiets her, putting up his hand, signaling for them to listen.

This time, a daunting, authoritative voice accompanies the pounding on the front door. "Police! Open up!"

Billy and his grandmother look confoundedly at each other.

"Don't answer it, Grandma," Billy protests.

"What do they want?" The elderly woman walks to the front window, peering through a sliver of the curtain.

Two men in full uniform stand on her front porch. One officer sees the edge of the curtain move and responds by firmly pointing at the window, commanding, "Open the door!"

Billy's grandmother looks back at her grandson, unsure of what to do. "It's the police."

"No, Grandma."

"What do they want?"

"I don't know. Don't trust them," is Billy's instinctive response.

Impatience has the best of the lead officer now, and he removes his nightstick to bludgeon the door again, shaking the night. "In the name of the law, open this door!" He will not be denied.

Billy's grandmother fully pulls back the curtain to communicate with officers. "What's this about?"

"Open the door, and I'll tell you what it's about!"

"Don't do it, Grandma!"

"Billy, I have to. It's the law."

Billy presses his weight against the door from the inside. Betty tries to be diplomatic. "Stand back. I'll talk to them."

"No, Grandma!"

The pounding persists—more pronounced. The officers are not going away.

"Yes, Billy."

"No, Grandma. You don't know what they...."

"I said stand back!"

Ultimately, the age and adamant tone of the grandmother subdue her grandson, and Billy with extreme reluctance retreats from the front door to the middle of the room.

Another round of pounding startles the woman. "This is the last time, and I'm not going to say it again! Open this door!"

Billy's grandmother gingerly unbolts the top lock before turning the doorknob.

Shocked, Billy watches as the officer who put him in cuffs in Ridgewood comes into view, and their eyes begin to wrestle.

Elvin Butler glares from under the brim of his department-issued hat, locking in and identifying the familiar young black before him.

Anger washes over Billy at the sight of the officer, and Billy cannot help but clench his fists at his sides.

"Remember me, boy?"

Billy keeps his mouth shut.

Stunned, Betty pleads, "What's this all about?"

"You! Stay back," the officer in the doorway decrees with no regard for the woman's concern or age. "We have some follow-up questions for this suspect."

"Suspect?" Betty debates.

"What are you talkin' about?" Billy holds his tongue no longer.

"I'm talking about follow-up questions...and don't talk back to me. Just obey," instructs the policeman while pointing fiercely.

The confounded countenance of the grandmother shifts back and forth between the officer and Billy as she clutches her robe from fright.

"That's crazy," Billy refuses to back down. "That was weeks ago. What are you trying to do?"

"Yes. This isn't right," Betty interjects.

"Lady, we need to speak with him," the lead officer addresses her directly, "and this doesn't concern you."

"Of course, it concerns me. This is my home!"

The second officer grows tired of the futile exchange between Elvin Butler and the elderly woman. "What he's saying is we need to speak to Billy on the front porch, right now!"

Billy freezes—they know his name. The defiant teen shakes his head, realizing the officers have never set foot in the house. *They can't*, he considers. Billy knows he is safe right where he is.

Officer Butler is only further enraged at the noncompliance. "Get out here, now."

Billy holds firm.

"Don't make me pull you out here...because I will."

Emboldened, the youth responds, "You can't! You can't come in here!"

"Boy, I will come in there and drag you out onto this front...."

"No, you won't!"

The two froth and volley as their voices escalate. Hostility is palpable in the room. Finished arguing, Officer Butler snaps, reaching just inside the door and clamping down on Betty's wrist, digging in his fingernails, causing the grandmother to shriek. "Come here!" the furious officer grunts at Betty through gritted teeth.

"No," Billy roars at the sight of the policeman putting hands on his grandmother, watching as Elvin Butler violently pulls her toward the door, causing her frail body to lurch.

"Stop!" the woman screams.

The athletic young man lunges across the room, spanning the distance in an instant, now latching on to the arm of the officer.

Elvin Butler is shocked by the teeth of the young man's grip as the two come face to face, eye to eye.

"Hey!" the other officer yells, stepping into the fray.

The four bodies converge in a tight space in the doorway.

"Billy!" his grandmother yells. "Get back! Get back!"

"Too late," Officer Butler declares as he releases his grip on the woman and clamps both hands on Billy's protruding right forearm, wrangling him toward the front porch.

The screams of the woman drown the ears of her grandson.

This time, it is Billy who snaps. The fury with which he shoves the officer catches the man off guard and sends all three males through the front door. Billy lifts Elvin Butler from the ground, the force ripping the screen door from the hinges, the wreckage falling limply to the porch boards.

"Jail time, boy!" the other officer yells while grabbing Billy by the neck.

"Get off me!" Billy's yell is muffled.

Elvin Butler regains his footing and goes back after the muscular teenager. The policemen and the enraged youth spar in the night, and if not for the odds against him, Billy would have run Elvin Butler straight over the railing and into the thorn-riddled bushes below.

The second officer gains position and thrusts his nightstick under Billy's chin and across his throat, pulling back.

"Ahhh," Billy screams in rage.

Betty's knees give out as she falls into the doorway, her crumpled body half in and half out of the home. "Help!" she calls for anyone to hear. "Help us!"

As Billy gets brought around, he sees his grandmother on the ground, crying, futilely reaching for him with a weathered hand.

As the officers and Billy spin as a group, Elvin Butler is annoyed by the woman's wailing. With Billy watching, the policeman kicks at the grandmother's extended hand, Butler grunting a profane word at her.

Another surge wells within Billy as the athletic teen with bloodshot eyes bucks and pulls both officers further onto the porch with him.

Laying against the doorframe, Betty watches powerlessly as the policemen ultimately gain leverage, sending Billy down the front steps end over end. Both officers descend the steps and soon stand over Billy's body. Brandishing nightsticks, both men begin to beat the defenseless teen as he fights for his life on the ground.

Billy yells in pain from a direct hit between the shoulder blades…and another…and another…without mercy.

"Billy!" his grandmother cries his name. The woman witnesses the flailing arms and legs of her grandson in futile self-defense. Billy lays on his back while kicking and swinging to try and block the blows from above.

Five, six, seven times—the clubs connect again and again.

Billy rolls over to cover his face from the barrage.

The voice of the woman coupled with the sounds of violence have roused the neighbors.

Even so, any help is too late. The final blow from Elvin Butler catches Billy across the skull, filling the night with an unmistakable sound of wood on bone.

"Hold on, hold on." The second officer puts out his hand. Both men look down and watch Billy's eyes roll back then jolt into a blank stare, the rest of Billy's body waning limp, his once swinging arms falling to his side.

"No, Billy!" the woman sobs as she begins to crawl across the porch.

Out of breath from a flurry of strikes to the young man's torso, the officers stand back to gather themselves, observing the elderly woman pitifully crawling down the steps on her hands and knees to drape herself across the body of her grandson.

"No more," Betty's voice quivers, her words emerging through her tears. "No more. No more. No more."

By now, curious eyes and feet move in the direction of Betty's home from the surrounding houses.

Unsympathetic, Officer Butler admonishes the woman while standing over her. "You better shut up."

His threats fall short as Betty laments, her voice muffled with her face in Billy's chest, tears drenching her grandson's shirt. "No more. No more" is her hollow cry.

As alarmed neighbors gather, the second officer steps to the front of the crowd to stunt their progress. Elvin Butler opens the squad car door to radio for back up. More shouting ascends into the night air. The officers keep one hand on their revolvers to send a message.

"Get that dog out of here!" yells Elvin Butler at the sight of a pit bull on a chain.

Eventually, more police arrive, and the officers load Billy's limp body into the back of one of the vehicles.

The officers leave Betty to be comforted by a neighbor woman; the scratch on the elderly woman's forehead is noticeable.

The police cars—to the background of more shouting—ultimately exit the neighborhood and drive into the darkness.

• • •

The piercing ring of the telephone jostles Roger, and he struggles for his bearings in the night. Snaring the receiver to his ear, he hears the voice of Principal Bullock.

Roused from her sleep as well, Karen listens attentively and hears only her husband's end of the conversation. "What? I just saw Billy after practice, gave him a ride home…. The hospital!"

Karen gasps as Roger's voice crescendos.

"Is he going to be okay?" Dissatisfied with the lack of information, Roger ends the discussion with, "I'll meet you there."

"What is it, Roger? What about Billy?"

After flipping the light switch, the man fumbles about the bedroom. "The police, Karen. The police were at Billy's home tonight."

"The police? Why?"

• • •

As Roger enters the emergency room, he sees Charles Bullock.

Roger's first words are, "How is he?"

The principal takes Roger by the arm and leads him a few steps away from Billy's grandmother and those neighbors who console her in the waiting room.

"The police came to Betty's house, and things got out of hand."

"What do you mean, out of hand? Why were they there in the first place?" Roger does a poor job of controlling his tone.

Charles Bullock squeezes his arm. "His grandmother said there was pounding at the door after she'd gone to bed, and it was the police. They wanted in."

"Why would they need to come in?"

Principal Bullock sighs to keep Roger and himself calm. "Follow-up questions...."

"Follow-up questions?"

"Follow-up questions based on that afternoon in Ridgewood months ago."

"What about it?"

"I don't know, Roger, but we are going to get to the bottom of this, I assure you."

"Is Billy okay?"

The Principal struggles to keep up with Roger's questions.

"Is Billy okay?" Roger persists.

Charles Bullock leans forward to whisper in the man's ear. "It's bad, Roger. It's terrible."

"What do you mean, terrible?" None of the answers given are satisfactory to Roger, and the answers cannot come fast enough.

"They hit him with clubs. Some neighbors ran to help, but by that time Billy was on the ground. He wasn't moving."

Roger is numb at the words. The man can hardly bring himself to ask the question, but he must.

"Is Billy going to die, Charles?"

Principal Bullock doesn't respond.

"Answer me, Charles."

"He's not dead, but he's not conscious either."

As the coach and principal speak, Roger looks over the man's shoulder and sees Billy's grandmother; the woman is beside herself, stewing in misery and sorrow. Roger leaves the principal to kneel before her. Roger takes her hands in his.

Lifting her weathered face, her eyes moist and weary, Betty whimpers a prolonged, hollowed exhale. "Oh, Mr. Stevens."

"Roger, ma'am. Call me Roger, and I'm here. I'm here."

"It was awful," Betty recalls through another sigh. "Awful. Those policemen, they just...just...just grabbed him and hit him and...." Her breath becomes choppy at her memory of the attack. "And beat him while he was down... and beat him and beat him." More sobbing overtakes the grandmother.

Roger gently rubs the woman's hands; he cannot stand it. He does not know what else to do. The only action he can take feels like inaction. Even so, it is the only action he has in reserve. "Pray with me, ma'am. We must pray for Billy."

Betty nods. She knows prayer is all they can do.

As Roger and the woman bow their heads, the neighbors pull close and encircle the two, including Principal Bullock who now stands in solidarity, placing a hand on both of their shoulders.

• • •

Ten minutes later, the attending nurse escorts Roger Stevens to a holding cubicle in the emergency room. As she reaches for the curtain, a white woman, she first turns briefly toward Roger, attempting to brace him for what he is about to see.

Billy is unrecognizable. His face is bloated, and a bandage wrapped completely around his head amplifies the severe swelling. His forehead and right side of his face are both badly bruised. There is a bandage on his lower lip to cover a serious cut. His head hangs to the left. His large, athletic frame is anything but right now. Billy simply lays supinely and motionless, confined to a standard-issue hospital bed.

Roger swallows the giant knot in his throat. His eyes moisten involuntarily. He vacillates between sadness and rage as he stares helplessly at the young man. The coach quietly shuffles to the right side of the bed. There he stands, not sure what to do. Before speaking or touching the stricken teen, Roger scans the critical patient from head to toe.

"Oh, Billy," is all the grown man can muster through a feeble whisper, next placing the soft palm of his hand on top of the blanket where Billy's hand might be. "Oh, Billy…. I'm so sorry." Roger raises his free hand to cover his own eyes. Other than the hissing of Billy's oxygen tank, silence permeates the room. *I don't believe this*, Roger thinks incredulously. *I do not believe this. Why God? Why?*

There is no response to the man's query. Instead, his silent thoughts are met with more silence.

Roger uncovers his eyes and looks down at Billy again. At this moment, the man could not care less about the teenager's ability as a small forward or his grace and power on the basketball court. Instead, Roger just wants to see Billy open his eyes, grasp his hand and say something, anything. What Roger would give in exchange for such conversation right now!

It is unfathomable to Roger. The two were sitting and talking in his car earlier today. From then to now, from there to here seems impossible. *Why God? Why?*

"Billy," the coach breathes. Roger labors for what to say. Instead of searching for the right words, he speaks the first words that flow from his heart. "I love you, son. I love you." Roger stands at the bedside of his player for the next several minutes, his hand resting on the teen's still body, the man whispering fervently in prayer, pleading with God for Billy's life.

● ● ●

Roger exits the holding room and paces slowly back toward the waiting area.

Principal Bullock sees him emerge and discerns his sadness.

Roger sees the principal, and, out of the corner of his eye, he sees someone else. The coach swivels his head, looking left.

Roger halts and his eyes lock on three men standing near a side entrance for hospital personnel.

There, conversing with the ER physician on duty, are two policemen, and Roger immediately recognizes one of them from the incident that fateful afternoon in Ridgewood.

The eyes of Officer Elvin Butler lift from a cup of coffee as he recognizes Roger Stevens as well.

Roger squints hard without relenting.

The officer quickly interprets the stare down in the same way he understands all stare downs: disrespectful, especially coming from this man.

Roger does not know which officers were at Billy's home earlier tonight, but he can venture a guess: *him. It's got to be him.* The hyper-emotional coach turns his entire body toward the officer and—without realizing it—begins moving in his direction.

Principal Bullock senses conflict, although he is not exactly sure what is happening.

Undaunted, Butler stands tall, peeling back his shoulders at the sight of the oncoming man.

Roger senses no remorse from the officer, no regret. The officer's body language screams to Roger: *I did it, and I'm proud of it.* Images of Billy flash through Roger's mind—the boy lying in a hospital bed, the bandages, his motionless body, and his weeping grandmother. *This man doesn't feel guilty about what's happened?*

The second officer detects Roger approaching as well.

The doctor steps back.

The second officer steps in.

Roger and Butler keep their eyes locked as Roger closes the distance, and Roger is first to speak.

"Were you at their home tonight?"

"Whose home?"

"I asked you a question! Answer me!"

"You don't talk to me that way!"

Principal Bullock accelerates towards the scene and gently corrals his basketball coach by the shoulders. The placating words of the principal are gibberish to Roger. He tunes them out, and he is not going anywhere.

Elvin Butler begins to step around his partner and advance toward Roger. "You don't get to ask me anything. You understand me?"

"Elvin," his partner utters, trying to defuse the palpable volatility.

"You had no business being there," Roger barks over the shoulder of Principal Bullock. The coach is weary of decorum.

"Roger don't do this," advises Charles Bullock.

"You want to go downtown and discuss it?" shouts Officer Butler.

"Let's talk about it right here!" Roger retorts.

"You must calm down, Roger," Principal Bullock repeats.

The tension has spilled over and grabs the attention of everyone in the waiting area.

Betty wearily glances up to see the men verbally sparring.

"This doesn't help anyone, Roger." The Principal draws as close as he can to the ear of his basketball coach to deliver a firm whisper. "This doesn't help Billy."

With those words, Roger's aggression ceases. As he attempts to regain his composure, the Head Coach of Macon South High School, a public figure at all times whether or not he wants to be, glances back over his shoulder and sees a gaggle of onlookers. He also sees the still moistened eyes of Billy's grandmother. The last thing he wants to do is burden the poor woman any further.

The pacifying words of Principal Bullock begin to bear fruit, and with each passing moment, Roger's pulse decelerates.

Officer Elvin Butler, on the other hand, still appears ready to have it out right in the middle of the hospital waiting area, witnesses and all.

Roger reverses and allows Principal Bullock to steer them back toward Billy's grandmother and the rest of the group. "I'm sorry," Roger acknowledges to his supervisor, realizing how obstinate and disobedient he has been in a fit of rage.

"I'm sorry, sir. I'm sorry, ma'am. I'm sorry, everyone," he offers to Billy's grandmother and the rest of the group, tears now coming to Roger's eyes.

The group from the Macon South community collectively receive and embrace the man back into their fold.

Several feet away, Elvin Butler is less than willing to call a truce.

"Come on, Elvin. It's over," his partner pleads.

Butler is slow to respond, staring at Roger across the waiting area, watching as the man surrounds himself with blacks from the south side.

A squawking police radio grabs Butler's attention. Seconds later, he and his partner exit the hospital.

28

Friday, December 20
Game Six
Macon South vs. Pattonville
Record: 5-0

The ambiance in the pre-game locker room is predictably somber; Roger rehearsed and rehearsed a positive spin, but he can find no such words. Billy's absence is tangible. When he is here, Billy undoubtedly exudes a commanding presence, and the rest of the team strides behind his broad shoulders—even Kevin. Even Kevin, the coach's son, the team's starting point guard, the reigning Georgia State Player of the Year has relished Billy's role on the team. Sure, Roger and Kevin know Billy has been a handful at times, but those troubles are distant memories, and the coach and son would give anything to have Billy back. Now, in the light of Billy's absence, all the burden shifts speedily back to Kevin Stevens.

The Macon South coach steps into the midst of his players as usual. "It's time, men. Let's do what we have to do." He extends his bottom hand into the middle of the group. His players follow his lead; although, doing so with less exuberance than usual. "South on three: one...two...three: South!!!"

• • •

The hesitant energy conveyed by the Muskrats before the game immediately translates to the court. Tyler is not himself. Leonard has misplaced his rough-and-tumble persona in the paint, and Dwayne looks lost in general. If not for Kevin, the game versus Pattonville could easily be a double-digit deficit for South. Instead, the game is tied halfway through the second quarter: 19-19.

Kevin has disappointed no one by scoring fifteen points in the first twelve minutes of action. Everything is clicking for the coach's son tonight, which has been a huge blessing to his father; Roger does not feel altogether present either—Billy's condition has been on the man's mind incessantly.

Pattonville has no answer for the South point guard. Kevin hit five outside jump shots on five consecutive trips downcourt. Aside from Kevin's prowess, his teammates continue to struggle. When the Pattonville big men have rotated to defend Kevin's penetration, the savvy point guard has dropped multiple deliveries in the laps of Tyler and Leonard. However, again, both South post players have been off; Tyler fumbled a pass out of bounds that hit him softly in the hands with no one anywhere near him, and, likewise, Leonard blew an assist for Kevin by missing a point-blank zero-footer with no one else in the lane. Even so, Kevin has stuck with it, allowing his dogged persistence to avail; no doubt from the DNA of his father.

"Ninety-nine," Roger calls the play from the bench as Kevin dribbles across half court.

"Ninety-nine," the Coach's son echoes.

If Tyler and Leonard aren't scoring tonight, Roger thinks to himself, *Then let's put them to good use elsewhere.*

At the sound of *ninety-nine*, Tyler and Leonard simultaneously run to the top of the key, providing Kevin with a double screen, giving the ballhandler the option to go in either direction. Roger dialed up this play not so much because his son needs a screen to beat his man; much to the contrary—Kevin has successfully beat his man off the dribble all night. Instead, the coach wants to pull the Pattonville big men out of the paint, giving his son less congestion when he arrives at the basket.

With Tyler and Leonard giving their teammate two options, Kevin chooses to set his man up to the right before rubbing off Tyler's screen to his left.

The opposing point guard becomes easily lost in the wall of bodies and can only call for help once losing Kevin altogether.

As Kevin drives with his left hand down the left side of the lane, the Pattonville defender on the left wing tries to close the gap. The defensive rotation is close but too late, and Kevin goes airborne, putting up a soft floater.

Roger watches the play unfold from the bench.

Kevin's eyes are on the basketball as it glides toward the backboard and not on the protruding foot of the defender, and Kevin takes his landing for granted, doing so on the outer edge of the opponent's sneaker.

The first sensation is not one of pain, but of overextension, one of elasticity as Kevin's left shoe plants awkwardly then bounces back. Next comes the pain as the rest of Kevin's weight thrusts downward, his left foot buckling.

Roger sees the landing in real time. Kevin's left foot gave out, and Roger watches the body of his son plummet to the hardwood in a heap.

A shooting, burning sensation scalds Kevin's left ankle as he immediately recoils his foot, pulling his left knee into his chest while flat on his back, clutching at the injury.

The whistle blows. Play stops and for the Macon South players, coaches and fans time stops as well. Kevin's teammates quickly come to his aid, surrounding their wounded brother.

Never one to exaggerate or show unnecessary emotion, Kevin holds back any initial sounds. However, the severity of his anguish becomes evident as Kevin can no longer contain a lamentable shout from filling the gymnasium.

From the stands, Karen Stevens stands to her feet.

From the bench, Roger Stevens stands to his feet. As he would for any of his players, he begins the long trip across the court to survey the damage firsthand. As he walks, behind his stone façade is befuddled contemplation. *This can't be happening. Billy's out and now Kevin is hurt.* The man attempts to keep coaching in his mind, but he cannot concentrate over the torturous howl discharging from Kevin's lungs. Roger's heart sinks in his chest.

Coach Stevens calmly pushes his way through the bodies surrounding his son before kneeling at his side. "Kev? Kevin? You with me buddy? You okay?" he queries, placing a supportive hand on the teen's ribcage, moving his hand each time Kevin rolls from side to side.

The star player only responds with more wailing.

Karen and the entire contingent from South observe with bated breath from a distance; a woman nearby places a tender hand on the mother's shoulder as they watch.

"Is it your ankle, son? Your knee?"

Kevin manages to answer. "Ankle."

"Do you think you rolled it? You didn't hear a pop, did you?"

Kevin does not answer this time.

"Can you walk, son?" the official inquires. The ref does not mean to be insensitive; however, the game must go on.

Kevin's hesitation tells his father all the man needs to know, and Roger discerns it is not worth the risk of further damage.

"Don't try it, son. We'll help you." Roger gives a glance and he and the South big men all take hold of Kevin to help him to his feet.

The grimace on the young man's face is revelatory. His brow is rumpled. He grits his teeth, and pain is written all over his face. Kevin hisses as he tries to keep his balance and not put any weight on his left foot.

Tyler and Leonard each swoop under an arm to relieve the pressure of gravity.

"Let them help you, Kev," Roger instructs. "Thank you, men. Easy. Easy."

Eventual applause replaces the silence inside the gymnasium. South fans lead the way; though, some courteous Pattonville fans join as well; not everyone claps—some sneer.

Tyler and Leonard provide much-needed strength. The South bench parts to allow ample room for their injured teammate.

"We need your sub, Coach," the official instructs.

As much as the father wants to attend to his son, he must leave him in the hands of his assistant coach as Roger motions for Jeremiah Jenkins to replace Kevin. Furthermore, if the man thought his team looked out of sorts in the absence of Billy, add the loss of Kevin and the fearful countenances abound on the bench. Roger slaps his hands together in frustration. "Come on, men! Get locked in! Let's go!"

Subbing at the free throw line for Kevin, Dwayne toes the stripe and quickly feels the pressure, lofting a knuckleball that almost misses the rim entirely. Hearing it from the Pattonville crowd, Dwayne's second offering misses just as badly to the opposite side, allowing the opposing team to snare the rebound.

"Get back!" bellows Coach Stevens, sneaking an attempted-inconspicuous peak down the bench to see how his son is doing; the boy's face is still a portrait of anguish. Meanwhile, Pattonville runs a set play with numerous screens, losing Tyler in the fray as his Pattonville counterpart gets off a clean shot. Adding insult to injury, embarrassed and overzealous, Tyler foolishly swipes at the ball from behind and manages to strike the opponent across the shoulder, permitting the nearest official to call the foul and send the Pattonville player to the line for a potential three-point play. Even worse, Tyler picks up his third foul of the first half.

"Oh, Tyler!" Coach Stevens froths, releasing steam at the poor exhibition of defense. Immediately, the man signals down the suddenly thin bench for another replacement.

"Come on, Tyler," the coach gives the player an earful as he passes by, following his lumbering 6'6" frame down the bench. "Use your head. Kevin's out, and now you go and pick up a silly foul."

It is obvious Tyler knows he is fully in the wrong, the beleaguered teen hanging his head low.

Roger is emotional, and the man knows it. He wants to take out his frustration on someone, and part of him wants Tyler to backtalk to give the man the green light to unload. Instead, with his wife watching, Roger thinks better and turns to walk back to the lead spot on the bench. From there, the frustrated coach watches Pattonville score the final ten points of the half with little resistance from his squad. The truth is glaring. With Billy, Kevin, and now Tyler off the floor, Macon South is a vastly different team with no room for error.

• • •

Unfortunately for Roger and his team, the end of the first half was a harbinger of things to come in the second half. Macon South was unable to establish any semblance of flow during the third and fourth quarters, and Pattonville, conversely, was advantageous. Roger cannot remember the last time his team was out of a game by the start of the fourth quarter, and, after a while, the man relented barking any orders whatsoever. The veteran coach knew it was not going to happen on this night, and the Pattonville faithful relished that fact. Tonight's game had been billed as undefeated Macon South travelling to play a slightly above average Pattonville team. However, the final score proved to be far different than anyone anticipated: Pattonville 55, Macon South 34.

As Roger Stevens exits the court after shaking hands with his counterpart, he realizes this is his worst loss as head coach in the past eight years.

• • •

There are many things on Roger's mind now: Billy's critical health, Kevin's injury, the response—or lack thereof—of his team to adversity. It is difficult for the man to comprehend: just yesterday he was sitting in his car and talking with Billy; the two had their best conversation to date. As of today, Billy's in the hospital, clinging to life, and Kevin's undoubtedly set to see a doctor about his ankle which blew up like a basketball once they removed his sneaker. Add the fact the rest of the team looks completely lost without its two best players, and what was once a promising season for Macon South has taken a drastically pessimistic turn. With Christmas a few days away, Roger cannot help but feel less cheerful this year.

29

Roger always felt badly for hospital patients during the holiday season. It is Christmas Eve, and all is quiet throughout the facility as Roger pushes open the door to Billy's room. Betty sits in a chair near the window, sleeping, her hand propping up her chin. Looking to his left in the hospital bed, Billy is awake but laying silently. Roger waits for Billy to acknowledge him with permission to enter, but Billy never does.

The sound of shuffling feet wakes Betty. The elderly woman slides down her glasses from the top of her head and recognizes the man before her. "Oh, hello, Mr. Stevens."

"Don't get up, ma'am, please," Roger insists at the sight of the woman laboring to stand.

"No, that's okay," Betty replies. "It just takes me more than once to do it these days, that's all."

"Then let me help you," Roger lends a hand. "You look good. Are you getting rest?"

"Oh, you know; spend a whole lotta' time praying. Praying for this one," the grandmother motions toward her grandson in the hospital bed.

Roger turns to look at Billy as well. "How's he doing?" he whispers.

"I think he's getting better, but I'm just glad he's alive."

"Amen," Roger responds. "And you? Are you healed and well?"

"Oh, don't worry about me. At this point, I just add any bruises to the ones I already have."

Roger smiles. Betty's soft heart despite a harsh life has always fascinated the man.

"I'm gonna' let you two be while I step down the hall for a few minutes."

"Yes, ma'am," Roger obliges.

"Billy, I'll be back in a little while. You talk to coach, okay?"

Billy gives a slight nod but speaks no words.

Roger moves to Billy's bedside. "Hey, my man," he offers in an encouraging tone.

"Hi, coach." The response from the teen is brief.

Trying not to stare, Roger runs quick inventory of Billy from head to toe. The young man is debilitated, yes. Still, compared to nearly dying, Billy is improving. "Just came by to see how you're doing. Do you mind if I sit?"

Billy gives the impression he does not want to talk much, but, because it is Coach Stevens, the teen acquiesces.

Roger pulls up a chair. He notices the swelling in Billy's face has decreased significantly. The man knows the best thing Billy has going for him is his youth. A young body heals faster than an older one. Still, it has been gut-wrenching to watch such a strong, able-bodied young man laid up in a hospital bed like Billy Taylor has been. "Ready to get out of here, I imagine?"

Billy stares past Roger and out of the window—an aura of numbness about the teenager.

"I'm ready for you to get out, I know that," Roger adds. "It will be great to see you back in school again."

No response is given.

"That's the plan, right?" the coach inquires, jovial yet subdued. "We have to get you graduated."

Nothing the coach says has much effect on the motionless teen. The place where Billy is staring is not one of hope or optimism.

Roger leans into Billy's line of sight, the coach's tone growing serious. "What can I do, Billy." Roger does not want to overdo it, yet he wants to see Billy Taylor out of this bed and out of this hospital. "If it's possible for me to do, I'll do it."

"Tell me how." Billy's succinct statement surprises his coach.

"What's that, Billy?" Roger inquires.

"Tell me how this will ever change. Tell me how I will ever be more than just a black man."

The question saddens the coach and causes him to think. Only Roger knows it, but the man is praying fervently inside for the right answers to Billy's questions. "Why be anyone different than who you are, Billy? If God created you to be black...then be black. Be who God created you to be?"

Though genuine, Roger's words fail to win over the bed-stricken victim. The man continues. "God loves the way you are, Billy. That's not a consolation prize, either, son. God created you to be who you are, and God loves you the way He created you, and so do I. I can't imagine you any other way."

"It doesn't matter if God...." Billy's body shifts for the first time since Roger has seen Billy in the hospital. However, the teenager does so out of frustration, and Roger does not want anger the young man.

The room falls silent.

"I don't want to upset you, Billy. I feel like I am making you angry. All I want you to know is I love you, son, and I want you to get out of this bed and hospital and go live the life God has for you."

This time, Billy closes his eyes to shut off the conversation.

Roger takes the hint. The coach stands to his feet and pauses to see if Billy has anything left to say; Billy does not. "Like I said, I love you, son, and I'll be back to see you again if okay with you."

No response is given.

Roger begins his walk to the door.

"Nothin' on this earth can undo what's been done," Billy states, causing Roger to halt. "Nothin' on this earth…. It's bigger than all of us."

Roger stands in amazement, knowing the young man just hit the entire issue on the head. "You are absolutely correct, Billy. The only answer to this problem must come from above."

Waiting but hearing nothing more, Roger ultimately moves to the door. He stops one final time as the man cannot keep himself from saying the words, "Merry Christmas, Billy."

• • •

Christmas morning brings sunshine and so does the optimism of Rufus, the driver of the Muskrat team bus. "Merry Christmas, Coach Stevens and Mrs. Stevens."

"Merry Christmas, Rufus," Karen replies in kind as she climbs the short flight of steps, clutching her coat to her body in the chilly December air. "You're a sweetheart for doing this."

"Rufus," Roger pauses to lock eyes with the man behind the wheel, "I cannot thank you enough for giving up your Christmas morning. God bless you, sir."

"I think it's a great idea, Coach, and I'm glad to be part. Where to first?"

Roger checks his chart. "Let's get Reggie first, please."

• • •

The young men on the team were all ready and waiting, impressing their coaches. Roger was equally impressed by the cooperation of all the parents and guardians. Every family connected to the South basketball team allowed themselves to be inconvenienced this morning, all of them realizing their inconvenience does not compare to being hospitalized on Christmas Day.

The hospital is lighter and more festive today. Roger hears Andy Williams playing on the radio at the nurses' station as the team walks the hallway.

The Head Coach enters the room first and finds Betty faithfully by Billy's side; the grandmother and grandson have been up talking.

"Mr. Stevens?" Betty is perplexed at the sight of the man. "On Christmas morning? What are you doing, sir?"

"Merry Christmas," the man salutes the elderly woman with a hug.

Betty focuses her eyes over the man's shoulder. "Oh, Mrs. Stevens."

"Merry Christmas, Betty." Karen presents the elderly woman a bouquet of flowers, the two embracing as well.

"Merry Christmas, Billy," Roger moves to the side of the bed.

The young man's eyes are open much wider today. "Coach, what are you doing here?"

"It's not just me, Billy. I found some guys along the way. You might know them."

The surprised countenance of the patient blossoms further as several more visitors enter the room—his teammates.

"Billy.... Hey, Billy.... Good morning, Billy.... Merry Christmas, Billy." The greetings roll out one after another.

Betty and Billy are stunned by the influx of loving faces as each young man makes a point to not only greet Billy with a handshake but hug his grandmother as well. The elderly woman cannot hold back tears of joy and relief, knowing it can get lonely in a hospital room day after day.

After Dwayne, Jeremiah, Kevin, Leonard, Tyler and the entire team stride to and from Billy's bedside, the young man notices an additional face across the room.

The players part and allow room for Rufus to say a few words. "Merry Christmas, my man," Rufus shares while touching Billy's hand. "I hope you get up real soon."

Billy displays the kindest expression Rufus has ever seen from the normally tough kid. "Thanks, man. Merry Christmas, Rufus."

"We brought you something," Dwayne steps forward, plopping a basketball in Billy's lap.

Billy smiles yet demonstrates a look as if to say, *What am I supposed to do with this thing?*

"We all signed it," Dwayne adds.

Billy sees what Dwayne is talking about, the signatures of his teammates scrawled across the smooth surface of the ball.

"Here," Leonard offers a marker to his teammate in bed. "You sign it, too."

Billy appreciates the gesture but lifts his right hand to show the team his cumbersome, plaster cast.

"Oh," Leonard retracts. "Sorry about that, man.... Just... sign it later...when you feel up to it."

"I will."

Following an hour-long visit from his coaches and teammates on Christmas morning, Billy exhibits a smile as they filter out of the room one by one.

Betty was equally moved by the gesture. "Well, wasn't that something?" she exhales while sitting in her chair.

"Yes," Billy agrees. "That was cool." The young man looks at the ball in his lap and all the signatures, snickering at bad penmanship by some of the guys. Billy wishes he could sign the ball as well. Instead, the star player secures the basketball in the palm of his free hand, his left hand, and begins to work on his release and follow-through.

30

January 1969
Games 7-10
Record 5-1

The doctor's visit regarding Kevin's ankle could have been worse and could have been better. The sprain was severe. However, according to the underwhelming resources in the Macon Hospital, there appeared to be no indication of a fracture of any kind and, based on the doctor's best guess, no ligament damage. Of course, updated medical equipment in Atlanta would provide a better diagnosis should the Stevens family choose that option.

Kevin saw the doctor on Monday morning following a Friday night game. Despite the potentially enormous setback, Kevin and his family began to see noticeable improvement throughout the subsequent week, the teen's ankle responding better each day. Kevin continues to favor his left side markedly, but, with the assistance of some temporary crutches, at least the young man has been getting around.

As far as Kevin's basketball schedule: everything is on hold for now. It could easily take another week or two, if indeed there is no further damage, to work his way back onto the court, all of it coming at a very inconvenient time in the middle of the season. Even so, considering the initial appearance of the injury, the plummet to the court and raw anguish, Roger had prepared himself for much worse. The man has seen a ton of ankle injuries in his time, and this one looked particularly violent.

It's about that time, Roger confirms to himself. The veteran coach knows there is a crossroads in every basketball season when momentum collides headfirst with adversity, and Roger knows, as far as this season goes, that time is now. Therefore, if Roger and the Macon South Muskrats are going to assume an overcoming persona, they will have to do so quickly, or this season will get away from them just as quickly.

• • •

In the game of basketball, Roger knows January waits for no one—*your squad better be ready to roll.* Coach Stevens' team looks shaky in the first half against Leetown but not fraught with fear. It appears the South players are coming to terms with reality. Despite the losses of Billy and Kevin for the time being, the players acknowledge the season must continue.

"Guys, I believe in you," Roger fires off. "You! Those of you in this huddle—I know we've had a bad stretch, but there's nothing we can do about that. All we can do is play tonight's game. Now, you know the scouting report. Trust it. It's there for a reason. Remember, I believe in you; now I ask you to believe in me and our game plan." *Now*, Roger thinks to himself, *if only this message can penetrate the hearts of these young men and not just their minds.*

The man extends his hand to the middle of the huddle to begin the second half. "Everybody in here! Let's go!"

A litany of hands joins his.

"South on three: one...two...three...South!"

• • •

As the game versus Leetown moves into the fourth quarter, and though the man has been in the throes of frustration for most of the night, Roger cannot entirely discard his team's performance. Macon South has stayed in striking distance of Leetown, a deficit between five and ten points throughout. There have been instances when it appeared to Roger South was going to get over the hump and put a run together, but inexperience would rear its head at inopportune times.

"We need a stop!" calls Coach Stevens from the bench, his team trailing 37-32. He knew offense would be a problem with his top two scorers sidelined. Where his team has lacked on offense, however, the boys have compensated with effort on defense. Anchored by the steady improvement of Tyler in the middle and Leonard's rock-solid rebounding, Leetown has struggled around the basket and thus been unable to pull away.

It's now, or never, the man hears his thoughts as the clock decreases to under three minutes remaining.

Leetown moves the ball patiently around the perimeter, trying to steer clear of Tyler's 6'6" frame in the middle. To Tyler's credit, the Leetown center has given up calling for the ball inside, not so much because he cannot get the ball but because he does not want the ball. Tyler has sent back four of his shots so far, one in each quarter, and the Leetown player is still smarting from embarrassment.

Pass...pass...pass: the ball continues to swing as Leetown rapidly drains thirty precious seconds.

"Get in the passing lanes," bellows the Macon South Coach, his panic level increasing with every tick of the clock. "Jump the passing lanes!"

For the first time all season, a surge of assertiveness hits Dwayne, and suddenly it dawns on the young man no one else is going to do something if he does not. *It would be worse not to go for it*, Dwayne considers, *than to let them run out the clock.*

With that thought in mind, as Leetown attempts to swing the ball from the far wing back to the top of the key, Dwayne makes his move. His eyes are as big as the basketball as he leaves his man and lunges forward. He sees the ball. Here it comes. With all his quickness and momentum, he extends his left hand as far as possible.

There it is, Roger identifies from his angle, *Dwayne's got an edge.*

Unfortunately for Roger, Dwayne and the entire Macon South team and fans, the ball grazes the tips of Dwayne's fingers but has enough velocity to reach its destination in the hands of the Leetown point guard.

With Dwayne out of position, the ball is swung again, this time to Dwayne's man who stands unattended on the opposite wing from where the ball began. Wisely, the player drives to the basket unimpeded, setting off a chain reaction.

Instinctively, both South post players rotate. As they do, the Leetown power forward is left alone in the middle of the lane. The rotation of the defense cannot keep up the pace and plug all the holes. With touch and efficiency, the Leetown swingman drops off the ball in the paint. Tyler and Leonard watch the pass coast by, the ball landing in the hands of the Leetown power forward who lays a soft shot over the front of the rim and in for two more crucial points, extending the late-game lead to seven.

Roger grunts at the missed opportunity. "Go! Go!" he commands, the clock weaponized against them.

To no avail, Macon South fires up a shot which falls in the hands of a Leetown rebounder. With that, the Muskrats are forced to foul and watch their opponents convert successfully on all remaining free throws. Thus, the game ends, and South falls for the second consecutive game.

Though the man detests losing with a passion, admittedly, Roger saw a few items this night he attributes to progress.

"Dwayne," he stops the young man on their way into the locker room, the young man with his head held low. "That's what I want to see—you, jumping the passing lane. Good effort, son. Good effort."

The encouraging words and pat on the back are trademarks of Roger Stevens. More times than not his contemporaries would chew out a player under such circumstances or ignore the player out of disgust altogether, *but what would be the point of that* is Roger's opinion. *The kid tried. He just didn't get there on time; a fraction of a second too late. Next time*, the coach believes, *Dwayne will get there.*

Dwayne jogs ahead after the compliment from his coach. *At least Dwayne's feeling better*, Roger thinks to himself. *Wish I could say the same for me. Our team is in trouble.*

• • •

The next three games without Billy or Kevin on the floor were classic examples of one-step-forward and two-steps-back. After a promising showing against Leetown, a game on which there was a semblance of progress to build, South was on the wrong end of an eighteen-point loss to Trenton, which included another technical foul by Coach Stevens. Yes, Roger thought the game was officiated poorly, but what bothered the veteran coach the most was how he felt the referees disrespected his players. From the outset, neither official looked interested in meeting Roger or hearing a word he had to say. Of course, Roger knows he can get over junk like that. However, once the disrespectful tone and demeanor became directed at his players, it set him off.

The next game versus Westport was analogous to the Leetown game, and Roger and his players found themselves in the game with two minutes remaining. However, a dangerous combination of an inability to get a crucial basket plus get a crucial stop proved to be the difference, and South dropped the game at Westport 55-50.

Again, just when Coach Stevens thought his Muskrats had crossed a significant threshold, they ran into a buzz saw versus, of all people, his old friend Tom Chaney and Ridgewood High. Even though the double-digit loss came at the hands of an old buddy, the sentiment was still not enough to assuage the bitter sting of defeat, and there have been many defeats lately.

"Good game, Tom," Roger exchanges sportsman-like words with his friend following the game.

"Thanks, Roger. I know you guys are hurting right now." Tom Chaney is gracious in victory. "Once you get Kevin back, you guys will be tough to beat."

Roger musters as much congeniality as he can before he begins what is quickly becoming routine: a long, frustrating, lonely walk to the locker room following another Macon South loss. The stellar 5-0 start to the season has faded quickly, and the coach's team has tumbled to 5-5.

• • •

Karen is a wise woman, and she keenly discerns tonight is not the night to discuss the game with Roger—sometimes she does, and sometimes she does not.

Roger is not talkative anyway, and the man falls into bed to do nothing more than stare at the ceiling. *This is rock bottom,* he considers. Immediately, the man corrects himself, *Billy would beg to argue that point. What he wouldn't give to be back on the court.*

Karen lays alongside her husband, joining him in staring straight up.

"Dad." Kevin unexpectedly stands at the door to his parents' bedroom.

Both Roger and Karen prop themselves up in unison. "Hey, Kev," the father answers. "What's going on?"

"Sorry to wake you guys."

"You didn't wake us, honey." Karen replies.

"Can I talk to you for a minute?"

Knowing his son never likes to inconvenience anyone, Roger welcomes the unoffensive intrusion. "Sure, buddy. Come in. What do you got for us?"

• • •

Raymond Huddler stands with his back to a weathered wooden fence, his coat collar fending off the cold night air. Waiting impatiently at the northern edge of the old Terminal Station, cigarette smoke pours from his nostrils and mouth. The man is startled by the stealth of the voice behind him from the other side of the fence.

"I assume this is important," speaks the voice out of the darkness.

"Of course, it's important. Is there someone inside my group?"

"Don't be ridiculous," the voice scoffs. "That would be counterproductive, now wouldn't it? Stop your paranoia and focus."

"I am focused, and it's time to do something," Huddler answers, offended by the man's inference.

The voice pauses then states the obvious. "We are doing something."

"That's not what I mean. I'm talking about Stevens," Huddler demands.

"We can't get things out of sequence, you know that."

"So, what then? Stevens just gets to keep living…without threat of consequence?"

"We had everything in place before he ever arrived, remember that."

"Yes, but now he's here, and he is a menace who's against everything we stand for."

"He's your menace," the voice responds from the other side of the fence. "Look, another six weeks or so and we'll be free and clear. Until then, whether you want to or not, you must lay low and keep first things first, and the same goes for your lackeys on the police force. That was supremely foolish of them to beat that black kid, and I know you gave the go-ahead. All of you, knock it off and stick to the plan. After that, you have my blessing to do whatever you want."

Huddler's blood is percolating. "I don't need your blessing. I want Stevens dead, and if you're not willing to do something about, then I will. Besides, at least the men on the PD are loyal to instructions and know unrighteousness when they see it, and they're willing to do something about it, willing to protect our town and our state. That's more than I can say for you and your men from up north, all of you influenced by perverse ideology...." Raymond Huddler gets the feeling he is talking to himself. "Are you there?" No answer is given, and Huddler walks several steps around the end of the fence to see a man with his back to him in the distance, blending with the night. The FBI agent is gone.

31

The whistle blows and the players gather at center court. Five straight losses would normally equal an extremely tough practice at the hands of their veteran coach. However, as Roger prepares to address his team, the man seems a little less stressed and a little more jovial than how his team expected him to be this afternoon.

"I'm not going to lie: it's been a rough stretch, guys." Coach Stevens begins to pace back and forth before his players, squeezing the basketball chest high.

The collective attitude of the team is heavy. The coach is correct: it has been a rough stretch for everyone.

"Be that as it may, what I say next might surprise you, men: that's life. If life were easy all the time, if there were never any challenges or adversity or hills to climb, we would never grow. We would never strengthen as players or as a team or even as people. But not you: you men are tough. You men are resilient. You men are strong and in shape from hard work and dedication. You are tough on the outside and on the inside. In fact, that's why I call you men. You are not boys; you are men."

The coach scans his team. "Tyler, without Billy here, you have become more assertive. Dwayne, without Kevin here, you have learned to look for your shot. All of you have shown a new level of grit and resolve. Now, do I want to win every game? Oh, you bet I do," the man squeezes the ball even tighter. "More importantly, regardless of our record, and our current losing streak, we are building something here. We are in a marathon, not a sprint. You are getting better as individuals, as a team, and I'm proud of you."

A sense of relief permeates the entire squad; they thought they were in huge trouble today following their recent performances. Instead, they bask in the apparent good news: *Coach is in a good mood. We aren't going to die from running line drills today.*

"So, as we prepare for the second half of the season, I think it would do us some good to add a player to our roster to give us fresh legs and energy coming down the stretch."

The South players look to each other for help, confounded, speculating: *Is there a new kid at school? A transfer we haven't seen or don't know about?*

Coach Stevens lifts his whistle to his lips and delivers two, quick, high-pitched blasts.

Kevin Stevens emerges from his hiding spot on the Ridgewood stage, the reigning Georgia Player of the Year. As he lowers himself to the court, the customary limp of late is no longer noticeable. Instead, Kevin's teammates watch in surprise as the point guard picks up the pace and glides across the court with no evidence of an ankle injury.

Pumped at the sight of their teammate, the Muskrat players are quickly caught up in the moment. "Yeah, Kev. Right on" are some of the words heard as Kevin melds into the swarm of teammates who rub his head and shake his shoulders.

Though relishing the visual before him, Roger cannot help but think of the one player who is missing from this scene: Billy. Even so, adding Kevin is a great blessing, not only from an improvement standpoint but for the sake of comradery. Furthermore, the coach knows it is time to put his foot back on the gas. Roger blows his authoritative whistle again. "Okay, let's go to work."

32

Friday, January 24
Game Eleven
Macon South vs. Junction County
Record: 5-5

Even though the loss of Billy has been heart-wrenching, given Kevin's reemergence, the Muskrats have embraced a fresh surge of confidence at the halfway point of the season. Roger is banking on other teams running out of gas just as Macon South is gearing up. Tonight is their first opportunity to turn the tide as Junction County rolls into the Ridgewood gym.

As both teams gather at half court, Tyler assumes his customary place in the center for South. That is until he feels a tap on his right shoulder.

"Just for tonight, Tyler," Kevin petitions, surprising his teammate, speaking privately in Tyler's ear. "I need this."

Tyler recognizes a determined countenance to go with Kevin's determined request. "Sure, Kev," Tyler gladly concedes, extending his hand for a low-five. "Go get 'em."

Kevin slaps Tyler's hand and steps to the middle of the floor.

Karen watches intently from the stands.

Roger curiously observes from the sideline as his son invades the center circle. The coach is in the dark about what is happening. However, after seeing the display of unity between Tyler and Kevin, the coach grants his players the benefit of the doubt.

A shrill from the referee's whistle demands respect, and the man releases the ball in the air. The entire gym watches as Kevin elevates just beyond the reach of the Junction County center and pushes the ball into the hands of Dwayne to his left.

As the home crowd shows their appreciation for Kevin's effort, as soon as he lands on his feet, the South point guard runs to Dwayne with determination and receives a handoff from him. Once assuming possession, Kevin turns the corner and goes.

The Junction County defense backpedals.

Kevin gets downhill rapidly. Beginning 25-feet from the basket, the South point guard weaves with the dribble through a maze of defenders, a few of them futilely swiping at the ball, as if the orange sphere is an optical illusion; one moment it is before their eyes, the next moment it is gone.

In fewer than five seconds, Kevin has penetrated the lane as the Junction County power-forward retreats on his heels. With the appearance of stepping into an easy 12-foot jumper, the coach's son draws the defender to him while keeping his dribble alive, carving a perfect circle around the cumbersome opponent and laying the ball sweetly off the backboard and in for two points.

The South crowd roars in acknowledgment: Kevin Stevens is back, and relief is felt by every Macon South fan and player, and especially the teen's parents.

• • •

The spectacular opening basket was simply a precursor to the rest of the game. Kevin used this night not only to mark his valiant return from injury, not only as a tune-up for the rest of the season but to make a statement. Kevin is still the reigning Georgia Player of the Year, and despite the tumult once heaped on the Macon South season, going forward, Roger knows his team will be very tough if not impossible to beat with his son on the floor.

The South coach watches as the final seconds tick down. Kevin now sits beside his father on the bench after a 27-point return performance, padding a 20-point lead. Roger took him out early in the fourth, knowing there was no need to play Kevin any more tonight. The young man proved his point—he is back. The final score is Macon South 65, Junction County 45.

• • •

Roger and his team find themselves rolling as they cross from January into the crucial month of February. Though it was difficult, the absences of Billy and Kevin thrusted the remaining players front and center. Tyler looks like the best center in the City at times. No one from any team has been able to match Leonard's strength. Both Dwayne and Jeremiah have become more than serviceable at the guard positions. Hence, insert a superstar like Kevin Stevens on a team with height, rebounding, supplemental scoring, defense, and good role players with good ball movement, and the formula for a Macon South post-season run is on the table, and Roger knows it.

The veteran coach is constantly pushing himself as well. He lives on the competitive edge, shifting back and forth between commending his players on their proficient play and prodding them to reach topflight potential—*who knows the next time such a collection of talent will come along for the school.*

Further evidence the Muskrats have hit a mid-season groove are the scoring totals during a spate of February games. The numbers nearly look like duplicates from one game to the next:

- Kevin, 23, Tyler, 15, Leonard, 11, Dwayne, 10, Jeremiah, 9.

- Kevin, 20, Tyler, 16, Leonard, 10, Jeremiah, 10, Dwayne, 9.
- Kevin, 25, Leonard, 14, Tyler, 13, Jeremiah, 9, Dwayne, 8.

As the regular season concludes, Macon South already has accomplished more than anyone thought was possible, including their head coach. The team finished with a record of 15-5 thanks to a 10-game winning streak. The Muskrats also won their conference for the first time in nearly a decade, since Assistant Coach Reggie Dawkins played at South, and Roger's team has earned the top ranking in the district.

For the first time since arriving in Macon, Roger feels a rhythm to this season, his team, and even his life. Overall hostilities seem to be less of late. Of course, the man misses Billy terribly, but even Billy has been showing steady improvement in his rehabilitation. Kevin is healthy again. Therefore, despite some daunting setbacks, Roger deems the plan of attack to be full steam ahead; next stop, the district playoffs.

● ● ●

Raymond Huddler dials the number, hanging up after one ring. He pauses. Thirty seconds later, Huddler dials the same number—this time, hanging up after two rings.

● ● ●

Blair Yokum sits in the dark corner of his bedroom and listens as the phone rings once then ceases. He leans back and exhales a vapor of cigarette smoke into the air. He waits. Thirty seconds later, the phone rings twice then ceases.

Yokum stands to his feet and walks into the hall, opening a door leading to the basement. A single bulb illuminates the flight before him. His rugged boots stomp all the way down. He retrieves a familiar suitcase with care from beneath the stairs. He places the case on a nearby workbench and views the contents inside, satisfied with what he sees.

Outside, the man cautiously loads the suitcase in the passenger seat of his car. He then circles the vehicle and climbs behind the wheel before driving into the darkness.

• • •

Unlike his good friends a few hours away, Reverend Jordan walks his kitchen floor in Augusta, pacing back and forth in prayer. His sleep was mysteriously interrupted—he just lurched forward with an urgency to intercede. The faces of Roger, Karen and Kevin flash before the pastor's eyes more than once.

"Thank you for protecting the Stevens family, God," the man utters again and again. "The name of The Lord is a strong tower," he begins to whisper the scripture at the forefront of his heart and mind. "The name of The Lord is a strong tower. The righteous run into it, and they are safe. The name of The Lord...."

• • •

As the car slowly turns onto a bumpy country road beyond the southern edge of town, the jostling of the vehicle causes Blair Yokum to wince while glancing at the suitcase to his right. Five minutes later, he kills the headlights and pulls to the side—the Anderson home is in the distance. Opening the suitcase, the man delicately handles the same model of timer he hid behind the walls of Macon South High School. Meticulously, he begins final assembly. Wires are carefully laid in place. Satisfied, the man leaves his door ajar and circles the car. Yokum looks to the house in the distance: there is no movement, everyone sleeps. Opening the passenger door, he takes a deep breath before reaching for the device—it is armed and ready for collateral damage.

• • •

"The name of The Lord is a strong tower," Reverend Jordan paces and prays 120 miles away. "The name of The Lord...."

• • •

Secretly, silently, by the light of the moon and headlights from multiple pickup trucks, men work surreptitiously in the night; hoods and street clothes on this occasion and not full robes.

Maxwell gives his best attempt to stay at a distance, keeping his hands clean of the evil, yet showing the appearance of his involvement. His mind races: he cannot put his fingerprints on an act like this; he would never forgive himself. Instead, Maxwell tries to lighten his conscience with repeated trips back and forth to the vehicles, fetching canisters of gasoline and taking them to the other men, allowing them—not him—to douse and pour.

Raymond Huddler stands across the front of the property and watches as the men employ his instructions. More specifically, he watches Maxwell's every move.

Maxwell reciprocates, keeping an eye on Huddler with his peripheral vision.

"Freddy," Raymond calls, getting Maxwell's swift attention. "Start pouring gas around the base."

His insides churning, Maxwell nods, speciously showing his support. Grabbing a canister, he heads around the back, out of sight.

Once safely hidden from view of everyone, Maxwell sloshes gasoline in the canister, pouring out some in the grass and splashing himself to worsen the smell of his clothes.

After a few more seconds, a commanding voice affirms, "That's it! Let's move out!"

Exhaling with relief, Maxwell scampers around the front of the building to join the other men with his empty can in tow.

The culprits lay a seemingly incalculable number of metal canisters in the backs of the trucks; they do not want to wake anyone from their sleep. In the dead of night, the men eagerly look to their leader, awaiting his cue.

Huddler, his face and scar covered by a white hood, walks to the forefront and turns to view the entire group. He next lights a homemade torch, the end of it wrapped in a cotton cloth and saturated with gasoline. The end of the torch ignites and illuminates the dark as he hoists it high in victory above his head. Huddler scans the line of Klansmen before him.

Maxwell is nauseated. The undercover agent wants to vomit as the flame of the torch undulates in the night air. He tried his best not to take part in this sinister strategy, but he knows he must.

Huddler continues to peer through the eye holes in his hood, evaluating the men one by one...until he finds Maxwell.

Maxwell holds his breath to stabilize and compose his outward appearance.

Extending the torch in Maxwell's direction, Raymond Huddler bids: "Come, Freddy."

Hesitating without hesitating, Maxwell steps forward with pseudo-eagerness, approaching the man who summoned him.

The men watch with semi-jealousy. Many of them desire to be chosen this night, yearning to set their hand and enact purification.

Maxwell stops short of the man, unsure of the leader's motives as Huddler points the end of the burning torch directly at the agent. Maxwell's clothes are saturated in gasoline.

Raymond pauses before cryptically asking the question. "Are you worthy, Freddy?"

The empty eye holes stare into Maxwell's heart as Freddy thinks carefully upon a plausible response. "Yes. I have proven to be."

Huddler assesses the statement. After thoroughly vetting Frederick Collins, Huddler learned the man had indeed been arrested in Decatur, Alabama just as Freddy had said; Huddler's source with the Decatur PD confirmed as much. "Then take it, brother," Huddler calmly responds. "Take it from my hand. Do us the honor. Light with night sky with the fires of purification."

Drenched in gasoline, Maxwell assumes the torch then steps back. Once at a safe distance from the Klan leader, Maxwell nods in agreement and turns toward the edifice. Under a white hood, the countenance of the agent swoons from guilt. However, there is no time to hesitate; they are all watching.

Maxwell assumes a committed pace toward the structure, regretting every step. He takes one final stride and tosses the torch into a bed of gasoline-saturated cotton cloth at the base. The undercover FBI Agent who did not want to apply the slightest splash of gasoline to the building is now lighting the fire.

Flames spread quickly, shooting vertically up the walls, forcing Maxwell to step away as he looks on with remorse.

The devoted gathering watch with satisfaction.

Maxwell must appear complicit in the act; although, he finds the sight demoralizing. He impersonates a man entranced by the fire. He stands as a man in repentance.

Huddler signals to another Klansman. Without Maxwell's knowledge, the other man steps behind the FBI Agent, out of Maxwell's sight, a shotgun resting in the Klansman's hands.

• • •

A woman in the South neighborhood opens her front door in her robe, banishing a bothersome cat to the porch for the night. The woman halts and lifts her head at the distant echo of a shotgun blast. She cannot place where it came from, but the sound did not seem far away. The woman squints: flames give off a yellowish-orange hue over the horizon. She back-peddles, scurrying to wake her husband.

• • •

Maxwell never had the chance to turn around. Lying face down in the grass, the FBI agents gasps futilely for breath.

The group of Klansmen watches without utterance as Raymond Huddler approaches the wounded man and hovers over him.

Freddy clutches clumps of grass in his fists, hopelessly trying to pull himself forward, trying to get away, but there is nowhere to go.

Bending at the knees, Raymond Huddler disrespectfully pulls the hood from the dying man to address him. "FBI Agent Nathan Maxwell," the leader of the Klan declares, pausing to observe the swiftly spreading flames before looking down again. "You will burn in this fire tonight."

Maxwell hears the man's voice but cannot register what he is saying as his life fades rapidly.

The emotionless leader stands uprightly and ultimately decrees over the Federal agent, "May God have mercy on your soul...because I will not."

The flames have quickly engulfed the building. Huddler looks to the group of men, many of them stunned by the turn of events but willing to trust and not call his decision into question. Huddler points at two men and gives a final command: "Throw him in."

Agent Nathan Maxwell lies motionless in the cold grass as his remaining breaths seep through his open mouth. Never married and no children, Maxwell thinks of his parents as his eyes begin to dim; he hopes he did them proud. *God, tell them I said goodbye*, is his fleeting last thought. *Tell them....*

Maxwell is dead before the hands take hold of his body, lifting him from the ground.

• • •

Blair Yokum assumes possession of the explosive, taking pride in his work as he does. Suddenly, the eyes of the man widen at the sight and sound of the timer unexpectedly jumping ahead.

In disbelief, the timer winds forward on its own, striking the trigger with the mechanism resting in his bare hands. The man has no time to speak the word on his lips. The only thought crossing his mind is *how*. It is the moment all bombers fear..., and it has come to Blair Yokum.

• • •

Roger and Karen are both startled to consciousness by the sound in the distance.

"What was that?" Roger inquires, still groggy though roused to his feet.

"I don't know?" Karen responds, out of bed first. "Was it inside or outside?"

"I'll check Kevin." Roger scampers down the hall.

"Roger!" Karen calls panicked from the bedroom.

Her husband returns.

"Look. Dear, God," she exclaims with the curtain pulled back.

Roger Stevens steps to the window. He strains to see outside. Down the road, illuminating the night sits a car ablaze as flames jut out both windows.

"What is it, Roger...? I mean, what happened?" Karen stammers.

Bewildered, Roger glares harder, trying to place the vehicle, but it is impossible for him to do so. "I don't.... Where are the Andersons? Where is their truck?" Roger sprints to the far window to find the Andersons' truck parked in its normal spot. Roger can see lights appearing in the windows of the Anderson cottage. They have been stirred from their sleep as well, but, as far as Roger can tell, the Andersons seem to be okay.

Roger lunges back to the first window.

Kevin emerges. "What's going on?"

As Roger stares intently, the car is unfamiliar to him. Regardless of who it is or who it was, the hungry flames show no mercy—fire has consumed the vehicle in the distance, surely killing whoever was inside.

The blaring phone startles everyone in the house, causing Karen to shriek.

"Yes," Roger answers in the dead of night. "What! No! No!" Karen inches closer to listen.

"Oh, please, God, no. Who's there now?"

"Roger. What's wrong?" his wife pleads.

"Okay." He pauses for a moment to gather his thoughts amid the swiftly unfurling events of the overnight. "I'll be right there." Coach Stevens hangs up the phone with force and begins rifling through clothes in a nearby drawer.

"What is it, Roger!"

The man looks at her: "It's the church, Karen. It's burning."

• • •

As the Stevens family draws near, the illuminated night sky tells the tale. The night is in its pre-dawn darkest moments, which makes the yellowish-orange background that much more striking and fearful.

"God, please, no," Roger utters.

"Oh, Roger," are the words escaping Karen's lips before she quickly covers her mouth in shock.

Kevin's face from the backseat reflects the horrific image before them now.

"Stay here!" Roger barks as he parks the car near a group of bystanders. As he steps outside, his first sensation is that of intense heat across his face. An inferno now engulfs Second Baptist Church of Macon, its flames ascending high and licking the dark sky above.

All the faces aligned and witnessing the blaze radiate a mixture of emotion: some crying, some horrified, some catatonic. One of the unresponsive faces is that of Pastor Jenkins, the reverend watching powerlessly at a safe distance at the stern behest of the Macon Fire Department. The wife and son of Pastor Jenkins stand on either side of him, the man paralyzed with emotion, a witness as the building implodes, collapsing on itself more with each passing minute. In stark contrast, his wife wails under his arm, crying aloud as she grips the shoulder of her husband's jacket with both hands, burying her face; the man allows her to tug at him violently with no response.

Roger grunts, torn between standing back from and rushing to the fire. The power of the flames ensures no one is to challenge or come close. Even the firefighters attempting to fight the raging blaze do so from a logical distance, given the fact 80% of the building has fallen to the ground. Still, Roger wants to do something. They all do—but there is nothing to be done. Apart from the familiar facade of the church with the once-charming stained-glass windows on opposite sides of the front door, this house of worship has become unrecognizable; it is now merely a pile of searing rubble.

As Roger adjusts his eyes, an eerie image comes into focus across the landscape of the church property, and the sensation washing over Roger Stevens is one of both debilitating fear and seething anger. Just to the left of the front walkway that leads to the front steps of the church, still blazing with ferocity, is a message; a signature of the men who have been here this night.

Roger stares at the burning cross. His stomach is tossed about by a storm of emotion. *They were here, on this property. They walked on holy ground, and they showed no respect, no shame. What evil! It makes no sense. How, God? How could you let this happen?*

Karen emerges from the car and walks to the side of Sister Jenkins, the woman turning loose of her pastor husband and falling into Karen's embrace, both women weeping in unison.

Kevin walks to the side of his father, the young man with far more questions than answers regarding the sight he beholds.

As the witnesses futilely stare, one final, startling crash is felt. The remaining standing portion of the church, the façade, gives way and falls to the ground, reflecting a surge of heat across the dejected faces of the gathered. It is down. The church on the south side of Macon is down.

Powerless, Roger looks at those looking on, and the man cannot help but think this has to do with him. This church was standing as of last fall before he brought his family to Macon, and now he is here, and the church is not. No one glances at the man; they watch the fire blaze. Nevertheless, Roger feels every eye burning right through him as he is convinced: *I brought this trouble on them. I brought nothing but heartache with me. I am a walking disease. Everything I touch, everywhere I go is unclean. These poor, poor people. Forgive me, God. Forgive me.*

Charles Bullock has arrived. The principal walks to Roger's side, and he finds the man with his face buried in his hands. The principal touches Roger softly on the shoulder and whispers, "Let's go stand by Pastor Jenkins."

Roger wants to decline. He wants to stand and stew in his own misery, but Roger cannot stand idly by and let his Pastor stand alone.

Both men soon flank Pastor Jenkins on either side. Crackling flames and sobbing are the only sounds left to be heard.

Kevin sees Jeremiah Jenkins. The coach's son steps next to his teammate, lapping his arm over the shoulders of the preacher's son.

Jeremiah emerges out of his trance. The son of the pastor does not smile, although it is obvious Kevin's presence has brought relief. Jeremiah lays his arm over Kevin's shoulders as well.

The two teammates stand before the burning church. It is all they can do—watch together.

33

The first shred of daylight reveals the charred rubble. Vapors of hot steam climb from the underbelly of the wooden heap as melted debris pops and hisses.

Dawson, Dennison and a team of agents comb the church property for evidence; although, the extinguished, crude wooden cross at the front of the property is undoubtedly the signature of the guilty.

"Seen this before," Dawson declares as he and Dennison take in a panoramic view of the smoldering church. "Too many times…with no end in sight."

"Agent Dawson," another agent respectfully summons him, "we're ready for you."

Both Dawson and Dennison walk to a remote area of grass where several agents, including Wheeler and Hopper, stand around a white sheet on the ground. One of the men can no longer tolerate the pungent smell and discreetly steps away.

"Coming through," Dawson announces as the men part before him. The sheet is pulled back, and Dawson and Dennison view the remains of a body burned beyond recognition, still hot to the touch.

"Not much to go on," an ancillary agent interjects. "Might be a Klansmen for all we know. But why?"

"A double cross, maybe?" another Hopper offers. "They've been known to turn on one another."

Dawson stands over the deceased and peers at what was once a face. He next looks at Dennison. "Can you tell?"

Dennison moves closer, and, at first glance, he offers nothing conclusive. He asks, "Does someone have a clean rag or towel?" As Dennison waits for an answer, none of the men are helpful. Impatient, Dennison removes his jacket, rids himself of his tie and begins unbuttoning his shirt. "Let me check something."

A nearby agent takes Dennison's coat and tie. Dennison strips down to his undershirt and slacks, revealing his torso trim from years of biathlon training. "Baton," he requests, and a baton is quickly presented to him by one of the agents. Pressing his dress shirt firmly against his nose and mouth, Dennison kneels near the still smoldering cadaver for a closer look. The agent takes the baton and extends it toward the corpse.

"What are you doing?" Wheeler asks in disgust.

"Just hold on," Dennison asserts. Carefully pushing what was the upper lip with the end of the baton, the agents watch as the mouth of the victim falls open. Dennison next presses the rod against the skull of the burnt body, pushing slightly to the left, exposing teeth still intact despite the consuming fire. All the teeth are there except for those teeth noticeably missing to one side, prompting Dennison to speak the name, "Maxwell."

• • •

A knock at the door interrupts the somber conversations of those who have gathered at the home of Pastor and Mrs. Jenkins early in the morning. Many people have been in and out this morning to show their love and support. Pastor Jenkins opens the door to find Agents Dawson and Dennison on his front porch with Dawson presenting identification.

"Sir, I am Special Agent in Charge Harold Dawson of the FBI, and this is Agent Dennison. May we speak to you? In private would be best."

Pastor Jenkins motions for one of the men in his home to draw near and speaks to him in a low tone. Nodding, the man proceeds to kindly clear the living room of all guests to allow the pastor and his wife to meet with the federal agents.

Roger and Karen comply, and as they exit through the front door and walk onto the front porch, Roger sees additional agents looking at him more intently than any of the other guests. One agent in particular smirks as Roger walks past.

• • •

Roger and Karen await out front of the Jenkins' home with several other concerned members of Second Baptist. The visitors are spread out, sadly contemplating the desecration of the church quietly. Roger glances to ensure his following words will remain private between his wife and him. The man hesitates, torn between what he should say and what he does not want to say.

Karen discerns her husband's anxiety. "What is it, Roger?"

Roger beings to speak…then stops…then starts again. "I can't protect you here, Karen," the man lowers his head. 'I am ashamed to say it, as a man, as a husband, as your husband, it embarrasses me to say the words: I cannot protect you in Macon."

"But you have protected me, Roger. You've protected both Kevin and me, and you've protected us for years."

"That was then, Karen. That was up until now, but now…." The man rests a hand on his wife's shoulder and speaks with his eyes and his heart. "I can protect Kevin; he's with me at school. You, though, I'm fearful to leave you during the day."

"I have the Andersons," Karen responds. "I am with them pretty much every day, and, if push comes to shove, Mr.

Anderson has a gun. He knows how to protect himself and his wife and me if necessary."

"I know, Karen, but that's not his job. Protecting you is my job."

As much as Karen appreciates her husband's intentions, she is a woman who has never felt in need of twenty-four-hour care. "God looks after me, too, Roger; don't forget."

"Of course, He does. I know. I know, but I have a part to play in all this, and I am worried—if anything ever happened...."

Karen lays her head against her husband. "I don't believe anything will, honey," Karen pauses, trying to use as much wisdom as faith, "but I know what you're saying."

Roger pulls back, staring at his most-prized possession on earth. "I hate to say this because I hate to be away from you, but I think you should go be with your parents for a while. It never hurts for you to visit your mother anyway, and I would...I would just feel better if you did."

Her husband's suggestion causes Karen to ponder. She had been thinking of visiting her mother anyway, but she did not want to abandon Roger and Kevin at the same time. "I've already been thinking about it," Karen confirms. "but what about you and Kevin? It's not fair for me to up and leave both of you during this time."

"We are fine," Roger affirms. "Like I said: Kevin is with me. We are together most of the time, and we can take care of ourselves. I think Kevin is big enough and strong enough to help take care of me to be honest."

Karen flashes a smile. "He's grown into a young man overnight, hasn't he?"

Roger nods.

"And you've made him that way," Karen adds. "He reminds me of you."

"He reminds me of you," Roger counters. "I love you."

"I love you, too."

Roger and Karen proceed to hold each other without words, each one entertaining the thought of what the future holds.

The front door to the Jenkins' home opens, and a cluster of FBI agents abruptly emerge. Agent Dawson surprisingly walks the length of the porch to find Roger Stevens.

"Sir, could I ask you to walk with me?"

Roger turns a mystified countenance toward Karen and the other guests around him. Karen returns a confounded look in his direction as well.

"Yes. Sure," Roger stammers, standing to his feet and walking behind Agent Dawson; Karen watches with suspicion all the way.

Dawson leads, Roger walks behind him, and Dennison is behind Roger. Once the men are at a safe distance from the home, Agent Dawson turns to Roger.

"I am Special Agent in Charge Harold Dawson of the FBI. I am based out of Atlanta, but I have been assigned to Macon since the school bombing. I think it's time we talk—off the record."

Roger looks briefly at Dennison who stands nearby before shifting his focus back to Dawson. "That's fine."

"I know who you are," Dawson reveals, "and most of your story; more than you know, I'm sure. And I know you didn't start the hostility down in these parts because it's been going on for years." The man from the Bureau has Roger on his heels by the deluge of blunt information. "Nevertheless, your presence certainly has added fuel to the fire, wouldn't you agree?"

Roger is at a loss and still caught off guard by the conversation. "I'm not sure what you're saying, sir." he responds.

"If you don't understand, then you're not as smart a man as I think you are. You left an all-white school in Augusta for an all-black school in Macon; a town that already suffers from significant racial unrest. Did you think a decision like that would go unnoticed?"

Roger tries to process the forward tone and demeanor of the agent. The coach thought everyone here was on the same side. "No, sir. I knew it would draw a good amount of criticism."

"Well, we're way beyond criticism now. I just came from a church that has been burned to the ground, and I lost a good agent." Dawson pauses, knowing—in his frustration—he has said too much.

Dennison listens, not about to interrupt.

"I want to make certain you comprehend the severity of the situation," Dawson resumes, looking up a few inches at Roger but by no means showing an iota of intimidation. "You have put yourself right in the middle of it. Do you acknowledge that fact?"

It does not take Roger long to reply to the agent with honesty. "More than you know, sir."

The conversation has become fruitless to the frustrated agent; he has said everything he wants to say. "Have a pleasant day," Dawson salutes tersely before turning his back on Roger Stevens and walking away.

As the lead agent moves toward his vehicle, Agent Dennison steps in front of Roger. "He's to the point," Dennison states the obvious. "I feel badly for you and everybody who attended that church."

Roger adjusts from the curtness of one agent to the empathy of another, part of him wondering if this is some good-cop bad-cop routine. However, if it is, then Dennison plays the role well since the look in his eyes appears wholly genuine. "Is it true?" Roger quickly inquires. "Did an agent die?"

"A friend," Dennison confirms.

Roger nods grimly—yet another casualty in the wake of him coming to Macon. "I'm very, very sorry, sir."

Appreciating Roger's concern, the agent reaches into his wallet and displays a card with a phone number, handing it to Roger. "You think of anything that might help in any way, give me a call."

Roger receives the card with appreciation; appreciation for knowing someone in high places might be watching out for him, even if others are not. "Thank you, sir."

"Nice to meet you," Dennison offers as he too turns and walks away.

Roger looks down at the contact information in print. As he does, the shadow of another man casts across his hands. Looking up, FBI Agent Hopper stands before Roger now.

"There are many eyes on you" are the agents only cryptic words accompanied by an ambivalent grin. Hopper excuses himself, walking behind Dawson and Dennison toward their vehicles.

As the FBI agents eventually drive away, Roger is left to watch and consider: *Are they for us or against us?*

• • •

The raid begins shortly after the FBI leaves the Jenkins' residence. Dawson and his agents race and work from a list. All over the City of Macon, men are pulled from their homes on a sleepy Saturday morning whether directly or indirectly linked to the Klan in the slightest.

So much for building an admissible case against all these guys, Dennison considers privately, not thrilled with the Bureau's actions this morning but realizing they have no choice. An agent is down, and Dawson is on a mission. "This next guy is Raymond Huddler," Dennison proclaims. "He might be pretty high up the ladder, but no one's been able to confirm that."

"I've heard of him," Dawson acknowledges. "He's been around town for a long time but keeps a low profile. Too low to be that high up in my opinion."

A cluster of FBI vehicles converges on a small house to the west of Macon about ten minutes into the country.

"Check around back," Dawson instructs a handful of agents. The Special Agent in Charge spares no mercy with a heavy hand on the door. "Raymond Huddler! FBI! We have a warrant to enter your home and search your property!"

Dawson does not give a second warning. Stepping back, he signals for the agent behind him to prybar the front door. The multiple locks are no match, and the agents enter.

"Search every room." Dawson strides into the center of the home, slowly turning all the way around for a panoramic view of the contents.

"No one is here, sir," reports an agent.

The back door to the home swings open as more agents invade. "No vehicles anywhere."

Dawson stands in silence and his men comb the house.

"Sir," an agent summons his superior. "You want to see this."

Dawson and the men following him enter the kitchen and gather around the table to look at the lone piece of paper awaiting them. The note simply reads, "Knew you would be here.... long gone."

Dennison senses the frustration of his supervisor. ""We still rounded up plenty today," Dennison states with optimism. "It's a good place to start."

"I wanted everyone," Dawson replies, staring at a painting of Jesus on the wall with a Confederate Flag unfurled and displayed next to it. "But you're right: it's a good place to start. I think the tide has turned and the war is about over. Let's get back to the office and start talking to these guys. I will personally lead all interviews."

34

The first conscious thought Roger has on this early Sunday morning is the sun is shining brilliantly. Karen left yesterday for her parents' home in South Carolina per her discussion with her husband; however, Karen wanted to make a stop along the way. Roger pulls back the curtains completely. *It's a new day*, he observes. *After everything that has happened, it's a new day—a day The Lord has made.*

The phone next to the bed rings. Roger hesitates, wrenching at the thought of more bad news. Even so, he must answer; it might be Karen. "Hello."

• • •

Pastor Jenkins begins his day as he does most days, praying on his front porch. The reverend is especially praying on this Sunday morning, preparing his heart to meet his congregation for the first time since Second Baptist burned to the ground. Graciously, Charles Bullock will open the Roosevelt Center later this morning for the church to hold their service on schedule.

Roger and Kevin drive speedily to the home of Reverend Jenkins, bearing good news—great news, even phenomenal—and Roger cannot wait to see the man's face.

The pastor shields his eyes from the dominant sunshine as the father and son step from their vehicle and draw better into focus. "Good morning, men."

"Pastor," Roger replies with vigor, rapidly approaching the reverend. "I have news you will want to hear as soon as possible."

• • •

The two men and the coach's son enter the home on a mission to find Mrs. Jenkins who is—like her husband outside—praying inside.

"Honey," her husband yells, stomping through the house, startling the woman.

Mrs. Jenkins emerges hastily from the bedroom. "What is it?" she asks, afraid to know the answer. The woman is greeted by her wide-eyed husband and his countenance of astonishment.

"Come with me, sweetheart" is the man's only request.

Roger and Kevin stand in the downstairs living room as the husband and wife turn the corner.

"Mr. Stevens," the woman addresses the coach, surprised to see Roger and Kevin this morning. "What's this all about?"

"Good morning, ma'am," Roger salutes. "Can we all sit together?"

The woman looks at her husband and then back at Roger as anticipation builds; she can tell from their faces they have information. "Sure, let's sit. That way someone can tell me what's going on."

With everyone seated, Roger looks to the minister for consent to share—it is his home.

"Please tell her, Roger," insists the reverend.

Roger clears his throat. "Pastor and Sister Jenkins, I will spare you all the details, but to make a very long story short: as you know, a gentleman bought our home from us in Augusta, which helped us make the final decision to come to Macon. Well, my wife Karen, on her way to visit her mother in South Carolina and desperate to do something about the church, stopped in Augusta yesterday to share your story, the story of the church, with the same man who bought our home."

Roger sees confusion on the face of Mrs. Jenkins.

"I hope you don't mind us sharing your business, ma'am, but Karen thought the gentleman—who is a Christian by the way—might be sympathetic or know some people who might be sympathetic to the situation. Anyway, Karen spoke with the man yesterday and continued her drive to her parent's home." Roger pauses to cast an even bigger smile. "Karen just called a little while ago, Mrs. Jenkins. The gentleman who bought our home was moved with compassion about your story, to say the least."

For the pastor's wife, Roger can't get to the point fast enough. "What are you telling me, Roger?"

"Well, ma'am, Karen's hope was for the man to think about it, pray about it and get back to us, and he did. He called Karen at her parents' home this morning after a night to sleep on it, and he told my wife he would like to donate toward our cause."

Reverend Jenkins does not stare at Roger as the man speaks. Instead, the pastor stares at the love of his life while she hears the news for the first time.

"Well, ma'am" Roger continues. "The gentleman who bought our home doesn't just want to make a partial donation. He wants to pay to replace the entire church."

Roger chokes up as he delivers the news. Kevin smiles from ear to ear. Pastor Jenkins' eyes moisten, and Mrs. Jenkins clasps her hands over her mouth and gasps from joy, unspeakable joy.

"Oh, Jesus!" The woman proclaims, tears bursting from her already weary eyes. "Oh, thank you, Jesus!" Mrs. Jenkins throws her hands toward heaven then lunges to throws her arms around her husband, both suddenly immersed in tears and laughter. "Oh," the woman cannot contain her praise. "Oh, I believe in you, Jesus. I believe in you!"

"What the enemy meant for evil," the pastor preaches, "God has turned for good."

Roger turns to Kevin, and the father cannot help but put his arm around his son's neck. Kevin gives his dad a hearty hug in return.

Trying to sleep in, Jeremiah Jenkins lumbers down the stairs at the jubilant ruckus. "What's going on?"

• • •

Later that night, Dawson sits alone in his office. He sent the night shift home and offered to cover it himself on a hunch he might get a call. The phone on his desk rings, conjuring an eerie sensation since normally it would be Maxwell calling during odd hours. Dawson lets the phone ring a few more times before bringing the receiver to his ear. The agent offers nothing, not his name nor a greeting.

"You know who this is," the voice of Raymond Huddler speaks confidently. "I knew you would be there. This is probably around the time your informant would call, isn't it?"

Dawson listens.

"Stevens has mocked me long enough," Huddler continues. "An example must be made. It's time to do something?"

"You're kidding me, right?" Dawson pushes back. "Do something? What do you want to do, kill the man, lynch him in broad daylight? You have already done enough, haven't you? You bombed a school. Framed a man and had him killed. Had a black kid beaten within an inch of his life by your lackeys on the police force. Tried to bomb the Stevens' home in the dead of night while burning down a black church, not to mention killing an FBI agent in the process...."

"Based on your information." A long pause ensues between the leader of the Klan and FBI Special Agent in Charge Harold Dawson.

Eventually, Agent Dawson resumes. "There is too much at stake right now, and you know that. I gave him up for you in an act of good faith."

"You never should have put him here in the first place," Huddler retorts. "Besides, you lied to me about your man."

"I had him there to keep your mind on people inside instead of people outside. Now, I just swept a bunch of this away, but if you move on this now, you will do nothing but shed more light on us, which will make it difficult to do what we need to do. The time will come. I have no problem with that. Stevens has caused me more problems than I need, but everything must be done at the right time."

"I want Stevens dead," Huddler gives his singular response.

"It sounds like you're having trouble closing that deal," Dawson pokes at the man.

"Shut up," Huddler froths back. "I just want your guarantee you or your men won't interfere."

"My men won't be in the way, but Stevens is not priority."

"He's my priority."

"Let's be clear," Dawson decrees to his unhinged co-conspirator, "if you get caught…I won't get caught. Do you understand?"

"There is no getting caught," Huddler rebuffs.

The two men allow more silence.

Dawson gives the bottom line. "We are at the doorstep of finishing. Once it is done, I will be gone, and you can do whatever you want to the man, but you must wait at least one more night. Do you understand?"

The line goes dead.

Dawson hangs up as well. His goal was to stabilize the situation, but the Special Agent in Charge knows he must dispose of Raymond Huddler to stay his voice.

35

Tuesday, February 18
District Playoffs
First Round
Macon South vs. Jeffersonville

Roger has assigned three parts to the basketball season so far: a great start (five straight wins), tragedy in the middle (five consecutive losses), and, since Kevin's return, unstoppable momentum down the stretch (ten straight wins). Leading the team to a regular-season record of 15-5, Kevin Stevens averaged over 20 points per game during the final winning streak of the season, topping the 30-point mark on three different occasions—30, 32 and 33 respectively.

Furthermore, Roger knew Kevin proved to be what the team needed: a star player to absorb the brunt of opposing defenses, allowing Tyler, Leonard, and Dwayne to let the game come to them without any extra pressure, exclusively versus one-on-one matchups. In retrospect, the five-game losing streak without Billy or Kevin proved to be instrumental. It was not pleasant to Roger nor to his team—losing never is. However, the supporting cast strengthened and gained essential playing time during the brutal stretch of losses, and, once Kevin got back on the court, Macon South was firing on all cylinders for the stretch run.

Up next: The district playoffs. Two district victories would advance South to the regional round. Two wins at the regional level would buy the school a trip to the State semifinals at Georgia Tech in Atlanta, a place Roger never thought he would see again and certainly not while coaching at Macon South.

Ironically, the first team facing the Macon South Muskrats is Jeffersonville High, a repeat of the first game of the season, and a team South handled easily in the opener. Although, South had Billy Taylor on the floor that night which will not be the case going forward.

As the beginning of the first-round game unfolds, unfortunately, so do the nerves of the South supporting cast. Predictable, big-game jitters rise to the surface: lack of focus, errant passes, and short free throws; tightness abounds. Still, Roger knows all this can be overcome, once again, if Kevin Stevens is on point.

So far in the first half, Kevin has been okay but not stellar. The point guard came out firing, knowing his team would need to lean on his playoff experience and alpha-dog mentality. Even so, the senior has only shot at a 35% clip, which has been good enough to keep his team even with Jeffersonville.

Watching from the bench, Roger Stevens weighs emotions that are not mutually exclusive. He is glad to be here, but, while his team is here, he wants to make the most of it. Roger knows all too well a close game in the postseason is a dangerous premise. It simply takes a random bounce of the ball here or there to cause a team to advance or send a team packing, and there is nothing the man detests more than the inability to put a team away. Instead, South continues to let Jeffersonville stay with the Muskrats stride for stride.

With fifteen seconds remaining before halftime, Kevin dribbles near mid-court, holding the ball for the final shot.

With eight seconds left, the veteran point guard motions for Leonard to set a high screen.

Leonard sprints to the top of the key.

Kevin sets up his man to the left, then peels back to the right to hang him up.

Failing to get his feet established, Leonard overzealously engages Kevin's defender before coming to a full stop.

The illegal-screen call for the official is easy as the Jeffersonville player goes flying from the impact.

"Ahhh," Roger grunts from the sideline. "Leonard."

Leonard's face tells it all—the teen with the adult torso appears almost weepy, afraid to glance at his coach.

Roger chooses to move on. "Get back! Find your man!" he instructs.

"Fourteen! Fourteen!" the Jeffersonville coach bellows with just seconds remaining in the half. In well-drawn up, end-of-the-quarter execution, the Jeffersonville point guard takes the inbound pass and rushes up the court. The two Jeffersonville post players set a screen for the shooting guard at the left block, allowing the would-be shooter to scrape off and run cleanly to the opposite baseline. The pass from his teammate is on point as the guard squares for a textbook jump-shot with the entire gymnasium watching, the 17-footer splashing through at the buzzer.

Roger groans in anger. The man just watched a four-point swing erase his team's once small lead. Not to mention, he knows a buzzer-beater is always a big lift to the team who scores it. Halftime arrives, and the score is Macon South 24, Jeffersonville 24.

Coach Stevens covers x's and o's from the moment his team enters the locker room to the moment they leave. "Listen to me!" the coach exclaims while slapping his hands together. 'We must make our move now. I've seen it too many times, men, and you must trust me. If we let them hang around, something bad will happen in the end. We must play this first part of the second half like the rest of the game depends on it...because it does. Don't wait! Whatever you're going to do, do it now! Everyone get in here," the man decrees as he puts his hand to the middle, his team matching him with energy and newfound confidence. "Men, what do you say we go win our school its first playoff game in a decade?"

"Yeah! Come on! Let's go!" is the chorus.

"That's what I want to hear. South on three: one…two… three…South!"

Any tentativeness harbored by Macon South in the first half has been left in the locker room. The Muskrats sprint to a ten-point lead to begin the second half—Kevin has an eight-to-nothing spurt of his own.

It is clear Jeffersonville senses a tectonic plate of momentum shifting beneath their feet: Macon South has that look. Worse than that for Jeffersonville, Kevin Stevens has that look as the Muskrats extend their lead to 14 by the end of the third quarter.

The fourth quarter shows no signs of Kevin Stevens slowing down. Running through his mind are his father's words: *You must finish the other team while you have the chance.* Such championship mentality is on full display as Kevin and his teammates drive the final nail in the Jeffersonville coffin. Macon South notches the school's first playoff victory in a long time—Macon South 64, Jeffersonville 45.

36

"This guy should have something to say," Dawson affirms. He, Dennison, and Wheeler stand in the hall, looking at Officer Elvin Butler of the Ridgewood PD through the glass in the door.

"Test..., test," Agent Dawson checks the microphone concealed in the collar of his dress shirt.

"You're good," Wheeler confirms, listening through a pair of headphones attached to the sound equipment.

"Here's your recorder as well." Dennison hands Dawson a smaller tape recorder by the handle.

Dawson wastes no time and enters the room with purpose. "Not in uniform today, huh?" The veteran agent sarcastically pokes at the officer in his white t-shirt and brown trousers.

Elvin Butler stares at Dawson from under a bedraggled head of hair; the agents pulled the officer from his home. Butler had to hold his pants up the whole time because the agents did not allow him to grab a belt.

"This is a shameful predicament for you, Officer Butler," Dawson pours it on. "Here you are, a policeman, a paid public servant, a man of stature in your community, and you are now the subject of an FBI investigation."

"I don't even know why I'm here," Butler futilely responds.

"If you think I'm stupid or in the mood for stupidity, say that again," Dawson leans forward, brandishing an intimidating scowl. "I am the FBI Special Agent in Charge, and you will not waste my time, do you understand?"

Butler looks away, not wanting to acknowledge he is on the short end of authority in the room.

"Here is what's going to happen," Dawson proceeds, setting the tape recorder in plain view on the table. "You are going to be brought up on federal civil rights charges, and I will personally extradite you to Atlanta for your hearing because I can easily convince a judge you cannot receive a fair trial in Macon due to coverage of the press. Or," Dawson continues, pushing a pad and pen across the table, "You can give me the names of all those involved in the local chapter of the KKK in exchange for leniency."

Butler attempts to process the information on no sleep; his bloodshot eyes telling the story. "How would I know anyone in the Klan?"

Dawson was ready for the man's token reply. "Because I've already had three different Klansmen under questioning identify you by name as a longstanding member. Not to mention you went to the home of a black kid and beat him within an inch of his life."

"That's not why we went there," Butler interjects.

"That doesn't matter because that's what happened," Dawson puts the policeman back in his place. "Not a good look for you, is it?"

The once-tough Ridgewood Officer sits in silence, his mouth beginning to quiver.

"So, let's start over." Dawson presses the play button.

Butler stares at the tape recorder on the table before him.

"I want every name you know, and, again, make it worth my while."

The two men sit across from each other.

Dennison and Wheeler surround the sound equipment outside the room, both wearing headphones. Wheeler prepares to document the conversation once Butler gives his consent.

The veteran agent discerns the officer's apprehension. "I'll tell you what...." Dawson turns off the tape recorder. "Now, it's just you and me talking."

Butler continues to sit silently. The gesture is not enough to win his confidence. "That recorder doesn't matter...because you're probably wearing a wire."

Dawson smiles. "I can tell you're a good policeman."

Dennison and Wheeler exchange a curious look; they are a little thrown by the words of their superior.

"Just for you..., out of common courtesy," Dawson begins ridding his dress shirt of the wire running through it, "from one law enforcement officer to another...." Dawson disconnects the wire before pulling it completely through and laying it on the table between the men.

The audio recording goes dead in the office.

"What's he doing?" Wheeler objects.

"I don't know," Dennison replies, frustrated, standing to his feet to look through the glass.

Dennison watches as the two men talk for several minutes. No one knows what either of them is saying from outside the makeshift interrogation room.

"Have you seen him do this before?" Wheeler asks, befuddled by the unorthodox measures taken by the Special Agent in Charge, fearful anything shared would be inadmissible.

Dennison continues to twist his neck in observation. "No. I'm not sure what he's doing."

Dawson eventually emerges from the room and is greeted by his two curious understudies. "Relax, men. Relax."

"But, boss," Dennison interrupts.

"I know, Dennison. It's not Bureau SOP. Trust me. I needed to talk to him off the record to get him to go on the record. I'm going back in there to do it for real this time. I just needed to know if we are wasting our time or not."

"Well, are we?" inquires Wheeler.

"No. Butler just named the bomber, Blair Yokum, as the leader of the Klan in Macon, and it was Yokum who led the church burning and Yokum, not Phillip Barlow, as we suspected, who bombed the school to begin with."

Dennison's eyes widen at the thought of bringing the case to a long-awaited close.

"So, men," Dawson begins to replace the wire in his shirt. "We are about to wrap this up. Butler is willing to go on the record. He just wanted to make sure the deal would be worth him naming names."

"What deal are we giving him?" asks Dennison.

"I will talk with 'H' about that," Dawson responds. "Now, let's check the audio and start from the top. We're about to go home and finally leave Macon, and I can't wait."

• • •

Principal Charles Bullock, displaying a child-like grin, sits at his desk, plopping down two separate issues of the Macon Telegraph. Rapidly, he flips to the sports section. As would a surgeon, the man steadies the newspaper with one hand while systematically incising the articles with the other. The two pieces read:

Saturday, February 22, 1969
Macon South Disposes of Clinton, Advances to Regionals

Behind another stellar performance from Kevin Stevens, Macon South claimed the District Championship with a 59-50 victory over Clinton Tuesday night. Stevens scored 27 points, and South also received a noteworthy contribution from Tyler Washington who chipped in 15 points and 15 rebounds as well.

"I was proud of Tyler tonight," commented Head Coach Roger Stevens when asked of his center's performance. "It was clear what they (Clinton) were trying to do, so we discussed it during a time-out. I told Tyler they were going to foul him hard rather than let him score. He knew he would have to produce at the free throw line, and he did. He accepted the challenge."

The win punches the Macon South ticket to the Regional round where the Muskrats will ironically play Ridgewood High School in the Ridgewood gymnasium, which will technically be a home game for Macon South as the higher seed. After the much-publicized bombing of Macon South High School last year, the entire student body was displaced. Macon South classes were moved to the former Roosevelt war depot in Macon for classes, and the basketball team was provided a gym for practices and games at Ridgewood thanks to the longtime friend and former college teammate of Roger Stevens, Tom Chaney, Head Basketball Coach at Ridgewood High School.

When asked if he has ever been involved in such a scenario or even heard of a similar situation, playing a home game on the opposing team's court, Coach Stevens commented, "No. I don't believe I have. Either way, the school and I are extremely grateful to Coach Chaney and Ridgewood High School for allowing us to practice and play in their gym. Otherwise, well, I don't know what we would have done."

The final remarks of Coach Stevens took on a light-hearted tone. When asked if he would feel badly in the event of his team beating Coach Chaney's team on Ridgewood's home court, the Macon South Coach responded, "I can say this because Tom (Chaney) and I go way back: nothing would make me happier than beating my good friend on his home court."

Wednesday, February 26, 1969
Improbable Run Continues for Macon South:
Muskrats Win Home-Away-From-Home Game vs.
Ridgewood

A home game played on the road versus the host school. Confused? That was the scenario everyone in attendance had to accept at the regional game between Macon South and Ridgewood on Friday night, played at Ridgewood High School. Macon South notched a hard-fought 53-48 victory, advancing to the Regional Championship. Kevin Stevens led the South Muskrats in scoring with 32 points. Leonard Sweetwood owned the paint with 19 rebounds.

Last year, the horrific bombing of Macon South High left the school scrambling for a location to hold classes. Thanks to the temporary conferment of the Roosevelt war depot by the Mayor of Macon, the high school opened on time for the fall semester. That solved one problem; however, a temporary home was needed for the basketball program. A longtime friendship between two coaches came to the rescue, and Ridgewood Coach Tom Chaney and Macon South Coach Roger Stevens agreed on arrangements for both schools to share the gym at Ridgewood High.

"All kidding aside, this is a bittersweet win," admitted Coach Stevens in the team locker room following the game. "I know us coaches joke quite a bit about winning at all costs, and I wanted to win badly tonight, but I would have been happy if Tom's team had advanced because Tom is a great man. Tom took a lot of heat by sharing his gym with our kids this year. Coach Chaney has a very good team at Ridgewood, and his team could easily be playing in the next round. I congratulate them on a great season."

As for the game itself, both teams traded strategic punches for the first half as the lead swung back and forth. The Ridgewood game plan was obvious from the start: keep the ball out of the hands of Kevin Stevens, the South team's star point guard who happens to be the coach's son. However, as two experts in a chess match, Coach Stevens and his team were ready for such a tactic, and when a double-team would run toward younger Stevens, the South ballhandler would quickly pass and then get the ball back almost immediately, leading all scorers.

Ridgewood looked up to the task of denying Stevens early, but as the game progressed, Ridgewood could never fully gain the advantage. Despite Ridgewood's best efforts, Stevens still accounted for 15 first-half points.

When asked why his team moved away from this defensive approach in the second half, Coach Tom Chaney explained, "According to the score, it looked like our game plan was working. Still, Stevens was getting whatever he wanted, and the flow of the game felt helter-skelter and too up tempo for us, which plays into their hands with the athleticism they bring. No matter what any team tries to do, Macon South is tough to beat, and Roger is a great coach. They deserve to move on."

Coach Chaney enacted change and dropped his team into a box and one zone against Macon South and their point guard for the entire third quarter. However, Kevin Stevens displayed his versatile talent by trading quick-cutting penetration in the first half for bulls-eye jump-shooting in the second half.

In the end, a late full-court press applied by Ridgewood failed to force turnovers, and, behind six free throws from Stevens in the final minute, Macon South held on to advance to the Regional final Tuesday night versus Maryville. The winner of that game will advance to the state semi-finals in Atlanta.

● ● ●

Roger listens nervously for the phone. Something feels off to the man. He believes Karen already should have called—she always checks in by now from her parents' home. Roger glances at the clock, pondering, *Her parents should be sleeping. I don't want to bother them if they are. Maybe Karen fell asleep early as well. She deserves it if she did.*

The man tries to rest, but he cannot.

Something rattles from outside the bedroom, coming from downstairs. Roger hastens to the top of the steps. A figure has moved through the outside door to the home and quietly turns the knob to the inside door. Roger grips the bannister—he may have to protect his son this night.

The door opens, and Karen steps into the faint light.

"Karen," Roger breathes.

The voice of her husband startles her. "Oh, Roger. You scared me."

"You scared me," the man replies, descending the stairs in double time. "What are you doing? I can't believe you're here."

Karen gladly receives the arms of her husband, the wife exhaling in his embrace. "I had to be here." She pulls back from her husband to look at him. "I want to be here; no matter what."

Roger discerns the courage in the tone of his wife, coveting her resolve. "Sweetheart," he whispers, pulling her close again.

Karen rediscovers the eyes of her husband. "God hasn't brought us this far to leave us, Roger. He'll go with us all the way, regardless of what life may bring."

The strength of his diminutive wife empowers Roger. *She's right,* he concludes. *Whatever we face, we face together.*

"Is Kevin asleep."

"Yes."

"Oh, I want to surprise him."

"You can surprise him in the morning," Roger quietly decrees, taking his wife by the hand to lead her upstairs.

37

Friday, February 28
Regional Championship
Macon South versus Maryville

Kevin Stevens is at full strength. Each game presents individual challenges to the star player; some teams pose size, some quickness, some double-team ability. Regardless of what faces the coach's son, however, one common weakness lingers among all the teams opposing Macon South: none of them have an answer for Kevin. He once again looks to be the best player in Georgia.

Case in point, another zone defense this night and another walk in the park for Kevin. His jumper is clicking, and he is hitting consistently from 17, 19 and even 21 feet. There is no three-point line, but if there were, the coach's son would average three to five more points per game.

Beginning the game in a zone, Maryville switches to man midstream, trying to give Kevin and South a different look. Kevin identifies the change as soon as it happens, and the seams quickly appear in the defense. Maryville has good size inside, and the team's hope is their post-men will at least alter some of Kevin's shots once they push him into the lane. To no avail. Stevens is playing with too much confidence and too much aggressiveness, getting downhill whenever he wants against his counterpart and slipping past the bigger bodies in the lane.

Versus Maryville, Kevin and Tyler have been working in concert. As the opposing big men step out, Kevin has been passing over the top to Tyler. The passes have been so on-point, Tyler has learned not to come back down with the ball. Instead, Tyler has been using his height and athleticism to catch the ball high over the defense and lay it over the front of the rim in one smooth motion, a play none of the schools had seen before playing Macon South. When Roger drew it up, he knew it would be nearly impossible to defend an athletic big man who could catch a well-placed pass just in front of the rim. Roger has not been sure exactly what to call the play, so, for now, he calls it a lob pass.

Despite playing from behind for most of the night, Maryville has hung tough, staying within striking distance.

• • •

Less than two minutes remain in the game, and South holds a steady five-point lead, each team bidding for a berth in the state final four. Maryville rebounds following Leonard's miss at the free throw line. Out of a set play, the Maryville point guard swings the ball to the right wing to his teammate who curls off a pin down screen. The player wastes no time in getting the ball into the Maryville center who cuts across the lane.

A step behind, Tyler overzealously leaps as his counterpart gives him a ball fake. The opponent wisely leans into Tyler with his shot attempt, forcing the official on the baseline to call the foul.

Roger shakes his head repeatedly on the sideline, and the man knows what his assistant is going to tell him.

"That's five," Coach Dawkins confirms.

Tyler walks to the bench with slumped shoulders. As he does, Coach Stevens sees in an instant the player Tyler once was and the one he has become, and Roger cannot help but be pleased.

"Good effort, Tyler," the coach sings the praises of his center. "You showed up big tonight."

The words are music to Tyler's ears.

Meanwhile, to Roger's dismay, the Maryville center, normally a 50% free throw shooter, knocks down both free throws without breaking a sweat. Roger has that old feeling—*this game could get away from us.*

Nursing a slim three-point lead with fewer than two minutes remaining, Kevin exudes confidence, as usual, the entire roster drawing from him as an energy source. The point guard crosses half court in command of the dribble.

On cue, Maryville sends a second man to initiate the double team, wanting the ball out of Kevin's hands. He sees it coming and offers a hard dribble to his right, causing the double team to lurch, exposing a gap between the two defenders. Instinctively, Kevin drops a hard, low dribble to the floor, pushing the ball out in front of him, splitting the trap in two, racing into the clear. It is just Kevin, Tyler on his left and the Maryville center in his way.

Kevin drives to the basket and draws the bigger defender to him. Seamlessly, before the Maryville center knows it, Kevin loops a beautiful pass behind his back to Tyler.

The crowd clamors at the sight of stellar ballhandling.

Embarrassed, the center from Maryville knows he has been duped. He turns in time to see Tyler shooting an uncontested layup. Meanwhile, Kevin did a circle around the larger defender, and the coach's son has nestled on the opposite side of the basket from Tyler. There, Kevin waits, just in case Tyler misses the point-blank shot. The Maryville center is too late to do anything about Tyler's shot, so the muscular 6'6" opponent takes out his frustration on Kevin. The Maryville post player acts as if he is fighting for position while coming high with his forearm and elbow, violently catching Kevin in the back of the head.

The thud of the contact gets the attention of the nearest ref, and he blows his whistle.

A dazed expression brushes Kevin's face. The coach's son thinks to move his feet to keep his balance, but his thoughts and actions do not line up. Instead, Kevin closes his eyes and goes weightless, falling face-first to the court.

Roger did not have a clean look from the bench; although, he knows something is wrong.

Everyone on the court freezes. Time stops as well.

In the crowd, already on her feet with the rest of the South faithful, Karen cups her hands over her mouth as her son lays face down on the court.

Leonard shoves the Maryville center out of the way, and the big man from Maryville returns the favor. Other players begin to lock arms as the refs and their shrilling whistles try to break it up.

A Maryville player loses his balance amid the pushing and shoving and falls on Kevin, the Macon point guard breaking his fall.

Roger is in a dead sprint. "Get off of him!" Roger yells at the Maryville player who uses Kevin's body as leverage as the player pushes to his feet.

"Knock it off!" yells one of the refs at the tussling players. Eventually, the skirmish dies down as all eyes look to the fallen point guard from Macon South.

Roger rolls Kevin over to get a better look. Kevin's eyes are closed. "Kevin! Kevin!" his father bids. "Kevin," the father yells again, this time slapping his hands together an inch away from his son's face.

Kevin jolts in response. The young man's vision blurs and then focuses as the face of his father appears. Kevin sits up quickly as his hand finds the rapidly growing knot on the back of his head. He pushes a little from the floor then plops back down.

"Easy, Kev," exhorts his father. "Easy."

Karen watches from the stands, heartbroken. *He's trying to get up.* "Oh, honey," she pleads under her breath. "Stay down. Stay down."

"I can get up," Kevin announces.

"Take it slow," admonishes his father.

Coach Dawkins stands in a support capacity as well, and both coaches assist in pulling the point guard gingerly to his feet.

The crowd, still stunned, begins to emerge from its catatonic state—a smattering of clapping dominos among the spectators. Soon, the gymnasium is a box of collective applause in support of the injured player who is back on his feet again—both sets of fans getting behind the kid's effort tonight.

Coach Stevens and Coach Dawkins help South's leading scorer to the bench. Kevin continues to open and close his eyes. All Roger can do is pat his son on the shoulder and then turn his back to coach the rest of the game.

Roger sends in reinforcements.

To his credit, the nearest ref was on top of the rough play, assessing a technical foul to the Maryville center for the flagrant elbow to the back of Kevin's head. The technical sends Macon's choice of players to shoot free throws. Roger motions for Dwayne, and the young man steps to the line. The rest of the players from both teams stand near their team benches and watch.

As Dwayne toes the line, the crowd noise begins to crescendo.

"Shooting two," the ref informs Dwayne as he hands the ball to him.

Sweating uncontrollably, one dribble...., two dribbles...., three dribbles, and Dwayne sends his first shot airborne. To his disappointment, his first offering is on line but hits the front of the rim and kicks back.

The crowd reacts accordingly.

Dwayne lines up his second attempt.

The basketball hits the right side of the rim...then the right side of the backboard before falling off.

"This is getting away from us," Roger tells himself aloud while looking straight at the floor. His team's three-point lead is scant.

The game is late, but there is no need for Maryville to rush, working the ball from the right side of the floor to the left while running their motion offense.

After several seconds and nothing to be found, the opposing coach bellows from the bench, "Fifteen! Fifteen!"

"Fifteen," the Maryville point guard repeats the command from his coach.

"Tough D!" Roger counters.

With his team now set, the opposing point guard dribbles to his right as his teammate on the wing clears that side of the floor.

On cue, the Maryville center steps out to set a screen.

Leonard follows closely.

At the last second, the Maryville center keenly slips the screen and flows toward the basket, leaving Leonard with his back to the action. The Maryville center receives a perfectly placed pass over the top and converts an easy layup, shrinking the South lead to one and bringing the Maryville faithful to a fever pitch.

"Timeout!" is Roger's predictable response—his final timeout. The veteran coach discerns his team's low self-esteem as they saunter to the bench. "Come on! Come on!" he rides them. "Hustle!"

The remaining South players plop down on the bench. Kevin is out, Tyler has already fouled out, and Billy has been long out of the picture. Roger is quick to read their faces. "Look! If you want to quit and give them the game right now, then pack up your stuff and get on the bus! I didn't come here to quit—no matter what happens. Do you hear me?"

"Yes, Coach," a few voices trickle from the roster.

"What?"

"Yes, Coach," they repeat with strength and vigor.

Roger takes several steps away to consult with his assistant.

"What do you think?" inquires Coach Dawkins, clutching a clipboard in his right hand.

Roger responds with a sigh. "I'm not sure. I'm concerned about our ball-handling with Kevin out of the game."

"True," Reggie agrees. "They have momentum right now, and they're going to keep coming."

The two men talk with their backs to the bench, knowing a decision must be made. The veteran Head Coach reaches his conclusion. "Let's try to get Leonard a shot. He might score. He might get fouled."

Coach Dawkins concurs and hands the clipboard to the head coach.

Roger returns to the bench and squats in front of his players as the man begins to scribble furiously. "Here we go. They're going to expect us to stall, but I'm not going down without a fight. Dwayne, bring up the ball. I want a triple screen at the top of the key by our two, three and four men. Leonard, you are still the five with Tyler out, and I want you to stay on the block. Dwayne, come off the screen and get Leonard the ball. Leonard, when you get the ball, go to work. Either score or get fouled. Just do what you do best and draw the contact."

The players confirm what their coach wants from them.

"South on three: one…two…three…South!"

Roger and his assistant were correct. Maryville comes out of the timeout with aggressive pressure on the ball.

The Maryville point guard hounds Dwayne, getting a hand on the ball as Dwayne tries to spin away.

Roger's heart drops as the ball squirts free, but Dwayne regains possession. "Protect the ball, Dwayne!"

The Macon South guard successfully crosses half court despite the smothering defense. The triple screen is set at the top of the key, and Dwayne uses it moving from left to right.

Down low, Leonard flows with the action and establishes position on the right low block.

Dwayne delivers the pass.

Leonard receives the pass and—with the voice of his coach ringing in his ears—goes to work. One hard dribble, a second dribble, a little incidental contact, and Leonard gets separation, turning his body to the left to shoot a five-foot touch shot toward the rim.

The opposing center leaps out of desperation and catches Leonard on the shooting hand.

The referee blows his whistle.

Roger and the bench jump to their feet as the ball touches the front of the rim with a possible three-point play hanging in the balance. "Get in there!" he grits through his teeth.

To no avail. Leonard's touch on this shot is too soft, and the basketball rolls gently backward and off the rim; no basket, but Leonard is going to the free throw line for two crucial shots. Thirty seconds remain, and Macon South leads by one.

"Knock em' down, Leonard," the voice of the coach undergirds his player.

The wooden bleachers begin to vibrate beneath the Maryville fans.

"Two shots, gentlemen. Relax on the first one," are the instructions given by the official who presents the ball to Leonard.

Taking a deep breath, Leonard wisely decides not to overthink the moment. Instead, as soon as he feels comfortable, he shoots, and the orange sphere goes up—and in. The Macon South lead is back to two points.

"Ya, Leonard! Way to go, brother" are the words coming from the South faithful. "One more!"

Employing the same strategy on the second free throw, Leonard lofts his second offering. This time, the shot hits the heel of the rim and kicks out, falling into the hands of the opposition.

"Get back!" Roger erupts from the bench, the man bemoaning a missed free throw but realizing one is better than none.

He knows with South on defense and a two-point lead, the best Maryville can do is tie and send the game to overtime.

"Fifteen!" the opposing Coach repeats his previous command.

"It's the same play, Leonard," Roger projects his voice over the crowd. Leonard, you know what's coming!"

As the clock bleeds precious seconds, the Maryville point guard moves his defender to the top of the key. Again, the off-guard clears the right side of the floor. Out steps the Maryville center to set a screen for the point guard. This time, Leonard hangs back, not allowing the Maryville center to slip to the basket again.

The Maryville center sets a solid screen, and Dwayne is easily picked off. Even worse for South, Leonard is playing back to prevent the slip. Thus, the Maryville point guard rolls off the pick with a clear lane to the basket.

Dwayne reacts but is too late.

Roger next watches as the unthinkable happens. As Dwayne chases, the Maryville point guard stops to pull up for a ten-foot jumper, causing Dwayne to run into the opponent from behind. The whistle from the nearby ref shrieks at the contact. Furthermore, the Maryville shooter contorts his body just enough to get the shot airborne. In a pivotal moment of the regional championship, the ball kisses off the backboard and in for the game-tying basket. Plus, thanks to the foul call, the Maryville player will step to the free throw line with a chance to give his team the lead with twelve seconds remaining.

Hysteria engulfs the gymnasium, some feeling elation and some deflation.

Coach Stevens lowers his head; he told his squad what can happen when another team hangs around late in a game. Even so, Roger is determined to coach to the very end. "Dwayne!" he motions for his backup point guard.

Dwayne hustles over.

"Look! Shake it off! We are still in this game. Whether he makes or misses, you must push the ball to get us a basket."

The man talks a mile a minute. "Just go to the basket and get the best shot you can, okay!"

The young man, clearly jittery from his foul, nods in acknowledgment.

The lead official situates the young men along the three-second lane accordingly. Soon, the Maryville point guard will have the ball in his hands to shoot the go-ahead free throw with little time on the clock.

As in the past, in surreal fashion, at crucial moments of certain games during his career, life grinds to a halt for Roger Stevens. He stands alone on the sideline. There is no crowd, there is no score, and there is no game. There are only the thoughts racing through the coach's mind as everything else becomes background and scenery. His sense is they will lose this game, and more times than not he is correct. The fourth quarter has shown an erosion not only of his team's lead but their self-confidence as well. Even if Maryville misses, overtime will be difficult to overcome given the monumental emotional shift in the game since Kevin went down.

If this is the end, the man considers, *what a ride!* It will certainly end a chapter Roger never thought was possible. First and foremost, Roger cannot believe he is even here, at this moment, standing on this sideline, coaching basketball for Macon South High School.

Roger calmly turns to find the eyes of his wife in the section behind him.

Karen can read his face, the serene smile, the countenance of calm. She discerns his thoughts based on his satisfied facial expression. *This is it*, she surmises. *Roger thinks this is it. They won't be able to hold this game. We are going to lose.* Karen tilts her head, smiling back at her husband while accepting the end of the road to another season is here—in her opinion, her husband's best coaching job ever.

Down the bench and across the court, Roger sees the beleaguered, sweaty faces of his players. *Look at them.* He considers. *They've come so far and played so hard. It's okay for the season to end here. Regionals—we made it. Just one step short of the final four. Who would have thought? We beat other teams, beat the refs, beat the crowds, beat the odds. Despite all the difficulty and adversity, Billy, Kevin and a white coach at a black school, I couldn't be prouder of my guys, and no one will ever be able to take....*

• • •

Roger's moment is interrupted by a hand gripping his shoulder.

A towel drenched in sweat drops to the floor on the Macon South sideline.

"Sub!" A commanding voice calls from behind Roger, surprising everyone, especially the Coach of Macon South since he is not the one who yelled it.

Stunned, turning his head, watching in disbelief, the father sees the back of his son, Kevin, upright, sauntering to the scorer's table.

Roger is not the only one. The players on both teams are shocked. The coaches and the fans are shocked. The refs are shocked, too. Even so, the nearest official waves Kevin back into the game.

"Kev...," Roger stammers, unable to get his son's name out of his mouth in time to stop the young man from checking into the game.

"Come on, ref," the Maryville Coach complains. "We were about to shoot a free throw."

"He hadn't given him the ball yet," the nearest official responds.

Roger watches incredulously as his son takes control of the game.

"Box out!" Kevin yells to his post players.

Dwayne—astonished like everyone else—rushes to talk with his injured teammate. Kevin pulls him close by the jersey, staring him in the eyes. "You gotta' get me the ball on the left low block. No matter what."

Dwayne nods.

Kevin repeats. "No matter what."

"I got you," Dwayne confirms.

Kevin glances at his father, and the teen begins to walk to the other end of the floor with a slight wobble.

Roger watches as his son struggles in the opposite direction, heading to the offensive end of the court. Roger looks to Karen. Karen shakes her head as if to say *no. Kevin's not ready.*

Roger looks back to Kevin. His son has made it all the way to the far end of the floor.

"Box out!" Dwayne calls to his teammates; the player is clearly more optimistic with Kevin on the floor.

Under the basket, Leonard and Jeremiah dig in.

The crowd yearns for a resolution to this riveting back-and-forth display.

Trying to conceal his surprise at Kevin's re-emergence, the Maryville point guard dribbles three times, then puts up his best shot.

Innumerable eyes strain at the ball dancing on the rim before falling through: Maryville has come back to take a one-point lead.

Dwayne rushes to take the inbound pass; ten seconds remain as he jets near half court. With seven seconds remaining, Dwayne pushes to the left side of the floor per Kevin's instructions.

The point guard from Maryville has sprinted back and settles in behind Kevin, giving him a little bump for good measure.

Kevin is not deterred, pushing back.

"Watch it, men!" warns the nearest official.

Kevin, with all the strength in him, wills his body, establishing a low base and pinning his defender behind him, setting up on the left low block. Glancing at the time, Kevin sees the clock has dwindled to five seconds.

"Ball! Ball" commands the South point guard.

Not to be the one to deny Kevin, Dwayne does his part and ultimately delivers a bounce pass that finds Kevin's grip.

Four seconds.

The Maryville center forsakes all to run and help, recognizing his teammate is one on one. Injured or not, it is clear to everyone the star player from Macon South is going to either win or lose this game with the final shot.

Three seconds.

Kevin inhales deeply. With one bounce of the ball, he leans left. Kevin bodies his defender, striving for just enough separation.

Two seconds.

The Maryville center arrives on Kevin's left to help, but Kevin turns away from both him and the point guard, drifting toward the baseline

One second.

Roger watches as his son commits to his patented, baseline, turnaround jumper, Kevin keeping his defenders just enough at bay and out of reach as he eyes the basket.

Both Maryville defenders leap and lunge to close the distance.

As Kevin turns, despite the previous blow to his head, for a micro-second, the former Academy point guard sees the unobstructed basket and thinks to himself, *there it is.*

His body fading toward the baseline, Kevin gets off the shot, the ball leaving his fingertips, ascending from his hand.

The explosive blast of the horn fills the gymnasium; the shot got off in time.

The defenders crank their necks in midair to watch the ball that escaped their reach by an eyelash.

The ball finds its zenith then flattens out as it continues its path.

Once done with everything he could do, Kevin's heart, mind, and soul go limp. So does his body as he falls toward the hardwood floor, not worried in the least about the impact.

The Maryville coach cannot believe what he is seeing. The South player who had worked his team over all night, the same player who looked to be severely injured and left the game has now returned and just got off a clean shot that, if it goes in, will seal Maryville's fate.

Roger, as well, watches in disbelief. The last few moments—from the time his son put his hand on his shoulder to right now—seem like a mirage. *If this shot goes in....*

As Kevin crashes to the floor, he does so under the force and weight of the opposing two players, both overextending and falling on the shooter after the buzzer.

The ref ignores the contact after the shot, mesmerized by the leather sphere floating toward the basket.

Karen and the entire South body are witnesses as well.

Kevin watches from the floor as his turnaround baseline jumper…drops cleanly through the net, and Macon South wins the regional championship at the buzzer.

A deluge of emotions descends on the gymnasium: joy, pain, exhilaration, exasperation, faith, and disbelief.

Every hand on the Macon South bench, including those of the coaches, is in the air. The Macon players are now on the floor, running to the aid of their hero lying on his back.

All Roger can do is place his hands on the side of his head, covering both ears. He immediately turns and looks for Karen; she is doing the same thing, taking the same posture, looking back at her husband with mouth agape.

Miraculously, all pain had left Kevin's body, that is until his teammates yank him from the floor. Leonard steps to the front of the group and bear hugs the Coach's son, lifting him off his feet; the other players close around them.

"Great game, Coach," Roger extends a hand of sincerity toward his counterpart, the opposing coach still reeling from what just happened.

"Yes. Good game" is all the man can muster.

A jubilant Coach Dawkins corrals the boys from Macon and sends them to half court to shake hands with the opposition.

Once the line is complete, Roger can speak with his son for the first time since the kid called his own number. "I would ask if you are okay, but I think you are, so…."

Kevin smiles as hysteria flails around him. "Yeah. I'm okay."

With that out of the way, Roger admonishes his son privately in the teenager's ear. "One time," the father says. "That was the one time you ever get to go over my head."

His father looks as if he is half-kidding, but, then again, he is Roger Stevens. Therefore, Kevin replies with a token yet wise response: "Yes, sir." Kevin wisely changes the conversation to something more upbeat. "We're going back to the Final Four by the way."

"We're going back to Atlanta," Roger affirms, unable to prevent a smile from beaming. "Can you believe it?" Roger lifts his head and voice for all around him to hear. "We're going to Atlanta!"

Screams of excitement ascend to the rafters. Thanks to some late-game drama, Macon South has grabbed the regional title, its first ever in school history. Now, it is on to the State Final Four in Atlanta, Georgia. Little does Roger know, across the state in a different regional game, another winner has advanced tonight, filling the final slot on Macon's side of the State semi-final bracket. Up next for the Muskrats is Roger and Kevin's former school: The Augusta Christian Academy Patriots, coached by Bart Newhouse, Sr.

38

Thursday, March 6

"Heading back to Atlanta tonight, Wheeler?" asks Agent Dennison. The roundup of the Klansmen is complete, and the agents' time at the makeshift FBI office is done—the two men emptying the last few items from their desks.

"No. I have an uncle who lives about an hour from here," Wheeler responds. "I am going to visit and stay for a night. My family's always busting my chops about me never taking the time to see them."

"You're preaching to the choir," Cy Dennison concurs. "I haven't made it up north in quite a while."

"This job's probably why most of us around here are still single and haven't found a nice woman to settle down with," Wheeler adds.

Dennison cannot agree with Wheeler this time. "No. I'm not married because I'm not married. I hear everything changes when you do."

As the men exit the building, Dawson's office appears to still be in use, although, the Special Agent in Charge is nowhere to be found.

"I thought Dawson said he was leaving today," says Wheeler.

"He said he'd get out later," responds Dennison. "But you know Dawson: first one in, last one out. I just saw him earlier. He had me inspect the truck for transport back to Atlanta."

"Who's driving the transport? Runyon?"

"Yeah, Runyon and Southerland." Dennison stops to turn and look behind him one final time. The once-bustling Macon office is now still.

"Everything okay?" Wheeler asks, stopping with his fellow agent.

Cy Dennison pauses. "I am sorry Maxwell isn't leaving with us."

• • •

It never ceases to amaze Roger how the details of life can swing wildly, and he and his loved ones have clung to the volatile pendulum by the grace of God. On the one hand, the City of Macon has lived up to its reputation as a hotbed of racial tension; conversely, the Stevens family has come to know an alternate side to the town and the people, a citizenry unjustly labeled by public perception through the years.

Roger, Karen, and Kevin have met an endless number of loving souls who have captured their hearts and changed their lives. More specifically, the players Roger has inherited at South have been nothing less than phenomenal, and the man loves the kids on his team and cannot imagine life without them.

"Need any help packing?" Karen inquires, one night before the family heads for Atlanta with nearly all south Macon in tow, the community eagerly anticipating the trek to the capital.

The Stevens believe the caravan will be a proud procession. Before the road trip, tomorrow is the huge, school-wide pep rally, and, from what Roger can gather, Charles Bullock has pulled out all the stops: banners, confetti, the school band, the city newspaper—no detail will be spared. The Principal is elated beyond words at the school's first-ever appearance in the state semifinals, and he will not let this grand opportunity pass unannounced nor unnoticed.

Roger continues to fold clothes and does not mean to ignore his wife's question; his mind is all over the place right now.

"Did you hear me, honey?" Karen queries; her husband is obviously deep in thought.

"Oh, sorry, babe. I was thinking about what I should say at the pep rally tomorrow."

"What are you going to say?"

"That's just it. I'm not sure. There's so much to say, but I don't want to overdo it. I don't want to undersell it, either. These boys deserve a special weekend they will remember for the rest of their lives—no matter what happens in Atlanta."

"Or who we play?" Karen broaches the topic for the first time with her husband. She has been waiting for him to say something for days, but, peculiarly, he has not.

Roger glances at his wife then slowly takes a seat on the side of the bed. "Can you believe it? Can you believe we're playing the Academy in the state semifinals?"

Karen finds a soft landing next to her husband and exhales. "No, no I can't. Not in a million years, but it will be nice to see everyone again."

"True," Roger agrees; snickering, a name comes to mind, and Roger speaks the name aloud. "Bart Newhouse."

Karen tilts her head. "What about him?"

Roger cannot help but chuckle as he massages his brow. "I can't make this game personal. It's about the kids, but I would be lying if I said I don't want to beat Bart Newhouse more than anyone in the world."

Karen offers a half-smile of her own.

"Bart's not such a bad guy," Roger assesses. "Chalk it up to competitiveness. My personality and his have never jibed, and neither have our coaching styles, for that matter. But in the end, the guy's a good basketball coach with a good record; I'll give him that. He got the Academy back to the final four. There were no guarantees I would have done that."

"I think you would have done just fine coaching at the Academy this year."

"Thanks, sweetheart." The tender moment is short-lived as Roger's mischievous chuckle resumes.

"What?" Karen asks.

"No. I shouldn't say it."

"Come on. Say it."

Roger concedes after one final chuckle, already feeling guilty. "I don't think I like Bart's kid either."

"Roger," Karen admonishes under her breath, sorry she made him say it. "He's just a boy." Karen stands to her feet.

Her unruly husband catches her by the arm and playfully swings her onto the bed, his fingers locating her ticklish ribs. "Don't you want to win?" Roger asks. "Don't you? Don't you?"

Karen's shriek of surprise laughter fills the room and travels down the hall.

"Don't you want your husband to win...or do you want Bart Newhouse to win?" Roger chirps mischievously in a cartoon-character voice out of nowhere. "Is that it? Are you cheering for Bart Newhouse? Don't you love your husband more than Bart Newhouse? Huh? Huh?"

The outburst of laughter pries Kevin from his room, and the teenager finds his parents wrestling on the bed. The teenager shakes his head as he quickly exits. "Weird."

The night draws to a close. Tomorrow is the big day. The family lays down to rest. All is well this night.

• • •

Dennison is ready to sleep in his own bed in his Atlanta apartment—his driving speed bears witness to that desire. Granted, he and his fellow agents did not get everyone, namely the Huddler guy. Even so, the Macon area chapter of the Klan has been, at the very least, decimated. Dawson said he spoke with "H." The makeshift FBI office is officially shut down. Plus, Dawson said the FBI is tired of paying for hotel rooms, insisting all agents leave town at once, and Dawson said he would see everyone back in Atlanta in a day or so.

Country mile-marker after country mile-marker blend with the night. "I don't even know where I am," Agent Dennison speaks aloud to himself. On the right side of the road is a dive bar. The man cannot believe it, chuckling at the sight of a Bureau vehicle in the gravel lot. To everyone else in the world, the vehicle is unmarked. To Dennison, it screams *FBI*.

The country and western music blares as Dennison enters, the man surprised to see Agent Runyon across the room.

Sitting by himself, Runyon spots Dennison. "Cy! Get over here!"

"I thought you were in charge of transport tonight," Dennison asks, perplexed by the change in plan.

"The truck is fine," Runyon answers without a care in the world. "Southerland is sitting in the truck around back."

Dennison is a team player but seems less than thrilled with this lapse in protocol.

"Come on, Cy. We're going home tonight. What's one hour give or take? The truck is safe. No one knows we're here."

Just any FBI Agent driving down the highway is Dennison's thought. "If you and Runyon are driving the truck, then whose car is out...."

"Hey, Dennison," speaks a voice behind the agent.

Cy Dennison turns to see Travis Hopper and his signature sneering smile. Dennison pauses in surprise. "Hopper."

"Funny seeing you here," Hopper continues. "Are you here to join us or get us in trouble?" Hopper circles the table to sit next to Runyon.

"Just on my way back to Atlanta and saw the car, which I guess you are driving."

"Come on, Cy. Sit down," Runyon pleads again. "Let's enjoy a round together; celebrate a job well done. We won't tell if you won't." Runyon makes himself laugh.

"Fine by me," Hopper gives his consent.

"What can I get you, sugar," a waitress sidles next to Dennison.

"Just one bottle, please."

Thirty minutes later, and Agent Dennison sits behind two empty bottles. Surprisingly, Hopper is not as unbearable as Dennison thought he would be—Hopper is still full of himself, though. Plus, Dennison already knew Runyon to be the type of guy who, once you get him away from the office, knows how to have a good time.

"All that waiting and then things wrapped up pretty quick," Runyon comments.

"No complaints here," Dennison replies. "I'm ready to sleep at my own place."

"I guess we all are, except Dawson, of course," adds Hopper.

"What do you mean?" Dennison queries.

Runyon takes the bottle from his lips. "I don't know. He stayed for some reason."

Dennison is confused. "In Macon? Tonight."

"Yeah," Runyon answers.

"Why?" Dennison sits perplexed.

"Beats me. He stopped me right before Southerland and I left. He said he needed to correct the shipment."

Dennison cannot hide his confusion. "I'm losing you."

"I don't know. He switched out some boxes. Had us take the ones off the truck and put new boxes on. I didn't care. I was ready to get out of that place."

"Why did he do that? What did he say?" Dennison persists.

Runyon cannot get another word in edgewise because of Dennison's spate of questions. "I don't know, man. He told me to hold on, so, I did. He opened a box, checked the barrels on a few guns and had us switch everything out. That's all."

Dennison sits in bewilderment.

"Something's eating at you, Cy," Hopper comments while bringing a bottle to his lips. "Dawson didn't get your permission. Is that it?"

Runyon snickers at Hopper's quip.

Agent Dennison is too deep in thought to be annoyed by Hopper's smug sarcasm. "He specifically had me log those guns for analysis in Atlanta, and then the shipment was supposed to transport to D.C from there...."

"Well, he's the boss," Hopper cannot help but add to Dennison's agitation on purpose.

The eyes of Agent Cy Dennison widen as he grabs Runyon by the wrist. "Get up. Come on."

Nearly nodding off, Agent Southerland is surprised to see Agents Dennison, Runyon and Hopper all approaching the transport with haste. "Where did you come from, Cy?" inquires Southerland after stepping from the truck.

"Open the back."

Caught off guard, Southerland begins to stammer.

"Now, Southerland." Dennison spins his colleague by the shoulder and begins to walk him toward the back of the truck.

"Okay, Cy, okay. What's going on?" asks Southerland.

Runyon and Hopper follow the men.

Southerland unlocks the back of the truck, barely getting out of the way as Dennison pushes past and climbs inside the covered bed of the Bureau vehicle.

"Look, Cy," Runyon chimes in, "I know we aren't supposed to make stops like this on the job, so if you're here to rat us out...."

All the chatter is background noise to Dennison as he grabs one rifle, then another, then another, checking under the barrel of each weapon.

Runyon continues to ramble. "And don't tell anyone you saw us drinking, because you had a couple, too."

Caring little about Runyon covering his backside, instead, Dennison is much more concerned with the weapons in the truck. He proclaims, "These guns don't have etches under the barrels. These aren't the guns I approved for transport."

• • •

Crammed inside a telephone booth at the end of the lot, Dennison feverishly summons the operator. "I need the number of all residents with the last name Wheeler for Macon, Georgia and all surrounding areas. This is an emergency. I am Agent Cy Dennison of the Federal Bureau of Investigation."

39

"Stevens!" The calm of night is torn asunder by the violent yelling of a name. "Stevens! Stevens!"

Roger lurches upright in bed.

Karen heard it, too. She gasps. Her eyes widening in the dead of night. "What was that?"

"Stevens!" The angry voice commands again.

Roger vaults from their bed, staggering to his feet. "Stay here," he commands. With no light, the man groggily feels his way past the bedroom door, scaling down the hall toward Kevin's room.

"Stevens!"

"Kevin," the father calls in a loud whisper. "Kevin." He enters his son's room. The boy is fine but slow to wake. "Kevin, get up."

Roger clumsily turns the corner, awkwardly finding the banister. His steps are cautious, his way vaguely and strangely lit by the orb of yellow and orange light ascending the staircase and originating beyond the front living room window.

"Roger," Karen calls from behind her husband.

"No! Stay"

"Dad?" Kevin emerges into the hall.

"Go in with your mother. Stay with her, Kevin. Don't come down."

The son obeys.

"Stevens! I'm calling you, Stevens!" The voice persists, hostile, impatient, filling the night.

Roger arrives at the bottom of the staircase and looks to the clock—12:15 a.m. He takes a few more tentative steps. The light beyond the curtains grows brighter as Roger enters the front sitting room. He holds his breath, summoning the courage to peer through the curtain.

"Dad!" The son startles his father, calling to him from the top of the stairs; Kevin looked through the second story window across the front lawn. "There are men out there. A bunch of men. And they are wearing..."

"Stevens! If you don't come out, we will come in!"

"My God!" Karen screams, causing Roger to run back to the bottom of the staircase, his wife and son not sure whether to join Roger downstairs or remain upstairs. "Call the police, Roger!"

The man moves across the poorly lit room the best he can, reaching for the telephone receiver: rapidly, his heart descends, and the man feels as dead as the phone line.

The woman watches her husband lower the receiver from his ear as he turns to look at her without words. "Oh, dear God!" She covers her mouth with her hands.

"Come down next to me, and stay behind me out of sight," he commands. With those words, Roger presses against the far wall and peers past the curtain.

There they are. Roger's eyes try to adjust. He sees a man. He sees men, all dressed alike. "Oh, no," the words escape his lips.

Roger peers into the night again. The first man in full view stands about 20 feet from the front door, covered nearly head to toe in a white hood and robe, the holes in the hood giving way to a pair of lifeless, dark eyes, the silhouette of the man perfectly outlined and illuminated by the intensely glowing light behind him. Arrayed from there is a company of men, all clad the same, all staring at the front of the Anderson home where the Stevens family now resides, waiting for the man and his loved ones to show themselves.

Kevin and Karen clutch each other, the much larger teen attempting to comfort his mother.

"Stevens! Listen to me, Stevens! We have the home surrounded! You will come out!"

"Kevin, keep low but look out the back window. Tell me what you see. Don't turn on any lights."

The son feels his way through the dark house.

"Roger."

"Pray, Karen" is all the man can advise his wife at this moment. "It's the Klan. Pray."

Her fingernails dig into her husband's arms. "They're here. Oh, God. They're here."

Kevin returns. "Dad, there are men out back, too!"

Roger grimaces at the news. Looking past the curtains, he tries to identify how many men are outside. He sees and hears the one clearly, but it is hard to get a count—there are at least a half dozen or so. Soon, another man draped in white emerges and comes into Roger's focus across the front lawn, and the man is not walking alone.

"Oh, no." Roger cannot contain his fear.

"What is it, Roger?"

A tremor pulsates Roger's spine, the man watching through a slit in the curtains as another member of the Klan ruthlessly corrals Mr. and Mrs. Anderson toward the front of the house. The Klansman yells incoherently at the older couple, advancing them by force, raising the end of his shotgun toward the backs of the homeowners.

"It's the Anderson's. They've got the Andersons," Roger covers his mouth in angst, his words now muffled. "God help us."

"God, please, no!" Karen prays breathlessly.

The lead Klansman offers a horrific proposition at the expense of the Anderson couple. "Who should we shoot first, Stevens? How about the woman?"

The cloaked gunman holding the Andersons hostage takes his cue from his leader, irreverently lifting his right foot and placing it in the lower back of Mrs. Anderson, shoving her in front of him and into the open, the woman screaming and tumbling helplessly to the ground.

"No!" Mr. Anderson shouts from both fear and fury, lunging for his wife, dropping to his knees and shielding his wife from the gunman.

The shotgun-brandishing Klansman fumes with anger, flipping the barrel of the weapon in his hands, swinging the handle like a cudgel, striking the protective husband with a blow to the back of the head.

Mrs. Anderson cries in terror as her husband's limp body loses his grip on her and slides to the ground. "No!" she shrieks.

Before she can tend to her wounded husband, the gunman in white grabs her by the top back of her robe and pulls her away, standing her up. The Klansman next takes two steps backward, raising his shotgun in full view, pointing the barrel again at the defenseless woman's back; Mrs. Anderson can only groan and sob.

"What's it going to be, Stevens?" the lead Klansman grows weary of giving commands. "You're coming out of that house one way or another, whether this woman lives or not. I'll burn you out. I'll burn all of you out!" The man pauses for a response from the house…but there is none.

"Don't go, Roger!" Karen spurts toward the door, clutching the back of his shirt.

"They're going to kill her if I don't!"

"They're going to kill you both if you do!"

• • •

Wheeler cuts through the night at 70 mph, driving speedily toward the Anderson property per Dennison's phone call. Dennison told him not to inform anyone else, agents or the police. Thus, Wheeler goes alone.

• • •

Dennison covered the distance back to Macon faster than he thought possible. With his headlights off, the agent pulls the steering wheel hard to the right to land abruptly yet softly in a grassy plain next to the side of the country road. In the distance, he can see a light illuminating the night, a flame, a fire.

• • •

Standing in the dark and out of view to the side of the Anderson home, another agent listens to the commotion coming from the front of the property.

• • •

Dennison lunges from his car and circles to the back, springing the trunk open. A long-range rifle appears. Taking the weapon in hand, Dennison quietly closes the trunk, breathes deeply, and then embarks on a steady jog across the field toward the illumination in the distance.

• • •

"Shoot her!" The leader commands the gunman.

Mrs. Anderson screams, her body tensing to brace for gunfire.

The deadbolt lock to the front door turns, and the door comes ajar, "Wait!" a voice calls from inside the home.

"Wait," the leader orders the execution to cease.

"Don't hurt her!" the voice calls again behind the front door.

"Then show yourself!"

There is no response.

"Now!"

• • •

"No, Roger. I'm begging you!" Inside the foyer of the Anderson home, the debate fraught with fear continues between Roger and Karen.

The man turns to his wife, trying to stabilize his trembling body and quaking voice. A hard decision must be made, and the man will not allow a helpless woman to give her life for his. "Karen, I must."

Karen begins to sob heavily on the shoulder of her husband, and instead of pleading her cause with him, she pleads with God.

Roger Stevens lays his head against his wife, fiercely holding back tears himself. "That's it, honey. Pray for me."

Roger next looks to his son, the teen's mouth quivering by the surreal moment. Roger's face is resolute. "Stay with your mother, Kevin. Do not open this door; not for anything. Do you understand?"

Kevin Stevens cannot believe this is happening. He cannot believe they are having this conversation. All the young man can do is nod tentatively at his father's instructions, attempting to process all of it in a microsecond.

"Listen to me, son. Don't come out, and if the house starts…" the man's voice begins to choke up, but he quickly pulls it together. "If the house starts to burn, still don't go outside. Do you understand? Take your mom to the basement, find cover, and pray for someone to send help. That will be your best move."

The boy cannot believe the words his father just spoke to him.

"Answer me, Kevin."

"Yes, Dad."

Roger pauses one final time—the opportunity to watch his son come of age has been cruelly thrust upon him. "I love you, Kev."

Tears starts to form in the eyes of the teenager.

Karen whimpers as her husband places her in the arms of their son.

"Take your mother."

"That's it, Stevens!" The lead Klansman outside is tired of waiting, desiring action.

In an instant, Roger's sentimentality turns to white-hot anger as he pivots to address the belligerent man through the opening in the door. "I'm coming out! You hear me? I'm coming out!" Roger fearfully looks into the night; several Klansmen ominously litter the property, a large, intensely burning cross behind them.

• • •

Agent Dennison hearkens back to his days as a biathlete as he steadies his breathing through the vacant field in double-time, his rifle draped over his shoulder—the blazing orange light in the foreground leading his way.

• • •

Going from memory, Agent Wheeler passes a perpendicular road in the night, then slams on his brakes, performing a U-turn in the middle of the deserted country road. Changing direction, the man accelerates down what he hopes is the way toward the Anderson property.

• • •

The front door fully opens. Roger shows one hand to the men on the lawn, then the other, and then, reluctantly his head.

"Don't hurt her." he pleads. "She's not the one you want."

The leader watches Roger Stevens eventually step and reveal his entire body from behind the door, both his palms showing at shoulder level. Beneath the white hood, the lead Klansman smiles before snapping back to anger.

"You're not in a position to educate me on anything," the sinister voice speaks from behind the dark eyeholes. "She's dirt…, but you're lower than dirt."

Roger shuffles forward. His breathing sporadic. His eyes shifting continuously; Klansmen stand variously positioned in his line of sight. Flames ascend as the wooden cross crackles and hisses.

The leader of the men is twenty feet from Roger—dead ahead. To Roger's right, another Klansman holds Mrs. Anderson at gunpoint. She is wailing uncontrollably.

The leader begins to approach Roger Stevens. Upon closing the distance, he gives an order. "On your knees."

Roger hesitates, his hands still elevated.

"On your knees!" the Klansman shouts. "I won't ask again."

At those words, the shotgun clicks into final position.

"Okay, okay," Roger concedes, dropping quickly to one knee...then both knees.

The Klansman relishes seeing the man in submission before him. "Roger Stevens: we finally speak face to face." The leader of the men calmly and eerily clasps his hands, scanning the frightened man up and down. "I just had to get a closer look at you. I just had to get a closer look at a man who would betray his people, his kind, his country and, most of all, God in heaven to intermingle and yoke yourself so unevenly with such an irredeemable race."

Roger listens but does not absorb much, all of it coming across as background noise as Roger keeps an eye on Mrs. Anderson.

"And for what?" The hooded man continues his diatribe. "To die? To die as a martyr with no reward? That's the worst kind of death there is."

From behind Roger and inside the house, Karen screams amid sounds of a scuffle. Roger whips his head around, gritting his teeth. "Karen!" he yells.

A gruff male voice accompanies the cacophony from inside the front door, and soon, to Roger's dismay, Karen and Kevin both emerge reluctantly, forced outside by another Klansmen who entered the back of the home and now holds them at gunpoint.

"Karen," Roger calls, beckoning his wife to run to his side.

"No, no!" the leader decrees. "Separate them!"

On cue, the masked gunman who forced the man's wife and son from the home grabs Karen by the arm.

Roger instinctively balls his fist and does his best to resist from his knees. At the first sign of Roger's rebellion, the gunman lets loose of Karen and his raises his shotgun, aiming the barrel directly at her.

"No!" Roger shouts. "No!"

Slowly backing away, Kevin lifts both hands and pulls at the sides of his hair in panic, a helpless witness.

"Go, Karen!" Roger insists. "Go stand with Kevin. Go, now!"

Through a flurry of tears, the woman heeds and falls back into the arms of her son, both nearly collapsing on the porch.

The nearby gunman now points his shotgun at both the mother and son.

"Stop pointing at them!" Roger commands. "I'm here. I'm the one you want. Leave them alone!"

Before Roger can turn around, he takes the brunt of an open hand across the side of his face. Roger starts to involuntarily froth and spit from anger. Behind Roger and to his left, his wife and son are at gunpoint. To his right, Mrs. Anderson is at gunpoint. Before him, the leader of the Macon Klan has his hand poised to strike again.

● ● ●

Oxygen rushes in and out of Dennison's lungs. He halts his run; the Anderson home is now in the near distance, and there is a commotion. Dennison bends on one knee in the desolate field. He swings the rifle from his shoulder, his hands comfortably gripping the smooth steel. Bringing the scope to his eye, his still rapid breathing moves the gun up and down. Dennison calms himself, adjusting the scope. Through the lens, he surveys multiple men spread across the front lawn, all of them draped in white—Klansmen.

A burning cross illuminates the night sky in the middle. One Klansman stands over another man—looks to be a civilian—on the front porch, the defenseless man on his knees with his hands in the air. To the right of the men on the porch, a young man holds a woman in his arms as a gunman keeps them at bay. To the left of the porch and in the yard, yet another gunman holds a weapon to the back of a woman, a black woman. A body next to her lies motionless on the ground.

Dennison cannot hear the conversation; still, the situation is critical, and time is of the essence. Fighting uncertainty, the FBI sharpshooter swings his scope back and forth among the gunmen and the leader, calculating, *Who to target first? Hit one gunman and the other may fire. Hit the leader and both may shoot. Or hit the leader and maybe the rest will scatter.* With that thought, Dennison sharpens his aim, burrowing his sight into the upper back of the leader of the KKK who stands over the defenseless man on the front porch.

• • •

FBI Agent Wheeler rumbles up a country road, still five minutes out.

• • •

Two hours away, a reverend paces the floor as in the past. "The name of The Lord is a strong tower," he repeats in prayer. "The righteous run to it…and are safe."

• • •

"We are here as representatives of the Kuklos, the righteous circle of brotherhood, to uphold sacred values and enforce morality," decrees the voice from beneath the hood of the leader. "And we do this in the name of The Lord."

Roger looks to his left to see his wife trembling and shrinking in the arms of their son. Kevin holds her, holding himself up at the same time. Both the mother and son are paralyzed with fear. Roger knows he should pray, but he cannot overcome the fury welling inside, and, against all common sense, he blares his opinion of the Klansman to his face.

"You know nothing about the name of The Lord," Roger stares deeply into the dark eyeholes of the hood. "You misuse Scripture to filter hatred through your twisted view of the world. The only thing good about you is you're a dying breed."

The pulse of the Klansman accelerates. He wants to kill Stevens right now. However, he senses fear behind the tough words of the treasonous white man, and nothing would satisfy the leader of the Klan more than watching Roger Stevens watch his wife and son die first.

The Klansman leans forward, raising his hand.

Roger flinches, expecting the man to strike him again.

The man does not. Instead, the leader lifts the hood from before his face.

Roger first recognizes the jagged scar, and after a few moments he ultimately places the man as the one who stared at him across the aisle at the church in Ridgewood. Roger is speechless as he tries to put everything together, his mind generating one question: *why?*

The look of Raymond Huddler is one of great satisfaction. The man never enjoyed wearing a hood and robe. The man always believed the things he did should be done in the open without remorse. Furthermore, Huddler knows the time for which he has long waited has come. No more secret meetings. No more hiding. No more reservations. No more seeking consent or permission. The breath of Roger Stevens ceases tonight. "I want you to see the face of the man who killed your wife and son...and you."

Raymond Huddler pulls the hood over his face again and turns to walk in the opposite direction. "It is written that judgment begins in the house of The Lord, and we are here to execute said judgment…, and I have the honor and responsibility of pronouncing said judgment." Huddler turns to face Roger Stevens one final time.

• • •

Dennison gives pause at the leader taking several steps back, but the situation still reads as critical. Gingerly, the sharpshooter massages his finger along the trigger, maintaining the leader of the group in his sights. In his mind, he begins to time his heartbeats, ready to shoot at the bottom of an upcoming breath, aiming between the leader's shoulder-blades.

First, Dennison pauses again; there is more movement.

• • •

"Halt," an unexpected voice calls from somewhere in the night.

The attention of every robed man in the front yard shifts.

Soon a hand with a badge can be seen extending around the side of the house and into the open. "Halt!" the voice repeats. "FBI."

The gunman on the porch steps back to point his weapon at the distraction emerging from the dark.

The leader of the Klan watches as the man steps into full visibility.

• • •

FBI Special Agent in Charge Harold Dawson continues to display his badge as he presents himself in the open. "Federal agent! Lower your weapons!"

• • •

Dennison's blood runs cold at the sight of his superior through the scope.

• • •

Confidently, Agent Dawson addresses his audience. The information Elvin Butler provided was right on point; time, location, everything—the Ridgewood Officer gave up Huddler and his inner circle then skipped town. "Lower your weapons!"

"What are you doing here?" Huddler asks from behind his hood.

The agent does not answer at first but instead brandishes a weapon of his own. "First, have your men lower their weapons."

Huddler looks to his subordinates and nods, causing the men to lower their shotguns for the time being. "I asked, what are you doing here?"

Despite the high tension, Dawson strikes a tone of humor. "Just checking up on you men. I didn't know they still burned crosses in the South. An outdated concept, don't you think?"

The leader of the Klan is unamused. "I have this under control. I am in charge here."

"Oh, you are," Dawson responds, unimpressed, moving closer to the action but not too close, stopping ten feet away from the woman and her son. "Let's not get in a discussion about jurisdiction, men. I win that every time. Besides, it looks like you have taken hostages here. You know I can't condone that."

Roger Stevens peers from his petrified state. Initially, he was relieved at the sight of the FBI agent, recognizing Dawson from the morning following the church fire and failed bombing of their home. However, the more the agent and Klansman speak with familiarity, the more Roger knows the situation is amiss.

"Help us," Roger pleads, his risen hands trembling as he does.

The FBI agent looks at the man with an utter lack of respect. "You've made your bed, sir. Now, you have to lay in it."

"It's best if you're not here," Huddler reengages Dawson.

"You don't blame me for verifying, do you?" Dawson retorts. "Ensuring you finish the job tonight, especially after the mistakes of the past?"

The man seethes beneath his hood.

"Besides," Agent Dawson turns to again look at Roger Stevens. "This man has caused us tremendous problems and cost us tremendous amounts of money."

The more banter that passes between the federal agent and the lead Klansman, the more Roger comes to grips with the fact none of them—not he, his wife, his son or the Andersons—will live to see another day. *This is it*, Roger resolves internally. He brought his family to Macon on a hunch, to do nothing more than get them killed.

Roger, still on his knees, vacillates between pleading for mercy and speaking his mind. Not about to go quietly, just as he addressed Huddler earlier, the man's rage wins the battle. "You're a disgrace," Roger speaks directly at Harold Dawson.

The FBI agent glares in furious disbelief at the man on his knees, offended by not only his words but his presence. Dawson responds by stepping toward Roger and pointing his gun squarely in the face of the unarmed man. "You have no right to address me. Not you, of all people."

Karen begins to shake and cry again. It is clear no one is here to help her family tonight.

Roger tries to remain strong, but the formidable image of an oncoming gun forces the man to flinch and cringe as he braces for the impact of a bullet.

· · ·

Dennison is locked on Dawson through the scope of his rifle, watching the veteran agent approach the man on the porch, gun drawn. As part of an out-of-body experience, Dennison has FBI Special Agent in Charge Harold Dawson in his sights, his boss, his superior, his supervisor, his mentor. Dennison pauses, lowering his rifle, searching for sanity, casting his eyes to the ground. *How can I shoot another federal agent?* Dennison ponders, but there is no time to spare; a decision must be made and must be made now, right or wrong. Dennison answers his own question by speaking aloud and swinging his rifle back into action. "He's no longer a federal agent."

• • •

Agent Wheeler swings his car wildly into the final turn, desperately hoping to make it in time.

• • •

"Oh, God, please," Karen mutters under her breath, her face buried in the shoulder of her son, his arms enveloping her.

"Stand up straight, like a man!" Dawson commands Roger.

Roger does not want to dignify the agent by obliging.

"I said get up!" Dawson rages, stepping back to point his handgun at the mother and son to his left. "Do you want your wife to get shot? If I don't do it, these animals will! And I will let them!"

Huddler watches Dawson's every move, wincing at the thought of the man spoiling his prize.

Both Klansmen with shotguns track Dawson as well, unconvinced by the man's motives and presence here.

To protect his wife and son, Roger finds the strength to wobble to his feet and eventually stand tall.

Dawson walks toward Roger again, drawing closer until the end of the agent's handgun is inches from the face of the defenseless man.

Roger twitches, almost closing his eyes at the sight of Dawson's finger on the trigger. Roger's life begins to race through his mind…from childhood to adulthood…to marriage to fatherhood…to the faces on his Macon South team. "I did what you asked, God," Roger breathes quietly.

"What did you say," Dawson bids in disgust.

"I did what you asked," Roger repeats.

Dawson readies to pull the trigger, his face filled with fury; the agent is ready to send a message to everyone here—he is still in charge. "Open your eyes," he addresses Roger Stevens for the final time, ready to shoot. "Say to me what you said before. I dare you."

Karen and Kevin grip each other tightly, both looking away before the sound.

The gunshot is sensed and heard by Roger more than felt, the sniper's bullet sailing past Roger's head by mere inches and hitting Dawson in the upper torso, near the neck, jolting the man, causing an instant convulse as he stumbles backward.

Karen screams.

Kevin ducks, pulling his mother down with him.

Huddler drops his head from the sound of the bullet that pierced the air just above him. The man next whirls to see where the shot came from, to see which of his men did it—the shot was not fired by any of his men.

Falling against the house, Dawson felt the metal instantly pass through skin and muscle, shattering his clavicle as bone fragments are now shrapnel inside his upper chest. His mind boggled, the agent knows it was not the blast of a shotgun that hit him. Dawson's rolling eyes scan the group of Klansmen before him. They all appear equally befuddled by the gunfire, looking to each other for answers. The veteran draws one fleeting conclusion: a sniper. Dawson's thoughts flicker from nausea and blood loss as the man falls to the porch near Karen and Kevin's feet. As he begins to lose consciousness from a severed artery, a name crosses Dawson's mind: *Dennison.*

With weapon still in hand, Dawson twists his neck and tries to find Roger with the end of his gun. Instead, Dawson's waning reflexes cause him to fire at the first object that moves, the gunman on the porch.

Dawson misses Roger and strikes the Klansman, a splatter of blood instantly painting his white robe from the inside as the man collapses from a gunshot wound to the stomach.

Kevin lays his body over his mother to protect her.

Roger's countenance is of shock at the unfurling scene.

The Klansmen shuffle and pivot in bedlam, scanning their eyes to find the culprit, but no one is to be seen.

Another phantom bullet in the night takes flight. This round hits the gunman behind Mrs. Anderson, dropping him to the ground with a precision kill shot from distance. The woman screeches and wisely falls on the body of her husband, Mr. Anderson jolting back to consciousness.

Huddler swivels his neck, dumbfounded, jarred: he and his men are under attack.

The remaining Klansmen are discomfited, yelling at one another with audible incoherence as they scramble to take cover from the invisible gunman. Another Klansman near Huddler takes his shotgun and fires wildly into the nightly at the hidden sniper.

"Look!" shouts one of the cloaked men, pointing to the east. "They're coming!"

The Klansmen turn to see the rapidly approaching FBI vehicle of Agent Wheeler, the flashing light atop his car flooding the once dark horizon.

The robed gunman who fired aimlessly into the air stumbles backward and falls, his shotgun discharging again.

Amid the tumult, Huddler—crouching in the front lawn from anxiety over airborne bullets—looks to the front porch where both Agent Dawson and the other gunman lay motionless. The leader then focuses his attention on the family, the three of them now hunched and bundled together—father, mother, and son—shrinking to avoid gunfire as well. Huddler's blood waxes hot. He grits his teeth beneath his mask. He turns and scampers toward a nearby shotgun in the grass, the weapon left in a panic by one of the fleeing Klansmen. Huddler grabs the firearms and turns to the front porch.

• • •

Wheeler rolls down his window and fires into the air at the sight of the men in robes scurrying. The light atop the agent's car was so bright it caused the Klansmen to believe ten cars were coming instead of just one.

Vaulting from his car, Wheeler fires another shot for good measure into the air. "FBI, everyone down on the ground."

Another Klansman—still draped in pride—is furious at the sight of surrender from his fellow men. Clutching his rifle, he exclaims in the night, "Fight, my brothers!"

With those words he fires at Agent Wheeler, the bullet missing the man but not by much, hitting the top of the windshield. Wheeler reacts instinctively, shooting the gunman dead, bringing the other Klansmen into immediate submission as the group collectively falls face first to the ground.

• • •

Dennison beholds through his scope the lead Klansman refusing to surrender. The man in white has retrieved a weapon and is now sprinting toward the family on the front porch. Dennison calmly refocuses and takes aim at the aggressor, lining him up. In between heartbeats, Dennison exudes a breath and pulls the trigger....

Nothing happens. The rifle jams. Dennison feverishly recalibrates. The gun jams again as he watches the gunman in the distance arrive at the edge of the porch.

• • •

Raymond Huddler is out of breath but has enough of his bearings to plant his feet and steady his aim at Roger Stevens and his family, a shotgun resting in the hands of the leader of the Macon KKK.

Roger assesses the threat but can do nothing about it. Instead, the husband and father presses himself atop his family, pushing them to the wooden boards. "Stay down!" he yells over his wife and son, the man taking the only action he can: putting his head down.

Raymond Huddler pulls the trigger.

• • •

Wheeler has his weapon pointed at the group, too far away for a shot.

• • •

Dennison watches helplessly through his scope. "Oh, no."

• • •

The hammer drops but the shotgun does not engage. Both Huddler and the family on the porch hear the empty click; the Klan leader failing to realize both shots were already fired by the previous gunman. Huddler curses loudly as he tries to fire the weapon again, but to no avail. Among the swelling chaos of the night, heard above all is the silence of Huddler's empty shotgun.

• • •

Lifting his head, Kevin Stevens pushes off the protective arms of his father. Replacing the normally kind, amicable gaze of the teenager is an enraged glare. White eyes with red veins burn through the would-be murderer before him.

Raymond Huddler—with an inoperable weapon in hand—recognizes the look of a boy who is suddenly a man...and begins to backpedal.

Kevin Stevens has had enough. Blood instantly rushes to his calf muscles as—without thinking any longer—the athletic teen bursts from his crouched position as would an Olympic sprinter from his blocks.

Roger feels the rush of energy blow past; all he can see now is the back of his son as Kevin vaults from the front porch. "Kevin! No!"

Karen looks on in terror. "Kevin!"

Kevin Stevens leaps the entire set of front porch steps and hits the ground running, rage ballooning with each heartbeat.

Once backpedaling, Raymond Huddler now pivots at the sight of the oncoming bull and begins to run, stumbling and almost falling as he does. Despite his scamper, the middle-aged man in a robe is no match to outrun the 6'4", 180 pound, 18-year-old specimen that is Kevin Stevens, and the youth closes the distance with ferocious speed.

Kevin feels empowered with each exhale, his pulse resonating throughout his body. His arms flexing, his legs flexing, he has never felt stronger, faster, or more laser-focused in his life. As a lion hunts prey across the plain, Kevin has the man who tried to kill his family in his sights.

Powerless, Roger and Karen watch from the front porch.

Raymond Huddler, breathing sporadically, his world crumbling, runs for his life, but it does not feel fast enough. Huddler turns his head to see how much cushion he has: he has none; Kevin is there.

To keep from being overrun from behind, Raymond Huddler spins his body toward the aggressor, his weight carrying him backward. The face of Kevin Stevens is in view now, every detail, every protruding vein—a look of vengeance.

"No!" Karen screams from the house.

The Klan leader grabs at Kevin to keep from falling.

The youth shows no remorse; he has been pushed too far tonight—beyond the cliff of mercy. Kevin rams both hands through the feeble defense of the backpedaling man and grabs Huddler's cloaked shoulders with fists of iron. Kevin's momentum surges as he hoists Raymond Huddler completely from the ground, the teenager digging his feet in the soil while pumping his legs.

Huddler is at the bulging teen's mercy, and Kevin sees eyes fraught with fear through the holes of the mask.

It is now Raymond Huddler who whimpers in anguish as the vengeful young man plows him backward.

• • •

From long range through his scope, Dennison watches Huddler and the young man wrangle, but there is no clean shot.

• • •

The violent struggle in the front yard catches Agent Wheeler's attention. He sees the direction the two are heading.

• • •

"No!" Karen screams in horror at what is about to happen.

"Kevin," Roger speaks with hollow breath as he watches his son attack the leader of the Ku Klux Klan.

Kevin feels as if he could run Huddler right out of Georgia. Little does the teen realize, behind the man and out of Kevin's line of sight is a horrific collision waiting to happen, and Kevin unwittingly uses the man as a battering ram, the two crashing into the burning cross in the middle of the Anderson front yard.

Previously frozen in fear, Roger leaves his wife and sprints for his son.

"Kevin!" his mother screams as the impact flattens the cross in the yard, emitting a secondary burst of flames, flames that momentarily engulf both Kevin Stevens and Raymond Huddler as they tumble to the ground.

The impact flips Kevin completely over the man, and the teen is chewed up and spit out by the collision, propelled several feet beyond the cross and onto the ground, head over heels. A searing hot pain immediately takes hold of Kevin's left arm from the shoulder of his short-sleeved shirt up to his neck—he is on fire. Kevin instinctively rolls and rolls…, frantically pulling his shirt off as he does.

Suddenly, everyone on the front property of the Andersons—Kevin, Roger, Karen, Mrs. Anderson, the FBI agents, the scattering remnants of the KKK—stops at the overwhelming screams of horror.

Raymond Huddler vaults to his feet in delirium, his white robe engulfed in flames. Wildly grasping at nothing and everything, the burning man stomps around an imaginary circle as his arms flail, spontaneous outbursts of pain discharging from his lungs.

Kevin's eyes reflect orange and red flashes of light as he retreats from the aimlessly spinning human torch in the darkness, the pitch of the wailing man's voice ascending higher and higher in searing anguish, the white robe melting to his skin.

"Kevin!" Roger runs toward his son and helps pull him further from the burning man. The two take several steps backward together.

• • •

Dennison watches through his scope in disbelief at the image of a man swinging his arms, reaching for help where there is none. There is no water, no blanket, and no relief—only fire.

• • •

Wheeler stands over the remaining members of the Klan who look on with fear and dismay at the sight of their burning leader.

"Raymond," one of them gasps.

• • •

Mere seconds last forever as Raymond Huddler convulses, flaps and whirls, his actions only giving further breath to the blaze. The body of the man once cloaked in pride from head to toe plummets lifelessly to the ground, face first. Screams draw silent, and there Raymond Huddler is consumed, his burning body taking the place of the cross since extinguished.

Breathless, Karen arrives to stand by her husband and son.

Roger shields his wife from the horrific sight, the man turning his head as well. Roger looks to find Kevin still staring—mesmerized—at the man's body ablaze on the ground.

"Kevin," Roger speaks to get his attention.

The teen does not blink, staring straight ahead, oxygen pouring out of his nose and mouth.

"Kevin…. Kevin," Roger repeats. This time the voice of the man is accompanied by tender hands turning the teenager's face toward his own.

Kevin emerges from his trance to recognize his father.

"Look away, son." Roger speaks softly. "There's no need to look anymore."

Sudden remorse overtakes Kevin's countenance as the teen falls into his parents' arms.

The father lays his hand on the back of his son's neck. "It's all right, son. We don't need to look anymore."

40

The next day, Charles Bullock is the first to greet Roger Stevens in his Geometry classroom, and, to the principal's surprise, Roger has a guest on his arm.

"Good morning, sir...and ma'am," Mr. Bullock salutes Roger and his bride, both smiling yet ostensibly weathered by the overnight events. The concerned principal strides past the teacher's desk, gazing proudly at his coach. "Oh, Roger.... I thought you might be here, but you don't need to be. There's no way you got any sleep last night."

Roger offers his best smile through a fog of exhaustion. Following the near-death experience for him and his family in the middle of the night and the subsequent lengthy question-and-answer sessions with the local police and the FBI, Roger's days run together; the past year is one long extended haze. Even so, Roger has faced the fire, figuratively and literally, and he is still here. "Sir, the team leaves for Atlanta today." Roger declares. "Nothing can stop me from being here."

Awash with amazement, the principal answers, "I know, I know. At least you could have waited to arrive for the rally. I would have found someone to cover your class. For heaven's sake, I would have taught it for you."

"I know you would have, sir."

Mr. Bullock shifts his sympathetic eyes and attention to Mrs. Stevens. "And you, Karen? How are you making it today?"

Karen matches her husband's honorable effort. "We are here," she replies with all sincerity. "Just...glad to be here, thank God."

The principal does not want to belabor the obvious, and yet he does not want to breeze callously past it, either. Again, Mr. Bullock looks to Roger. The two men smile at each other amid a student-less classroom, and, without words, they both relive the surreal events that have transpired since the first day they met over a year ago—a long line of deadly and miraculous events. A school bombing with no one killed, a church fire with no members injured, burning crosses, corruption, dead FBI agents, dead Klan members, and all of this while Macon South has advanced to its first ever state basketball tournament. Furthermore, the team, their coach, and half the Macon South community leave for the Georgia capital later today.

"Roger." Principal Bullock pauses, looking to the floor, shaking his head. "I.... I don't know what to say. I knew it would be a tough situation for you, for all of us, if you came here. But I didn't know it would be...." Principal Bullock brings his eyes level to lock with those of Coach Stevens. "If I had known all of this would happen, I never would have asked you to come here."

Never a man to take pleasure in the suffering of others, Roger must admit it is pleasant to hear and feel he has company at this moment in life, desolate yet full and exhilarating. His players are about to board a bus for the final four in Atlanta to play—of all teams—his former school. Roger reconciles: it is just the way the past year has gone; ups, downs, mountains, and valleys.

"I know you well enough by now, Principal. You didn't want any of these hard times for us, and, frankly, neither did we. I certainly didn't want to bring any hardship on you or the wonderful people of Macon South. I can't stand here and tell you I understand everything that's happened or that's going to happen, but in the end, after all the ups and downs and close calls and miracles and near-death experiences for all of us, my conclusion is that this situation is so crazy, I know God must be right in the middle of it. What else can I do at this point but trust Him to see us all the way through to the other side?"

With those words, Karen squeezes closer to her husband's side, standing in agreement with him.

• • •

The energy in the makeshift auditorium is electric; the student body is about to send its basketball team into uncharted waters. The South cheerleaders face each other, forming a boulevard of elated support as the players file through. One by one, the players are introduced over a squawking, secondhand P.A. system, and by the time Kevin Stevens jogs across the floor, the room reaches a fever pitch.

Standing last to be introduced, Coach Stevens cannot help but smile at how Macon South has embraced this team, his son, his wife and even him as head coach. It has been a long and tough journey. It has been an unpredictable road, but the blessings of God have been undeniably good, more than he could have asked or thought them to be.

"And last but not least, the Head Coach of your Macon South Muskrats, Coach Roger Stevens!"

The South faithful erupt in cheer. The faculty and student body are on their feet. It is clear: they accept him, and he accepts them.

The energy from the crowd gives Coach Stevens a boost as his venerable walk soon becomes a jovial jog, the man disappearing into the assemblage of his waiting players with high-fives all around—everybody is fired up.

Eventually, the coach re-emerges and ambles to the microphone.

"Thank you." Roger tries to part the excessive volume with his humble words. His first attempt fails to dent the cacophony of noise, so he tries again. "Thank you. Thank you. I greatly appreciate your kindness."

Ultimately, the crowd yields; the room is full of youthful vigor.

"I greatly appreciate your display of support for your team, and my family and me. I am proud of this group of players, their work, their effort, the sweat, the commitment day after day to the school, to me and each other. I could not be prouder of them, and, oh, by the way, in about one hour this team is getting on a bus to Atlanta!" Roger cannot help but raise his voice and his fist, his tone causing those in attendance to vault to their feet again for another standing ovation.

"Thank you. Thank you. Oh!" Roger exclaims, bringing his fingers to his chin, posing as a man deep in thought. "I think I forgot something. Men," Roger pivots to face his players on the front row, "I think we forgot something, didn't we?"

"Yes, we did, Coach. You know we did," ring the voices from the Muskrat players.

Roger shifts to the crowd again. "Macon South, I apologize. I need to introduce one more person, one more player. Ladies and gentlemen, let's hear it for Mr. Billy Taylor!"

The student body and faculty are caught by surprise, and they immediately start to applaud as a side door is thrown open by two attendants. It takes a few moments, and the pause causes the handclapping to wane. Eventually, through the door rolls a wheelchair. Seated in the chair is a young black man with an elderly black woman proudly pushing from behind. The crowd is astonished at the sight of Billy Taylor, and those present are conflicted: should they celebrate, or should they show restraint? The sight of the once athletically proud teenager is jarring.

Billy's frame is visibly thirty pounds lighter, and his legs hanging from the front of the wheelchair lack noticeable muscle. The once rough and tough teen who prowled the halls of Macon South has been reduced to an average-sized guy in the eyes of his peers. The faces of shock prevent Billy from fully embracing the moment with joy. However, more than anything, Billy is just glad to be alive.

Roger takes over and begins to applaud again, sending a signal to the rest of the assembly, and the others in the room take the hint. The members of the Muskrat roster stand to their feet at the sight of their former star. Following suit, those in attendance eventually stand to their feet as well.

Billy's grandmother Betty seems to be the happiest person in the room as she brings her grandson's wheelchair to a stop next to his teammates on the front row. The players surround Billy and overwhelm him with a deluge of kind words and pats on the shoulders.

Billy Taylor looks as humble and open to compassion as he ever has.

Roger gives a long pause, letting his players greet their teammate and allowing the crowd to take their seats.

Karen smiles through tears as she watches the reunion among the kids.

Roger resumes. "It's obvious there has been more to this basketball season than just basketball. As I have often said, life is not all about sports. There are more important things in life than sports. But while life is not all about sports, sports can be about life. The importance of unity, teamwork, hard work, perseverance, surmounting the odds, faith in each other through challenging times: these lessons endure for a lifetime. Furthermore, basketball seasons come and go, classic games come and go, great teams come and go, but the relationships can last forever. I still have friends to this day who are my friends because we played basketball together over 30 years ago.

"Men," Roger pivots to look at his players on the front row, the group listening closely. "My advice to you is this—make these relationships last forever."

The players heed the words of their coach, several nodding in response while looking to one another.

Roger clears his throat, his tone becoming somber. "As some of you may know or not know, my family and I are blessed just to be here this morning. In case you have not heard, in the dead of night, a group of Klan members came to our home and targeted my family."

A fearful hush falls. Word of the attack had moved through some circles of the South community, but not all. Those in attendance look to each other with alarm. Every ear listens intently.

Roger allows the low drone in the room to settle as the details remain fresh in his mind; he can still picture the men who donned white robes and hoods. "They came to our home while we slept. They burned a cross in the middle of the front yard, they forced us from our home, and they even held us at gunpoint..."

As Karen hears the words, she closes her eyes while reliving the harrowing memory from just a few, short, fateful hours ago.

On the front row of the rally, Kevin drops his head, his lips pursed.

Some nearby teammates pat Kevin's back in support.

The South faithful gasp at the news.

"Nevertheless," Roger proceeds, his tone growing in optimism, "by the grace of God—and I must emphasize by the grace of God—the FBI arrived in time to save our lives and bring the guilty men to justice."

Though still stunned, the crowd releases more applause.

"Thank you.... So, here we are, all of us in a similar boat. During the past year, Macon South High School was bombed. Thank God, that plan killed no one—a miracle. As many of you probably know, there was a plan to bomb our home several days ago as well, in the middle of the night while we slept, with my wife lying next to me and our son down the hall, but that attempt failed and killed no one—another miracle. Many of us in this room attend church together, and many of us saw Second Baptist burned to the ground. Again, thank God, no members of the church were injured."

"These evil events that have taken place, they have not just happened to one of us, but many, if not all, of us. To be even more personal this morning, I dare say I am not the only one to be called horrible names in my time here at Macon South. Some of your families have received death threats, and I know this because you have told me the stories. Please understand, I don't recall and cite all these dreadful details to cast us down any further. No, I highlight these details for us to stop and reflect. There are many hardships you and I have in common. When I think on all that's been done to us, to me and you, I cannot help but think of some other words I've read before."

Roger opens the book before him and begins to read. "'Three times I was beaten with rods,'" the man begins, his voice coming strong. "'Once I was stoned; three times I was shipwrecked; a night and a day I have been in the deep; in journeys often, in perils of water, in perils of robbers, in perils of my own countryman,' and on the list goes." Roger closes the book.

"Those words are from Paul in the New Testament, but, if I may, I would like to add some personal commentary," Roger interjects. "I've been threatened, I've been shot at, I've had a burning cross staked in my yard, I've had a player almost beaten to death, I've had my church burned to the ground, I almost had my house bombed, and I had my school bombed...."

A sense of pride washes the South faithful as they hear Roger Stevens refer to their school as *his* school.

"Therefore," Roger's voice ascends with passion, "I hope you don't mind if I'm just glad to be alive this morning! I hope you don't mind if I'm just glad to be here, and I hope you don't mind if I take a few minutes to speak what's on my mind!"

The crowd matches the man's surge with another round of applause—an *amen* or two even filters through the crowd as the longtime Sunday school teacher rounds into form.

"Because the truth is, when you've stared down the barrel of a loaded gun, for some reason, you gain perspective. Some of you know what I'm talking about. When you almost die, you come to appreciate life more than ever. So, as I stand in the middle of what we call a public school, I'm not ashamed to admit the truth; and the truth is I believe in God. Yes, I said it. I said it in a public school. I believe in God."

"All right!" A voice makes its way through the crowd, accompanied by laughter and more applause.

"God help us as we begin to phase His presence out of our schools. I shudder to think where our school systems might be in 50 years."

"God help us," echoes an anonymous voice from the audience.

"So, the day may come when they drag me out of a public school for exercising my faith in God, but until then, I'm going to get my money's worth and talk about God to my heart's content."

"Yes, sir! Yes, sir!"

Principal Bullock cannot help but smile from his nearby seat, not about to pull the plug on the speaker of the hour. Instead, the principal settles in for more.

"That was my introduction, and now I'm ready to begin."

Roger Stevens is on a roll, and the crowd is with him—more laughter permeates the masses.

"Let me put it like this.... I teach Geometry, and as a Geometry teacher, I love discussing angles. Now, I realize that topic might not be exciting for some of you, but as for me—I love discussing all angles. More specifically, as long as I can see the angles, the angles make sense to me. But with God, here's the thing: He is God, and I am not. So, whether I see all the angles in life or not is up to Him. Whether I understand all the angles in life or not is up to Him. And none of it, regardless of what I see or don't see, changes the fact that He is God and I am not."

"And that's how I describe the last year of my life. I came to Macon South without seeing the angle God was working. This past year has given me the highest of highs and the lowest of lows. There have been moments of pure, unadulterated exuberance. I mean from the first play of the season when Billy dunked the basketball to the game-winner Kevin hit in the regional final, and all the wonderful moments in between as these young men and I have come to know one another. I had a reporter ask me a question the other day. He asked me, 'How's your son adjusting to playing basketball at Macon South?' to which I replied, 'Which son are you talking about? I've got about twelve sons now.'"

Roger motions toward the entire basketball roster on the front row, the crowd again letting the team hear their support in the background.

"And then, there have been times—let's face it—that have not been so good. There were times over the past year when I thought the worst decision I ever made was coming to Macon. At times it seemed to be the worst decision for me, the worst decision for my family, and even the worst decision for all of you."

The pace at which the man speaks begins to slow as he searches carefully for his next words. "I don't like to admit this, but I might as well for the sake of transparency. There was a fleeting moment, when I had a gun in my face last night..., there was part of me that thought me dying and being out of the way would be best for everybody, that all of this would end, and everyone could go on with their lives."

"No," a voice disagrees. "Don't even think it."

"However, I've come to the following conclusion: whether I'm here or not, whether I die or not, even whether all of you are here or not, this hatred is not going to end. Let's be honest with ourselves. This hatred has been in the world for a long time, and, I'm sad to say, it will be here for many years to come. How do I know this? Because there is evil in the hearts of men and women, and there's nothing either you or I can do to change that. Please understand: I'm not saying all of this to discourage you. No, I'm telling you this to get all of us to the truth. And here is the truth: neither you nor I can change someone's heart...."

"Now, the older I get, the less time I have for things that don't work in my life. I am always open to new things, of course, because I am the first to admit I don't know it all. But once it becomes clear to me a certain idea isn't working, I am quick to move on. So, let me share with you an observation I have made over the 45 years of my life so far. I've met many people—black and white, young and old—and, after a lifetime of observation, there is one common theme among them all: the only genuine, lasting, positive change I have ever seen in the hearts of men and women is when people repent of their sins and ask forgiveness of God. That's it. That's what I have seen."

The words of the man serve as a lightning strike to those under his voice.

"Don't get me wrong. I know there are nice, kind, well-intentioned people out there who don't believe in God, nor do they seek the forgiveness of God, and I love and embrace them, too. You see, I can't love only those like me, because if I love only those like me, I deny the very love I claim to believe in. I am sharing with you my observation, an observation I have made time and time again. And, ladies and gentlemen, after a while, it becomes increasingly harmful to deny the truth, whether we want to believe the truth or not. The truth is the asking and receiving of forgiveness changes hearts and lives."

"Are there those who claim to love God, but their actions don't align with their words. Absolutely! I've observed many people like that as well, but what I find is over time truth and sincerity will rise to the top. I'm talking about lasting change of the heart with lasting power."

Principal Bullock walks to the microphone and serves his basketball coach a glass of water.

"Thank you, sir," Roger acknowledges the man. "You are a blessing to my life." Roger drinks, trying to assess his speech so far. The silence means either they are absorbing everything he is saying or impervious to his impassioned plea.

"I try to keep my testimony and my answers in life very simple. People ask me to this day, 'Roger, how do you know God is real?' My answer is simple. Before Jesus, there were things in my life I couldn't change. I wanted to change. I intended to change; I just didn't have the power to change. Then, once I asked forgiveness of God and asked His Son to change my life, life started to change. And this is what I tell people: 'Don't you know if I could have changed my life on my own, I would have changed it? But I couldn't...not until Jesus entered my life.' And that's how I know God is real. He changed my life. And if He changed a hopeless case like me, then the scripture is true: 'whoever calls on the name of The Lord shall be saved.'"

As Roger pauses, the vibration of his voice through an echoing sound system moves in waves among the people.

"Here's the secret many of us miss. We can't perform the change in other people. I can't perform the change in you, and you can't perform the change in me. When we can't change others is when the frustration brews and festers to the point where we start to hate those who hate us, and, remember, whoever does not love does not know God, because God is love."

"Now, here comes the hard part. You might be sitting there saying, 'Coach Stevens, you just told us the hard part. The hard part is to live among people who hate you, who despise you, who loathe you, people who even want you dead if they could have their way.' I hear what you might be saying. However, I need you to listen to what I'm saying. Better yet, I don't want you to necessarily hear what I'm saying but hear the words of the only One who can change the hearts of men and women."

"'A new commandment I give to you, that you love one another....'"

"'And whenever you stand praying, if you have anything against anyone..., forgive him, that your Father in heaven may also forgive you....'"

"'Our Father in heaven, hallowed be Your name.... Give us this day our daily bread. And forgive us our debts, as we forgive our debtors.'"

"'For if you forgive men their trespasses, your heavenly Father will also forgive you. But if you do not forgive men their trespasses, neither will your Father forgive your trespasses.'"

"'For all have sinned and fall short of the glory of God.' This includes you and this includes me. And this is what I'm here to tell you today: more than me leading a pep rally, more than me trying to inspire you, more than me talking about basketball, which is frankly just a game. I want to tell you something else, something of more value, something with staying power, something that will bring change..."

"We often hear talk of the word *hatred*, how ugly it is, how evil it is, how unfair it is, how rampant it is, and how difficult it is to stamp out, all the while we fail to realize hatred is a trap. Hate is a two-way street, and it needs reciprocal hatred to keep it burning. So, what do we do? We resort to hating those who hate us, and sometimes we don't even know that's what we're doing. As a result, we don't end up extinguishing the hatred. Instead, we inflame hatred further. Therefore, if we're going to talk about eliminating hatred, we must first realize that hatred cannot defeat hatred. Hatred can only be defeated with love, and love comes from God; not imperfect human love but perfect love from a perfect God."

A thousand eyes are on Roger.

"I get it. I know: easy for me to say, right? Let's get down to it: I'm not black. I spend much of my time these days around black people, but I don't know what it's like to be black and live in Georgia in 1969. I haven't been in your shoes when people have glared at you for doing nothing more than walking down the street, looking at you like you're dirty, like you need a bath to wash away the color of your skin. I haven't been in your shoes when you walk in a store, and someone begins to follow you. I haven't been in your shoes when you walk past a police officer, and they rest their hands on their wooden clubs. I haven't been in your shoes. But I must tell you this with all kindness and respect: you haven't been in my shoes, either."

Roger's neck oscillates as he pans the gymnasium; the entire room is looking back at him. "I don't share this story very often, because, honestly, I'm not proud of it. I was born outside of Atlanta to a teenage mother. My mother wasn't married when she had me. My father, I later learned, was the son of a prominent preacher in the area with a huge church. I'm not going to name names because there's no need. It's already passed. My mother was *encouraged* to keep quiet about her pregnancy, and when I use the word *encourage*, I mean whatever it took to get the point across; condemnation, bribery, blackmail. I say this next part with a little bit of sarcasm. I'm sure some of you have faced undesirable people in your life, but you haven't seen determination to ruin someone's life until you've had a church board secretly come after you."

"My mother just wanted to marry the man, but that was not going to happen. She had me with the help of some very kind women at a shelter run by a different church. I believe my mother was brave to have me because she had every chance in the world not to do so. If she didn't, I never would have met my wife, and we would never have had our son, and I would not be here with you today. Still, the whole situation was too much to bear, and, one night, my mother kissed me, left me in the care of the women at the shelter, and she left. She never returned. Two days later, they found my mother's body along the banks of a river after she had taken her own life."

The Macon South contingent sit aghast and heartbroken; they had no idea. Principal Bullock had no idea. Karen and Kevin, of course, knew. However, they know these words are hardly spoken by Roger.

"My father and his father, the pastor, were approached by the women of the shelter. Even upon news of my mother's death, the pastor's family was not interested in raising me. Conveniently, a sizeable donation was made by the church to provide for the shelter as the shelter provided for me. In other words, to keep the situation quiet. A few years later, I was adopted by a wonderful man and his wife, Reverend and Mrs. Jordan Stevens of Augusta, Georgia, a couple who couldn't have children of their own."

"As I grew, just like any child, my curiosity grew. I started making observations and comparing notes. I eventually realized everything wasn't adding up regarding the Stevens as my biological parents. Reverend and Mrs. Stevens sat me down and were honest with me. The day came they had been dreading, and I requested to meet my birth father. I was twelve. Reverend Stevens drove me to Atlanta to a large church on a Sunday, and we heard a man preach."

"During the message, Reverend Stevens leaned over to share with me the man preaching was my father, and my father had followed in the footsteps of his father. I was riveted by the words of his message—so pure, so powerful—and I believe so was everyone else. And I must tell you, as I heard the man preach, a sense of pride came over me as if to say, 'That's my dad.'"

"Following the service, Reverend Stevens and I waited in the large foyer of the church as a long line of people spoke to my father, the pastor. Once the line ended, Reverend Stevens got up from the bench we were sharing, and he approached the pastor of that large church, and the two of them spoke quietly for a few minutes. I watched from across the room, not sure what was about to happen. All I knew is I was ready to spring to my feet should they, especially my real dad, call for me. And, as if it was yesterday, I remember the moment when my biological father stopped speaking with Reverend Stevens, and my father looked at me from across the room for a few seconds."

Roger pauses for another drink, his hand shaking a bit.

The assembly leans into the man's story, desperate to hear the remaining details.

"*This is it*, I thought. *This is the moment—the moment of a lifetime.* I was so nervous. I wasn't sure what to do, so I made sure to sit up as straight as I could. I tried to fix my hair. I tried to think about what my dad was thinking. Did he like the way I looked? Did he see something in me that reminded him of himself? Had he looked forward to this day as much as I had? I remember the lump in my throat to this day; I can almost feel it if I let myself. I was ready. I was ready to run to him. After everything, after all the lost time and even after all the unfortunate circumstances, I was ready to move on and embrace this man as my father. And I remember the moment when my real dad stopped looking at me, and he looked back at Reverend Stevens and shook his head, and I could see his mouth form the words 'No, thank you.' After that, the pastor of that large church, my real father, turned and walked away."

A blanket of silence is cast across the room.

"It's hard to describe the crushing sensation that came over me. In essence, my real dad said *no thank you* to the thought of knowing me. He said *no thank you* to the opportunity to play catch with me or shoot baskets. He said *no thank you* to the thought of watching me grow and marking my height against the door frame with a pencil. He said *no thank you* to watching me graduate from high school, maybe even college, maybe even getting married and maybe even having a son of my own. In one swift moment, my real dad said *no thank you* to all of it. Like someone casually refusing seconds on dessert, my real dad said *no thank you*…to me. So, by the age of twelve, not only had my mother chosen to leave me with someone else, but so did my father."

Principal Bullock winces; he had no idea.

"Fast-forward many years, and I was a young married man, and we had an infant son of our own—he's now a senior in high school. I think you know him."

The lighthearted gesture does the room some good.

"I made a point, often against the wishes of my wife, to get up at 4 a.m. each morning to work an extra job as a farmhand for two hours per day. I set aside that money, and one day I went back to that same large church in Atlanta. I sat through a very inspiring church message, and I waited for the line of people to file out as they had years before. This time, unlike years ago, I walked across the foyer to speak with the pastor of that church on my own. I looked him in the eye and handed him one-hundred dollars, which took a long time for me to earn. I told him I was his son and that I now had a son, and I didn't know how much he gave to the shelter to raise me, but I returned whatever was donated in the form of one-hundred dollars to represent re-payment of his church's gift. But those were not the only words I spoke to my father that day. I also thanked him for turning away from me because it taught me never to turn away from my son."

Kevin nods gently, the young man holding back the tears.

Karen is not so successful across the makeshift auditorium; neither are many of those in attendance.

"I said these things to him not out of spite but out of sincerity. And the final words I spoke to the man were a struggle for me to say, but I did it, and I said it because I meant it in my heart. I told my father I forgave him. To all of you hearing my voice right now, I promise you: that is when a surge of freedom came to me."

Roger prays in his heart; he wants desperately to say this the right way.

"Here is the truth. We can all sit around and compare stories and notes and try to outdo each other when it comes to who has been wronged more in this world. We can talk about it all day and night, and all week or all month, and for the rest of our lives, but in the end, we won't be any closer to solving any of our problems. In fact, we will only be more frustrated and angrier and full of vengeance toward others, and, if we are not careful, we will be guilty of the same sin as those who hate us. Mark my words: racists discriminate, but racism does not. Racism and hatred can infect any heart, anywhere, anytime: white against black, black against white—it does not matter."

Billy Taylor stares at his coach, knowing of the paralysis of hate.

"So, just as I said a few moments ago, the moment of forgiveness is when freedom came to my heart regarding my real father and me. Please hear me: my father didn't give me freedom. Forgiveness gave me freedom. My father's heart didn't change toward me and give me freedom: forgiveness gave me freedom. Even if my real father tried to deny me freedom, it would not have stopped me from gaining freedom...because forgiveness gave me freedom. From that lesson, I have learned the following, and my prayer is all of you will remember these words for the rest of your lives: the one who has the power to forgive...has the most power."

Roger allows time for his words to saturate and penetrate every ear before repeating his statement. "The one...he or she... who has the power to forgive...has the most power. You can't change someone else's heart, but the one who has the power to forgive has the most power. You can't change what someone thinks of you or someone's actions toward you. Even if someone hates you to their very core, their hatred does not have power over you unless you hate them in return. Instead, the one who has the power to forgive has the most power."

"I'm not here to give you a church sermon, but what's true is true, no matter who tries to deny it. Let me ask you a question. Has anyone forgiven more offenses committed against Him than God has? Lying, stealing, jealousy, murder? And not only has God chosen forgiveness despite the offenses against Him, but He chose how all offenses and sin would be forgiven. It took Him who knew no sin to bear the sin of the world on His shoulders. But after Jesus was put to death for my sin, for our sin, for the sin of the world, Jesus did not remain dead. No. Jesus rose from the grave, and what do the Scriptures teach us Jesus said after raising from the grave? 'All power...is given to me in heaven and in earth,' which includes the power to forgive. And if the Son of God sincerely resides in us, we have the power to forgive and find freedom. Why? Because the one who has the power to forgive has the most power."

Roger's heart beats with desire and sincerity as he concludes.

"So, Macon South High School, I leave you with this. You have a decision to make. We all have a decision to make, and this decision will steer us in one fateful direction or the other for the rest of our lives. Are you going to sit and wallow in your hatred, depending on vengeance to reconcile all your disappointments, which it won't...or are you going to forgive the past and forge ahead? Will you dare to know the freedom of forgiveness? Remember, the one who has the power to forgive...has the most power."

And with those words, Roger Stevens leaves an empty microphone to stand alone in the middle of a silent crowd.

41

Friday, March 7
Georgia State Semifinals:
Macon South High School vs. Augusta Christian Academy

The hype is palpable. The time is near. The most anticipated game in Georgia high school basketball history will soon come to fruition in Alexander Memorial Coliseum on the famed campus of Georgia Tech.

Macon South works through their pre-game routine at the west end of the court following the first semi-final game. The first game was the appetizer. The next game will be the main course. Roger Stevens studies his players carefully; the kids do not seem nervous as much as they seem anxious to get the game underway, which is good in Roger's opinion. Nervousness sometimes speaks to a lack of readiness. Anxiousness speaks to eagerness.

Coach Stevens and Coach Dawkins stand on the sideline together, observing their boys as they get loose.

"What do you think of this place?" Roger asks, looking as high as he can to the arena ceiling.

"It's nice," Dawkins responds. "Big…really big. Probably gets loud, too."

"Yeah, it gets pretty electric in here."

The conversation between the two is cut short as the opponent emerges from the east end of the arena, accompanied by a resounding cheer. With great confidence, the Patriots of Augusta Christian Academy sprint from the tunnel, led by Bart Newhouse, Jr. and bookended by Bart Newhouse, Sr.

Roger knows great fans when he sees them, and Augusta has great fans. The Academy faithful easily fill the section behind the Augusta bench and stretch many rows high and wide. Several of the ACA fans called to Roger earlier from the stands to kindly greet him as he walked onto the court. Many memories and decade-long relationships are on display tonight. On cue, two familiar faces run to the sideline to greet their former coach in person, Reynolds Green and Trevor Hopkins.

"Hey, men," Roger extends with a smile.

The two young men are quick to embrace their one-time leader respectfully.

"Hey, Coach."

"Hi, Coach."

"I don't remember you guys being this tall. Make sure you take it easy on us tonight, okay? Have a great game…but not too great."

"Thanks, Coach. You, too,"

"Thanks, Coach. We miss you."

"Get back in line, men," a voice interrupts the reunion.

Roger turns and there stands Bart Newhouse, Sr.

"Coach Stevens."

"Hello, Coach Newhouse."

Bart Newhouse, Sr. has not lost that familiar countenance through the years in Roger's opinion: the appearance of a smile with a dash of condescension; his salt-and-peppered flat top always perfectly in place.

"Congratulations on getting to Atlanta," Roger offers amicably.

"You, as well, sir." The two engage in a firm handshake, Newhouse making certain his grip is firmer than that of his coaching counterpart. "Congratulations to you as well. Who would have thought it, right?"

It is difficult for Roger to discern if Newhouse is delivering a compliment or delivering it with the back of his hand.

"Well," Roger responds, "They're a hard-working group."

"With one of the best point guards in the state," Newhouse adds, granting Roger a hearty slap on the shoulder.

Typical Newhouse, Roger thinks to himself, the man going out of his way to say *one of the best in the state* as opposed to the best in the State. The man knows how to rub people the wrong way, and he seems to relish the opportunity. Therefore, Roger does what he finds most useful in situations such as this; he ends the conversation as cordially as possible.

"Coach Newhouse, I wish you the best tonight, sir."

"You bet," the opposing coach barely acknowledges the comment as his eyes find someone else in the arena, walking past Roger as his words are still suspended in air.

Coach Dawkins extends his hand, but Newhouse, Sr. does not see it.

Roger chuckles as he looks down at the empty hand of his assistant.

Dawkins offers a half smile. "Nice guy."

"If you say so," Roger replies with a sarcastic grin of his own.

Soon, a much sincerer face appears before Coach Stevens. "Principal Mize," Roger embraces his former employer from the Academy.

"Good to see you, Roger. Congratulations on getting back to Atlanta. You have been here many times, but to bring two different schools is extraordinary."

"Thank you, sir. It's great to see you again as well."

"Excuse me, Coach. It's time," Dawkins points to his watch, indicating warmups for the team are over and time has come to enter the locker room for final pre-game assignments.

"Got it. Thanks, coach." Roger is proud of his assistant. "By the way, Principal Mize, this is our Assistant Coach, Reggie Dawkins."

Both men share in the cordial introduction.

Coach Dawkins signals Kevin who summons the rest of the team. The Macon South squad and Kevin jog past half court where Kevin gives both Reynolds and Trevor fun-loving punches in the arms. His former teammates and current friends greet him as well; tonight, they will play against each other for the first time.

• • •

Inside the bowels of the arena, the South players sit facing yet another chalkboard in yet another building. However, this locker room is not the typical locker room. Rather, this locker room is the largest, most amenity-laden facility they have witnessed so far: the Georgia Tech visiting locker room. Augusta Christian is one of the teams to receive the home locker room, but that is okay in Roger's opinion. When he coached the Patriots, his teams were such frequent visitors to the final four in Atlanta the home locker room became a home-away-from-home. So, tonight, just as has been the case with everything this season, the veteran is seeing everything from a different vantage point, a different angle.

Coach Stevens and Coach Dawkins finish their final private conversation off to the side, and the two men soon surround their players, Coach Dawkins standing behind and Coach Stevens taking his place in front. After turning to survey tonight's game plan on the chalkboard for the thousandth time, the veteran coach returns the chalk in his hand back to the ledge of the board. He next finds a miscellaneous chair and drags it in front of his team, taking a seat.

After a substantial pause, the veteran coach speaks. "You guys know this stuff. You guys know what they're going to do. They're going to run everything through Reynolds Green, their center. We know they have size. We know they have athleticism. We know their coach is tough-minded—so is his team. We know all of this, or at least we should know all of this, right? For crying out loud, I coached there for a decade. I'd be the worst coach in America if I couldn't come up with a scouting report against my former team, huh?" The humor ushers a brief wave of levity into the locker room.

Roger clasps his hands, glances to the floor then looks up again. "What a season! What a ride!" The man's pace slows, a look of contemplation in his eyes. "I want to tell you, men, what I think of you before we go out there tonight, and I'm not going to sit here and lie and tell you I don't want to win... because I do. I'm not going to sit here and tell you I don't want to beat the school where Kevin and I came from, because I do, and so does Kevin, badly." The man exhales. "I know one of the worst mistakes a coach can make is to tell a team it's okay whether you win or lose a particular game, especially a game of this magnitude...because once you do, the game is over before it starts. I know all of that. Even so, there is something more important on my mind than basketball right now."

Roger Stevens looks down a second time, waits. then lifts his face, making eye contact with the team collectively. "I want you men to know you have changed my life. I am a different man after knowing you than I was before I came here. I am a changed man, a better man."

Every countenance is visible, every heart and mind absorbing his words.

"I know people credit me for leaving a white school to coach a black school, but I didn't do it for anyone or any other reason than I felt it's what God had me do. I didn't even do it for me," Roger surveys the entire team, "But I'm glad I did.... I'm glad I did.".

"But what people don't understand is this: it wouldn't have made any difference for me to come here if you had not received me. You, men..., you in this locker room..., all the progress we've made, on and off the court…, none of it would be possible without you, and I will be forever grateful for that."

Kevin echoes his father's sentiments by nodding and leaning forward to look down the row of teammates

The remaining players in the locker room appreciate feeling appreciated. If nothing else, to his players, that is what Roger Stevens has brought them: a feeling of appreciation and dignity.

"I don't know what the future holds," the man resumes, "But I know this: I can face anything now because…, thanks to all of you…, God has given me the courage to see the impossible come to pass, no matter how hard, no matter how difficult…, no matter what. So, I want to thank you for receiving me as your coach. I feel like we are family, and I don't mean to embarrass my son because Kevin is a wonderful son. For whatever reason, God only knows, we could only have one child, one son. Now, as I look around the room at you guys, I feel like Karen and I have many sons, including Billy. That's how much I think of you."

The boys nod, some feeling more appreciated and wanted now than they have at any point in their lives.

"Thank you, Coach," Leonard speaks up with a soft voice from a large frame. "I've learned more about basketball this season than I ever knew was out there. And it's because of you."

Roger smiles back at the young man. "I am honored to be your coach and for you to be my player, Leonard."

"Yeah, thanks, Coach. You're the best man I've ever met," Tyler adds.

"Yeah, Coach. I like it because you treat me like a man and teach me how to treat others the same way," Dwayne offers.

Overwhelmed with the feedback of his team, Roger is at a loss for words, and all he can do is close his eyes and smile with gratitude, fighting back a tide of emotion.

"The knowledge and wisdom we've received this season, men, have been worth more than any amount of money," Coach Dawkins affirms from behind the group.

"Thank you, Coach Dawkins," Roger responds. "You've made my life richer because of your commitment and friendship.

I believe the sky is the limit for your future in basketball and life."

Then Kevin Stevens adds, "I'm blessed to have you as my coach...and my father."

Roger cannot take much more, but the coach holds on.

"Well, you're not the only one, Kev." Toward the middle of the cluster of seated players, Jeremiah Jenkins, the son of Reverend Jenkins, speaks up, garnering everyone's attention. Reaching for the top of a long, nearly knee-high, white sock, Jeremiah removes a piece of paper folded many times over.

The sight is peculiar. Roger tilts his head and observes the teen's surprising and humorous action.

"I forgot about this until I was packing for Atlanta," Jeremiah continues. "Sometimes I write down prayer requests and file them away until they get answered. I wrote this one down because I knew we needed a quality basketball coach at South. Nothing against Principal Bullock. I mean, he did the best he could, but he is a principal at heart." Jeremiah leans forward and extends the crumpled paper to his coach. "I guess I filed this one in my sock drawer."

Roger accepts the paper with a curious glance. "Not sure I want this if it came from your sock drawer, Jeremiah."

The players smile and snicker.

"My clean sock drawer," Jeremiah adds with a smile of his own.

Roger unfolds the weathered piece of paper and privately reads the sentiments from Jeremiah's hand. His players watch as the countenance of their coach suddenly changes. Whatever safeguards have kept Roger Stevens from emotion fail miserably as the eyes of the grown man immediately fill with water. Even more, tears quickly turn to audible sobbing as Roger lifts both hands to cover his face, the note still in his grip.

The players look to each other, incredulously.

Kevin observes his father, knowing something has struck him at his core.

Roger continues to hide his face.

The players next look to Jeremiah. "What does it say?" one of the boys whispers, perplexed.

"Like I said," Jeremiah responds, "it was a prayer request."

"Well, what did you pray for?"

Jeremiah Jenkins looks at his teammates and answers: "I wrote, 'Dear God, please send us a coach…who will love us like a father.'"

Roger continues to cry before his players with little control.

Coach Dawkins stands in awe.

Kevin's eyes moisten as well, the teen realizing what his father now realizes: his father is supposed to coach at Macon South. His family is supposed to be in Macon. They are right where they are supposed to be.

Just when Roger cannot take any more, Jeremiah Jenkins adds one more angle. "By the way, I didn't realize it until I reread my prayer request. I dated that paper like I do all my prayer requests, and the date on that paper is February 15 of last year, which was the day before the bombing of our school."

Ashamed of how he must look, Roger brings the note back in front of his face, tears splashing against the page as the man confirms what Jeremiah just said. Etched in the upper left corner is the date February 15, 1969. The man cannot help but softly drop from the edge of his chair to his knees. Deep sobbing persists, and the man cannot stop it.

Kevin moves to his father's side as do the other players, the man on his knees in the middle of the locker room.

Roger's mind is swirling. All those times he fought God, fought coming here, all the second-guessing, all the pain and grief, all the dark nights…, it all meant something. It all was part of the plan and look at what he would have missed if he had said no, choosing to live life his way. What a missed opportunity this would have been.

"We love you, Coach," declares on the of players, several of them agreeing and echoing the same sentiment while patting the man on his back on shoulders.

Overwhelmed with utter amazement, Roger does his best to pull it together. He drops his hands down and reveals a red, swollen face with watery eyes, offering the best most messed-up smile he can. All he can see through his tears are the smiling faces of his team looking back at him—all beautiful black faces except for one beautiful white face. With a thousand words to say, Roger settles from the most concise message he could give. "You guys are the best," Roger declares, standing to his feet with the aid of his players and extending his hand to the middle. Rapidly, his hand disappears under a stack of hands, and then the coach places his other hand on top. Surveying the young men before him who have grown up quickly this season, he knows it is time. The man gives his final admonition before the state semifinal game: "Let's go have some fun. South on three: one…two…three…South!"

• • •

The National Anthem has been played. The starting lineups have left their benches and approach half court, both sides shaking hands at the behest of the lead official who stands at half court.

Kevin and Newhouse, Jr. find each other, paying mutual respect. Even so, there is no love lost between the two on this night.

"Give me a player in the circle from each team, gentlemen," decrees the ref.

Reynolds Green steps forward for Augusta Christian.

Tyler Washington does the same for Macon South.

Equal in height, their eyes confront one another.

The youthful athletes around the center circle exhibit every nervous tendency imaginable; some sway, some tug at their shorts, some wipe the bottoms of their shoes, some swing their arms.

The throbbing crowd noise swells. Every high school basketball fan in Georgia has been waiting for this one. A larger than usual contingent of general fans made the pilgrimage to Atlanta this year; the state semi's instantly became a hot ticket as soon as this matchup took shape.

A multitude of press aligns the front row, insulating the players from the rest of the arena.

Each time one fan base gets a chant going, the other fan base interrupts with one of their own.

Everything is set. There is only one box left to check: play basketball.

The lead official gives a short blast of his whistle before stepping between Tyler and Reynolds. "Straight up, gentlemen."

With those words, the second semi-final of the Georgia Final Four is underway.

As the brownish-orange sphere ascends, several press photographers capture the athletic image of two opposing centers rising high in the air to compete, their arms and hands stretching to the basketball heavens.

Tyler edges Reynolds, tipping the ball straight back to Kevin Stevens, and the Macon South crowd reacts as if they just won the game.

Kevin wastes no time. While players from both teams jog into position he weaves in and out of bodies with his dribble, as if changing lanes on a highway, bolting toward the offensive goal.

Bart Newhouse, Jr. is immediately frustrated, trying to track Kevin through the shifting trees—the Macon South guard is tough enough to cover as is. By the time Newhouse, Jr. locates him, it is too late.

Kevin jets past eight players and then a ninth on his way to an effortless finger-roll off the backboard. Two points: Kevin and Macon South strike first.

The Muskrat fans lose their minds over scoring the opening basket.

The Macon South bench explodes to their feet.

Coach Dawkins pumps his fist.

Roger Stevens allows no time for celebration. "Sky!" he bellows the defensive call immediately. "Sky!"

On cue, the Muskrats hit ACA with an athletic full-court press.

"Press-break!" Newhouse, Sr. calls from the bench.

"Press-break!" Newhouse, Jr. calls from the court.

The Patriots are caught flat-footed.

"Press-break! Get to your spots!" Newhouse, Sr. clamors again from the sideline.

"Press-break! Newhouse, Jr. echoes near the free throw line, flustered by Dwayne who is aggressively face-guarding him.

Three...four the official on the baseline counts with the wave of his arm.

"Get it in bounds!" The angry Augusta Coach commands.

Trevor Hopkins breaks for the ball.

Kevin sees it coming and takes away the passing lane.

The in-bounder for ACA stands, shaking the ball feverishly over his head with no options in sight.

A long blast of the whistle overrides the action. "Five seconds!" the ref exclaims.

The Muskrat players clap wildly from forcing the turnover.

The South bench is still on their feet from the play before.

The South crowd cannot get enough.

Roger Stevens is pleased.

Bart Newhouse, Sr. is furious.

The Academy players and fans are stunned.

Dwayne takes the ball out of bounds under the offensive basket. "Twenty-four!" he calls. "Twenty-four!"

Newhouse, Sr. recognizes the name of the play matches the number on Stevens' jersey. "Watch Stevens! They're going to Stevens!"

"I've got him!" Newhouse, Jr. announces, angrily stepping through the stack of bodies to get to his defensive assignment.

With a slap of the ball, Muskrat players disperse accordingly. Kevin is last to move, first awaiting a screen.

"Watch the screen!" Newhouse, Sr. yells from the bench.

Tyler sets a screen for Kevin.

Kevin draws three defenders as he juts hard to the right.

Leonard arrives behind Tyler.

The Muskrats screen the screener, and Tyler is suddenly wide open in the lane.

On target with the pass, Dwayne hits his teammate chest high.

With adrenaline pumping, Tyler receives the pass, takes a power dribble and explodes into the air for an authoritative two-handed slam.

The Academy players watch from below with disbelief.

The Macon fans scream.

The Augusta fans groan.

Newhouse, Sr. foams at the mouth.

Roger refuses to relent. "Sky! Sky!"

The smothering press resumes.

"Get in the press-break!" Newhouse, Sr. fulminates again.

Newhouse, Jr. slips free. When he does, Dwayne and Jeremiah are right there. The Academy point guard attempts to beat the trap to the sideline, but Dwayne disallows it, forcing Newhouse, Jr. to pick up his dribble.

"Help him!" The agitated coach calls from the Augusta sideline.

The baseline official is counting again.

Newhouse, Jr. turns and attempts to fire a pass. However, Jeremiah gets a finger on the ball, deflating its trajectory.

Kevin cuts in and intercepts, dribbling for the paint at full speed.

The Augusta in-bounder is no match for the oncoming train, and the defender futilely tries to draw a charge.

Kevin elevates with reckless abandon. Knowing there will be contact, the star player sets his mind and absorbs the impact down low while extending his right hand high above his head, forcing the ball over the rim for a spectacular one-handed dunk, causing the ref to blast his whistle again.

"Block!" the ref exclaims while bringing both hands to his hips before swinging his arm down hard. "Block and count the basket!"

Alexander Memorial Coliseum explodes. The Macon South wave is unstoppable. The Muskrats have ignited a frenzy. Augusta fans stand in disbelief: they have never seen anything like that, a player dunking while fouled at the same time.

The Muskrat players on the floor surround Kevin in a buzzing hive.

"Yeah, Kev!" "Yeah, boy!"

The Patriot players from Augusta stand in hushed awe and deference. They have never seen anything like that.

"Time out! Time out!" Commands Coach Newhouse to the nearest ref. The raging coach must ask a second time because even the officials have never seen anything like that.

Roger watches as the players on his bench rush past him and onto the court at the timeout signal. They blitz Kevin and escort him back to the sideline.

"Come on! Come on!" Roger motions, trying to restore order yet dumbfounded by what he just witnessed; the veteran coach has never seen anything like that. Roger strives to be all business, but he, too, is not immune to the electricity of the moment. "Okay, okay. Take a seat, men. Take a seat." Roger Stevens observes as Kevin Stevens passes by on his way to the team bench. The father joins in the momentary elation. "Not bad, Kev."

• • •

The Augusta Academy Patriots re-take the floor following the lambasting by Bart Newhouse, Sr., complete with airborne saliva.

Kevin sinks the free throw; Macon South spurts to a 7-0 lead to start the game. Once the ball passes through the basket, South resumes the same full-court press that has caused ACA countless problems.

Newhouse, Jr. is annoyed yet determined. In a burst, the Academy ball-handler breaks free of the South double team and catches the ball near the baseline. Without hesitation, Newhouse puts down a hard dribble and accelerates toward the sideline.

Dwayne tries to cut off Newhouse but is too late, his left foot tripping the point guard.

A whistle blares. The Academy fans and bench applaud.

"Finally!" Coach Newhouse sarcastically spews. "A call for us!"

South resets their press.

ACA resets their press-break. Newhouse, Jr. shakes loose again, receiving the pass and racing for the same sideline.

Dwayne is quicker to react this time, cutting off the drive while planting both feet with the stance of a statue.

Newhouse, Jr. plows forward, running down the South defender.

The impact elicits yet another whistle from the referee. "Block, block!"

"What!" Roger stews in disbelief, ambling toward half court. "What are you talking about? He was there! He was completely there!"

Before the South coach realizes it, he is several steps onto the court, thus testing the boundaries and patience of the lead official who jogs to the scorer's table. "Take a step back, coach," the ref warns, not thrilled with the animated gesture.

Coach Dawkins does the job of a good assistant, grabbing Roger's arm from behind to help subdue him. "Easy, coach."

Half the crowd loves the call while the other half despises it.

The grin on the face of Coach Newhouse conveys his opinion of the ref's decision.

Amid the emotion and excitement, an important issue now looms for South: Dwayne just picked up his second foul very early in the game, and Roger has a decision to make. "Go get Dwayne," he instructs one of his bench players.

As Dwayne returns to the bench, Coach Stevens pats his shoulder.

"I was there, coach," Dwayne protests. "I was set."

"I know. I know. It's okay. Just get a breather."

Dwayne's replacement is still working out the kinks, and Newhouse, Jr. exploits the jitters, receiving the inbound pass and jetting up the sideline, easily evading the trap.

Kevin retreats.

Newhouse, Jr. throttles ahead, crossing half court and getting to the right side of the free throw line.

Kevin rotates to pick him up, but his counterpart sidesteps him nicely while keeping his dribble alive.

Both Tyler and Leonard take the bait and rotate impulsively, not wanting to surrender an easy basket.

With textbook presence, Newhouse, Jr. dishes an effective bounce pass beneath reaching hands, the ball kissing off the court and springing into the hands of Reynolds Green who cleanly takes the pass and lays in the bucket.

It is the Academy faithful who now show approval; their team is on the board, putting a stop to the furious South run.

Kevin takes the inbound pass and jogs the ball up the court, studying the defense as he does.

Newhouse, Jr. picks him up 25-feet from the basket.

Kevin bellows a command.

In an instant, a second Academy defender bolts toward the ball-handler.

Recognizing the double team, Kevin swings the ball to Jeremiah.

Jeremiah is stunned to be so open. Given the bright lights, the size of the crowd, and the enormity of the stage, the eager South player shuffles his feet before his first dribble.

The nearby ref is quick to assess a traveling violation.

Roger grunts but remains upbeat. "Shake it off! Let's go! Sky! Sky!"

South resumes the press.

Newhouse, Jr. eludes the trap and wisely takes the pass up the sideline on the run.

Kevin sprints from half court to cut off the opponent. Crouching low with ultra-quick hands, Kevin taps and changes the direction of the ball, stripping Newhouse, Jr. cleanly.

Unfortunately, both Stevens, father and son, and the entire South contingent cannot believe it when another whistle intervenes, the ref pointing directly at Kevin.

"Oh, no! No way!" Roger exclaims.

The ref strides past the disgruntled coach to the scorer's table: "Reaching foul..., Macon South..., number twenty-four."

Kevin looks incredulously at his father who shares the same expression: the man shaking his head. "That was clean, sir!" Roger conveys to the official who made the call.

"No, sir, coach."

Bart Newhouse, Sr. on the other hand celebrates the call, as does Newhouse, Jr., both clapping their hands loudly and annoyingly. Newhouse, Jr. makes a point to walk past Kevin while clapping, trying to get under the skin of his counterpart. "Good call!" the ACA point guard lauds the ref's decision.

Kevin sees and hears the antagonistic display, though he chooses to ignore it.

In response to three quick fouls, Roger pulls the Muskrat defense out of the press.

Augusta capitalizes in their half-court offense, getting the ball inside for two.

"Watch the screens!" Roger admonishes his team.

Kevin brings the ball up the court, certain he will see a double team again. Once the second defender breaks in his direction, Kevin veers hard right, forcing Newhouse Jr. to sprint to his left to keep up. Not only does the second defender give chase, but now Reynolds Green leaves his man to assist—Kevin draws three defenders.

Picking up his dribble, Kevin feels obligated to give up the ball amid the traffic. He spots Leonard at the right elbow, and Kevin delivers a pass on point.

Leonard, to no fault of his own, is jacked up on adrenaline as well. Hastily, the South power forward squares up and launches a fifteen-footer, missing badly.

Roger can live with the miss. He liked Leonard's aggressive mindset.

Newhouse Jr. has the ball again and walks it up the court.

Kevin shadows him but soon feels the presence of a screen on his left. "I'm good. I'm good," the venerable guard calls out once he recovers under the screen.

Instead of coming off the screen hard, Newhouse, Jr. nonchalantly dribbles to the right corner, using the screen to get just enough separation to help his passing lane.

Trevor Hopkins, who set the screen on Kevin, turns and receives a back-screen form Reynolds Green.

Leonard gets caught among the thicket of bodies as Trevor slips away.

Trevor sprints to the weak side of the rim, looking skyward as the pass from Newhouse Jr. sails over the top of the defense.

Leonard closes on Trevor, but it is too late. To make matters worse for South, Leonard cannot put the brakes on his bulky frame, running into the back of Trevor who converts the layup and elicits yet another foul call from the refs.

The impressive play brings the Academy faithful to their feet and a fist pump from their coach on the sideline.

The same play brings anguish to Roger Stevens. "Guys!" he froths at the mouth. "What are we doing? Call out the back screens."

Just that quickly, once Trevor Hopkins steps to the line and nails the subsequent free throw, the Macon South lead vanishes. The game is now tied 7-7.

• • •

The remainder of the first quarter and beginning of the second quarter are back and forth: 10-10, 15-15, 19-19. It looks, at times, as if South's athleticism is too much for ACA. However, the Academy seems to respond with tactical precision, running a litany of screens to get guys open for easy baskets.

The easier the baskets are for the Academy the more frustrated Roger Stevens becomes. He does not take the bait, but Roger can see Bart Newhouse, Sr. staring his way down the sideline after each made Augusta basket.

"I want to beat this guy so badly," Roger mutters to himself on one occasion.

Just over four minutes remain before halftime, and Augusta Christian has edged to a 23-22 lead.

With a man on his hip and Reynolds Green in front of him, Kevin pulls up his dribble for a midrange half-jumper/half-running shot, lofting the ball safely out of reach, everyone watching the ball carom off the backboard and cleanly whisk the net. South regains the lead: 24-23.

"Call out the screens!" Coach Newhouse clamors. "How many times have I told you?"

At the other end of the floor, Newhouse, Jr. escapes the defense and hits an uncontested mid-range jump shot of his own. Augusta resumes the lead: 25-24.

The two ultra-competitive coaches manage to overpower the sold-out arena with their volcanic voices.

"Get over those screens, men!" Roger fumes.

"Hands up!" Newhouse shouts.

"Over the back!" Roger pleads.

"Three seconds!" Newhouse haggles.

"He lifted his pivot foot!" Roger protests.

"What game are you watching, ref?" Newhouse percolates.

Kevin maintains his balance, converting a gorgeous flip shot off the glass from the right side of the lane.

The South fans relish the result.

The Academy fans languish.

Roger Stevens pumps his fist.

Bart Newhouse, Sr. flings his arms.

Reynolds Green hits a soft five-foot turnaround jumper.

The Academy fans celebrate.

The South fans grimace.

Bart Newhouse, Sr. applauds loudly.

Roger Stevens wipes the sweat from his brow.

The lead vacillates between the two teams.

Leonard snares another rebound with twenty seconds before halftime.

Kevin runs to his side and takes possession. The point guard glances at the clock: eighteen seconds.

Still discombobulated by Kevin's twenty-point-first half, Augusta scurries on defense.

"Hey!" Roger gets the attention of his team, motioning with his fingers by rolling one over the other in quick succession.

Both Kevin and Leonard know what that means—rerun the high screen.

"Trap! Trap him!" Newhouse, Sr. bellows from the ACA bench: there is no way he will let the Stevens boy get the final shot before the half.

Trevor and Newhouse, Jr. run at Kevin again as the Macon point guard crosses the half court line.

Kevin tries a sudden move to get clear of the trap.

Trevor shows more aggressiveness this time, sliding his feet more swiftly to impede his opponent's progress. Trevor even manages to bump Kevin without a call from the referee.

The impact knocks Kevin off balance, and his dribble hits Trevor's leg, sending the ball rolling into the backcourt.

"Foul, ref!" Roger furiously exclaims.

Boos from the South crowd show their distaste for the no-call.

There is no time for Kevin to complain. Instead, the South guard sprints for the ball as it runs away from him—nine seconds, eight seconds, seven seconds. Kevin finally chases down the ball before it nearly goes out of bounds near his father's feet.

His son now within earshot, Roger encourages his best player. "Six seconds, Kevin! Go!"

Kevin turns and surveys Trevor and Newhouse, Jr. still giving chase. A hard dribble to the right creates a crease and a subsequent changing of hands grants Kevin the ability to split the loosely-fitted double team. What looked to be a non-existent path to the basket a second ago yields to Kevin's prowess as the South star dribbles back to the half court line— three seconds, two seconds....

"Shoot!" Roger greenlights from the sideline.

With a good three steps on his defenders, Kevin Stevens picks up his dribble and—with controlled breathing—the reigning Georgia player of the year gains his composure, securing another long stride before launching a shot from just in front of the timeline. Kevin follows throw, pushing the ball from his right hip high into the air, his momentum still carrying him forward after the shot is released.

The arena horn blasts halfway through the flight pattern of the basketball and holds a prolonged blast.

The entire coliseum falls victim to silence.

Coach Newhouse watches, his mouth agape. "Don't you dare," he mutters as if to threaten the basketball.

Roger looks on. He tilts his head slightly; to him, the shot looks right on line.

Kevin has an even better vantage point, thinking to himself, *It's right on line.*

The remaining players on the court watch as the basketball sails over their heads on its descent...then as it swishes and flips the net, causing the net to hang on the rim.

The arena quakes. South fans scream with power. The South bench explodes in jubilation.

The ref looks to the scorer's table to confirm the 40-foot shot is good, and Kevin Stevens calmly allows his momentum to carry him toward the locker room. Then, he mystically disappears into the tunnel like the high school basketball legend he is.

Smiling and shaking his head, Roger Stevens looks to the scoreboard as he begins to walk off the court. At halftime, his current team from Macon leads his former team from Augusta: 33-29.

• • •

In one locker room, one coach sings his team's praises.

In another locker room, one coach delivers a scathing reprimand. "When you run to double Stevens, run!" shouts Coach Newhouse, vehemently slapping his hands together. "Don't worry about your man. The stage is too big for the rest of them."

• • •

"Right now, they are in the other locker room making adjustments," Coach Stevens affirms to his squad. "And let me tell you what they're going to do. They're going to continue running another man at Kevin, probably as soon as he crosses half court."

• • •

"In fact," Coach Newhouse continues, "I want to run a third defender at Stevens. We are not going to let him beat us. If someone else beats us, that's fine. But Stevens will not beat us!"

• • •

"I won't be surprised if they try to triple Kevin," Roger kneels eye to eye with his team. "So, listen. The rest of you: Dwayne, Jeremiah, Leonard, and Tyler, you're back in, remember what got you here. Play free, have a good time, trust each other. If you get an open shot, I want you to take it. And if you miss, I want you to take the next one because I want your confidence high. Who cares about a big crowd? There's no pressure because we weren't supposed to be here, anyway."

A surge of belief and energy rises in the Macon South locker room.

"I'll go you one better: let's not just play the way we play. Let's go win the way we win." With those words, Roger Stevens stands to his feet and extends his right hand toward the group, gesturing for anyone who wants to join him.

The Muskrat players vault to their feet with a growl of aggressiveness, spouting, "Let's go! Come on! Yeah! We can do this!"

Roger Stevens scans the huddle before him. *They are ready. There are no more words to say, except….* "South on three: one… two…three…South!"

• • •

Much like the beginning of the game, Macon South storms through the opening stages of the third quarter only to watch the playoff-veteran team from Augusta withstand the surge and re-establish their footing. The Patriots continue to force Kevin into tough decisions: either give up the ball or be forced to beat three men.

Kevin agonizes. *I must get these guys going.*

Roger feels the same way at a distance, appraising the situation privately: *We must get Tyler more involved on offense.*

"Don't think, just play," Kevin speaks in the ear of his teammate as he passes Tyler during a dead-ball timeout, punching him in the shoulder in loving fashion.

Tyler looks at him and nods, knowing if South is going to do it, there is not much time left to do it.

The score: Augusta leads 44-40.

Kevin dribbles the ball to the offensive end as he and the Muskrats trail with less than twenty-five seconds remaining in the third quarter. Taking a risk, rather than holding for one shot, Roger's son puts his foot on the gas.

On cue, here comes the triple team again.

Kevin does not hesitate, busting to his right with a hard dribble and seemingly dragging Newhouse, Jr. down the sideline with him. Eventually, Kevin outraces the other coach's son and turns the corner near the baseline, plowing toward the lane with a full head of steam.

Reynolds steps in front as Kevin comes to a two-footed jump stop at the right low block. Next, Reynolds goes airborne as Kevin gives a nice shot fake and successfully gets the Augusta center off his feet. Kevin then nicely wraps the ball around the defender and drops it in Tyler's lap.

Tyler takes the ball without thinking and goes straight up, almost dunking but instead laying the sphere softly over the front of the rim, boosting his confidence—Macon South trails by two.

The Patriots take the ball out of bounds as Kevin employs an old trick, dipping out of sight behind Newhouse, Jr. By the time the in-bounder realizes a once-clandestine Kevin has emerged, it is too late, and the ball leaves the reluctant player's hands and into Kevin's, the crafty guard stealing the ball and laying it up and in for another basket, drawing the score even yet again.

The move generates a roar of applause from the South crowd.

"What are we doing!" Coach Newhouse bellows.

Embarrassed and determined to redeem his pride, Newhouse, Jr. brings the ball up the court in anger. He expertly weaves in and out of the South defense, digging his way close enough for a floater in the waning moments of the third quarter.

Tyler responds by exploding from the floor and rejecting the shot, sending the attempt several feet in the air in the opposite direction.

With two seconds remaining, Kevin snares the loose ball and pivots in the other direction. One second is enough time to take a dribble, gather his footing, and let fly a sixty-foot attempt.

The coliseum holds its breath as the shot looks good again. The shot is on line again. Every neck is cranked airborne as the ball soars seemingly through the arena rafters on its way to the basket.

"No way!" Coach Newhouse spews.

"No way!" Coach Stevens sings.

Amid dead silence from the crowd, the incoming shot is on its descent…and had there been another four inches of strength behind it, the shot would have propelled through the net instead of hitting the front rim and bouncing violently away.

Another rush of adrenaline puts the crowd in a head-lock, many people covering their faces with their hands as the roller-coaster continues.

Both teams jog to their respective benches to entrench for one more quarter to see who will advance to the State Title game tomorrow night. The score at the end of three quarters: Augusta Christian 44, Macon South 44.

As the South players attack the water cups on the team bench, Coach Stevens and Coach Dawkins step from the group to consult.

"What do you think, coach?" Roger queries.

"I think Tyler looks good, but I think we have to keep riding Kevin," answers Coach Dawkins. "We've come this far, and Kevin gives us our best shot to finish it."

Roger does not necessarily want to agree with him, but Coach Dawkins is correct. Tyler has shown flashes at times. Leonard is rebounding at a healthy clip. Dwayne and Jeremiah are playing solid defense. However, it is Kevin who is playing at a high level on the biggest stage.

Coach Stevens cannot help but let his mind wander for a moment. The man smiles and offers the following idyllic thought to his assistant. "Can you imagine if Billy were here?" Both coaches smile at each other as Roger proposes the utopic idea. "We would be in the driver's seat. Newhouse wouldn't know how to handle Billy."

Roger returns to earth: *but Billy isn't here. Tonight, it's all Kevin.*

Striding back to the bench, the veteran coach kneels before his players. "One more quarter, can you believe it?" He scans the oversized eyeballs staring back at him. "Look, men. Look around you. Look where we are…, and you are the ones who got us here."

The players from Macon South take the advice of their coach and begin to survey the coliseum around them, the packed arena buzzing with anticipation before the final quarter.

"Look how far we've come since the first game, since the first scrimmage." Roger pauses. "Since we first met."

Kevin stares at his father, still learning from the man's every word after all these years.

"So, here's the situation," the well-storied coach continues. "And I say this with all honesty: if we win, then great. If we don't, it doesn't change a thing. It doesn't change how much I love you guys. Of all the teams I've ever coached, this is my favorite team. You are my favorite team."

An immense pressure lifts from the shoulders of the Muskrat players; their faces shine with gratitude and pride.

The arena horn blasts to signal the start of the fourth quarter.

Roger stands to his feet and extends his hand to the middle of the pack; his players follow his lead. With every hand in unison, Roger concludes with these final words. "It doesn't matter if we win or lose," the man smiles, "So, we might as well win. South on three: one…two…three…South!!!!"

The force nearly knocks Roger back as his players nearly run their coach down, undeterred, undaunted on their way back to the court.

The official signals for play to begin. The fourth quarter is underway.

Kevin takes the inbound pass and begins the offensive attack.

Newhouse, Jr. is quickly joined by two teammates to form a triple team.

Kevin wastes no time, dribbling swiftly to his right before crossing back to his left, dribbling hard and low and splitting one of the futile traps. He spins a beautiful bounce pass on the run.

Again, Tyler does not think; he just plays. On a mission, Tyler takes the bounce pass and rockets from the hardwood, jamming the ball with two-hands: Macon South 46, Augusta 44.

Newhouse, Jr. advances; here come the screens again. The Academy runs an effective inside out play as Reynolds takes the pass then gives it right back to Newhouse, Jr. who eludes Kevin to an open spot on the floor, knocking down a seventeen-foot jump shot: Macon 46, Augusta 46.

Kevin throws a pass over the top of the triple team, hitting Leonard at the top of the key. Kevin next sprints past his defenders and receives a nice back-door pass from Leonard, Kevin laying the ball off the backboard for two more. Macon 48, Augusta 46.

Newhouse, Jr. screams the play from half court. He receives a high screen and swings the ball to the right wing. Trevor steps out to seemingly set a ball screen for his teammate then just as quickly slips the screen and fades toward the basket, losing his man in time to receive the pass and convert the basket unmolested. Macon 48, Augusta 48.

Newhouse, Sr. changes the defense from the bench, knowing they have been burned too many times. The Patriots drop into a zone except for Newhouse, Jr. who remains on Kevin.

Roger recognizes the gimmick immediately. "It's a box and one, Kevin!" Roger calls from the team bench.

Kevin hears the words of his father just as his mind processed the same thought: *it's a box and one.* Even so, Kevin does not decelerate. He signals Dwayne to come to the top of the key to set a screen. Dwayne plants his feet, and Kevin rubs Newhouse, Jr. into Dwayne's body before exploding and turning the corner. Trevor Hopkins steps from the bottom of the zone, and Kevin circles him as well, keeping Trevor to his back as Kevin contorts and floats a ten-footer. The South guard's shot goes airborne while seemingly lodged between his old teammates, Trevor and Reynolds, all three players watching as the gentle offering ascends, descends and splashes softly through the net to the satisfaction of the South crowd: Macon 50, Augusta 48.

Newhouse, Jr. looks more and more irritated on each trip down the court, and Kevin discerns this, knowing full well frustrated players often force the action and are prone to mistakes. Instead of waiting for Newhouse, Jr., to come to him, Kevin takes the fight to Newhouse, picking him up at half court. Hounding the opponent, Kevin slides his feet in a blur, keeping his hands withdrawn to show the ref he is not reaching.

Newhouse, Jr. lowers his shoulder and increases his speed. However, Kevin forces Newhouse to speed up to the point it causes Newhouse to errantly dribble the ball off his right foot and out of bounds.

The blast of the official's whistle further antagonizes both Newhouse, Jr. and Sr. "Come on, boy!" The Academy coach shows disgust. "What are you doing? Take care of the ball!"

Kevin takes the inbound pass and surveys the Academy defense. He has that feeling—the feeling the action on the court is in slow motion, there is no one who can guard him, every shot is going in, and every decision is going to work. He feels like the best player in the State of Georgia again.

Kevin analyzes the box and one again and summons Leonard to set the screen this time.

Tired of all the screens, picks and rubs, Newhouse, Jr. runs into Leonard but this time lowers his shoulder and tries to bull his way through the massive youth. Instead, all Newhouse manages to do is spin himself completely around and flop on the floor. Now sitting on the court, he looks helplessly at the nearest ref with his palms up, begging for the call.

The ref fails to acknowledge his plea.

Kevin cannot help but snicker as he dribbles past his fledgling counterpart.

Terrified, Trevor Hopkins is on an island with his childhood friend again.

With Newhouse, Jr. out of the picture, Kevin takes his time and backs up his dribble, forcing Trevor into a decision. At first, Trevor tries to play Kevin halfway, far enough back to take away the drive but close enough to take away the outside shot.

Kevin jabs, jabs…and then raises his eyes toward the goal.

Trevor takes the bait and makes a fateful step forward.

With Trevor now leaning, Kevin leaves Trevor in the dust, taking the baseline and reaching the right edge of the lane.

Reynolds lunges.

Never empty of surprises, Kevin picks up his dribble and spins, whirling around Reynolds as Kevin shows his back to his other childhood friend, keeping the ball safely out of reach. Once completing his spin move, Kevin lofts up a soft, one-handed shot. The shot is so gentle it lightly bounces twice on the side of the iron before rolling over the rim and through the net.

Kevin is unstoppable at this moment, and both teams know it. What is demoralization for one side is elation for the other, and the fans from Macon South cannot get enough. With that basket, the Muskrats extend their lead to 52-48.

Roger senses a shift in momentum. He sends his team back into their full court press. "Sky! Sky!"

The pressure and quickness of Macon South are thorns to the Academy, most evident by the face of Newhouse, Jr. who uses an elbow to separate from Dwayne's stellar defense.

"Oh! The elbow, ref?" Roger decries the contact.

No call comes from the official, though a few boos come from the Macon crowd.

Newhouse, Jr. swings the ball back to the in-bounder, and then the Augusta point guard sprints to his teammate's side to retrieve the ball.

Trevor appears open near half court.

Newhouse propels a long pass.

Tyler anticipates the pass beautifully, leaping from behind Trevor and knocking the ball forward to himself.

The capacity crowd emotes accordingly.

With adrenaline racing, Tyler picks up the pass and tries to fire it across the court to Kevin.

Newhouse, Jr. returns the favor and jumps the passing lane, instantly sending the action the other way. The Academy point guard is full speed ahead, and the Patriots have numbers on the fast break.

Kevin refuses to give up on the play.

Leonard is the only defender back.

Newhouse drifts to the left side of the lane to make Leonard commit.

Leonard activates the teaching of his coach, stepping with his hands up toward Newhouse to stop the ball.

Newhouse, Jr. drops a perfect bounce pass to Trevor at the right block. With no one in his way, Trevor sizes up his layup attempt.

Expecting to watch his shot carom off the backboard, instead, Trevor is in shock when, from above, out of nowhere, Kevin Stevens appears even with the basket, sailing high, cutting through the air, swatting Trevor's attempt into press row.

The Macon South fans go to a new level of ecstasy at the sight.

"Oh!" Newhouse, Sr. bellows at the painful sight of another missed opportunity.

"Whoa!" Roger reacts at the sight of his son shot out of a cannon.

• • •

As Kevin returns to earth—in a moment—he is reminded how quickly everything can change in the game of basketball. As the star guard watches the ball sail into the stands, Kevin's focus is not on his landing. Thus, when his left foot plants awkwardly on impact, the immediate, shooting pain cruelly reminds him of his previous injury.

A surge of tenderness yet intense heat rushes to the same spot in his foot, causing his ankle to buckle under the weight of his body. Putting his arms down as quickly as he can, Kevin does all he can to brace himself. Nevertheless, gravity thrusts him mercilessly to ground, his body sliding across the hardwood floor for several feet and into an area of cheerleaders.

A collective gasp is heard from the crowd. Those sitting near the fall both hear and feel the impact of Kevin's body smacking against the unforgiving court.

Roger cannot see his son from the vantage point of the bench, but the crash landing does not keep Roger from immediately speculating, *Is it the same foot? How do we compete without Kevin? This could be the ball game, right here.*

More aggravated than injured, Kevin Stevens struggles back to his feet quickly; although, he does not have the strength to move just yet.

It is all Karen can do to keep from leaving her seat in the stands to join her son on the court.

Roger arrives at his son's side, encouraged to see the teen already back on his feet. "Talk to me. Kev?" Roger's question receives no response, only grunting. "Is it the same ankle?"

Kevin manages to hear and speak. "Yeah." The coach's son is a gamer. He despises the thought of another setback. Kevin stumbles forward.

"Nice and slow, Kev," Coach Dawkins encourages. "No hurry."

Kevin's next several steps are painstaking hops.

A faint yet supportive round of applause begins somewhere in the stands and soon consumes the arena, both sides coming together to back the star player.

Coach Stevens and Coach Dawkins guide Kevin through a crowd of teammates. All of them holding their breath yet engaging their fallen leader at the same time.

"Easy. Go easy" are the words of wisdom from those around him.

Once arriving at the team bench, Kevin spins around and gingerly finds a seat. The former star player from Augusta, now the star player from Macon, vigorously rubs his lower leg and ankle: "It's okay. I'm okay. Just give me a minute."

The solemnity of the moment is interrupted by the referee at Roger's shoulder. "Sorry, coach. We need a sub for twenty-four."

Roger responds, "Timeout?"

Granting his request, the official steps back from the South bench and blows his whistle. "Timeout, Macon."

From the stands just behind the team bench, Karen wants to do something. She resorts to observing Roger from a distance, trying to read his face to gauge just how dire the situation is.

Roger does not dawdle. His remaining players are visibly stunned by Kevin's re-injury; they need leadership right now. Roger quickly positions himself before the team bench. "Okay, men. We must roll with the punches. We can't undo what's been done, and we're not going to quit. Tyler, we're going to run some plays for you on offense. Leonard, crash the weakside boards hard in case he misses." Roger shifts his attention back to Tyler. "Hear that, Tyler. It's okay if you miss. Leonard will be there."

Tyler and Leonard both nod.

"Stay tough on defense," the veteran coach continues. "We're in front. They can't win if they can't score. We've seen the plays they are running. We know what they're doing. If they were going to put us away, they should have done it before now." The volume of the fearless leader's voice crescendos with each passing instruction. "We're more athletic than they are, we've worked harder to get here, and we want it more than they do."

The arena horn blares in the background, summoning both teams back to the hardwood.

Roger vaults to his feet and extends his hand to the middle. Working through a fog of reluctance, his players one by one join the call. In customary fashion, Roger places one hand on the bottom and one hand on top of the stack. "South on three: one...two..." The fiery chant is interrupted by one more hand on top of the pile: Kevin's hand.

Roger looks to his son.

Kevin's face has normalized since the initial, burning pain. "I think I'm okay," Kevin declares.

The news is well received by Roger and the rest of the team. "Kevin's going to be all right." The man confirms. "But let's show them for a few minutes we're a good team whether Kevin is on the floor or not. You men deserve to be here whether Kevin and I are here or not. Let's go. South on three: one… two…three…South!"

Reggie Dawkins respectfully moves to the other side of Roger to allow the father and son to confer.

"You sure you're okay?" Roger inquires.

"I just need a breather."

Augusta is awarded the ball out of bounds and under the offensive basket. The Academy aligns in their familiar stack down the right side of the free throw lane. The in-bounder slaps the ball. Patriot players quickly pop in every direction, confusing the defense. Trevor Hopkins breaks free, calling for the ball just to the left of the basket. The pass is on the money as Trevor scores an easy two: Macon 52, Augusta 50.

Roger can barely curb his fury. He holds his tongue, instead opting to rock back and forth in frustration.

With the Stevens kid out of the game, Coach Newhouse shifts his focus to Tyler. "Two-one-two," he instructs his team as his players pack into a tight zone, taking away the athletic Macon center and daring the South guards to shoot from the outside.

"Move the ball against the zone," Roger counters from the Macon sideline. Dwayne initiates the offense as the Muskrats skirt the basketball around the perimeter. Inside, Tyler looks diligently for an opening, but the big men from Augusta Christian stifle him at every turn. The Patriot defense retreats and packs further and further in the lane.

Roger can see the anxiety in Dwayne's demeanor as the guard is unable to get the ball inside. "Don't force it" is the coach's admonition. To Roger's dismay, force the pass is what Dwayne does, the young man trying to thread the needle but instead sending a deflected pass into the arms of the opposition.

Newhouse, Jr. pushes the ball up the court. Macon South does a quality job of getting back. However, the Academy point guard wisely refuses to force the action and waits for the secondary break to develop. On cue, Newhouse, Jr, hits Reynolds with a pass at the free throw line, and the skilled center knocks down an uncontested jump shot.

Just that quickly, the South lead is gone: Macon 52, Augusta 52.

"Dwayne," Roger rockets to his feet. "Don't force the ball against the zone, son. If they give you a clean look, take it. Knock it down."

Dwayne acknowledges with a nod and proceeds downcourt. The zone he faces is again packed tightly.

The Macon big men work fervently to get open, especially Tyler, and his frustration is evident.

"Three seconds!" Newhouse, Sr. speaks of Tyler to the officials. "He's camping in the lane!"

"Take your shot, Dwayne!" Roger encourages the tentative player.

Acting on the endorsement of his coach, Dwayne receives the pass as the ball works back around the perimeter. Stepping forward with semi-confidence, Dwayne eyes his target. Exercising his mechanics, he follows through and watches with the rest of the arena as his shot hits the heel of the rim and kicks out.

Trevor Hopkins gathers the rebound for the Academy, giving his team the opportunity to take the lead at the other end of the floor.

Vacillating in his mind, Roger teeters between calling a time out or letting his boys play it out. *Let's go*, he decides, slapping his hands together, summoning inner strength. *Let's play. They can do this.* "We're okay!" the veteran coach calls for all his team to here. "Now, D'up!"

Tyler takes the vote of confidence to heart, and as Reynolds receives the ball for ACA and attempts a five-footer in the lane, Tyler springs from the hardwood, leaping high in the air and not just blocking but stopping the trajectory of the shot in its tracks, Tyler pulling the ball down from ten-feet in the air with one hand and arm, controlling the ball all the way.

"Oh, yeah, Tyler!" Roger praises from the sideline as several Muskrat players on the bench vault to their feet.

It is now up to Dwayne to initiate the offense, and, at first, the replacement point guard looks shaky as he brings the ball up the floor.

"You're fine, Dwayne." Roger encourages. "Just run the offense."

"You can do this, Dwayne," echoes Kevin from his dad's side on the bench.

Dwayne and the Muskrats to go work against the Academy zone with the game tied in the fourth quarter. Dwayne works the ball to Jeremiah…back to Dwayne…then to Leonard at the high post.

Leonard turns to face the basket as Tyler finds a crease in the defense and flashes his hands, showing hard across the lane. Leonard hits him in the palms. Tyler does not hesitate, extending up and over the outstretched hands of Reynolds Green, banking in a desperately-needed, ten-foot basket for two points: Macon 54, Augusta 52—four minutes remain.

"Great job!" Roger affirms. "Now 'D' up again! Watch the screens!"

Seated next to his father, Kevin continues to massage his lower leg and ankle, and the feeling of not being out there empowers his body with each passing second.

Roger watches as his former player Reynolds Green calls for the ball, which is what star players do in crucial moments. "Stay on your feet, Tyler," Coach Stevens shouts. "Stay on your feet!"

Reynolds gives a textbook head fake and gets Tyler airborne. Fortunately for Roger and Macon South, the shot circles the entire rim before spilling over the side.

Before Roger can finish exhaling, Reggie Dawkins is in his ear. "That's four on Tyler."

Roger next looks to the scoreboard: his team leads 54-52. He next looks to the clock: 3:15 remaining. He next looks down the bench for a comparable alternative, and other than his son rubbing to get life back in his sore ankle, there is no one to replace Tyler. Thus, the man is forced into a tough decision;

the type of choice that forces a head basketball coach to earn his salary.

"Stay in," Roger mouths to Tyler.

Tyler acknowledges as he and the other players align the free throw lane accordingly.

Reynolds steps to the line for the Academy. Poised, calm, seasoned, the Patriots' leading scorer for the year knocks down the first attempt to the delight of the Augusta crowd.

Even Roger cannot help but feel pride as he watches his former player excel on such a big stage this night. The man can only guess how many hours Reynolds and his son spent together in the Augusta gym.

After three more dribbles, Reynolds hits his next attempt and pulls the Academy even again: Macon 54, Augusta 54.

Coach Newhouse considers pressing Macon with Kevin Stevens out of the game. However, he does not want to over-extend and give up anything easy. Plus, Macon has not been effective against the zone given their current lineup.

"Move the ball, Dwayne! Get a good one!" Roger instructs.

Again, the Patriot zone is stalwart, and the Academy big men have closed the loophole from last time. Nothing... nothing...nothing is available as the ball swings around the perimeter.

Roger winces on the sideline, wondering who will step forward and lead with Kevin out of the game—lead whether in victory or failure.

Dwayne has seen enough, and despite the fact his jumper has not fallen all night, without cumbersome analysis, he receives a pass from his right and steps into the same jumper he missed a few minutes ago.

Roger watches, pleasantly surprised. Whether the ball goes in or not, he loves the way Dwayne fires his shot with confidence.

This time, Dwayne hits the mark, as if the South guard has been shooting well from the start. Thanks to the young man's fearlessness, Macon retakes the lead in a see-saw battle: Macon 56, Augusta 54.

"Yes, Dwayne! Yes!" Roger claps on the bench. Even Kevin unadvisedly rises on his bad ankle to show support.

"Easy, Kev," his father admonishes.

"I'm feeling better, dad. Just give me another minute."

Without relenting, Augusta is back on the attack, and despite the fact Macon knows what is coming, the Muskrats seem powerless to stop it.

Newhouse, Jr. again successfully feeds the ball to Reynolds, and the Academy center immediately draws a crowd as both Tyler and Leonard gravitate toward him. Reynolds, playing with supreme confidence, pivots and drops a pass inside to Trevor Hopkins with no one else around, the Academy converting and re-tying the game: Macon 56, Augusta 56.

The game clock rolls under two minutes.

Roger glances at Kevin to quickly check his status between plays.

Kevin continues to rub his ankle, wincing as he does.

Dwayne again initiates the Macon offense, confronted by the same, obstinate zone defense. With no success inside, Dwayne keeps his confidence alive and steps into another jump shot from the same spot between the free throw line and top of the key.

Roger groans as the shot bounces off, but the man's anguish is short-lived as Tyler Washington displays great agility and athleticism, somehow weaving his way through a mass of bodies and leaping high enough to get a hand on the putback, hanging unbalanced in the air, tipping the ball just over the front of the rim and in.

A barbaric roar ensues from the South faithful: Macon 58, Augusta 56.

The Patriots feverishly work the ball around the perimeter, looking for an opening.

The clock displays a scant 1:15 remaining in this State Semi-final matchup.

Since Reynolds cannot get the ball down low, he pops up high. Newhouse, Jr. passes to his now open teammate, and Newhouse, Jr. wisely cuts, running past Reynolds as the two execute a perfect give and go, giving the point guard a clear path to the basket.

Tyler leaves Reynolds and closes on the ball as Newhouse, Jr. sends a floater airborne from the left side of the lane. Tyler makes a clean block up high. However, thanks to slight contact to the body and a great acting job by Newhouse, Jr., the nearest official brings the worst nightmare of Macon South to fruition.

"Foul, right there…with the body! Two shots!"

"No!" Roger fulminates from the South bench. Before he realizes it, the man is five feet out on the court while pleading his case.

As the official reports to the scorer's table, Roger is a mere few feet from him, giving the man an earful. "How can you call that now? That's garbage!"

Roger quickly draws a look of fury from the official who stands whistle in hand—not afraid to use it.

"Let them play!" Roger thunders. "No one came to watch you ref the game!"

With impeccable timing, Coach Dawkins steps between the two men and begins to walk Roger back in the opposite direction. "Let it go, coach," he speaks in a docile tone. "Let it go."

"Stay on your bench, Coach!" admonishes the irascible referee. "I'm not going to tell you again."

The Macon Head Coach yields to the calm voice of his assistant coach. Roger next looks to his right and sees a slump-shouldered young man walking his way. Tyler carries all five fouls with him to the bench, feeling as if he has failed, as if he has let his team down.

Much to the contrary, Roger grabs Tyler's arm and pulls him close. "Great game, Tyler. Great game. Proud of you, son."

The words do little to console Tyler as he saunters to the end of the line and plops down, his face in his hands.

Out of desperation, Roger looks to see if Kevin is anywhere near ready. The man looks among the bodies, but Kevin is not there. "Where's Kevin?" is his befuddled query.

"Behind you, Coach," points one of the players.

Roger wheels to find his son already reporting to the scorer's table. Whatever pain the star player felt was pushed out when Tyler picked up his final foul. Kevin told himself, *there isn't time for pain.*

Kevin bends and then jumps to get loose. Upon landing, the Macon point guard winces and hobbles before regaining his balance.

Roger soon stands before him. "You good to go?"

Again, Kevin pushes away the pain, wiping sweat from his forehead and then wiping the bottom of his sneakers with the same hand for traction. "I'm good, dad. I'm good."

Karen watches like a hawk.

The reemergence of the star player onto the court provides a spark to his team. The other four in the lineup welcome him back. In a nice gesture, some of the Augusta players check on him as well, most notably Reynolds Green and Trevor Hopkins. Bart Newhouse, Jr., on the other hand, remains at the free throw line and does not budge, awaiting his foul shots.

"We're shooting two, gentlemen," the referee instructs, handing the ball to Newhouse, Jr. who calmly knocks down the first attempt to the roar of half the crowd, moving the Academy within one point.

Between shots, Kevin walks the width of the court to build endurance in his tender ankle.

Newhouse, Jr. knocks down the second shot as well, and, again, the game is tied: Macon 58, Augusta 58.

Kevin, with under one minute on the clock, defers to Dwayne to bring up the ball. Soon, Newhouse, Jr, knowing there is no mercy in sports, comes chest to chest with Kevin, bumping the injured player off balance as they both jog downcourt, Newhouse, Jr. lifting both hands high in the air to give the illusion of innocence.

Kevin grunts from the flash of pain. Ultimately, he finds the left block.

Dwayne can tell Kevin wants the ball, and Dwayne does his best to sneak the ball inside. Kevin comes free just enough to harness the bounce pass from Dwayne.

"Double him!" bellows Bart Newhouse, Sr. "Double him!"

Roger watches helplessly from the bench as his counterpart shows no mercy.

Trevor Hopkins runs toward Kevin, but without the normal burst of speed, Kevin is unable to elude both defenders as usual. He attempts to spin away, yet he almost loses the ball in the process. Roger can see Kevin is not himself.

"Timeout!" pleads the South coach from the bench.

The nearest official acknowledges the request.

Kevin feels relief at the sound of the whistle, and the entire team heads for the bench.

As Coach Dawkins walks with his Head Coach, Roger Stevens wastes little time in analyzing the situation. "We're tied, and we can't afford to give the ball back. I know there's still 50 seconds, but we've got to play for the final shot. I don't think Kevin can go up and down and play defense right now."

Coach Dawkins concurs.

Both coaches return to the huddle.

The crowd buzzes in anticipation. The anxiety oppresses both fan bases.

"Okay, men," Roger intercedes. "We're playing for one shot. Dwayne, they will no doubt double Kevin, so be ready to handle the ball again. You're doing a great job. You need to play catch out high with Jeremiah. Jeremiah, at the ten-second mark, screen for Dwayne to get him open in the direction of Kevin on the left block. Kevin will post his man. Give him a good pass, Dwayne. Kevin," the coach turns to look at his son, "hit the shot, buddy, and send us to the title game."

The assemblage around the coach exercises collective faith in the man's decree.

• • •

Jeremiah receives the ball from the nearest ref on the sideline.

Dwayne sets himself behind Leonard, ready to pop out and receive the inbound pass.

Jeremiah slaps the ball.

Roger winces as Trevor Hopkins nearly jumps the passing lane for Augusta, almost coming up with a crucial steal, knocking the ball further into the back court.

Dwayne regains his composure and brings the ball across half court—45 seconds remain. Instead of attacking the basket, Dwayne delivers an innocent pass to Jeremiah well above the top of the key, then Jeremiah back to Dwayne, then Dwayne back to Jeremiah, each pass about three seconds or so apart—the clock dwindles to 30 seconds remaining.

Kevin bends at the waist at the low block, conserving his energy.

Bart Newhouse, Sr. discerns the Muskrats are holding for the final shot. Normally, he would have his players hold tight and play straight up. With Kevin Stevens not handling the ball out front, the man decides to test the other South guards. "Pick them up!"

The Patriot defense extends.

The pulse of the crowd intensifies.

Dwayne receives a pass from Jeremiah; however, Jeremiah is no longer open so Dwayne cannot pass back.

"Move, guys!" Roger calls from bench. "You gotta' get open!"

With 17 seconds remaining, Jeremiah jukes to rid himself of his defender.

However, the stomach of every Macon South fan, player and coach drops as Dwayne and Jeremiah misread each other, Dwayne passing the ball in one direction as Jeremiah cuts in another.

This time, Trevor Hopkins does not miss, and the athletic Augusta power forward runs down the errant pass and breaks for the goal.

A crush of volume fills the arena as Jeremiah gives chase.

"Oh, no," Kevin laments, unable to sprint to help, watching the action from behind.

Roger is powerless as well, fearful such a well-played game by his roster will come down to such a cataclysmic mistake.

The capacity crowd holds its breath for a moment as Trevor out runs the defense, laying the ball up and in to give the Patriots the two-point lead with 11 seconds on the clock. The arena rumbles with thunderous vibration.

Newhouse, Jr. takes the opportunity to relish the moment. "That's the ballgame," he proudly brags in Kevin's ear.

Roger watches as the seconds drop to 10. "Get it and go, Jeremiah!"

With no time to pout, Jeremiah grabs the ball out of bounds and turns to find Dwayne who calls for the ball under the Patriot basket.

Nine seconds remain.

Dwayne pivots and throws it into high gear, racing his dribble forward.

Seven seconds remain.

Kevin sees the fight in his teammates and begins to gravitate toward the left block again.

Newhouse, Jr. thought the game was over and now moves as Kevin moves.

"Get back!" commands Newhouse, Sr.

Roger watches as Dwayne crosses half court. "That a boy, Dwayne."

Four seconds remain as Dwayne hits Kevin with another clean bounce pass as Kevin successfully holds off Newhouse, Jr.

Three seconds remain.

The feel of the leather sphere in his hands takes Kevin to another place, and the sensation of slapping the ball with his free hand ushers Kevin's mind past any pain he might feel in his body.

"Double!" screams Coach Newhouse, the man running down the sideline as close to the action as allowable, as if he wants to run on the court and play defense himself. "Double!"

Reynolds Green was already on his way when he saw the pass go to his former teammate.

Kevin senses Reynolds approaching and takes a hard dribble into the chest of his longtime friend.

Two seconds.

Kevin next picks up his dribble and begins to whirl in the opposite direction, turning toward the baseline.

Reynolds has seen this movie before. "Watch the turn-around," he calls to Newhouse, Jr.

Newhouse, Jr. closes out the best he can as Kevin, who once showed signs of a foot injury, begins to float gracefully as if in perfect health, somehow finding the athleticism and strength to leave the floor without any complications.

Kevin smiles, familiar with his sweet spot on the floor, knowing when he finds it no one can stop it.

Roger watches as the clock over his son's shoulder hits one second—the ball still in Kevin's hands. With that, the man takes a deep breath, as does everyone else in Alexander Memorial Coliseum.

Fading away and toward the baseline, Kevin gets off a comfortable turnaround jumper over the outstretched arms of both Reynolds Green and Bart Newhouse, Jr.

Leonard would normally move in hard for the offensive rebound, but there is no need as the arena horn blasts while Kevin's shot is in the air.

All remaining Macon players watch from their bench.

Coach Dawkins leans slightly to try and send a little body-English Kevin's way for good measure.

Karen is awash with anxiety, almost covering her eyes.

Roger is no longer a coach but a spectator like everyone else.

It looks good from here, Kevin considers. *It felt good, too.* As if his job is done, as if there is nothing left to do, Kevin watches the result of his effort by falling safely to the court, his backside cushioning the impact. His arms send the basketball star sliding away from his defenders, giving him an unobstructed view; Kevin watches the ball touch nothing but net as it passes cleanly through the iron cylinder, sending the crowd into a frenzy and this State semifinal game into overtime; Macon 60, Augusta 60.

The South bench explodes as players rush the court. Roger is lassoed around the neck as Coach Dawkins corrals him in joy.

The remaining Muskrat players pounce on Kevin as the coach's son holds up his hands to protect himself against the oncoming stampede. Even the Macon fans seated nearby storm the baseline to get in on the action.

"Come on, ref!" What is this?" an agitated Coach Newhouse complains. "The game's not over!"

Roger Stevens, trying to remain calm amid the hoopla, waves his arms vigorously to get his players off the court and back onto the team bench. "Please go get them, Coach," he bids his assistant.

Soon, Kevin Stevens and the rest of the team emerge and arrive at the South bench. Roger could say a million things to his son right now. Instead, he settles for, "Nice shot," as the coach rubs the teenager's flattop as he passes by.

With a long exhale, Roger steps from the huddle and looks to the scoreboard. As glad as he is with Kevin's heroics, the man also knows the game-tying shot has only forced the game to overtime, and now his team must find a way to forge ahead for five more minutes. Not to mention, Kevin is not at full strength.

"We've got to find a way to slow this thing down," he confides in Coach Dawkins. "Five minutes feels like an eternity. Not to mention, we don't have Tyler for the overtime."

• • •

On the opposing bench, Coach Newhouse gives an earful to his squad for the fact they are even in this position since Stevens hardly played in the second half. "Pour it on!" is the coach's theme to his team for the overtime session. "Pour it on!"

• • •

"Okay, settle down. Settle down," Roger exhorts, wading through the celebratory bodies. "We still have a game to play." Roger checks the first item on his mental list of priorities. "Kev, how are you feeling?"

Adrenaline overwhelms pain at this moment, giving Kevin his second wind. "I'm good, Coach."

"You sure?"

"Yes. I feel good."

"Okay, men. We are going to shorten this overtime. So, let's go back to Dwayne and Jeremiah working the ball back and forth out top. Leonard, come to the top of the key to give them an outlet if they get in trouble. Once the defense slides out high, let's go to Kevin on the block again. Let's not make this more complicated than it needs to be."

• • •

"I don't know if Stevens will play the whole overtime or not," bellows Coach Newhouse at the other end of the court. "If he's in there again, they'll probably put him back in the low post. If they do that, I want to double him again, but this time I want a good trap," the man admonishes, looking squarely at Reynolds Green and his son, both players feeling the crushing weight of their coach's stare.

• • •

As his players stand to their feet and surround him, Roger Stevens brandishes a smile that cuts through the ultra-intensity. Putting his hand to the middle, he mundanely addresses his players, "Look around, men. We're at the Georgia Final Four. Where would you rather be?"

The light-hearted comment has the desired effect on the faces of his players.

"Besides," the man continues, trying to raise his voice above the pounding of the capacity crowd. "I have nowhere else to be tonight. I canceled all my plans to be with all of you."

The Muskrat players smile at the well-timed antics of their head coach.

"South on three: one…two…three…South!"

Both teams reunite at center court for the second jump ball of the evening.

In Tyler's absence, Leonard steps to the center circle to represent Macon.

Reynolds Green counters.

Tyler is dying inside as he watches the commencement of the overtime session without him.

The crowd has received a generous portion of quality high school basketball, but they are hungry for more.

"Straight up in the air, gentlemen," the lead official reminds the competitors as he steps between the two towers and lofts the ball into the air.

Reynolds re-directs the tip to Trevor Hopkins who kicks the ball back to Newhouse, Jr. to set up the offense.

After two passes and three screens, Reynolds comes free on the baseline and Newhouse hits him with his tenth assist of the night as the Academy draws first blood in overtime; Macon 60, Augusta 62.

Kevin does the abnormal again and relinquishes the ball as point guard. The injured warrior lumbers down the court to the left block.

Dwayne and Jeremiah resume their game of catch out high.

Newhouse, Sr. allows the stall tactic for a little while but eventually sends pressure to speed up the action.

Dwayne gets a screen from Jeremiah and goes right back to Kevin on the low block.

Everyone in the gym knows what is coming, but it does not seem to matter. Kevin releases and hits another textbook, turnaround-baseline jumper over the top of the defense; Macon 62, Augusta 62. Four minutes remain in overtime.

"What are we doing!" a livid Coach Newhouse excoriates his players from the sideline, zeroing in on his son especially. "You know it's coming."

Macon South retreats to the defensive end of the floor as Newhouse, Jr. angrily dribbles the ball up the court.

"Call out the screens!" Roger admonishes from the team bench.

"Call out the screens!" Kevin simultaneously admonishes from the floor.

Here come the screens from the Academy; two screens, three, popping Reynolds free on the baseline again.

Clearly frustrated, Leonard runs down one of the screens like a bulldozer in sneakers.

As Reynolds converts the lay in, a whistle is icing on the cake for the Academy. "Count the basket! And a push, right here!" exclaims the official, pointing at Leonard.

Every basket is crucial in overtime, and Roger grimaces as his former team is awarded the basket plus additional opportunities. "It was a moving screen, ref!" petitions the Macon coach.

"No, no, it wasn't," the official retorts on his way to the scorer's table. Meanwhile, the Academy goes on top again; Macon 62, Augusta 64.

Stepping to the line, Trevor converts on his first free throw attempt; Macon 62, Augusta 65. However, his second attempt kicks off the rim.

Leonard grabs the rebound and looks for Kevin out of habit.

Bart Newhouse, Jr. craftily sneaks behind Leonard and pokes the ball away.

Roger shakes his head as momentum has shifted; the Patriots have possession with a three-point lead in overtime; 3:30 remaining.

It is obvious where the Academy wants to go with the ball.

Keenly, Kevin takes away the passing lane, shading toward Reynolds.

Torn between forcing the pass and taking an uncontested jump shot, Newhouse, Jr., never too shy to shoot, takes the jumper with exactly three minutes to play.

The shot is off, and Leonard shows his physical superiority by snaring yet another rebound, this time holding the ball high and free from reaching hands.

Kevin takes the handoff from Leonard then hands the ball to Dwayne. Kevin next takes a light jog to the other end of the court, favoring his left side.

Dwayne and Jeremiah begin to pass to one another out high again, and Bart Newhouse, Sr. is content to let them do it with the Patriot's three-point lead.

Roger knows he must act, or he will be outdone by his counterpart. "We can't wait, Dwayne. We've gotta' go!"

Dwayne rolls off Jeremiah's screen again, but the Patriot defender successfully hedges and impedes Dwayne, causing the ball-handler to dribble the ball off his foot and out of bounds; 2:39 remaining.

Roger exhales deeply: *overtime has been too sloppy already.*

Newhouse, Jr. looks for Reynolds at the other end. With all the attention gravitating toward the skilled Academy center, Trevor pops free for an open mid-range jump shot. However, the moment proves too big for the anxious teen, and Trevor leaves his attempt short, Leonard snaring another carom.

The Academy is allowing Macon South to hang around. The Augusta lead still stands at three. The clock continues to dwindle—under two minutes remain.

"You're fine," Kevin encourages Dwayne in the backcourt, showing confidence by giving him the ball again. "Just get it to me."

Dwayne acknowledges and brings the ball up the floor, allowing Kevin time to settle at the same low block.

As Kevin posts up again, he is greeted with the same forceful hand in the back from Newhouse, Jr. Tired of the bumping and pushing, Kevin bumps back.

Newhouse, Jr. retaliates with a shoulder of his own, which prompts Kevin to whirl and face his opponent, the two competitors coming nose to nose.

A shrilling whistle intervenes. "My time!" declares the ref, leaving his place on the baseline to wedge between the two combatants.

Both fan bases take the side of their own, booing the other, causing hostility to fester.

"I'm not going to tell you two again," exhorts the official, clad in black and white stripes from the waist up, pointing at both Kevin and Newhouse, Jr. "Watch the contact! Do you understand?"

What began on the court spreads to the sideline as Bart Newhouse, Sr. whips around to eyeball Roger Stevens. "Tell your boy to back off!"

What has been boiling within Roger Stevens all night cannot be contained any longer. "You're kidding me, right?" Roger responds while advancing toward half court to verbally spar with the coach of his former team. "Your boy's a dirty player," Roger spills the beans. "And everybody knows it!"

"What did you say to me?"

More crowd noise swells as the coaches have words.

Both benches are on their feet.

Another official is quick to intervene as well as both assistant coaches.

Roger regains his composure. He often finds it a difficult road to walk, balancing the actions of a competitor with that of a good Christian man.

Newhouse, Sr. in the meantime, has never backed down from a fight in his life. "That's what I thought," he fires one final shot across the bow.

Once the refs restore order, which includes a final warning to both head coaches, the game resumes with the Academy in front.

Dwayne takes the ball and, this time, successfully navigates the screen of his teammate and the hedging defender. With a clear lane, Dwayne next gets the ball back into the hands of Kevin Stevens on the low block.

With his injury far from his mind, Kevin immediately reads the oncoming trap and wheels away just as he did previously. Playing with the defense as would a puppet master, Kevin pulls the string, not shooting but dropping a perfect pass under the basket to Leonard who Reynolds Green has left alone.

Leonard goes up strong and scores to the roar of the Macon faithful, pulling his team within one; Macon 64, Augusta 65 with 1:37 remaining.

Clearly frustrated, Newhouse, Sr. refuses to call a timeout—he knows they should have put away South by now. Instead, he flashes a hand signal to his son, who relays the same message to the other four Academy players on the floor. In synch, the Academy offense goes into a spread formation, protecting and moving the ball safely around the perimeter.

Roger discerns the opponent's plan to stall. Unable to call a timeout while on defense, Roger calls to Kevin and the rest of his team. "Pick up the pace! Deny the ball!"

On cue, the Muskrat defense steps up the intensity.

"Don't foul!" Roger adds. "Not yet!"

The next 45 seconds evaporate quickly and just over 50 seconds remain in overtime. The Academy moves the ball with precision, just out of the reach of the zealous defenders from Macon.

Kevin is as mentally tough as they come; however, his swollen ankle is inhibiting his lateral quickness.

The South crowd itches for a turnover. "Get the ball! Hurry!" miscellaneous voices fraught with fear can be heard in the background.

Forty-six seconds..., forty-four seconds..., forty-one seconds..., thirty-nine seconds; precious time continues to evaporate.

The Macon defense extends further, higher, frenetically, but the Academy players aptly handle the pressure.

Under 30 seconds remain. Roger's eyes shift back and forth between the action and the clock as he assesses the situation. *If we're not getting a steal, we need to foul.*

Newhouse, Jr. receives the ball again near the center circle at half court.

Kevin limps to challenge him.

Newhouse clasps the ball, shielding it with his body while swinging his arms, anticipating a foul from Kevin to stop the clock.

Surprisingly, Kevin chooses not to foul; not yet. Instead, Kevin has one more trick up his sleeve.

To avoid a five-second call, Newhouse, Jr. puts the ball on the floor and dribbles past Kevin.

Waiting for him to do so, Kevin reaches around the ball-handler from behind with a long, arching swipe, poking the ball free and propelling it forward just beyond his counterpart's reach.

Dwayne sees the ball rolling his way. He steps from guarding his man and intercepts.

Once jostling the dribble loose, Kevin allows his momentum to carry him down the court to the offensive end, signaling high for the ball as he does.

Trailing by one, Dwayne sees Kevin, and the pass is on target. Breaking away from the pack, the star Macon point guard dribbles uncontested into the lane and lays the ball gingerly over the front of the rim and in for the go-ahead score with twenty-one seconds remaining. Kevin had to protect his ankle at all costs—no more dunking tonight.

The crowd erupts as South—via tremendous perseverance and despite all obstacles—somehow takes the lead in overtime; Macon 66, Augusta 65.

"Timeout!" Coach Newhouse demands, his face red with fury, the lines in his forehead markedly pronounced.

As the Academy players saunter toward the bench, no doubt regretting the tongue-lashing soon to follow, the Muskrat players sprint toward Roger Stevens.

"Nice work, men!" Roger congratulates his players as they whisk past him. "Great pass, Dwayne! He pats the young man on the head as he runs past. "Great play, Kev!"

The fans from both teams are exhausted. The final stage is set, or so they thought earlier.

"We know where they're going," proclaims Coach Dawkins to the head coach.

Roger concurs. "Absolutely."

"Should we double Green?"

The veteran coach chews on the prospect for a few moments, doing his best to gather his thoughts among the hysteria, vigorously rubbing his chin as he does. In the end, Roger turns to his assistant to ask, "What do you suggest? Should we double him?"

Slightly caught off guard that the head coach would put him on the spot in such a moment of enormity, Coach Dawkins gulps noticeably before responding. "I think I would, coach. If they're going to beat us, let's make someone else beat us."

Coach Dawkins observes the vacillating facial expressions of his superior before Roger Stevens finally concludes. "I agree. You're a good coach, Reggie."

Roger steps to the middle of his frenzied pack of players. "Listen! Sit down! Listen! We haven't won anything yet, so stay focused. Eighteen seconds is a lot of time. We know where they're going with the basketball."

• • •

"Get the ball to Reynolds!" Coach Newhouse demands in the other huddle.

• • •

"They'll probably set a double screen for Green, Leonard, so watch for it!" Coach Stevens anticipates.

• • •

"I want a solid double screen for Reynolds!" Newhouse continues.

• • •

"Fight through the screen, Leonard, but don't shove and give them anything cheap. Make them earn it. If he hits a tough shot, then he hits a tough shot. But make it tough!" Roger concludes.

• • •

"When the big fella' fights through the screen," Newhouse looks directly at Trevor Hopkins, "be ready to flop because he likes to push his way through. Put the pressure on the ref to call the foul!"

• • •

"Jeremiah, leave your man and stand on the other side of the screen to wait for Reynolds. I want to deny him the ball. Let's not even let him get a touch. If your man beats us, that's okay. That's on me!"

• • •

"Watch for the double team, Reynolds!" Newhouse resounds, both coaches trying to cover every contingency. "I want you to take the shot, but if they leave Junior wide open, kick it to him."

• • •

Both teams step from their respective benches, all ten of them fatigued.

Roger turns his back to the court, exhales, then takes a drink of water. Giving a glance to the stands as he does, he looks for Karen; his wife is feeling the nerves of the moment as well, smiling with a roll of the eyes. Roger next looks down the sideline to see Bart Newhouse, Sr. looking back at him. Both men exchange stoic glances followed by a mutual nod, acknowledging it has been a classic matchup.

Augusta prepares to inbound the ball—down by one point.

Macon South will allow the opposition to dribble the length of the court.

The ref hands the ball to Trevor Hopkins who inbounds to Bart Newhouse, Jr., the Academy point guard pushing the ball down the court speedily to get into the offense, his team desperately needing a basket.

Kevin picks up Newhouse, Jr. at half court to apply pressure and disrupt the passing lane. However, Kevin has trouble side-stepping the oncoming screen, and Newhouse, Jr. has the separation he needs.

Meanwhile, under the basket, here comes the double screen.

Per the specific instructions of Coach Stevens, Jeremiah forsakes his man to drop down and pick up Reynolds off the screen while Leonard shadows Reynolds from behind.

The passing lane between Newhouse, Jr. and Reynolds is gone.

Twelve seconds, eleven seconds, ten seconds: a frantic look overtakes Bart Newhouse, Jr. He motions anxiously with the ball, but he cannot find a crease to get it to Reynolds—the Muskrat defense does its job. With nine seconds remaining, Newhouse, Jr. cannot wait any longer. Realizing he has an advantage over his injured counterpart, the Academy guard fakes left then goes right, getting away from Kevin just enough to launch a 10-foot floater on the move.

All eyes are on Newhouse's attempt as the ball hits the right side of the rim.

Roger feels optimistic; the ball is bounding away from the basket—his team may pull out an overtime win after all. Before Roger can finish his thought, Reynolds Green squirms between multiple bodies and gets a hand on the rebound..., just enough to tip the ball up and over the rim for the go-ahead score.

The Augusta fans jump, leap and spin.

Roger immediately calls the team's final timeout with six seconds remaining; Macon 66, Augusta 67. An aura of deflation replaces his team's previous excitement.

"It's okay, come on!" Roger motions to his players then claps his hands in support. "It's not over. Let's go."

His players plop down on the bench before him. They are spent. They have given the man everything.

Coach Stevens tries to carry their burden with his optimism. "Okay, men. Let's do it one more time. Jeremiah inbound to Dwayne. Dwayne bring the ball up quickly. Get it to Kevin on the low block. Leonard and everyone else, hit the offensive boards. Watch the clock, though. Everybody got it?"

A collective nod lumbers from the Muskrats. The magnitude of this State semi-final has been more exhausting than many of them imagined it would be. Nevertheless, if their coach believes they can do it, then the players believe they can do it.

"Kevin," his father asks in front of the entire team. "You got one more left in you?"

With all eyes on him, Kevin assumes the weight of the mantle with a nod. "I've got one more."

"Then let's do it, men," Roger affirms with confidence by pushing his right hand to the middle. "South on three: one... two...three...South!"

Both teams emerge yet again, the players beleaguered, sweaty, some even cramping.

Kevin conserves his energy as he walks down the court, staring at the hardwood floor as he does. He blocks out the anxiety-riddled masses around him, preventing any noise from entering his mind, leaving him to his repetitive thought: *get your shot. Get your shot.*

Roger reconciles the scoreboard again; Macon South is one-point down with six seconds left. *Well, someone's going home right here*, the man concludes.

Coach Newhouse barks final orders to his team.

Karen looks on; her hands clasped beneath her chin; her knuckles white.

The crush of volume from the capacity crowd is ever-present.

The ref hands the ball to Jeremiah.

With six seconds remaining, Jeremiah inbounds to Dwayne.

Dwayne turns and quickly pushes the ball up the court.

Reynolds rotates. He and Newhouse, Jr. double Kevin just as Roger expected. In fact, here comes Trevor Hopkins as well to triple team Macon's leading scorer.

Five seconds remain. Dwayne rushes closer.

Kevin strives against the smothering bodies on defense; he can barely see past them.

Four seconds. Dwayne crosses half court.

The defenders continue to swamp Kevin.

Three seconds.

Kevin can sense the truth: they will not let him catch the ball in his favorite spot. The instincts of the coach's son assume control. Kevin shocks the defense by lunging from the low block, drawing a burst of energy from who knows where, hopping away from the traffic on a bad ankle.

Dwayne sees the opportunity and delivers on point.

Two seconds.

Kevin catches the ball, and, with his momentum already moving away from the basket, he effortlessly turns into his shot, ready to administer his patented turnaround baseline jumper one final time.

The opponents from the Academy close fast, fraught with fear; somehow, he still got the ball despite their best efforts.

Coach Newhouse is equally bewildered, and the man has an utterly haunting view of Kevin Stevens sizing up the basket.

Despite the injury, Kevin embraces his familiar wreath of confidence. *They can try, but they can't stop my shot*, he appraises as he drifts in midair.

One second.

Roger watches as the final shot of the game leaves the right hand of his son.

Karen cannot watch, but she must.

The same goes for both fanbases.

The arena horn sounds as the leather basketball begins its descent, then as it barely touches the inside of the far portion of the rim, causing the ball to ricochet back and forth inside the rim in a blur, then as the ball climbs innocently over the right side of the rim and innocently falls to the floor. The shot is no good—Augusta Christian has defeated Macon South.

Kevin closes his eyes while lying flat on the hardwood floor, releasing the longest exhale of his life.

Much the same, Roger tilts his head back and closes his eyes.

With the clock showing all zeros, this classic State semi-final comes to an end. The final score: the Augusta Christian Academy Patriots 67, and the Macon South Muskrats 66. For Macon South, their season is over.

The volcanic eruption from the Augusta fan base soars through the arena ceiling.

The hopes of the Macon fans fell to the floor with the basketball.

Just as last season—when the Academy won the State title under Roger's direction—the Augusta players and fans swarm the court.

Kevin is almost the victim of a stampede as zealous bodies sprint to the celebration.

The huge hands of Leonard Sweetwood reach down and grab Kevin, lifting him safely to his feet. In a tender moment, Leonard puts his massive arms around his point guard's shoulders and ushers him safely through the crowd and back toward the Macon South bench.

With the image in mind of the ball ricocheting in and out, one of the few turnaround jumpers Kevin remembers missing, the former Georgia player of the year lets go of the painful thought long enough to acknowledge the strength and love of his teammate. "Thanks, brother."

"I got you, brother," Leonard responds.

Meanwhile, Roger Stevens lifts his eyes from the floor as the final shot did not stay true. Just as Kevin's other shots this evening, the final one looked to be online. *This one, however,* the man considers, *this one just didn't go in.*

Observing his players on the floor and looking behind to his players on the bench, Roger can sense the anguish. Instead of allowing his players to sulk, Roger opens his arms and welcomes his team to come to him, and, as a father would, he pulls each one of them close, hugging them and placing his hands on as many drooping shoulders as he can.

"Great game, guys," the man genuinely spreads the word among his troops. "Great game. Let's line up and congratulate the other team."

With little interest in doing so, the Macon South players, yet again, heed to the instructions of their worthy leader. At half court, they meet the players from Augusta.

From her seat behind the South bench, Karen watches through tears as the Muskrats concede graciously.

It is evident the Macon South players earned the respect of their counterparts from Augusta this evening; the Patriots take ample time to congratulate the Muskrats on a hard-fought, well-played contest, especially acknowledging Tyler and Leonard as they pass by. To no one's surprise, the players from Augusta take extra time to speak with Kevin Stevens and then Roger Stevens. Near the end of the line, Kevin Stevens and Bart Newhouse, Jr. find one another and express good sportsman-ship as do the coaches and fathers, Roger Stevens and Bart Newhouse, Sr. Both men stand toe to toe, eye to eye, and dig deeply to speak cordial words to one another, followed by a mutual handshake.

The buzz of the crowd slowly subsides over the next hour.

Those who lost stumble toward the exits.

Those who won walk on air.

Ultimately, by the end of the night, person by person, body by body, the capacity crowd dissipates. The arena is eventually empty, the hardwood court swept clean by a small crew of workers, and then the lights go down on Alexander Memorial Coliseum.

42

The Stevens family has driven to Atlanta many times, mostly from the Augusta-side. Today, they travel from Macon on the heels of making the same trek to the State tournament a week ago. Even so, everything is different on this trip—same scenery, different purpose.

Roger is still reeling. He left Augusta Christian after all those years, to go to—of all places—Macon South, only to face Augusta Christian in the State semifinals and lose in a thriller, a classic—a game people will talk about for years. Even so, Roger keeps reminding himself of the objective truth: what a season! Macon South had never advanced to the State Tournament, and to do it this season with a new coach while surrounded by the most unspeakable circumstances: how can this basketball season be viewed as anything other than a monumental success!

There has been, however, little time to relish the success, to codify all that transpired this season, both good and bad. Once the phone call came from Central Georgia College in Atlanta, requesting a meeting with Roger regarding a position on their coaching staff, the whirlwind season took another unexpected turn.

There is excitement at the thought of a potential proposition in Roger's mind, whether such an offer comes from Central Georgia or whomever. However, the man has a different reputation now. Formerly known simply as a great coach, a tactician of x's and o's, a developer and maximizer of talent, Roger Stevens—in the eyes of many—now goes by a different moniker: the white man who coaches at a black school, as if the latter wipes away the former, as if he cannot be both or as if the two are mutually exclusive. At the same time, Roger has come to a place where he would rather know what people think of him up front, regardless of how good or how bad, concluding, *it's best to know it now rather than find out after signing on the dotted line.*

During the ride to Atlanta, Karen does not say much. Her goal is to remain neutral. She does not want to influence her husband one way or another. This decision is between him and God. Certainly, she knows Roger will consult with her. Yet after all her husband has endured, after everything the man has sacrificed, Karen has decided to let Roger and God sort this one out. Instead, Karen stares through the passenger window while attempting to hide an uncontainable smile. As much as she has grown to love the people of Macon South, a new season might be dawning.

As is customary, Kevin rides in the back. Not quite sure what to think, the young man has seen more in one year than he has in his entire life.

• • •

Following their arrival to Atlanta and subsequent tour of the Central Georgia campus as provided by the Athletic Director, Benjamin Hamm, the Stevens family is led to a conference room within the administration building.

"Please, make yourselves comfortable." Mr. Hamm gestures toward a long table with a particularly glossy sheen across the pine surface. "Allow me, Mrs. Stevens," the gentleman insists, pulling out a chair for Karen.

"How kind," she replies.

A female assistant appears at the door.

"Everyone, this is Cindy, my assistant. What would everyone like to drink? We have coffee, tea, water. Kevin, how about a soda?"

Roger looks to his family, starting with his wife.

"Coffee would be wonderful," Karen confirms.

"Sure. A soda sounds good," Kevin replies.

"I'll take some water," Roger requests.

"Water for me, too, Cindy. Thank you." Mr. Hamm, a relatively young man for the position of A.D., assumes the chair at the head of the conference-room table. Still somewhat of a mystery, all Roger knows of Benjamin Hamm is he just completed his first season as head of the Central Georgia Athletic Department, but as much as Roger appreciates speaking in person with Mr. Hamm, Coach Stevens wishes Central's head coach of 25 years, B.B. Munson, was here as well. Roger knows it is Coach Munson who would be able to best give insight as to the vitals of the basketball program—coaching philosophy, recruits, the overall direction of the program. Roger's best guess is Mr. Hamm is maybe five years his senior, maybe less.

"Well, now that you've had the official tour and seen what we have to offer here at Central Georgia, may I ask for your initial thoughts?"

Out of courtesy, Roger looks to his wife to see if she would like to speak first.

Karen responds with an acquiescent smile, letting her husband know he speaks for the family today.

Roger shifts his attention back to Mr. Hamm. "Very nice, Mr. Hamm. You have a solid campus here with great amenities. Looks like a great place for a young person to attend college."

"And the facilities, our gym, locker room, track?"

Roger smiles. "Yes. Very nice. The gym is great, just great."

"Seats 10,000, you know," Mr. Hamm points at Roger with a smile. "We have a slightly smaller enrollment here, but we are home to big-time college basketball, and we play all the big boys: UGA, Tech, North Carolina."

Impressed, Roger returns a smile.

"Good place to play, Kevin." Mr. Hamm shifts his sales pitch to the soon-to-be college freshman. "Good place for you to keep hitting that famous turnaround baseline jumper of yours."

The smooth recruiting tactic elicits a smile from the high school senior as well.

"Everything looks great," Roger continues, "but may I ask if Coach Munson will be joining us? I thought he would be here, you know, for me to direct most of my questions toward him; no offense to you, Mr. Hamm."

Bearing a dubious look, Benjamin Hamm shifts forward in his chair, bringing his hands together on the table, interlacing his fingers. The assistant returns just in time to leave Roger's question suspended in air, putting a pause to Mr. Hamm's would-be response. Coffee, soda and water are all served with a southern smile as the Stevens family thanks the young woman. On her way out of the room, the assistant receives one final request from her boss.

"Cindy, would you be so kind as to close the door?"

The door closes, and Mr. Hamm resumes. "Coach Stevens, first and foremost, I've worked hard at preparing a sumptuous speech to try and entice you to join our staff here at Central. So, for the sake of my hard work, please let me start at the beginning and I will make certain to answer all of your questions along the way."

Roger sits back and gives the keys of the conversation to the Central Georgia A.D. out of courtesy.

"Coach Stevens, I, like many basketball fans in the South, have known about you for years based on your success at Augusta Christian: six state titles, nine city championships, an .800 winning percentage, and now added to that already impressive list is a third-place finish in the State tournament while coaching Macon South, a school that had never reached the State Tournament before, and you did that in your first season."

Roger listens with humbleness as Mr. Hamm rattles his stats back to him. *Wow!* Roger ponders. *It's surreal to have all your career accomplishments recited back to you in a sentence or two.*

Mr. Hamm again shifts his attention to Kevin and recites from memory.

"Kevin, the only accolades that might cast a shadow over those of your father are yours: All-City for three straight seasons in Augusta, once in Macon, All-State for two seasons while in Augusta and now once again while playing in Macon. Finally, Mr. Basketball in the State of Georgia for the 1967-'68 season. The truth is, if you had not been hurt for five games, you might have won it again this season while averaging 25 points in the games you played. Instead, the award went to the Wilson kid from Savannah Memorial."

As Roger sits and listens, he must admit the reciting of stats is impressive, and though Mr. Hamm may be relatively new in his role, the man has the sales-pitch aspect of the job down to a science. Regardless, the most flattering words cannot compensate for the absence of Coach Munson at this meeting. Roger cannot make a quality decision to join as an assistant without first meeting face to face with the head coach. There are several bridges to cross, multiple bases to cover.

During the conversation, Benjamin Hamm can discern, despite his best deliverables and pleasantries, Roger Stevens is not sold yet. "Coach Stevens, let's cut to the chase here." A narrower glare quickly supplants the once gregarious façade of the A.D. "I do not doubt that before your move to Macon you were a highly desired basketball coach and your son a highly desired player. I know this for a fact since I run in the same circles as many other A.D.'s, particularly in the South. Before this season almost any college program would have been thrilled to have your son as a player and you as an assistant coach. But I know you are a smart man, and I know the number of scholarships and job offers has lessened, and we both know why that is."

The smile Karen has manifested all day begins to wane behind visible disappointment. She knew it. They all knew it. The litany of recruiting letters had nearly come to a halt since the move to Macon. Many people in the South, even at the college and university levels, did not approve of Roger working with black kids. No one had to say it, but that is the reason. After everything her family has endured, it hurts Karen to think their heartfelt cause has been detested and reviled by so many. *Sad* is the only word the woman can muster in her heart and mind. *Just sad.*

Seated next to his wife, Roger cannot help but consider— *makes you wonder what it was all for and was it worth it.* A swift correction comes to Roger's heart as the faces of Tyler, Leonard, Dwayne, Jeremiah, Billy, and the rest of the team flash before him. A mild wisp of derisive laughter escapes the man. "I'm sorry to interrupt you, Mr. Hamm. I understand what you are telling me but let me state for the record: I wouldn't trade coaching at Macon South for anything in the world."

Karen looks at her husband with pride and reaches for him, resting their interwoven fingers on the table for all to see.

Kevin nods and smiles with satisfaction as well.

"That's great to hear, Coach Stevens," Mr. Hamm replies. "And let me tell you why. Allow me to address why Coach Munson isn't here." With those words, Benjamin Hamm stands from his chair at the head of the conference table and moves to take the seat next to Roger. "May I?" Mr. Hamm politely asks in advance.

"Of course," Roger responds.

Mr. Hamm settles in then leans toward the Stevens family. "Coach Munson isn't here because, after 25 years, he is resigning as the Head Coach at Central Georgia College."

The words bludgeon Roger Stevens, catching him completely off guard.

Mr. Hamm maintains his serious disposition and confidential tone. "Now, a very select number of people know this information, and a formal announcement is forthcoming."

Roger is still hung up on the man's previous statement.

"Now, I'm sure this information comes as quite a shock. It's been a great shock to us in the Athletic Department as well. However, to fully inform you, I need to speak to you off the record for a little while."

Roger consents with a nod.

"Between us, on the surface the announcement of Coach Munson's departure will emphasize the fact that he gave a quarter-century of his life to this college, and Coach Munson feels it's time for a change in his life, namely retirement. Certainly, Coach Munson deserves the promenade of acknowledgments and deference coming to him. I mean, for crying out loud, the man has been a contemporary of Coach Rupp's at Kentucky since the '40s. But what I share with you next, I do so in the utmost confidentiality. The truth is Coach Munson falls under the category of coaches I described to you earlier."

Roger and his family sit in silence, stunned as the information unfurls.

"I know Coach Munson contacted you about a possible position on his coaching staff in the past. He was once very high on you and very high on Kevin, and it's unfortunate to think anything other than your performances on the court changed his opinion of you." Mr. Hamm pauses, only guessing what all of this means to the Stevens family, not intending to overwhelm the man or his wife or son. "Furthermore, the fact that Coach Munson had cooled on you and Kevin would not have been that big of a deal…if not for the fact that I didn't cool on you. To the contrary, I grew fonder of you, Coach Stevens, once you made the courageous move from Augusta to Macon."

Roger mentally sputters in amazement, his thoughts trying to keep up. *What's going on here? What's he saying?*

"It was this difference of opinion between Coach Munson and me that precipitated his decision to step down. He did not approve of your actions, leaving a white school to coach at a black school. On the other hand, I felt your actions to be timely and ground-breaking. Of course, what Coach Haskins accomplished at Texas Western is not to be overlooked. However, as wonderful as his feats have been, El Paso is not considered to be the genuine South. But what you did in the heart of Georgia, sir, was a game-changer. I believe you to be a trailblazer. Unfortunately, Coach Munson did not see it the same way, and Coach Munson is leaving."

The revelations, coupled with compliments, still have Roger off-balance. He asks the next most logical question that comes to mind. "Are you saying B.B Munson is leaving simply because you are considering me as an assistant? No offense, Mr. Hamm, but the man gets to pick his staff. After all these years, he deserves it."

"Yes," Mr. Hamm cedes. "You are correct. However, I—along with our recently appointed College President—sense a trend coming, and that trend is the integration of more black players at colleges and universities in the South. We feel it's time to get in the flow of that trend, even get out in front of it, if possible. I made this suggestion to Coach Munson, asking him to consider bringing someone such as you onto his staff to help with that transition. He didn't take well to the idea. We talked. He agrees change is coming, and he is resigning publicly this week."

"If Coach Munson is gone," Roger queries, "who are you hiring to replace him?"

"Well, Coach Stevens," Mr. Hamm shifts in his chair, bringing his countenance back to a smile. "Let me tell you who I need as a head coach. I believe integration will play a primary role in the future of college basketball. I believe it's a new day, and the schools that embrace this new day by acclimating black players into their programs will lead the future of the sport, not only on the high school and college level but even the professional level. Furthermore, I just don't want black players or just white players. I want the best players, and I want the man best suited to coach the best players, no matter what they look like. I want you, Coach Stevens."

Almost in tears, overwhelmed by the enormity of the moment, Karen squeezes Roger's hand as tightly as she can just in time to hear Benjamin Hamm speak again.

"I am asking you to become the Head Men's Basketball Coach at Central Georgia College here in Atlanta."

"Me?" Roger nearly fumbles the word.

"That's what I'm asking, Roger."

Shock jangles Kevin's spine. Kevin looks to his father. Roger looks to Karen. Karen looks back and forth between Roger and Kevin.

Roger looks back at the A.D. as if to give Mr. Hamm one more opportunity to let everyone know this is a joke, but Mr. Hamm gives no such indication. Before Roger can speak, Mr. Hamm concludes with one more piece of insight.

"The truth is, Coach Stevens, one year ago, we would have relished the thought of bringing you to Central Georgia as an assistant with the prospect of landing Kevin as a future player. However, after what you did this season, leaving Augusta and going to Macon, working with black players, your son playing with black players and both of you leading your team to the State Tournament, what you did was enough to put me over the top. It did the same for our College President, and I have his backing on this decision. In fact, he wants to meet you in a few minutes to tell you in person. We are offering you this job, Coach Stevens, because you were brave enough to coach at Macon South High School. Had you not gone to Macon South...I wouldn't be offering you this job."

43

Dennison checks the knot in his tie for the eighth time this morning, desperately using the reflection in a glass picture frame in the Secretary's office as a mirror.

"You got it?" the woman asks with a slight smirk; Dennison is not the first agent she has seen shaking in his dress shoes over the years.

The phone rings on the Secretary's desk. "Yes, sir," she replies. Just that quickly, she hangs up and looks to the nervous agent in her office. "He's ready for you."

"Thanks…, I think." Dennison gathers himself, taking one more demonstrative breath. Exiting the sub office, he next steps through a heavy door, peaking his head in first. "Sir?"

"Have a seat, Agent Dennison," instructs the deep voice from behind the desk across the room, the man immersed in a document.

"Yes, sir." Dennison sits. Several seconds pass. The only sound is the ticking of a large clock on the wall keeping time with Dennison's breathing.

The document drops to the desk. The man speaks again. "I read your report, Agent Dennison. I am troubled to say the least."

Dennison cannot help but sense a wave of panic, thinking to himself, *what did I miss?*

"Not the format of the report but the content," clarifies the Director. "Dawson worked that region for years. I hand-picked him for it." The already pointed tone of the man behind the desk becomes terser. "I have no one to blame but myself, and I am deeply concerned with my lack of judgment in this matter."

"We were all caught by surprise, sir," Dennison breaks his silence. "Dawson taught me almost everything I know as an agent. He seemed to go by the book one-hundred percent of the time."

The Director narrows his stare at Dennison, surmising whether the young agent is sincere or merely trying to flatter him. "Nevertheless," the Director continues, "I summoned you today to ask if you have anything to add to your report?"

"Add, sir?"

"Do you need to supplement your report in any way?

Dennison included every descriptor and word he could deem useful in his report, staying up the entire night before he submitted it. "Not right off hand, sir. I feel the report is thorough in the...."

"You will not be charged in the killing of another agent," the FBI Director interrupts from behind his desk. "His actions warranted your actions."

A sense of relief tides over Cy Dennison; the man almost melts in his chair.

"Still, you will need to participate in a hearing, but the conclusion is not in doubt. Just stick to your report."

"Thank you, sir. I am truly sorry it happened, sir."

The Director is not interested in a lengthy commentary. "Are there any loose ends in Macon, Agent?" The Director interrupts. "Are we on solid footing there?"

Dennison attempts to remain reverent yet with a spine. "As far as we could tell before leaving the city, yes, sir, things are under control. Granted, Macon hasn't known much stability for decades."

"And what of the operation between Dawson and Huddler? Between Dawson and the Ku Klux Klan?"

"Shut down, sir. We shut it down; no more guns shipped through Texas, Georgia, Florida, or any other parts of the South. Not to our knowledge at least, sir."

"And you honestly believe the two had a hand in illegally distributing tens of thousands of firearms over the course of several years?"

"That is the estimation, sir. It was a goldmine for Dawson and Huddler, and Dawson was no doubt soon to take his share and leave the country altogether."

Despite all the information in Dawson's written report and the agent's commentary this morning, the Director still brandishes an agitated countenance of dissatisfaction. The FBI Director stands and circles his desk, eventually taking a seat next to the young and up and coming agent.

"Do you see what's happened here, Agent Dennison? I am as much to blame as anyone. I failed to detect Dawson's duplicity. I failed to detect a dissatisfied, aging Special Agent in Charge who lost faith in our system right under my nose. Looking back, it makes sense now. Dawson always accepted my assignments in the South with great eagerness. I just thought he was a good man who had developed strong ties and leads in that part of the country. But what he had was a pipeline. He knew intimate information about firearms and distributors. He even found a network of people to help him move the inventory. Furthermore, he still had enough ties here in D.C. to help him keep an ear to the ground. He was ahead of the game. He was ahead of all of us, including me."

Dennison, an honest man, cannot allow the blame to rest on the shoulders of one. "Dawson duped us all, sir. He was hiding in plain sight. It all makes sense now. We were down there for months. The local Klan knew exactly when to go underground. We tiptoed and circled around all their activity, but just as we would get close to a breakthrough, we would come up short, and now I know why."

Despite the momentary showing of contrition by the Director, he is not a man to wallow in the misery of past defeats. "Do you think we can both learn from our mistakes?"

"Yes, sir," Dennison replies swiftly. "I look forward to performing better next time, sir."

"Good," the Director responds. "Because next time is now. You are replacing Dawson. I am stationing you in Atlanta, but your jurisdiction will be the Southeastern United States."

Trying to remain confident, Dennison almost whimpers the words, Who, *me, sir*? Instead, the young, sometimes brazen agent catches himself and, instead, conveys a well-qualified projection.

"You might be wondering why you," the Director continues. "Sure, I could appoint someone from one of the other regions, but, frankly, no one else would want the job. The South is too volatile for everyone else. No, you are the one. You are the right choice."

Dennison is at a loss for words amid his gratitude and shock.

"Take your time to think about it and let me know in twenty-four hours." The Director of the FBI stands to his feet and re-circles his desk. "If you accept, I'll need you to offer a recommendation for an assistant to your position as well. I am open to hearing any suggestions you might have."

Dennison wonders if Wheeler will be up to working with him some more. "Yes, sir. Thank you, sir. I will let...."

"Thank you, Agent Dennison."

The meeting is clearly over as the Director has returned to reading documents. As far as the man behind the desk is concerned, Dennison isn't even in the room anymore.

"Yes, sir," Dennison replies, standing to his feet. "Thank you, sir." The agent turns to exit the office.

As Dennison reaches for the door, "H" poses one final question, causing the agent to halt his progress. "Agent Dennison."

"Yes, sir."

"I must ask—this man, this Roger Stevens. I am curious. Does he have any idea of the deadly situation that swelled around him and his family? Why would anyone insert themselves in the middle of something like that—a white man joining a black school in Georgia? Does the man have a death wish?"

Dennison gathers his thoughts. "Stevens knew part of what was happening but not all of it. Given the look on his face, he was a little amazed and overwhelmed when he put everything together in the end. I think he just wanted to help the youth in Macon."

"Even after the bombing?"

"I guess so, sir. He seems to be a genuinely good man."

"Huh," the Director scoffs. "He's fortunate we were able to protect him, you especially. The man almost died, him and his family."

As the two men in Washington D.C. discuss the simple basketball coach from Macon, Georgia, the face of Roger Stevens flashes in the memory of Cy Dennison, causing the agent to smile.

"Honestly, sir. He doesn't believe it was us who ultimately protected him."

The Director lifts his eyes from the document before him. "Oh. How so?"

Dennison recalls his meeting with Roger Stevens following the attempt on his life by the Klan. Dennison remembers the glazed look of the husband and father—the man had no idea how much peril surrounded them.

"He said he believes in God, sir."

"Really?" is the unamused reply from behind the Director's desk.

"Yes, sir." Agent Dennison momentarily relives his time in Macon and the corresponding events: violent racism, a school bombing, dead Klansmen, dead FBI agents, a dead friend and colleague, illegal shipments of firearms, and Roger Stevens surrounded by an encompassing vortex of unpredictability and danger.

"And you, Agent Dennison? Do you believe in God?" "H" stares intently.

Dennison tries to discern whether the question is just another part of the FBI psyche test. Attempting to offer a non-committal answer to placate the Director, Agent Dennison replies, "Whatever it takes to get the job done, sir."

44

The final days of the school year are swift at Macon South. It is amazing to Roger: parts of the year move briskly, and other parts hardly move at all. Parts of the basketball season race past and other parts stand still. Certain days are pulse-pounding, leaving little room to breathe and other nights seem to last forever as if the sun would never rise again; but it did. As Roger thinks on the ups and downs, the ebb and flow, the back and forth of the past year, all of it is reminiscent of life as a whole: fleeting, here and then gone, a vapor.

The two men face each other across the desk: Roger Stevens and Charles Bullock. Silence abounds for much of the meeting. Both men grin almost uncontrollably. Roger strokes his chin and looks to the floor. Charles Bullock leans back in his chair and looks to the ceiling. An inexplicable chuckle escapes the principal, a snicker that in turn causes his former basketball coach to laugh.

Principal Bullock accepted Roger's resignation without hesitation. Roger prepared a lengthy, extremely detailed address in vain. His boss had already witnessed the writing on the wall; not that the principal wanted Roger to go—not in the least. Both men mutually felt the burden lift after the season.

As Charles Bullock sits and looks at his friend, it will not be the basketball victories the principal will miss, and it certainly will not be the publicity the school has received. Charles Bullock can do without publicity for a while. Instead, what Charles will miss the most will be Roger: his face, his smile, his frown, his befuddlement, his wisdom, his presence. What Charles will miss most is Roger passing him in the hallway, even the idea of just knowing Roger is in the building. Even so, Mr. Bullock is prepared to release Roger Stevens and grant his blessing to the man and his family. To Charles Bullock, considering all Roger has meant to Macon South, it is the least the principal can do.

It is hard for Roger to get his mind wrapped around the fact: so many times, he dreaded the thought of entering this office and sitting across from Charles Bullock; not because he disliked Principal Bullock but because of the outside complaints, controversy, vile threats, and even police involvement. The two of them could write a book together. Both would agree not a single book could hold all that has transpired over the past year at Macon South High School.

What a man! Roger concludes to himself, studying the countenance of his friend. *Better yet, what a man of God!* Many people consider such a man to be found only in the pulpit of a local church. However, Roger knows this godly man is a rare find; a jewel for Macon, a treasure for Georgia, a diamond in the rough for the South and for America. Even though the relationship is not ending, since nothing could ever separate the eternal bond between them now, a phase of the relationship is—the daily relationship. From now on, memories must take the place of regular interaction, and Roger will remember Charles Bullock by drawing from a sacred place in Roger's heart.

"Well," Principal Bullock breaks the silence.

"Well," Roger responds in kind.

The exchange causes both men to pause before chuckling again.

"Hard to believe, isn't it?" Charles inquires.

"Which part?" Roger can only guess.

"All of it," the principal determines. "The bombing, the letters, the trip, the basketball season, the fire, the Klan, the FBI, the State Tournament—all of it. It's hard to believe you're sitting across from me right now. I mean, how'd I ever get you to come to Macon in the first place?"

This time it is Roger who initiates the laughter, closing his eyes and shaking his head in disbelief. "Sometimes, I wonder how you did it, too." Roger pauses then sighs. "Truth is…it wasn't you who got me here."

Principal Bullock affirms as his smile illuminates the room. "I know. It wasn't me. It wasn't me."

Roger surveys a wall with pictures of Macon South High School through the years, including the building that was bombed. "I guess there will be a new picture of a new building to hang in the near future."

"Yes," the principal concurs. "God has put so much light on us that the Governor and State Legislature have released special funding to ensure a new high school will be built."

Roger smiles. "Never thought I would say this last year, but I'm going to miss it here."

Charles Bullock leans forward, his forearms crossing before him on his desk. "You know, it's okay to miss us and embrace a new season at the same time. One doesn't have to diminish the other. That's what we're going to do around here. We'll miss you, but we embrace the new season at Macon South as well."

"And I believe it's going to be a great new season, Principal Bullock."

"I'm not your boss or principal any longer, Roger. If you will have me as your friend, please call me Charles."

"Accepted," Roger responds. "On one condition…." Roger smiles. "Friends for eternity. Here on earth and forever in heaven."

Charles Bullock stands to his feet and draws near Roger who does likewise. The principal extends his right hand. Roger receives it, and Charles places his other hand on top. Roger does the same. The two men slowly move their hands up and down in unison, resembling the unity in which they have walked for the past year.

"How do I begin to thank you, Roger?"

"No, Charles, how do I begin to thank you? If you never had the boldness to ask, I never would have come here. You've changed my life, and I am forever grateful."

"It was our Heavenly Father who gave me the boldness to ask, and it has been our Heavenly Father who has changed both of us."

The men hold a sturdy embrace for several seconds. Roger pats Charles softly on the back. Charles pats Roger softly on the back of his head. Eventually, the two separate and take a deep breath.

"So," Principal Bullock changes the subject. "Should we bring him in?"

"Oh, yes," is Roger's response. I've been looking forward to this all morning."

As the principal walks to his office door, Roger takes his chair and re-situates it beside the desk of Principal Bullock; Roger wants a perfect view of what is about to happen.

The door opens, and the principal speaks. "Mr. Dawkins, please join us."

Reggie Dawkins appears in the doorway with an indecisive look, not knowing what this meeting is all about. Furthermore, Reggie Dawkins did not know Roger Stevens would be present for this meeting. The assistant quickly acknowledges his head coach. "Good morning, Coach Stevens."

"Good morning, Coach Dawkins." The grin on Roger's face lends even more curiosity to the meeting as the former Macon South basketball coach stands to his feet to greet his peer. "Very glad to see you today."

"Make yourself comfortable, Mr. Dawkins. I suppose you are wondering why I asked you to meet with me this morning" are the final words of Charles Bullock before the office door closes behind the three men.

45

Roger Stevens is the first one out of bed this morning. He quietly slips through the door and sits on the front steps of the Anderson home, observing the sunrise, the dawning of a new day. The moments are surreal. He stares across the front lawn where a convergence of men with guns and fire and deadly intentions accosted the Stevens family. Even as Agent Dennison informed Roger of everything in retrospect, even several factors Roger had not realized, the husband and father cannot help but sit speechlessly, considering all the turmoil, danger, threats, and all of it beyond Roger's control. Yet here he is and here his family is: safe; protected by the hand of God from start to finish.

Who am I, God, Roger ponders repeatedly to himself on the front steps this morning? *Who am I that you are so mindful of me?*

In Roger's hand is the latest letter from Reverend Jordan. The envelope arrived two days ago. Once again, the encouragement and timing of Reverend Jordan Stevens has been impeccable as he jotted down the following words for Roger and his family:

Behold, I will do a new thing,
Now it shall spring forth;
Shall you not know it?
I will even make a road in the wilderness
And rivers in the desert.
—Isaiah 43:19

• • •

Karen has made Roger giggle several times this week. On one hand, she of all people, has shown remorse at the thought of leaving Macon. On the other hand, Karen has been in high gear for days, packing like there is no tomorrow.

As far as Kevin is concerned, no one had to tell him twice when it came to packing and loading the car; he was the first one on the job this morning.

Despite the volume of memories over the past year while living in Macon, Roger cannot bring himself to judge Karen or Kevin for their anticipation of a new season. They did it. Both Karen and Kevin made it. They went along with Roger, even going against all convention and common sense. They made the move. They vacated the safe confines of Augusta, including their home and their school, in exchange for the very unknown, uncharted territory that was Macon South High School. As Roger reflects, he does not know what was more miraculous: the fact his wife and son went along with him or the fact they did not disown him. Even more so, the faithful actions of Karen and Kevin affirmed to Roger their commitment to God—no matter what. It would be impossible for Roger to ask for anyone other than Karen and Kevin in his life; he stands today a man blessed beyond measure.

"Knock, knock," a friendly, female voice calls at the back door. The Andersons are here to retrieve the house keys and say goodbye. Mr. Anderson has healed up well since the dreadful incident on the front lawn weeks ago.

Karen and Mrs. Anderson share words and embrace. Roger and Mr. Anderson visit as well. Kevin appears in the foyer, wiping his hands as he does.

"I think that's everything. We're all loaded." All feel the young man's exuberance—Kevin is ready to roll.

A few more words and hugs later, and the Stevens family descend the steps of their once temporary home. A final wave, a turn of the ignition, a couple of tears from Karen, and down the road rumbles the Stevens' Plymouth Fury.

Though still beautiful, the scenery appears much different to the Stevens family on the way out of Macon than it did on the way into Macon. It is not the scenery that is different to Roger, Karen, and Kevin; rather, it is the weight of their hearts as they conclude it is time; it is time to leave Macon; it is time to leave this season; it is time for a new season, and there is no shame in any of it. The Stevens family did what God called them to do. Old things have passed away, and it is time for things to become new.

"I'll miss the cherry blossoms," Karen comments as they drive beneath a once-proud boulevard of trees. "I wish they lasted longer."

"Seasons change," her husband responds.

"Yes, they do."

"Aren't you glad they do or do like the same season to last forever?"

Karen smiles. "That's okay. Atlanta has maples and hickory and magnolias."

"Hey, Dad," Kevin asks from the back seat. "When's Tyler getting to Atlanta?"

"His father said next week sometime. He'll call before they leave Macon. He wants to give us a little time to get settled before he brings Tyler to us."

"I'm so glad Tyler is coming to Central Georgia with us," Karen affirms.

"Between us, Dad: how do you think Tyler will do at the next level?"

Roger nods his head as he chooses the right words. "I think Tyler has the potential to be a great player at the college level. He's athletic enough, and he might not be finished growing yet."

"Plus, he knows our system," adds Kevin. "Or do you plan to change things on the college level?"

"We'll make some changes, sure. But basketball is basketball…and life is life."

"I hope I grow some more," Kevin wishes aloud, the young man's heart very light on this day.

Karen turns to project a mystified glare at her son in the backseat. "No, no, you're tall enough, Kevin. I have a hard time keeping food in the house as it is."

"When is the Wilson kid from Savannah getting there?" Kevin queries again.

"I think next week as well."

"I love Reynolds and Trevor, but it was awesome to see Savannah Memorial beat the Academy for the championship," Kevin admits. "I look forward to playing with Wilson. He destroyed the Newhouse kid."

"It feels as if we're already putting together a good team," Karen interjects, "and we haven't even made it to Atlanta yet."

"Reynolds, too," Kevin adds.

"Yep," Roger agrees. "It will be fun to coach Reynolds again."

Before making their way out of town, Roger navigates a humble part of South Macon. A turn here, a turn there and the Stevens' Plymouth Fury pulls to the front of a small home.

● ● ●

Several minutes later, Kevin helps pack more bags. Soon the Stevens family begins to exit the neighborhood. Behind them, the steady hand of a proud and grateful grandmother waves.

As the Stevens family pulls ceremoniously onto Interstate-75, a load is lifted. All three members of the family share the same thoughts. *We did it. We passed the test.* Now, without any regrets, they can embrace the next chapter in their lives, whatever that chapter may bring. They can embrace it together, knowing if God did it then, He will do it again.

The faithful Plymouth Fury exits the city limits of Macon, Georgia; next stop—more basketball in Atlanta. All four passengers are all smiles: Roger Stevens, Karen Stevens, Kevin Stevens...and Billy Taylor.

WALKING THROUGH FORGIVENESS...
HAND IN HAND

AN EASY WORD TO SAY CAN BE A DIFFICULT WORD TO LIVE

The premise of Forced Turnovers is forgiveness. Just like the main character in the book, Roger Stevens, Tony Ceballos has come to understand the good news: forgiveness brings freedom. If you are struggling with an area of your past, do not be surprised if that area is linked to unforgiveness. Tony has assembled a resource guide to take you beyond Forced Turnovers. Take the opportunity to navigate this guide and let the ball and chain of bitterness fall to the ground as you propel into a joyful future.

The one who has the power to forgive has the most power.

START THE ROAD TO FREEDOM TODAY
tonyceballosauthor.com

BRING TONY INTO YOUR BUSINESS, CHURCH OR SCHOOL

AUTHOR. SPEAKER. PREACHER. TEACHER.

Tony strongly believes in choosing the correct speaker. The right one sets the stage for success and the wrong one for failure.

Tony's sincere approach combined with relevant content positions him as a top choice for businesses and nonprofits.

He customizes each message and training to achieve and exceed the objectives of his hosts.

CONTACT TONY TODAY TO BEGIN THE CONVERSATION
tonyceballosauthor.com

CPSIA information can be obtained
at www.ICGtesting.com
Printed in the USA
FSHW021857140719
60006FS